I0660983

REALMS OF FANTASY
A RETROSPECTIVE

Edited by Douglas Cohen
Oz Reimagined: New Tales from the Emerald City and Beyond
What the #@&% is That?

Start Publishing PD LLC
Copyright © 2024 by Start Publishing PD LLC

All rights reserved, including the right to reproduce this book or portions thereof in any form whatsoever.

Start Publishing PD is a registered trademark of Start Publishing PD LLC
Manufactured in the United States of America

Cover art: Shutterstock/Taisiya Kozorez

Cover design: Jennifer Do

10 9 8 7 6 5 4 3 2 1

ISBN 979-8-8809-1054-0

REALMS OF FANTASY
A RETROSPECTIVE

by Douglas Cohen

Foreword: My Lost Realms

Shawna McCarthy

Once upon a time, maybe even before you were born, in a world and time much like our own, a youngish woman walked into a bookstore (these were places that were full of books, actual physical books, that you could look at and touch and examine and buy and take home with you) and saw a magazine (these were paper pages with many words on them, bound in paper covers with pictures on them) called *Science Fiction Age*.

This discovery both excited and depressed the youngish woman, because not too long before, she had been the editor in chief of a certain famous science fiction magazine named after a certain famous science fiction writer. She thought, not unreasonably, *Why am I not the editor of this new science fiction magazine? Why have I been left bereft of short fiction while some other editor gets to do what I love to do?*

So she picked up the magazine and discovered it was published by a company called Sovereign Media, many miles away in Virginia. Was she daunted? No, she was not. She sat down at her word processor (this was before personal computers—imagine!) and typed out a letter to the publisher. In it she suggested that while the company might already have a science fiction magazine, what it really needed was a fantasy magazine. Fantasy, after all, outsold science fiction at that time by a factor of ten to one. She mailed the letter, and to her surprise got a quick response from the publishers (Hi, Carl Gnam! Hi, Mark Hintz!), saying that this was a very good idea and would she like to help them start one?

Would she???!!! And so, after the usual startup work which none of you want to hear about, *Realms of Fantasy* was born. The first issue came out in October 1994 and featured a cover by Michael Whelan and, of course, a dragon. Dragons (and scantily clad women) would be an ongoing cover theme which, for some reason, led some readers to imagine that there might be stories inside featuring either dragons or scantily clad women. There were some of the former but none of the latter. (There may have been some cognitive dissonance engendered by this dichotomy.)

As well loved and cared for young creatures do, the magazine grew and thrived until it became the bestselling fantasy magazine in the world. (This was not hard as there were no other professional fantasy-only magazines in the world, but let's not quibble.) There were a number of growing pains, not the least of which was the fact that the youngish woman had another full-time job and two full-time children and did not have the time to keep the magazine's wheels spinning as fast as they should, nor did she have the budget to hire a full-time assistant. A number of these came and went (Hi, Rebecca McCabe, hi, Carina Gonzalez) until the woman stumbled upon a young man even crazier than herself. While the editor worked for very little money, this young man was so devoted to the field that he was willing to work for free! And not only did he work for free, he did a hell of a job organizing the submissions process and reading the slush. For the first time ever *Realms* ran like a well-oiled machine. (Hi, Douglas Cohen!!!) You hold in your hands the tangible proof of his devotion and his organizational skills.

For seventeen years *Realms of Fantasy* provided the now-not-so-youngish-in-fact-kind-of-oldish woman a much needed outlet for her love of short fiction, and provided up and coming young writers a much needed outlet for their stories, and provided up and coming young readers a much needed way to sample the delightful fruits of the writers' imaginations.

But as the magazine and its editor stumbled into the digital age, it became more and more difficult for a paper-and-staples publication to attract the readership and advertising it needed to survive. After a series of new publishers, all of whom were able, dedicated, and professional (Hi Warren Lapine!!), it eventually became clear that even operating on a shoestring budget, *Realms of Fantasy* had reached the end of its magical road.

As the once-youngish and now-oldish editor in question, I'd like to state for the record that my years with *Realms* were some of my proudest and happiest. It was truly a labor of love, done because I strongly believe that short fiction is the lifeblood of our genre. I'm delighted to have helped begin the careers of so many of today's most lauded writers, and I want to say thank you to everyone—writers, editors, readers, and fans—for your stories, your encouragement, and your support over the years.

And if you should need someone to edit short fiction, well, I may know a certain oldish editor who is wise to the field and youngish at heart when working with the stories she so loves ...

Introduction: Expect the Unexpected

Douglas Cohen

I never expected any of this. That's the plain truth of it. In college I realized I wanted to be a writer of speculative fiction. The idea of *editing* this genre never crossed my mind. I suppose the first editorial seeds were planted when after graduating from college I attended the Odyssey Fantasy & Science Fiction Writing Workshop, a six-week workshop where young writers go to hone their craft. The director of the Odyssey Workshop was my very first Yoda in the speculative genre, Jeanne Cavelos. Jeanne came from an accomplished editorial background, and part of her process entailed teaching her students to consider fiction with an editor's eye, which enhanced our critical reading skills, along with our objectivity when considering our own writing for revision.

I absorbed her teachings like a sponge to water, so much so that after Odyssey's conclusion editing came to me far more easily than writing did. I'd be lying if I claimed that after Odyssey the idea of editing *still* never crossed my mind, but that's all it did: cross it. Each time it did, the notion was promptly dismissed. I was going to be a writer in this genre. This was *all* I was going to do in this genre. I didn't want to get sidetracked.

Until one day ...

While researching the latest short story markets, I came across a notice that Editor Shawna McCarthy's assistant at *Realms of Fantasy* had stepped down. On top of that, there was no mention of a replacement. Maybe it was because fantasy was my first love in the speculative genre and *Realms of Fantasy* was the premiere magazine devoted strictly to fantasy fiction. Or maybe after five years, those editorial seeds Jeanne had planted had finally taken root. Whatever the reason, the proverbial light bulb went off over my head. *I can do that*, I thought. For the first time I *wanted* to be an editor of speculative fiction. I had no editorial background other than my training at Odyssey, nor did I have any writing credits to my name. But I fired off an email to Shawna, expressing my interest in the position and mentioning my Odyssey background (and probably blabbing about my love for fantasy).

I never expected to hear back from her two hours later.

A week or so later the interview took place and Shawna hired me on an interim basis. There was a lot to learn (and a lot to read!), but I was excited, determined, and eager to work. Perhaps this explained why two weeks later Shawna removed the interim label.

I never expected the first piece of slush I passed along to Shawna to get accepted for publication, but I suppose this was a sign of things to come, because pretty soon I had earned Shawna's trust as her assistant. In fact, I started finding publishable stories for her on a regular basis. Along the way I also lowered our response times. I made us more organized. I provided more in-depth critiques on the manuscripts Shawna was considering (each and every one). I worked with authors from the general submissions pile on revisions if I thought some editing might lead to an acceptance (and it often did). I did everything I could think of that allowed me to do more work on the magazine.

Never once did Shawna instruct me to ease up, or tell me I'd overstepped my bounds. I imagine she appreciated my go-getter attitude and how my devotion to *Realms* was making her life easier and the writers happier. But more than anything, I think she saw something in me. I think she understood the best way to encourage my editorial spark was to give me fairly free rein, allowing me to learn through experience. To be sure she imparted quite a few bits of wisdom over the years, but her trust in me was as responsible as anything else for me growing as an editor.

And during all this time, it never once occurred to me that I should read the back issues of *Realms of Fantasy*.

Until one day ...

My good friend (and future co-editor) John Joseph Adams, who at this time was still Assistant Editor at *The Magazine of Fantasy & Science Fiction* (F&SF), mentioned to me how he had acquired the complete collection of F&SF. F&SF had been around since 1949. *Realms* had only been around since 1994. Almost immediately, I experienced something between shame and guilt. John had acquired the complete collection to a magazine that had been around for almost sixty years. What was my excuse for failing to do the same for *Realms of Fantasy*?

So I turned my attention to acquiring every last issue of *Realms*. Once I did, I figured I might as well read the stories. And as long as I was reading them, I reasoned that I might as well blog about them. Such were the beginnings of my retrospective series. As with everything I did with the magazine back then, it was purely a labor of love, something I never expected to change.

Until one day ...

Fast forward about two years. I'd been reading back issues and blogging about them steadily on my LiveJournal when news broke that the publishers were pulling the plug on *Realms*. I figured that was it. I was depressed but grateful for the opportunity to have worked on such a wonderful magazine. I also remained intent on blogging about the remaining issues of *Realms*. Yes, I wanted to finish what I started, but more importantly these retrospectives represented a means to hold onto the magazine more intimately, to stay *involved* with it a while longer.

With this in mind, I never expected my involvement with the magazine to *increase*. But this is exactly what happened when Warren Lapine bought the magazine and brought back both Shawna and myself. Perhaps a month or so afterward, he also handed me new responsibilities with the magazine, putting me in charge of nonfiction and artwork. *And now I was getting paid for it.* The pay was nice, but monetary recognition for my efforts was even better.

Warren and I had no previous relationship prior to him taking over *Realms*, so for him to show such confidence in me marked quite the leap of faith. But as with Shawna, I think he saw something in me. He noticed how I busted my butt during the transition from one publisher to another, and I think he realized that I would exert that same dedication and effort to the nonfiction and the artwork if he put me in charge of these departments (and I did). As a result, I learned a great deal more about the publishing business, and when you reach the later editions of these retrospectives, I'll be providing more insights regarding the artwork, the nonfiction, and other departments I would come to work on. (There were a couple of stumbles along the way as I grew accustomed to my new responsibilities, and yes, I'll be discussing these as well.)

All the while I continued writing the retrospectives on my personal blog as time allowed. I was getting paid now, but the retrospectives remained that labor of love, something I never expected to be an official part of the magazine.

Until one day ...

Some months after taking over the magazine, Warren informed me that he planned on giving the magazine a beautiful new website. Naturally he wanted input from the editorial staff concerning potential content. Since the artwork was such an integral part of *Realms*, I suggested we incorporate a cover gallery ...and then, ever so hesitantly, I suggested we include my retrospective series on the website. I pointed out how this would provide visitors a lot of potential reading content, and since the series was still ongoing, we could continue adding new retrospectives over time.

Warren never hesitated. "Sure," he said, "it's all content."

And like that my retrospective series was incorporated onto the *Realms* website, thus becoming part of *Realms of Fantasy* canon. I continued blogging new retrospectives on my LiveJournal, but now they were being posted simultaneously on the *Realms* website. Meanwhile *Realms* was struggling behind the scenes. Warren and the rest of us did everything we could think of to save the magazine (including the aforementioned website), but the age of digital magazines was now fully upon us, and full-sized glossy magazines with color illustrations like *Realms* were quickly becoming a thing of the past. About a year and a half after Warren saved *Realms*, he was forced to shut down operations. Soon afterward he managed to sell it, giving the magazine one last chance at life. The new publishers once again brought back me and Shawna, and not only did they keep the old website intact, they allowed me to continue posting new retrospectives there.

Realms lasted another year, and while creatively speaking we were having one of our strongest years in some time, the financial realities proved more bleak. So this time, when the publishers closed the magazine's doors, they stayed closed. This was in late 2011. At this point I had blogged about eighty-three of a possible 102 issues. The end was somewhat in sight, but it would be a year and a half before I wrote another retrospective on my personal blog. With *Realms* well and truly gone, I wasted no time shifting gears. I sold my first anthology to a major publisher (and have since sold a second one). I started selling my short fiction with a little more regularity. I completed my first novel (which currently remains in a state of publishing limbo I'm not at liberty to discuss). I had every intention of finishing my retrospective series, but with so much else on my plate I couldn't find the time to dive back into it.

Until one day ...

I received an email from my old publisher Warren Lapine, asking if I'd be interested in publishing my retrospective series as a book through his publishing company, Wilder Publications. Would I?! The last thing I ever expected was for my little old retrospectives to find their way into a book. But first I had to finish the series. With *Realms* no longer part of my daily routine, finding time to finish the retrospective series proved an incredible challenge. But each day I squeezed out a few minutes, until twenty-one months later I had blogged my last retrospective.

Only it didn't end there. All of these retrospectives had been written online. Getting them ready for a book required some editing. More months passed with me squeezing out more minutes each day to make these retrospectives book-friendly. With the online retrospective series complete, I was also able to enhance some of these retrospectives, adding new observations, new information, new reminiscences, etc. As a result, the book you find yourself in possession of is what you might call the author's preferred edition, because overall I consider it more comprehensive than the combined online versions.

That in something bigger than a nutshell is the story-behind-the-story of the *Realms of Fantasy* retrospectives. Sometimes it felt like I would never finish working on it. I've called it a labor of love, but as the years rolled on and the series remained incomplete there were times it felt like a labor of hate and a downright pain in my ass, as I would wonder why I'd been foolish enough to ever undertake such a massive project. But here at the end of it all, I'm glad that I saw this project through to completion. It makes for a nice posthumous chapter for one of the most important speculative magazines to come along in the last twenty years.

On top of this, I realize I'm going to miss these retrospectives. As I mentioned above, when the magazine folded for the first time, these retrospectives represented a way for me to stay involved with *Realms* after its demise. *Realms* has been gone almost four years now, but these retrospectives kept me involved long after everyone else moved on. They were like a comfort food that was always in the fridge, even on those occasions when working on them felt absolutely tedious. But once I'm done with this introduction, I'll be letting go like everyone else. Maybe that explains why for over a week I've been dragging my feet about finishing this introduction, and why it's so much longer than it needs to be (yes, it's more than just self-indulgence here). There are endings and then there is The End.

This one is the latter.

What a sweet ride it's been.

Welcome to part one of the Realms of Fantasy Retrospective Series. I will read the fiction in each issue of *Realms of Fantasy Magazine* and offer my thoughts as Assistant Editor of fiction. I will touch upon the art and nonfiction features as well. So, let's jump right in with the inaugural October 1994 issue, shall we?

The honor of the first cover ever for *Realms of Fantasy* (RoF) goes to artist Michael Whelan. The art was originally the cover to the novel *Skybowl* by Melanie Rawn. Inside, it was interesting to note a couple of features the magazine no longer has, such as the Editorial Column and the Letters Page. Also, contributor bios are in the back instead of the front. Other than Shawna McCarthy—the magazine's founding editor—there are almost no names in the masthead still with the magazine. The publisher and publisher/editorial director—Mark Hintz and Carl A. Gnam—are still around. While she isn't in every issue, Terri Windling is in the first issue with her popular Folkroots column. Other than this, the only other name I saw that you can still find in the latest masthead is Diane Bonifanti, the business manager. But the supporting editorial staffs are different, as is the art director and all the other people in various branches that help run a magazine. I suppose I shouldn't be surprised, because the magazine is in its thirteenth year. But it's still interesting to note. Since the art is such an important part of each issue, I will note that the magazine's original art director is Ronald M. Stevens.

When it comes to nonfiction, I will always note the columns each issue in order of publication. A rundown of our inaugural nonfiction columns is as follows:

The Book Reviews column is handled by Gahan Wilson. The first books he reviewed were *The Hollowing* by Robert Holdstock, *Year's Best Fantasy and Horror 7*, edited by Ellen Datlow & Terri Windling, and *Skin* by Kathe Koja. There is also a defunct mini-column called Books to Look For, but I'm going to skip listing each of those each issue, and I'll be skipping cover other mini-columns of this ilk. I am only willing to be so thorough. Our first Movie/TV column is handled by J.B. Mauceri, who covers *Frankenstein*, directed by Kenneth Branagh & produced by Francis Ford

Coppola. Our first Folkroots column is handled by Terri Windling, as she covers the Green Man and the Lore of the Woods. Terri also covered our first ever Artists Gallery, where she profiles Brian Froud. And in our first Games column, M.C. Sumner reviews *The Horde*, a 3DO Multiplayer and PC CD-ROM from Crystal Dynamics, and *Magic: the Gathering* from Wizards of the Coast.

On to the fiction ...

In terms of the stories, Shawna did an excellent job in this first issue of establishing that *Realms of Fantasy* is a magazine interested in publishing all sorts of fantasy stories. Since it was the first issue, to lure readers in it looks like Shawna went out and got stories by Roger Zelazny and Neil Gaiman. But we'll get to those stories in a moment.

The first story ever published in RoF is "Twixt Dust and Dawn" by L. Dean James. Accompanying artwork is by Luis Royo, which makes his work the first interior illustration to appear in the magazine. This is a high fantasy tale that starts, in, of all places, a bar. On the surface this seems rather cliche. However, there is nothing wrong with the tale itself, as it tells the story of a warrior-woman who tries to reclaim her ancestral throne from an evil magician with the help of a fey who has other ideas. And if Shawna selected the order of the stories in this issue (I'm uncertain whether it was her or Carl Gnam, the publisher/editorial director, handling this), I would propose this was her thinking: she wanted to lead off with a well told but familiar-feeling high fantasy tale, something the typical fantasy reader of the mid-nineties might expect. And from here it would be a launching point as she would publish fantasy stories across the board. In fact, I'm fairly certain this is the *only* high fantasy story that starts in a tavern in the magazine's entire run.

Next up we have "Pest Control" by Chuck Rothman. This one is a funny fantasy tale about a house infested with magical pests and the exterminator hired to deal with them. Of all the authors in the first issue, the only one I've seen submissions from since coming to RoF is Chuck. And just last year he published a story in our pages called "Spare Change." Art to this one was provided by Gary Yealdhall.

After this we have "The Land Down Under" by Billie Sue Mosiman. This is the first science fantasy tale published in the magazine. This one deals with a far-flung future where magic and science are practically indistinguishable, and the greatest healer of the time attempts to treat her granddaughter's sick mind. Art to this one was provided by Mary O'Keefe Young.

Then we have "The Shrouding and the Guisel" by Roger Zelazny. Zelazny's story is actually a tale from his popular Amber series, in which the great wizard Merlin wakes to find himself making love to a long-lost love, who happens to be in need of his help to defeat an unconquerable beast. To my surprise, I didn't enjoy this one. Everything I've read by Zelazny (admittedly, not enough by far) has always left me hugely impressed. In all fairness, I'll note that I haven't read any of the Amber books (yet), and this story takes place after the 10th book, which I believe was the last. Perhaps if I knew something about the world of Amber I would feel differently about this story. I expect that one day, after I've read the Amber books, I'll go back and give this piece another try. Art to this one was provided by Doug Andersen.

Following this we have "The Redemption of Silky Bill" by Sarah Zettel. This one kills two birds with one stone by being our first Wild West fantasy and our first deal-with-the-Devil story. As to the particulars, the cowboy Silky Bill is out to save his soul and those of all Native Americans in the ultimate card game with the Devil. Art to this one was provided by David Beck.

Next up we have "Troll Bridge" by Neil Gaiman. This one is the magazine's first reprint. (Interestingly enough, while the magazine reprinted a number of tales over the years, we never reprinted a single story after I joined the publication.) I'm afraid it isn't mentioned in the magazine where this one was originally published, though it's worth noting that the original publication of this piece earned a nomination for the 1994 World Fantasy Award for Best Short Fiction. As to the story itself, it's an adult fairy tale about a young boy who encounters a troll beneath a bridge who bargains to save his life. These bargains continue over the years, leading to an unexpected result. Art to this one was provided by Gary Lippincott.

Finally we have "The Beholder" by Jean Lorrah. This one is high fantasy with a romantic flare. I'd like to note that sandwiched between the first and last tales in this issue, which are both high fantasy, we have a funny fantasy set in modern times, a science fantasy, a Roger Zelazny Amber tale, a Wild West fantasy, and an adult fairy tale. In other words, enough content has already been provided to let readers know that this magazine will indeed cover all the realms of fantasy. I make a point of saying this because every so often I read or hear about people complaining that RoF was supposed to be a magazine all about high fantasy. No, it wasn't. It's clear from the fiction in the very first issue, not to mention that in the last line of Shawna's very first editorial she makes it plain that she has a very broad definition as to what fantasy is. As to the story, I believe Shawna's editorial byline sums it up best: "Challenged by a love-struck prince to break a wizard's hideous spell, a young witch learns a lesson about love's ability to defeat even the most powerful magic." Art to this one was provided Carol Heyer.

So that wraps up the premiere issue of *Realms of Fantasy*. And my favorite story? "The Land Down Under," by Billie Sue Mosiman. And my favorite artwork? David Beck's illustration to "The Redemption of Silky Bill."

Originally posted on douglascohen.livejournal.com on August 14th, 2007

December 1994 (Issue 2)

Part two in my comprehensive retrospective as I read the fiction in *Realms of Fantasy* and offer my thoughts. This time around I'll be discussing the December 1994 issue.

The cover to this issue is by Don Maitz. This cover has a copyright of 1989 on the artist's website, but there is no attribution for the artwork. Google searches didn't turn up anything prior to this cover, so I'm uncertain whether the art appeared elsewhere prior to this cover or was simply an order piece put together by the artist that was never purchased until this issue.

A rundown of this issue's nonfiction is as follows:

In Book Reviews, Gahan Wilson covers *Curfew* by Phil Rickman, *The Winter Prince* by Elizabeth E. Wein, *Black Thorn, White Rose*, edited by Ellen Datlow & Terri Windling, and *The H.P. Lovecraft Dream Book*, edited by S.T. Joshi, Will Murray & David E. Schultz. Also, newcomer Dan Silver covers *The Forest House* by Marion Zimmer Bradley. I must admit, John Jude Palencar's illustration to this book's cover has always freaked me out. Something about the woman's hands and the arch of her neck give me the heebie-jeebies. It's a lovely illustration, but I can never stare at it for too long without feeling disturbed. In the Movie/TV column, newcomer Dan Persons reviews the adaptation to Anne Rice's *Interview with a Vampire*. In Folkroots, Terri Windling covers the music of Faery, and how fantasy literature and folk music have their roots in Celtic ballads. Author Charles de Lint handles the Artists Gallery this issue and discusses the DreamWeavers traveling exhibition. In the Games Column, M.C. Sumner covers the computer game, *Companions of Xanth*, which incorporates elements of Piers Anthony's latest Xanth book (at the time), *Demons Don't Dream*. Also covered in this column is a pair of RPGs: White Wolf's *Vampire* & TSR's *Ravenloft*.

On to the fiction ...

This issue's fiction had a distinctly different feel from issue one, which probably did a lot to establish RoF as a market for all fantasy stories back during the magazine's early days. The lead story in this issue is "The Rusty Smith and Faer Linden" by Nancy Varian Berberick. While the fey made an appearance for the second issue in a row, this time they did so in a more traditional role, as this story seems to draw heavily on Celtic mythology as a less-than-stunning blacksmith pursues a beautiful fey who cannot escape the call of fate. Art to this one was provided by Mary O'Keefe Young, which marks her second illustration in the magazine. It also makes her the first artist to have to illustrate multiple pieces for RoF.

Next up is "A Rush of Wings" by Richard Rowand. This one is a contemporary fantasy, and also the first appearance of an angel (at least that's what I assumed the creature to be). In this one, a man recounts stumbling upon a dead creature washed up on the beach, and buries the creature, much the way his father wished him to bury his dreams. Art to this one was provided by Laurie Harden.

Following this we have "The Lazarus Chronicle" by Amy Wolf. There also a small note beside the illustration stating the following: "Translated from the Arabic by Phillip D. Monroe, Cambridge, 1977." This was our first piece of historical fantasy, with a setting during the Crusades, and it's also our first story featuring an anti-hero protagonist. In this one, an unrepentant nobleman by the name of Roger of York is shipped off to Palestine, where he is afflicted with leprosy and proceeds to recount the deeds of his wicked life. Art to this one was provided by Tom Simonton.

Then we have "Beyond Munchen Town" by Paula May. This tale is our first dark fantasy. It is very much a literary stew, as a band of gypsies clash with some German soldiers, all in the framework of a fairy tale twisted inside out as they unleash an ancient curse and cause all hell to break loose. Art to this one was provided by David Beck, which marks his second illustration in the magazine.

After this we have "The Other Land" by Andrea Schlect. This story felt very much like high fantasy, but it was set in this world, with references to countries we've all heard of. But there was also a certain fairy tale quality to this, especially the way a dark and secret land seems to beckon with all the charms of a Pied Piper. Of course, it beckons to an old man instead of a child, but still. Art to this one was provided by Ken Graning.

Finally we have "A Little Moonshine" by Connie Willis. This one is a reprint, the second to appear in the magazine, and it's a quirky blend of fairy tale, mythology, astrology, and astronomy. Art to this one was provided by Charles Demorat.

So that wraps up this issue. And my favorite story? "Beyond Munchen Town" by Paula May. And my favorite artwork? I'll go with Don Maitz's cover artwork, featuring a warrior that may be the very definition of bad-ass.

Originally posted on douglascohen.livejournal.com on August 28th, 2007

Part three in my comprehensive retrospective as I read the fiction in *Realms of Fantasy* and offer my thoughts. This time around I'll be diving into the February 1995 issue.

The cover to this one is by Bob Eggleton. It was originally the cover to Dragons Above, edited by Gardner Dozois and Jack Dann.

A rundown of this issue's nonfiction is as follows:

The Folkroots column is by Terri Windling, which discusses the transformation of Beauty and the Beast folktales. In Book Reviews, Gahan Wilson covers *Street* by Jack Cady, *Throat Sprockets* by Tim Lucas, *The HastuWorm*, and *The Shrub Niggurath Cycle*, all edited by Robert M. Price, and *Cthulu's Heirs*, edited by Thomas M.K. Stratman. In the Movie/TV column, Dan Person discusses Chris Carter's *The X-Files*. Nigel Suckling hanles the Artists Gallery, covering the work of J.K. Potter, and it includes an introduction to the artist's work by Stephen King. And in the Games column, M.C. Sumner reviews the PC game, *Master of Magic*, TSR's *Advanced Dungeons & Dragons Player Pack Survival Kits*, and the video game *Dragon's Lair*, available on PC CD-ROM, 3DO, and Sega CD.

On to the fiction ...

The lead story is "The Story Told By Smoke" by Tanith Lee, a Journals of St. Strange Tale. Art is by Mary O'Keefe Young. This is a story about a domineering man who spits in the face of tradition, causing the city he lives in untold suffering for many years. Art to this one was provided by Mary O'Keefe Young, which marks her third illustration in the magazine.

Next up is "The Chapter of Bringing a Boat into Heaven" by Noreen Doyle. Art is by Ken Graning, which marks his second illustration in the magazine. This story is a piece of Egyptian mythology about a young boy who draws upon the powers of the gods to sail a boat into the heavens. Art to this one was provided by Ken Graning, which marks his second illustration in the magazine.

Then we have "The Moon is Drowning While I Sleep" by Charles de Lint. Art is by Carol Heyer. This one is another reprint, coming from an Ellen Datlow/Terri Windling anthology. Like Neil Gaiman's reprint in issue one, this story was basically an urban fairy tale, about a woman who must unravel the riddle of the drowning moon in her dreams. It's also worth noting that when the story was originally published, it was nominated for the 1994 World Fantasy Award for Best Short fiction. Art to this one was provided by Carol Heyer, which marks her second appearance in the magazine.

Next up is "The Year of Storms" by Judith Berman. I think it's important to note that this story and Noreen's represent the first stories pubished in RoF by unpublished authors. This in itself is rather important, because it demonstrated early on that RoF was open to publishing new talent. As to the story itself, I was rather impressed with this piece as a first publication, especially considering it's the sort of fantasy I tend to gravitate toward. In this piece, a pair of revered twins must figure out why the revered salmon have stopped coming to the land, and they must figure it out before everyone starves. Art to this one was provided by Web Bryant.

Following this we have "The Last Waltz" by Richard Parks. I'd like to note that this is Richard's first appearance in the magazine. I note this because at this time Richard has appeared in RoF more than any other author. It's also interesting to note that this issue feature's Tanith Lee's first appearance in RoF, because after Richard she is the magazine's most-published author. As to the story, this one is a piece about Death. Only Death has grown tired from his work, so he takes the time to "live a little." Art to this one was provided by Paul Salmon.

Finally we have "Mission: Rescue Merlin!" by S.N. Dyer. This one is a lighthearted piece of Arthuriana about the media circus that ensues when the stone is removed from Merlin's cave and he is rescued in modern times. It's a nice enough story, but I had trouble connecting with it. This has nothing to do with the story or the author's skills, both of which are solid. But I prefer Arthurian tales of a more serious nature than the story in question. It's a personal reader tic. Art to this one was provided by Annie Lunsford.

So that wraps up this issue. And my favorite story? "The Year of Storms" by Judith Berman. And my favorite artwork? Carol Heyer's illustration to "The Moon is Drowning While I Sleep."

Originally posted on douglascohen.livejournal.com on August 19th, 2007

Part four in my comprehensive retrospective as I read the fiction in *Realms of Fantasy* and offer my thoughts on the fiction. This time around I'll be expounding upon the April 1995 issue.

The cover to this one is by Broeck Steadman. It was originally the cover to *Song of Seashell Archives* by Elizabeth Scarborough.

I'll mention that in addition to everything else, each issue I've been reading the editorials and letter pages. So in this issue it's worth mentioning how it was the first "Guest Editorial," i.e. someone writing the Editorial other than Shawna McCarthy. And of all possible people, it was written by Jeanne Cavelos. Jeanne is the director of the Odyssey Fantasy & Science Fiction Writing Workshop. I attended the Odyssey Workshop back in 2000, and am forever grateful to Jeanne for the countless lessons she imparted to me concerning writing and editing speculative literature. The first year of Odyssey was in the summer of '96, so when Jeanne wrote this editorial I'd imagine she'd already conceived Odyssey and was deep into the planning phases for its inaugural year.

A rundown of this issue's nonfiction is as follows:

In the Books column, Gahan Wilson reviews *A Plague of Angels* by Sheri S. Tepper and *Bride of the Rat God* by Barbara Hambly, while Dan Silver reviews *Exiles: Volume I–The Ruins of Ambrai* by Melanie Rawn and *Ships of Merior* by Janny Wurts. In the Movie/TV column, Dan Persons has been replaced by Michael Cassutt, who offers an examination of science fiction vs. fantasy TV programming, and how fantasy has played second fiddle for some time. Folkroots is again handled by Terri Windling, who examines the diverse ancient folk traditions of North America. Janny Wurts handles this issue's Artists Gallery, covering artist, Don Maitz. (I believe these two are married, in which case she would know his work quite well). And in the Games column, M.C Sumner reviews a pair of PC games, an adaptation of Margaret Weis & Tracy Hickman's *Deathgate Cycle*, and *Magic Carpet*, which as you might expect carries an Arabian flavor. And for RPGs, he reviews *Masque of the Red Death*, which is a supplement to TSR's *Ravenloft* campaign.

On to the fiction ...

Let's start by noting that this is the first issue of *Realms of Fantasy* with all original fiction. The first piece is called "Excerpts From the Diary of Samuel Pepys" by John Moore. I've got to say, this one felt more like science fiction than fantasy to me. So after I finished it I spent a few minutes thinking about why Shawna considered this piece fantasy. The best answer I have comes back to her editorial in the very first issue, wherein she offered her definitions of fantasy and science fiction. To sum up, fantasy=chaos. Science fiction=order. This piece certainly leaned much more toward the chaos side of the equation, so in this respect I could see why Shawna considered it fantasy. And there could be other reasons as well. And clearly the author had his own reasons for considering this fantasy. And while I'm certainly entitled to my opinion, at the end of the day it really only matters how John and Shawna saw this piece. As to the story itself, Puritans seek to figure out the mystery of a plague that is demolishing their city. Art to this one was provided by Janet Aulisio Dannheiser.

Next up was "His True and Only Wife" a very dark piece by Louise Cooper, in which a woman's childhood love runs too deep as she continues to love the same man into adulthood before eventually going mad from his rejection. What I liked about this piece was the way it completely messed with my expectations. It started off leaving me sympathizing with the protagonist, but with each successive scene the author kept taking me in a rather horrifying direction that seemed so at odds with the opening (but really made perfect sense). If nothing else, I had to keep reading to see how this one would end. Art to this was provided by Tom Canty.

Following this we have "The Hour of Their Need" by Amy Wolf. This one is a piece of Arthuriana that deals with Knights of the Round Table coming back to aid Britain during WWII. It's worth noting that Amy is the first author to have a second story appear within our pages. Art to this one was provided by Gary Freeman.

After this was "Random Noise" by Carol Ives Gilman. This was another piece that felt a lot more like sf than fantasy (to me), until the last few paragraphs when I suddenly decided it was in fact a contemporary fantasy about a woman trying to decipher the hidden language of trees. Art to this one was provided by Web Bryant, which marks his second illustration in the magazine.

Then we have "Breeding Lilacs" by Daniel Marcus. This one is a dark contemporary fantasy with an absolutely unexpected, shocking, and haunting ending. I won't soon forget it, as it explores how love for one's family can become utterly twisted around when a woman is given a second chance to spend time with her dead father. Art to this one was provided by Alfred Kamajian.

Finally we have "Hold Me Fast and Fear Not" by Margaret Ball. I see stories about selkies in the slush pile all the time (and I've actually grown rather tired of them), but this marks the first time a selkie tale appeared in the magazine's pages. The trend-setter, if you will, as we see a woman risking all to rescue her child from the selkies. Art to this one was provided by David Beck, which marks his third illustration in the magazine.

So that wraps up this issue. And my favorite story to this issue? "Breeding Lilacs" by Daniel Marcus. And my favorite artwork? David Beck's artwork to "Hold Me Fast and Fear Not."

Originally posted on douglascohen.livejournal.com on September 1st, 2007

Part five in my comprehensive retrospective as I read the fiction in *Realms of Fantasy* and offer my thoughts. This time around I'll be sharing my thoughts on the June 1995 issue.

The cover to this one is by Michael Whelan, which marks his second illustration to appear in the magazine. It was originally the cover to *Stronghold* by Melanie Rawn.

In the masthead, it should be mentioned that this marks the first appearance of Rebecca McCabe. Before Douglas Cohen, Assistant Editor, there was Carina Gonzalez, Editorial Intern, and before Carina Gonzalez there was Rebecca McCabe, Editorial Assistant (though her title would later change to Assistant Editor). Why each of us was given different titles, I don't know. Ask Shawna. I'm not going to. And while there were some differences here and there for each of us, we all filled the same primary role. The most important part is dealing with the slush. We are the ones responsible for crushing the dreams of new writers, and occasionally helping bring these dreams to fruition. Over the years other names have been mentioned in the masthead that use the term editorial assistant or editorial intern, but I checked with Shawna and none of them filled this role the way we did. They were down in the publisher's office in Virginia, and I can only surmise their roles were more in the areas of copy editing/proofreading. There have only been three slush readers (a term I don't like if truth be told, because it implies this is all I do for the magazine—it isn't, which is why I'm the assistant editor).

Rebecca was the first of us, and she held this role the longest. Going by the mastheads, she was there from June 1995 all the way through April 2002. That's forty-two issues, a stretch of seven years. To put things in perspective, as entrenched as I am here at the magazine, at the time I write this I've only been doing this two years and a little over three months, not even close to Rebecca's tenure. She was part of the team for a long time. If I'm discussing the fiction of *Realms of Fantasy* then she certainly deserves a mention here as one of its editors. There will be others as we move along.

A rundown of this issue's nonfiction is as follows:

Gahan Wilson and Dan Silver handle the Book Reviews column, with Gahan reviewing *Worldwar: In the Balance* by Harry Turtledove and *Holy Terror* by Josephine Boyle, while Dan reviews *Daughter of Prophecy* by Anne Kelleher Bush and *Sword and Sorceress XII*, edited by Marion Zimmer Bradley. In the Movie/TV Column, newcomer Eric Niderost covers *First Knight*, *Braveheart*, and *Rob Roy*. Folkroots is once again handled by Terri Windling, and she discusses how Native American legends inspire magical fiction, art, and music. In the Artists Gallery, Jane Frank profiles the works of artist, Les Edwards. And in the Games column, M.C. Sumner reviews *Kilk & Play*, which allows you to design your own game, *The Great Dalmuti* from Wizards of the Coast, another card game by the creator of *Magic: The Gathering*, and *Ecastia*, a game for the PC.

Onto the fiction ...

The lead story is "Bread Crumbs & Stones" by Lisa Goldstein. This story is a reprint from the Ellen Datlow/Terri Windling anthology, *Snow White, Blood Red*. It is RoF's first story involving people of the Jewish faith. Set in contemporary times, it uses the fairy tale of Hansel & Gretal as a metaphor for the ovens that Nazis used to kill Jewish prisoners in during WWII.

I would term this piece as surrealism, which would be the first surrealistic piece to appear in the magazine. While surrealism is often more complex than the definition I'm about to offer, for the sake of brevity I'll use the following definition: surrealism is fantasy that is primarily achieved through the use of metaphors and/or symbolism. The tangible element of the fantastical is often absent or slight in such pieces (please, no arguments–we could spend a week debating over what surrealism is, along with all its nuances).

This is actually one of two surrealistic pieces in this issue. And I think it's important to note their appearance in the magazine, as I believe surrealism is probably the most unrecognizable form of fantasy to the general reading audience. Including such stories so early in the magazine's run signals to readers that this truly is a magazine for all realms of fantasy.

If you rewind to ten years ago, I would have been one of these people who didn't recognize this as fantasy. Actually, I would have sneered derisively, convinced this was literary fiction with no place whatsoever in a magazine like *Realms of Fantasy*. Whether they like it or not, even traditionalists will recognize things like urban fantasy and magic realism as fantasy literature. It's just of a sort they don't like. But some people don't get surrealism, not if it's supposed to be fantasy literature. It all comes down to whether you're willing to accept stories that often rely heavily (or solely) upon metaphors and symbolism to achieve the fantastical (again, the disclaimer of a simplistic definition).

I'll admit this form isn't my favorite kind of fantasy. In fact I usually hate it. The metaphors and symbols that most authors rely on (in my slush anyway) are terribly plain. Sometimes I'll reject a piece of what's supposed to be surrealism and scribble a quick note along the lines of "There's some nice writing here, but I don't consider this fantasy." I'm sure some of these writers get annoyed because they figure I just don't understand surrealism. The thing is I do. The problem is that when the metaphors and symbols are plain or cliche, the story falls short of fantastical and becomes mundane literary fiction. The metaphor of hell-on-earth is cliche. So are most dream metaphors authors come up with. These are what I see most often in the slush. You need to reach for something more powerful, more beautiful (or ugly), more original and thoughtful to convince me this is fantastical fiction. Fortunately, both of the surrealistic pieces in this issue do precisely this. Art to this one was provided by Paul Salmon, which marks his second illustration in the magazine.

Next up we have "Thorns" by Martha Wells. This was a reinvention of Sleeping Beauty, as a family protects Sleeping Beauty from being awoken by a prince because it would be cruel to bring her into this modern world. Art to this piece was provided by Todd Lockwood. It was nominated for the 1996 Chesley Award for Best Interior Illustration, making it the first RoF illustration to receive an award nomination.

Following this we have "Outside the Walls" by Dan'l Danehy-Oakes. This is another reivented fairy tale, in this case for Little Red Riding Hood, wherein we witness Red Riding Hood break all the literary rules to deliver her basket of goodies to grandma. Art to this one was provided by Mike Wright.

Then we have "Mending Maris" by Anne Young. Anne's story marked her first fiction publication. I should mention here that other than my own slush survivors, I never know if someone is publishing with us for the first time or is a slush survivor unless it's mentioned in the bio page. So I may miss mentioning someone's first publication as I continue doing these entries. As to the story itself, I found myself debating as to whether it was science fantasy or high fantasy. Eventually I decided this was science fantasy that changes back to high fantasy, and hence high fantasy at its heart. In a nutshell, it deals with how a king and queen's reconciliation leads to the rejection of technology and a chance at a fresh start. Art to this one was provided by Mary O'Keefe Young, which marks her fourth illustration in the magazine.

After this comes "Mother Moves In" by Deborah Wheeler. This is the other surrealistic piece I was talking about, and it deals with a mother seeking to reconcile with her artistically tormented daughter before the mother dies. Art to this one was provided by Debbie Hughes.

Finally we have "The Purl of the Pacific" by Allan Dean Foster. This one is a Mad Amos Malone tale. According to Foster's bio, Del Rey published a whole book of these tales, so if you like this one you may want to hunt down the collection. Not sure how I'd classify this story, hence I'll call it unclassifiable. As to what it's about, Mad Amos Malone and his spunky unicorn attempt to foil an evil Native American sorcerer. Art to this one was provided by Web Bryant, which marks his third illustration in the magazine.

So that wraps up this issue. And my favorite story? The surrealistic reprint, "Bread Crumbs & Stones" by Lisa Goldstein. And my favorite original piece to this issue? "Mother Moves In" by Deborah Wheeler. Surrealism wins in a landslide! And my favorite artwork? Todd Lockwood's illustration to "Thorns."

Originally posted on douglascohen.livenjournal.com on August 23rd, 2007

Part six in my comprehensive retrospect.ve as I read the fiction in *Realms of Fantasy* and offer my thoughts. This time around I'll be examining the August 1995 issue.

This issue kicks off with some reprinted cover art that I recognize as an old cover to *A Darkness at Sethanon* by Raymond E. Feist, the finale to his bestselling *Riftwar Saga*. It's been ages since I've read this (over fifteen years), but if memory serves correctly I believe it's a picture of Tomas driving his sword into the Lifestone. The actual art to this one is by Don Maitz, which marks the second time his work has graced RoF.

A rundown of the issue's nonfiction is as follows:

In the Books column, Gahan Wilson reviews *The Unnatura*. by David Prill, *Moondog* by Henry Garfield, and *Mysterium* by Robert Charles Wilson. Jeanne Cavelos makes her first appearance in the Books column this issue, with a review of *The Magnifiecent Wilf* by Gordon R. Dickson, and Dan Silver reviews *Adventures in the Twilight Zone*, edited by Carol Serling. In the Movie/TV column, Eric Niderfrost reviews fantasy movies, *Pocahontas* and *The Indian in the Cupboard*. Folkroots is handled by Terri Windling, and she writes about the transformational power of fairy tales as they pertain to the hero's quest. Terri also handles the Artists Gallery this issue, covering the art of Thomas Canty. Mark Sumner handles the Games Column, reviewing Terry Pratchett's *Discworld* on CD-ROM, and the card game, *Shadowfist*, from Daedalus Games.

On to the fiction ...

There are a ton of firsts in this issue. The lead story was "Transfusion" by Deborah Wheeler. By having fiction appear in this issue, Deborah becomes the first author to have stories in successive issues (her story in the last issue was "Mother Moves In"). This was also the first time a piece of vampire fiction appeared in the magazine's pages, and the first time we ran a piece of post-apocalyptic literature. The premise was a fascinating one, as a man and a vampire end up sharing a deep physical, emotional, and spiritual link after a blood transfusion.

Besides all these firsts, there is one other noting. Two issues earlier, we reprinted a story by Lisa Goldstein called "Bread Crumbs & Stones." The protagonist in this one was Jewish, which actually made it the first story run in RoF that featured a minority as the protagonist. In "Transfusion," there are two protagonists, one being the vampire, the other being the man he shared the transfusion with, in this case a Jewish man. So "Transfusion" marks the first story original to RoF to feature a Jewish protagonist. Art to this one was provided by Michael Beck, which marks his fourth illustration in the magazine.

And speaking of minority protagonists, we see another one in the very next story, this by Beverly Suarez-Beard. The name of the story is "The Ruby," and it marks the first tale to appear in RoF featuring a protagonist of Far Eastern descent (Chinese-American). This story also contains the very first dragon to make an appearance in the fiction pages. The story delves into Chinese mythology, and it was a fascinating blend of characterization and tension. In it, a smuggler makes the ultimate sacrifice to save his son after he unwittingly destroys a dragon egg that looks like a ruby. Suffice it to say the the story is hardly the stock interpretation that comes to mind at the mention of this mythic creature, and I applaud the fact that our first tale about the great wyrm went in a rather different direction. Art to this one was provided by Web Bryant, which marks his fourth illustration in the magazine.

Next up was a piece of magic realism by Carrie Richerson called "Geckos." This is a very unusual piece, but in a good way. The protagonist undergoes a rather radical transformation as she slowly becomes a gecko, and while not everything is explained down to the final letter, I didn't much care. The writing is really solid, and what ultimately sold me on this one were how many risks the author was willing to take. Art to this was provided by Alan M. Clark, and it seems to be a reprint of his Cover to Geckos by Carrie Richerson, from Roadkill Press.

After this comes another reprint, "The Frog Prince" by our very own book reviewer, Gahan Wilson. As you might guess, this was a reinterpretation of the classic fairy tale, as the frog prince tells a psychiatrist is recurring dream wherein he kisses a princess. As with much of the fiction that Shawna reprinted early on, it came from the Ellen Datlow/Terri Windling anthology, Snow White, Blood Red. Shawna must really love this anthology, because at this rate Realms will end up reprinting the whole book! Art to this one was provided by Micahel Dubisch.

Next up is "Radiomancer and Bubblegum" by S.N. Dyer, a quirky tale that examines the clash of pop culture and the spirit of old-school America as a pair of old-school souls fight to save America's soul. Art is provided by Mike Wright, which marks his second appearance in the magazine. At this point S.N. Dyer had published one previous story with us. This is worth noting because this means this would be the first issue with stories by two previous fiction contributors, the other being the aforementioned Deborah Wheeler. So by issue six, Shawna was already building a cast of recurring contributors to the magazine.

Finally we have "The Evil That Men Do" by Brian Stableford. This was a high fantasy tale with a lush milieu as a fomer wicked king sets out to repent for his sins, no matter the cost. However, the true appeal of this piece stems from the moral and ethical dilemmas that the author presented to both his protagonist and his readers, and the atrocious ironies that riddle the ending. I wasn't quite sure how to feel after having read this one, but I was glad that I did. Art to this was provided by Jon Foster.

So that wraps up this issue. And my favorite story? Lots of good stuff to choose from, but I have to give the nod "The Ruby" by Beverly Suarez-Beard. I am most definitely a sucker for dragons. And my favorite artwork? The nod goes to Jon Foster's illustration for "The Evil That Men Do."

Originally posted on douglascohen.livejournal.com on September 14th, 2007

Part seven in my comprehensive retrospective as I read the fiction in *Realms of Fantasy* and offer my thoughts. This time around I'll be discussing the October 1995 issue. The cover to this one proudly announces this as the one-year anniversary issue, which is always a big deal. One never knows how long any magazine will last (especially in these uncertain times for print), so a year is no small thing. Cover art to this one is a reprint of Bob Eggleton's work, which marks his second illustration to appear in the magazine. It first appeared on the cover of issue 154 of *Dragon Magazine*.

A rundown of the issue's nonfiction is as follows:

In the Books column, Gahan Wilson reviews *Tales of Zothique* from Necronomicon Press, which collects a number of short fiction tales from Clark Ashton Smith, *The Ghosts of Sleath* by James Herbert, *The X-Files: Whirlwind* by Charles Grant, *California Gothic* by Dennis Etchison, and Jeanne Cavelos reviews *Storm Rising: Book Two of the Mage Storms* by Mercedes Lackey. In the Movie/TV column, Eric Niderfrost covers the silver screen flick, *The Prophecy*. In the Folkroots column, Terri Windling discusses the magical lore of Italy. In the Artists Gallery, Robert D. San Souci covers the art of Stephen Johnson. And in the Games column, Mark Sumner reviews the board game, *The Hobbit Adventure Board Game*, *Warcraft: Orcs vs. Humans*, and *I.M. Meen* for the PC.

On to the fiction ...

As is usual in these early days of *Realms of Fantasy*, this issue has some more firsts. I've yet to actually break everything down, but I would guess the average issue of RoF contains six stories. The first issue actually had seven stories, but this was the first issue to have as few as five. No surprise though. "A Matter of Honor" by Chris Bunch is a very long tale (and the second story in this issue as opposed to the first), taking up a lot of pages. Not that I'm complaining. This story was rollicking good fun, filled with exotic milieus and clever solutions on the part of the protagonist who is attempting to be reunited with his wife. It also marked the first time we ran a piece in the subgenre of sword & sorcery. Art was handled by Todd Lockwood, which marks his second illustration in the magazine.

Another first for this issue came in the lead story of this issue, "Tuli, Prince of the Monguls" by William F. Wu. The previous issue featured our first story with an Asian protagonist when we ran "The Ruby" by Beverly Suarez-Beard. But that story was set during modern times (not a knock at all, since that was my favorite story of the issue). This was the first story we ran that featured a story set in the ancient Far East. In this story, Tuli, prince of the Mongols, and a sad scholar both seek death, but the author poses the question of which of them truly has nothing to live for.

Yet another first in this issue was our next piece, which is a fantasy story that deals with sports. In "Magic Carpets" by Leslie What we are presented with contemporary fantasy tale in which baseball factors heavily into the story. The story isn't really about baseball, more about two sisters seeking a better life while living with an abusive father, but baseball factors into this story heavily enough that the sports aspect is worth a mention. On the outside this probably sounds like an odd mix to put into one story, but it works if you read it. Art to this one was provided by Paul Salmon, which marks his third illustration in the magazine.

Following this was an unclassifiable tale by L. Timmel Duchamp called "Promises to Keep," a story about a family that has been taking care of a primordial creature that's been living in its basement for many generations. It had a bit of a New Age flavor to it, something I haven't seen in RoF before. Come to think of it, I don't think I've read any New Age fantasy before this one, at least none that I can recall. Art to this one was provided by Broeck Steadman, which marks his second appearance in the magazine.

The last story in this issue was a short tale by Geoffrey A. Landis called "Tale of the Fish Who Loved a Bird." This story marks the first true fable we ran in the magazine. Going by the title, this sounds like a preposterous idea, but it's also intriguing enough that you want to find out just what the author is up to. It turns out to be a very beautiful tale, and come the end you absolutely believe it. Just goes to show if your imagination is fertile enough and the writer is skillful enough, any idea can be made to work. Art to this one is provided by Janet Ausilio Dannheiser, which marks her second illustration in the magazine. It's also worth noting that this is the first issue where the cover and interior illustrations are all by artists whose work has already appeared in the magazine.

So that wraps up this issue. And my favorite story? I have to give the nod to "Tale of the Fish Who Loved a Bird" by Geoffrey A. Landis. And my favorite artwork? Broeck Steadman's illustration to "Promises to Keep" by L. Timmel Duchamp.

Originally posted on douglascohen.livejournal.com on October 11th, 2007

Part eight in my comprehensive retrospective as I read the fiction in *Realms of Fantasy* and offer my thoughts. This time around I'll be discussing the December 1995 issue.

The cover to this one is illustrated by Michael Whelan, which marks his third illustration in the magazine. This was originally an unused illustration for the cover to *Dragon Fire* by Melanie Rawn. It ended up being published as a print from Glass Onion before finding its way onto the cover of RoF.

A rundown of this issue's nonfiction is as follows:

In the Books column, Gahan Wilson reviews *Candlenight* by Phil Rickman, *Traveling with the Dead* by Barbara Hambly, and *Zod Wallop* by William Browning Spencer, while Jeanne Cavelos reviews *Great Writers & Kids Write Spooky Stories*, edited by Martin H. Greenberg, Jill M. Morgan, and Robert Weinberg, as well as *Isaac Asimov's Ghosts*, edited by Gardner Dozois & Sheila Williams. In Folkroots, Terri Windling discusses the magical legends of the "Enchanted Lands" of Wales. In the Movie/TV column, newcomer Lisa MacCarillo covers the movie, *Jumanji*. In the Artists Gallery, Ric Meyers covers James Gurney's *Dinotopia: the World Beneath*. And in the Games column Mark C. Sumner reviews the video game *Pitfall: the Mayan Adventure*, *Panzer Dragoon* for the Sega Saturn, and the miniature paints and accessories line, *The Chessex Magic Wand Beginner Paint Gift Set*.

On to the fiction ...

The lead story is "Eagle's Beak and Wings of Bronze" by Deborah Wheeler, which marks her third appearance in RoF (the first author to reach this mark). This one is a fairy tale about a were-griffin and a were-dragon, along with the expectations and secrets revolving around these characters. I'll point out that while I've yet to read any stories in RoF about werewolves, this does mark the first story in the magazine with lycanthropes of some form. Art to this one was a reprint from Carl Lundgren.

Next up we have "Wings" by Patricia Duffy Novak, the first piece rooted in Greek mythology to appear in RoF. Here we have a retelling of the Icarus myth; if you substitute the sun with the moon you get the gist of the major component she tweaked. In terms of reinvention to a well-known tale, this is one of the more engaging ideas I've encountered in RoF. Art to this one was provided by Carol Heyer, which marks her her third illustration in the magazine.

The third story is "Good Help is Hard to Find" by William John Watkins, a vampire tale with a rather psychological bent. Told strictly through the point of view of one of the vampires, this tale focuses on the mindset of a vampire, why they do what they do, how they think. It didn't make me sympathize, but it did make me understand. Art to this one was provided by Mark Harrison.

So of the three stories I've discussed so far, one was a fairy tale and another story was a retelling. So I guess it's only appropriate that this fourth story was a retelling of a fairy tale, the Little Mermaid to be exact. I must confess that before reading this story ("Foam" by Dave Smeds), the only version of this tale I ever came across was early during my run as assistant editor at RoF. One of the first slush survivors I passed along was a dark retelling of the Little Mermaid, although at the time I didn't realize this was a retelling. It was just a cool story by a good friend, Alethea Kontis. Shawna passed on that tale, though Alethea did place it elsewhere and eventually sold us another story (to be discussed many many retrospectives from now). So yes, this means I've never even seen the Disney movie. (I'm so deprived!) But with this Little Mermaid retelling, we have the first story on RoF with a mermaid in it. Art to this one was provided by Gary Lippincott, which marks his second illustration in the magazine.

The next story is "The Perseids" by Robert Charles Wilson. This is a reprint ...sort of. As Shawna explained it to me, she accepted this story first for RoF, but it was first printed in the Canadian anthology, *Northern Frights 3*. The Locus Awards index lists this as being nominated for 1996 Nebula Award for Best Novelette, with *Realms of Fantasy* as the publisher. However, it also lists the nomination as being [deleted]. This all happened way before my time, but I think I can piece together what happened here. The story was first published in a Canadian anthology, and the Nebulas only recognize stories originally published in the U.S. Meanwhile, Sovereign Media neglected to print anywhere in RoF that this story was a reprint (perhaps because Shawna accepted it first). So I suspect that for a long time a lot of people thought it was eligible for the Nebula Award, to the point that it was nominated before everyone was made aware of the mistake. What a mess!

Anyway, while it never had a chance to win the Nebula Award, it should be noted that it won the Aurora Award in Canada for Best Short Science Fiction. And not to be left out, it was also nominated for the 1996 World Fantasy Award for Best Short Fiction (although the original publisher was listed as *Northern Frights 3.*)

This story has a heavy philosophical sensibility to it, questioning the very nature of evolution and life. Early on I was absolutely convinced this story was science fiction, but as I kept reading it, I came to see how this could be considered fantasy as well. To me, it doesn't fall neatly into any of these categories though. You can argue for it belonging to either one of these genres really. Given this, it could certainly be published as a piece of fantasy. In her editorial byline for this piece, Shawna describes it as blend of Arthur C. Clarke & H.P. Lovecraft. I agree, but I'd also add that something about the characterizations and paranoia also brings Philip K. Dick to mind. As to the story itself, it's really hard to describe. The best summation I could come up with is a philsophical exploration of the evolution of life in the gnososphere, an amalgam of art, culture, and technology. It had me thinking long after I was done with it. I may think about stories after I'm done with them, but this was something far rarer. It just had me thinking. Very heady stuff. Art to this one was provided by Ken Graning, which marks his third illustration in the magazine.

The last story this issue is "Stealing From the Woman Snake" by Fred Askew. It marks the magazine's first tall tale, a zany piece about a man stealing soil from an ant colony run by a coral snake. Kind of coincidence that I should read this so recently, since I'll soon be passing along the first tall tale I've ever fished out of the submissions piles. Art to this one was provided by Joel Napstrek.

So this brings us to the end of *Realms of Fantasy* for 1995. And my favorite story for this issue? I have to give the nod to "The Perseids" because of how thought-provoking it was. And my favorite story original to the magazine? "Foam" by Dave Smeds. And my favorite artwork? Carol Heyer's illustration to "Wings" by Patricia Duffy Novak.

Originally posted on douglascohen.livejournal.com on October 19ᵗʰ, 2007

Part nine in my comprehensive retrospective as I read the fiction in *Realms of Fantasy* and offer my thoughts. This time around I'll be discussing the February 1996 issue.

The cover to this issue is by Steven Assel. Attempts to determine the origin of this piece were unsuccessful.

A rundown of this issue's nonfiction is as follows:

In the Books column, Gahan Wilson reviews *The Off Season* by Jack Cady, *The Shape-Changer's Wife* by Sharon Shinn, *Cthulu 2000*, edited by Jim Turner, while Jeanne Cavlos reviews *The Merlin Chronicles*, edited by Mike Ashley, and newcomer Louisa Bourne reviews *The Book of Goddesses*, with words and pictures by Kris Waldherr. In Folkroots, Terri Windling writes about Eastern European Magic: alchemy, witchery, and puppetry in Prague. In the movie/TV column, newcomer Dan Perez writes about the thirteen best fantasy films you've never heard of. In the Artists Gallery, Jane Frank writes about the art in game and collector cards. And in the Games column, Marc C. Sumner reviews the RPG, *Everway*, from Wizards of the Coast, and the dice game, *Dragon Dice* from TSR. Obviously these reviews take place in the days before Wizards of the Coast bought TSR.

On to the fiction ...

The fiction leads off with a rather familiar title to all fantasy fans, this being "The Return of the King." And while this funny fantasy does indeed draw upon elements from Lord of the Rings and *The Silmarillion*, it also draws heavily on Norse mythology (as do LOTR & the Silmarillion, of course), and, of all things, Elvis. Quite a mix. And with the story being written by Susan Wade & Don Webb, this also marks the first time that RoF has published a co-written story. Art to this one was provided by Annie Lunsford, which marks her second illustration in the magazine.

Next up was "Diana of the Hundred Breasts" by Robert Silverberg. According to the records I'm keeping as I go along, this marks the fiftieth work of fiction published by *Realms of Fantasy*. I'm almost embarrassed to admit that this is the first piece of fiction I've read by Robert Silverberg. I've known about him and respected his accomplishments/contributions to our genre for some years, have at least a few of his novels in my room, but somehow I've never read any of his works. After reading this piece, I understand why it was Long Listed for the Locus Award in 1997 for Best Novelette, and was also selected for inclusion in the tenth annual edition of *Year's Best Fantasy and Horror*. As to what the story is about, in the broadest sense of the word it falls into the realm of Greek mythology, but really it is a character piece, and an observation about how lack of faith can be a kind of faith itself, and having this shattered can be every bit as powerful as having one's faith shattered. Very riveting, and I'm looking forward to reading more of Silverberg's works in the future. Art to this piece was provided by Web Bryant, which marks his fifth illustration in the magazine.

Third in the lineup is "Pacifica" by Julie Stevens. Sort of a historical fantasy piece, it's set in the in the milieu of Hawaii before the white men reached its shores. The author does an excellent job of conveying the milieu, the simple but fascinating way of life, as she tells the story of one man who rises to be the greatest of prophets among his people, but where she takes the tale is full of sad, powerful, and unexpected ironies. Art to this one was provided by Carol Heyer, which marks her fourth illustration in the magazine.

Jack McDevitt is generally known for his science fiction, but with 'Duex Ex" he shows that he can write fantasy as well. This is a quirky tale about thieves pulling off a heist in a house containing a rather eclectic assortment of artifacts. Elaborating will simply give away the story, so I'll simply add that there's nice undercurrent of humor here and leave it at that. Art to this one was provided by Michael Dubisch, which mark his second illustration in the magazine.

The final story is "Doll Skulls: A New Tale of Paradis" by Tanith Lee, which marks her second appearance in the magazine. I gave some thought as to how I would classify this story before settling on literary fairy tale. In the city of Paradis, a poor and beleaguered woman buys her daughter a pair of beautiful dolls at an extreme discount. As is often the case in such stories, the dolls turn out to be more than she bargained for. But Lee excels at keeping the reader uncertain what will happen next, and coupled with skill at weaving hypnotic prose and lush milieus, you find yourself being drawn ever deeper into the story before it reaches a rather satisfying conclusion. Art to this one was provided by Mary O'Keefe Young, which marks her fifth illustration in the magazine.

And that's it for February 1996. I liked a number of tales in this issue, but my runaway favorite is "Diana of the Hundred Breasts" by Robert Silverberg. I have a feeling this is one of my favorite authors waiting to happen. Just need to read more of his stuff before I can make such a bold statement. And my favorite art this issue? Carol Heyer's piece to "Pacifica" by Julie Stevens.

Originally posted on douglascohen.livejournal.com on November 20th, 2007

Part ten in my comprehensive retrospect:ve as I read the fiction in the *Realms of Fantasy* and offer my thoughts. This time around I'll be doing that with the April 1996 issue.

The cover to this issue is by Brom and was nominated for a 1997 Chesley for Cover Illustration. This illustration originally appeared as the cover to issue 197 of *Dragon Magazine*.

A rundown of this issue's nonfiction is as follows:

In the Books column, Gahan Wilson reviews a reissuing of *Ill Met in Lankhmar* by Fritz Leiber, *Love & Sleep* by John Crowley, and *The Bloody Red Baron* by Kim Newman, qhile Jeanne Cavelos reviews *The Book of Atrix Wolfe* by Patricia A. McKillip. In the Folkroots column, Terri Windling writes about Merlin and Melusine: legends from the Breton coast of France. In the Movie/TV column, newcomer Craig Reid discusses the TV shows *Hercules* and *Xena*. In the Artists Gallery, Michael Resnick discusses the art of Jim Warren. And in the Games column, Mark C. Sumner reviews PC games *Warcraft II* and *Shannara*, which is based on Terry Brooks' books.

On to the fiction ...

The first story is "Sarah's Window" by Janni Lee Simner. I would term this story is a middle grade fantasy, which marks the first time such a tale has graced the magazine. Interestingly enough, the protagonist isn't a young child, but the child's father as his quest to save his child leads to a dangerous rediscovery of his second childhood. In a very few pages, Janni manages to explore a lot of old and familiar tropes in fresh ways, all the while painting a rather vivid picture with powerful characterizations. Art to this one was provided by J.K. Potter.

Next up is "Snow" by Al Sarrantonio, another middle grade fantasy, but this time the protagonists *are* children. The story itself is fun, as it explores the old theme of being careful what you wish for. In this case the children wish for it to snow forever, which would have a number of obvious ramifications. Art to this was provided by Laurie Harden, which marks her second illustration in the magazine.

We move back to an adult protagonist in the next tale, "Pavanne For a Dead Pross" by Jo Clayton. This story is dark urban fantasy. So far I haven't encountered much urban fantasy in the back issues. For that matter, I've noticed we haven't run too much urban fantasy since I've come aboard, nor have I come across too many stories of this sort in the slush that have excited me. And this leaves me wondering something. I've heard a number of times (and have said as much myself) that it's difficult to write effective high fantasy in the shorter form. But based on everything I've read so far–these being the earliest issues of RoF and the most recent ones–I'd say we've published noticeably more high fantasy than urban fantasy. So maybe urban fantasy is another subgenre which lends itself more to the longer form (just as sword & sorcery often lends itself to the shorter form). As to the piece itself, it is a dark and tense tale in which a witch brings a rapist and killer to the justice of three other witches. Art to this one was provided by John Berkey.

Next up is "With Vorpal Sword in Hand" by Bruce Boston. Just about everyone is familiar with Lewis Carroll's nonsense poem dealing with the Jabberwock. This tale attempts to make some sense of the nonsensical, as it treats the Jabberwocky amd company as real characters with real motivations. A very outside-the-box tale, and I'm sure fans of Lewis Carroll's *Alice in Wonderland* will appreciate this one. Art to this onwas provided by Marc Sasso.

The last story is a high fantasy piece, "Leuka and Phlego" by Lisa R. Cohen. This has to be one of the longest stories we've ever run in RoF. If it's not a novella then it comes in as a very long novelette. In this one, a man fleeing a fey who enslaved him through his own voice takes refuge among a pair of sisters, one a warrior, the other a sorceress. The characterizations and ideas in this piece strike me as its biggest strengths. Each character is clearly defined, and some of the ideas–like a fey queen stealing a human male's beautiful voice for her own nefarious purposes–are quite engaging. Art to this one was provided by David Martin.

So that covers the fiction for April 1996. And my favorite story? "Sarah's Window" by Janni Lee Simner. And my favorite artwork? Marc Sasso's illustration to "Vorpal Sword in Hand" by Bruce Boston.

Originally posted on douglascohen.livejournal.com on December 18th, 2007

Part eleven in my comprehensive retrospective as I read the fiction in *Realms of Fantasy* and offer my thoughts. This time around I'll be tackling the June 1996 issue.

The cover to this one is provided by Keith Parkinson. It was originally the cover to issue 106 of *Dragon Magazine*. It's also worth ncting that this marks the first of *Realms of Fantasy's* infamous chicks in chainmail covers.

A look in the masthead reveals that Ronald M. Stevens is no longer the art director. His replacement is Stephen Vann.

A rundown of this issue's nonfiction is as follows:

In the Books column, Gahan Wilson reviews *Expiration Date* by Tim Powers, *The 37th Mandala* by Marc Laidlaw, *Common Clay: 20 Odd Stories* by Brian W. Aldiss, while Jeanne Cavlos reviews *Lammas Night*, created by Mercedes Lackey, edited by Josepha Sherman. In the Movie/TV column, Dan Perez covers the movie, *Dragonheart*. In the Folkroots column, Terri Windling writes about hounds, hares, and standing stones: the lore of England's west country. In the Artists Gallery, renowned children's author Jane Yolen discusses children's book illustrations. And in the Games column, Mark Sumner reviews the CD Rom games, *D* and *Psychic Detective*.

On to the fiction ...

The lead story is "The Emperor of Dreams" by James Killus. This story falls somewhere between the realm of surrealism and metafiction. It deals with alternating scenes between a fantasy author in search of the perfect ending to his story, and snippets from the actual story. At one point an ending is suggested to him (one we don't learn), and he discards it. Come the end, we get to read the end to the "author's" story, and I do think that it's right the one, both to the story and to the story-within-the-story. I suspect it's the ending he discarded, though there's no way to be certain. Stories like this usually fail, or if nothing else fail to hold my attention. This one pulled it off though. Art to this one was provided by Chuck Demorat, which marks his second illustration in the magazine.

Next up is "Sphinx Song" by the aforementioned Jane Yolen. This marks the third time I'm admitting to my pathetic inadequacies as a fantasy reader, because I'd never before read anything by Jane Yolen. When I originally posted this retrospective, it marked the first time I'd read something by Jane Yolen. (There is nothing like going through every issue of a fantasy magazine to throw a man off his pedestal of fantasy knowledge.) Since then I've read all her stories in RoF and was even privileged enough to work with her on a story she delivered to an anthology that I coedited. But the first time I read something by Jane (i.e. this story) I was struck by her honest and easy storytelling voice. It oozes unassuming charm. And I learned more about the different kinds of sphinxes than I ever expected, because in this piece they come in all shapes and sizes ...and voices. A short read, but a fun one. Art to this one was provided by Janet Ausilio, which marks her third illustration in the magazine.

The third and longest story of the issue is "The God at Midnight" by Thomas E. Fuller and Brad Strickland. This one provides a fascinating alternate version of Greece where several gods act as advisers to Alexander the Great, and Alexander himself, practically a god already, is on the verge of achieving immortality, courtesy of an Egyptian vampire that's forced to obey him. The word "vampire" is never used, but if you pay attention it's obvious enough what we're dealing with. This one is dark, lush, and rich with invention. Art to this piece was provided by Mary O'Keefe Young, which marks her sixth illustration in the magazine.

Next up was "Vanishing Acts" by Kelly Link, a magic realism piece, I think, although the age of the protagonist might leave one wanting to call this young adult. This story was one of Kelly's first published stories. I know this because over the summer Gavin J. Grant happened to mention to me that one of Kelly's first stories was published in RoF. As this is the only story she published in RoF, it's obviously the one he's referring to. As to the story itself, I have to describe it as a slow burn. Kelly really excelled at capturing the mundane details of life, and while I could appreciate the writing and her eye for detail, I wasn't sure if this piece was for me. But the more it went on the more it drew me in, until after a few pages I was devouring the words, and the mundane had smoothly and seamlessly become quite a fabulous tale in which we learn that people can vanish in all manners of ways, but usually it's through traditional means. Very skillfully done. Art to this one was provided by Michael Gibbs.

After this we have a rather silly tale called "Grandma's Blessing" by Frank C. Gunderloy, a story about how blessings can just as easily be viewed as curses, in this case in the form of cosmic beasties. Art to this one was provided by Michael Dubisch, which marks his third illustration in the magazine.

Finally we have the young adult tale, "Beth's Unicorn" by Lawrence Watt-Evans. On more than one occasion Shawna has mentioned to me how tired she is of unicorn stories, so I guess that means she must have really liked this one. It's an engaging enough tale, and I think it's the thematic content that puts this one over the top. Among the themes I detected here were how sometimes we blind ourselves to the magic right beneath our noses, and how we should never take gifts for granted. Art to this one was provided by Ken Graning, which marks his fourth illustration in the magazine.

So that's it for this issue. And my favorite story? "Vanishing Acts" by Kelly Link. And my favorite artwork? Keith Parkinson's cover.

Originally posted on douglascohen.livejournal.com on December 26th, 2007

Part twelve in my comprehensive retrospective as I read the fiction in *Realms of Fantasy* and offer my thoughts. This edition's focus will be the August 1996 issue.

The cover to this one is by Tim Hildebrandt. It was originally part of the 1991 *Visions of Otherworld Calendar*.

A rundown of this issue's nonfiction is as follows:

In the Books column, Gahan Wilson reviews *The Golden Compass* by Philip Pullman, *Remnant Population* by Elizabeth Moon, *Serial Killer Days* by David Prill, and Jeanne Cavelos reviews *Black Horse for the King* by Anne McCaffrey, and *Touch Wood*, edited by Peter Crowther. In the Movie/TV column, Dan Perez reviews Peter Jackson's *The Frighteners*. In the Folkroots column, Terri Windling discusses fairy tales in poetry. In the Artists Gallery, Harlan Ellison discusses the artwork of Barclay Shaw. And in the Games column, Mark Sumner reviews *Civilization II* for the PC, the miniature game, *Warhammer*, and the video game, *Resident Evil*.

On to the fiction ...

The lead story is a magic realism piece by Peni R. Griffin called "Goldfish." This one resonated with me, revolving around a premise that on the surface sounds extremely absurd: a man and a goldfish swap places. And no, this wasn't a comical piece. Far from it. It actually features some very deep characterizations, and at times the protagonist reminded me of Charlie from *Flowers for Algernon*, one of my all-time favorite novels (I've yet to read the shorter version of this story). Just goes to show you that if you have a story worth telling, it really doesn't matter how absurd your premise is. It's also worth noting that was the first piece in *Realms of Fantasy* that featured a protagonist of Hispanic descent. Art to this one was provided by Jody Williams.

Next up is "Death Loves Me" by Tanith Lee, which marks her third appearance in the magazine. This particular piece takes place in ancient Greece, and considering the author, it's no surprise that it features a lush atmosphere with rich language. Overall the fantasy element here is slight, but it plays a pivotal role as Lee delves into the world of charioteers in a story of love, lust, betrayal, and deception as a charioteer is made to believe he kills Death. Art to this one was provided by Todd Lockwood, which marks his third illustration in the magazine. This illustration was the winner of the 1997 Chesley Award for Interior Illustration, making this the first artwork in Realms to win an award.

The next story, "Remedy of the Bane" by Storm Constantine, also relies on a slight but essential fantasy element, and also relies on a whole lot of lust, deception, and evocative language. The characterizations here were perfect, as we read about a princess who takes delight in tormenting her protectors. For beginning authors I'd point to this story as an excellent example of characters creating plot through their behaviors and actions, to such an extent that there was no other way this piece could have ended. I saw it coming, and was very satisfied when the author delivered. And then she took it a step further, surprising me and taking the story to another level in the last paragraph. I love it when that happens. Art to this one was provided by Carol Heyer, which marks her fifth illustration in the magazine.

Following this is a short-short by Pat York called "A Faerie's Tale," in which the author spins a quick yarn about the lengths some fairies will go to protect that which is theirs. Art to this one was provided by Laurie Harden, which marks her third illustration in the magazine.

The last story in this issue is "The Women Kahele Loved" by Julie Stevens. With this story, Stevens returns to her milieu of a Hawaii imbued with gods and magic, which she introduced to RoF readers with "Pacifica" in the February 1996 issue. As with "Pacifica," a big chunk of the story's charm comes from the author exploring this rather exotic milieu. She also wields a deft hand with the characterization, telling the story of a chief's wife and his witch-lover working together to avenge his murder. And let's not look past an important first for the magazine, as this story also explores the lesbian relationship that develops between these women. Before this, the closest any story came to this territory was a tale by Tanith Lee back in the February 1995 issue called "The Story Told By Smoke: From the Journals of St. Strange." In that story, two female characters shared kisses and caresses, but before things were cut tragically short before anything might progress further. So "The Women Kahele Loved" represents the first story in the magazine to significantly explore homosexuality, and since both women had also shared a bed with Kahele (the aforementioned chief), one might also argue there is at least a passing exploration of bisexuality.

Of course, Kahele is dead when these women get together, and the fact that these women end up having sex with both sexes isn't something the author really focuses on. Still, it's worth mentioning. Art to this one was provided by Ken Graning, which marks his fifth illustration in the magazine.

So that wraps up this issue. And my favorite story? A lot good stories in this issue, but for me the runaway favorite is "Goldfish" by Peni R. Griffin. And my favorite artwork? Todd Lockwood's illustration to "Death Loves Me" by Tanith Lee.

Originally posted on douglascohen.livejournal.com on December 27th, 2007

Part thirteen in my comprehensive retrospective as I read the fiction in *Realms of Fantasy* and offer my thoughts. This time around I'll be discussing the October 1996 issue.

The cover to this one is by Sanjulian. Attempts to determine the origin of this illustration were met without success.

A rundown of this issue's nonfiction is as follows:

In the Books column, Gahan Wilson reviews *Resume with Monsters* by William Brown Spencer, *The Prestige* by Christopher Priest (man oh man, do I love that movie adaptation), and *Bereavements* by Richard Lortz. In the Movie/TV column, Dan Perez covers the ABC television miniseries based on Stephen King's *The Shining*. In the Folkroots column, Terri Windling writes about the story of Cinderella. In the Artists Gallery, Terry Brooks writes about the art of Keith Parkinson. And in the Games column, Mark Sumner reviews the PC game, *Quake*, White Wolf's role-playing manual, *Mage: the Ascension*, and a tarot deck designed to accompany the aforementioned item.

On to the fiction ...

First of all, I should mention something about the contributors overall. Prior to this issue, the most authors we've had in a particular issue who had previously contributed stories to the magazine were two. In this issue, there are four authors who have previously contributed fiction to the magazine. It should be noted that one of them, Charles de Lint, had only previously contributed a reprint, whereas the other three authors had contributed original fiction. Regardless, this strikes me as an important step in the magazine's evolution, as it demonstrates how Shawna was building up a stable of regular contributors on top of the new writers the magazine kept introducing.

As to the stories themselves, the first one is "Scapegoat" by Susan J. Kroupa. While she would go on to publish other stories with RoF, in this particular issue she is the lone author who is new to the magazine. This particular story dealt with rainmaking and sacrifices, drawing heavily on Native American mythology as a youth carrying the heritage of an extinct rainmaker clan must make it rain to save his people. It also marks the first story in the magazine that featured a Native American protagonist. Art to this one was provided by David Beck, which marks his fifth illustration in the magazine.

Next up is an urban fantasy tale, "Shining Nowhere But in the Dark" by the aforementioned Charles de Lint. It marks second story in the magazine, but as already noted, his first original piece. This was an interesting and thoughtful story, dealing with the links between life, death, and dreaming, and what happens when a woman who never dreams tries to keep it this way. Art to this one was provided by Mary O'Keefe Young, which marks her seventh illustration in the magazine.

Next up was "Nairich" by William F. Wu, which marks his second appearance in the magazine. This piece is set in 1906 San Francisco, right around the time of the Great Quake. It's very atmospheric ghost story, informing the readers about some of the darker practices during this time, all in the interests of making money. In this particular piece, a young Chinese woman discovers the truth about her parents and they once worked for in 1906 San Francisco.

Somehow I guessed the ending to this one. Growing up, I mostly read novels and it became a habit of mine to figure out the endings to books. Eventually, I got so good at it that I was guessing endings hundreds of pages in advance, not to mention lots of other twists along the way. So for me, if I didn't see the plot twists coming in a novel it would score big points with me. With short fiction it's a different bag of worms. Sure, I figure out some endings, but short fiction relies on a lot of literary tricks I'm not nearly as used to reading about (yet). Also, with a magazine like Realms, where we generally don't publish anything longer than 10,000 words, a story reaches its end very quickly. You don't have time to chew on the unfolding events like you do with a novel. You read, you blink, and it's over. It's more like swallowing stuff whole. So sometimes, before I can figure out where a story might be going, it's done. This particular story wasn't terribly long, and the ending was one that should have surprised me, I think, but somehow, halfway through it, I said to myself, "She must be [blank]." And she was. So maybe all this short fiction reading is making me better at figuring out the endings to shorter works, or maybe I got lucky. Either way, I'll give myself credit for figuring this one out, because I don't think I should have! Art to this one was provided by Web Bryant, which marks his sixth illustration in the magazine.

The fourth story is "The Beautiful Wassilissa" by Don Webb, which marks his second appearance in the magazine, and the first where he wrote the story himself. This was a dark fairy tale, a mixture of Cinderella components and Russian folklore about a girl who must accomplish impossible tasks for the witch Baba-Yaga. Despite its brevity, I found it rather engrossing because of its macabre presentation. Art to this one was provided by Annie Lunsford, which marks her third illustration in the magazine.

Finally we have "Hot Death on Wheels" by Geoffrey A. Landis, which marks his second appearance in the magazine. This was an enjoyable piece about a hot-rodder who never loses ...and then one day he must drag-race with Death. It was the voice that sold me on this one, because it was particularly strong. One interesting thing about this story though was the personality of the narrator. He slanders entire groups of people as he tells the tale, using terms such as "fags" and "coons" (being as this piece seems to be set in the 1950s, the insult of "coons" was a little more common then, I think). Now this is the sort of thing where people could take offense. Easily. But I have friends that are gay, and friends that are black, and I wasn't offended by the author's language. Why? Because I didn't believe these were the author's opinions, but the narrator's. There is a definite difference. With stories that deal with racism or other prejudices, ignorant/slanderous language is often used to help illuminate the themes of a given piece. But this piece wasn't about racism, and the terms were used in a very casual manner. So in a case such as this it falls to the author to get it across that these are the narrator's views, not his, and to do this without interrupting the flow of the story. And I believe he pulled it off, all through the voice of the narrator. Shawna must have thought so too, or she never would have published this. Also, given when this piece was supposed to take place, the language could arguably be viewed as a sign of the times. Art to this one was provided by Mike Wright, which marks his third illustration in the magazine.

So that wraps up this issue. And my favorite story? "Shining Nowhere But in the Dark" by Charles de Lint. And my favorite artwork? David Beck's illustration to "Scapegoat" by Susan J. Kroupa.

Originally posted on douglascohen.livejournal.com on December 29th, 2007

Part fourteen in my comprehensive retrospective as I read the fiction in *Realms of Fantasy* and offer my thoughts. This time around I'll be blabbing about the December 1996 issue.

The cover to this one is by Michael Whelan, which marks his fourth illustration in the magazine. It was originally the cover to the novel *Sunrunner's Fire* by Melanie Rawn.

A quick perusal of the masthead reveals that with this issue, Rebecca McCabe, the original master of slush* at RoF, was promoted from Editorial Assistant to Assistant Editor. When my own name first appeared in the RoF masthead, it was as Assistant Editor, but Rebecca still earns my jealousy. First, she was with the magazine much longer and was basically there from its inception, which is kind of cool. Second, back when she was the editorial assistant/assistant editor there was a letters page, something I've been enjoying reading as I go through the back issues. And in this particular issue, she actually got to *answer* one of the letters! Barring a miraculous resurrection of the letters page, this is something I will never get to do. Alas.

Moving on ...

A rundown of this issue's nonfiction is as follows:

In the Books column, Gahan Wilson reviews *The Panic Hand* by Jonathan Carroll, *Sheep* by Simon Magnin, *The Book of Hyperborea* by Clark Ashton Smith, edited by Will Murray, and Jeanne Cavelos reviews *Glenraven* by Marion Zimmer Bradley and Holly Lisle, and *The Cormorant* by Stephen Gregory. In the Folkroots column, Terri Windling discusses deer maidens and selkies. In the Movie/TV column, Dan Perez discusses thirteen dark fantasy films you should see but probably haven't. In the Artists Gallery, Linda D'Agostino Clinger discusses the art of Dean Morrissey. And in the Games column, Mark Sumner reviews *Daggerfall* and LucasArt's *Afterlife*, both for the CD-ROM.

On to the fiction ...

The opening story is "Where's the Luck?" by William Nabors. This is a dark and entertaining tale about luck, the absence of it, and creating it as a man tries to create new luck for himself during a heat wave in Texas. The fantastical element is rather ambiguous, but is presented in a satisfying fashion. Art to this one was provided by Janet Aulisio, which marks her fourth illustraton in the magazine.

The second story is "The Secret of the Mummy's Brain" by William Eakin. This story marks the first mummy tale to appear in the magazine's pages, although the mummy we meet is far different from the typical shambling ancient pharaoh wrapped in white tape. It's hard to describe this one, but basically a mummy falls in love with a fat woman in the town of Redgunk, Mississippi, and it's told in the second person. A number of these Redgunk tales have appeared in RoF, and this one is the first of the bunch. While these Redgunk tales tend to be character pieces, they're also heavily reliant on the atmosphere and style, which at times could give William Faulkner a run for his money in sentence length. Art to this one was provided by David Martin, which marks his second illustration in the magazine.

Next up is "Love Equals Four, Plus Six" by A.M. Dellamonica. To me, this story had a slipsteam feel to it: part fantasy, past sf, and part mainstream, exploring love in terms both mathematical and transcendental as a husband's accident lands him in a coma while overseas in London, and he and his pregnant wife use mathematics to bridge the gap between them. Some might not consider this one fantasy (and a letter in one of the subsequent letter pages suggested as much), but I can see the argument that it is. That said, recently I've noticed how much editors can influence the definitions of our genre. Some pieces are no-brainers concerning the genre no matter how you break it down. Everyone will agree that Conan and Lord of the Rings are of the fantasy brand. I, Robot and Ender's Game are unquestionably science fiction. But every so often a story comes along where it's not quite as clear what genre it falls in. Often, it doesn't really matter. Over the years I've come to appreciate George R. R. Martin's take on this stuff: he notes how his father just called all these kinds of stories–fantasy, science fiction, and horror–weird stuff. And it is. So long as you like it, cool. That's what matters most.

But ...

When you get down to the slicing and dicing, there are certainly different types of weird stuff. Readers of RoF expect fantasy stories. If they read a horror story in the magazine, it had best have a fantasy element. If they read something "science-y," it would be wise if it were of the science fantasy variety.

Except ...

With *Realms of Fantasy*, Shawna determines which stories are fantasies. Sure, I do it with the slush, but she makes the final call. And with stories that aren't explicitly fantasy, sometimes her determinations come into play. Shawna has published stories in the magazine I consider science fiction (Dellamonica's story isn't one of them). Just last week I learned about a story she enjoyed but rejected as too science fictional for *Realms of Fantasy*. I didn't feel this way at all. I loved the story, believing it to be an excellent piece that expanded the definitions of both science fantasy and fantasy as a whole. But so it goes. As long as Shawna makes the calls for the magazine's fiction, hers is the most important opinion as to what constitutes proper fantasy within our pages. If pressed, I'd say her definition of fantasy is a little broader than my own. On the other hand, she did reject that piece I consider to be fantasy enough for RoF. So you never know what might tickle an editor's opinion concerning acceptance or rejection of a particular piece when it comes to the underlying bones of its genre.

Art to this one was provided by John Berkey, which marks his second illustration in the magazine.

Next up is "The Stover Cut" by Calvin Horne. This dark fantasy is a ghost story relying heavily on voice and milieu. The milieu was particularly engaging, introducing readers to the nitty-gritty of the struggling shipping industry through swamps and marshes during the Depression as a man tries to haul a load of good through a haunted swamp. A well-researched and unusual milieu can do wonders for taking a story to the next level. Art to this one was provided by Gary Lippincott, which marks his third illustration in the magazine.

The fifth story is "Holding Pattern" by Jack McDevitt, which marks his second story in RoF. This one also gets into a lot of nitty-gritty details, in this case with airplanes ...or should I say ghost-planes, as a man tries to help land this phantom plane. Art tot his one was provided by Lawrence Ronald.

The last story is "Coyote Woman" by Margaret Ball, which marks her second story in RoF. This one was an interesting blend of feminism, male chauvinism, and Native American mythology, as it explores Navajo myths in some unusual ways as a professor in danger of not receiving tenure become inhabited by the god, Coyote. The ending proves abrupt but powerful. Art to this one is by David Beck, which marks his sixth illustration in the magazine.

So that wraps up this issue and the publishing year for 1996. And my favorite story for December 1996? "Coyote Woman" by Margaret Ball. And my favorite artwork? David Beck's accompanying illustration to this story.

*Due to all the work I did with the slush, there was a time at RoF where my livejournal and email addresses were slushmaster.

Originally posted on douglascohen.livejournal.com on January 4th, 2008

Part fifteen in my ongoing retrospective as I read the fiction in *Realms of Fantasy* and offer my thoughts. This time around I'll be offering my thoughts on the February 1997 issue.

The cover to this one is by Keith Parkinson, which marks his second illustration in the magazine. Parkinson labeled this illustration as "The Ice Dragon" on his website, which was the cover to a book he didn't name and I couldn't track down.

A rundown of this issue's nonfiction is as follows:

In the Books column, Gahan Wilson reviews *The Lost* by Jonathan Aycliffe, *Devil's Tower* by Mark Sumner, *Worldwar: Striking the Balance* by Harry Turtledove, *Even Weirder* by Gahan Wilson (yup, self-plug), and Jeanne Cavelos reviews *Enchanter's Glass* by Susan Whitcher. In the Movie/TV column, Dan Perez discusses the history of dragons in film. In the Folkroots column, Terri Windling discusses Tristan, True Thomas, and Morgan of Hed; Legends of Harps and Harpers. In the Artists Gallery, Tanith Lee discusses the art of Wayne Barlowe. And in the Games column, Mark Sumner reviews the card game *Dino Hunt* from Steve Jackson Games and the PC game, *War Wind*.

On to the fiction ...

The lead story is "From the Journals of St. Strange: Old Flame" by Tanith Lee, her fourth appearance in the magazine. This is also her second St. Strange tale to be published in RoF, making her the first author to have multiple tales that return to a familiar universe (although as best I can tell, the only unifying element between the first two St. Strange tales is the fact that they're both "From the Journals of St. Strange"). The story itself is a bit reminiscent of the old Romeo & Juliet story at its onset, but it quickly veers off in a fresh direction when the wedding is arranged and the old hostilities between the families are assumed to be a thing of the past ...except not all wounds are so easily healed, and there is one family member still quite interested in visiting pain and suffering on her old enemy. Art to this one was provided Mary O'Keefe Young, which marks her eighth illustration in the magazine.

The second story is "The Pretender" by Stephen Dedman, a piece of re-imagined Arthuriana. In this piece, Arthur is homosexual and Mordred is a product of incest between Morgause and Agravaine. Today I happened to be reading the letters page to the June 1997 issue, and it contained a letter from someone complaining about "The Pretender." In particular, the complaint focused around the character of Galahad and what he was and wasn't "supposed" to be.

I was glad Shawna chose to publish this letter, because it gives me the opportunity to take exception with it. There are lots of books dealing with Arthuriana I've yet to read, but I've read enough to consider myself fairly knowledgeable on the topic. And if there is one thing I've learned about Arthuriana, it's that there is no one version of the story. Tales of Arthur have existed since the 5th century. Those that haven't read any of the tales are often under the misguided impression that there is one version of events. Actually, the few events and people they know about (like the Sword in the Stone, or Nimue putting Merlin to sleep, Arthur visiting the Lady in the Lake to receive Excalibur, etc.) are simply the most famous ones, the ones that have transcended the story and the centuries to become iconic parts of our culture/literature/consciousness/etc. If there is one thing that all real authors of Arthuriana understand (and by real I mean those who endeavor to write more than cookie-cutter stories that use the events and peoples from these tales without understanding or conveying any of the mythic resonance and/or traditions) it's that the tradition of re-imagining this tale is not only accepted, it's expected.

Shawna understands this too, because her editorial intro to this story begins with (paraphrased) "There is something about the world of Arthur that demands retelling."

The fun of re-imagining Arthur is finding fresh ways to explore the old myth, to capture the romance and particularly the tragedy in ways that are different and yet somehow familiar. You veer off in new directions, but in other parts of the tale you follow the more familiar path quite closely. It's a balancing act, and those that manage to walk the tightrope are the ones who understand the stories and the traditions. Stephen clearly understands these stories and traditions, because he walks the tightrope and he succeeds. For a short work, he covers a tremendous amount of ground in the world of Arthuriana, and he takes the tale in some very interesting directions. It should also be noted that Stephen's tale is the first one in

RoF to explore themes of male homosexuality. Art to this one was provided by Alan Lee.

Next up is "Mother's Day," by Leslie What, which marks her second story in the magazine. This was a darkly amusing tale, dealing with the Pied Piper. Ever wonder what happens after the Piper steals the children away? This one provides an answer, with some rather quirky twists. Art to this one was provided Janet Aulisio, which marks her fifth illustration in the magazine.

After this we have "Falling" by Kristine Kathryn Rusch. According to her bio, this story was published shortly after she finished her run as the editor of *The Magazine of Fantasy & Science Fiction* (and was subsequently succeeded by Gordon Van Gelder). I love the premise behind this one, as it explores the idea of the guardian angel in a very interesting way. Basically the guardian angel is an imposter, attempting to get the protagonist to commit an act of evil, which is so deliciously twisted and hence right up my alley. Art to this one was provided by Michael Gibbs, which marks his second illustration in the magazine.

The last tale is "Trigger" by Dave Smeds, which marks his second story in the magazine. This is the first piece of superhero fiction to be published in RoF. The man's superpower in this one is an unusual one: he's able to smell murderers and those capable of murder. How he handles this superpower reminds me a bit of Marvel's Punisher, but with different motivations. But as with many superhero tales, halfway through the story he is faced with one of those life-changing decisions (to quote Peter Parker's Uncle Ben: "With great power comes great responsibility.") Art to this one was provided by Jon Foster, which marks his second illustration in the magazine.

So that wraps up this issue. And my favorite story? A bunch of good ones, but I have to go with "The Pretender" by Stephen Dedman. And my favorite artwork? Alan Lee's acompanying illustration to "The Pretender."

Originally posted on douglascohen.livejournal.com on January 8ᵗʰ, 2008

April 1997 (Issue 16)

Part sixteen in my comprehensive retrospective as I read the fiction in *Realms of Fantasy* and offer my thoughts. This time around I'll be discussing the April 1997 issue.

The cover to this one is by Don Maitz, which marks his third illustration in the magazine. It features a knight on a rearing horse. On his website, this illustration carries a copyright of 1991, but it was also nominated for a 1998 Chesley Award for Cover Illustration. So unless the rules have changed since 1998, going by what I learned perusing the Chesley Award rules this piece needed to be previously unpublished to earn a nomination.

Two retrospectives ago, I confessed my jealousy toward Rebecca McCabe when I saw that she got to answer a fan in our now defunct letters page. But with this issue I'm even more jealous . . .she got to *write* the guest editorial! And this feature is also defunct, which means I can't write one. Damn her! Not that this stopped me from begging Shawna to let me write a guest editorial. But her response was about all I could hope for, when she said the editorial page isn't a feature in the magazine anymore, but she'll keep me in mind if anything should pop up down the road. Sigh.* Also of interest is that in the letters page there is a letter from Mike Samerdyke. This is the same Mike Samerdyke that I attended the Odyssey Fantasy & Science Fiction Writing Workshop with in 2000, a little more than three years after his letter was published. Such a small world.

A rundown of this issue's nonfiction is as follows:

In the Books column, Gahan Wilson reviews *Brand New Cherry Flavor* by Todd Grimson, *The Bell Witch* by Brent Monahan, *The Dealings of Daniel Kesserich* by Fritz Leiber, and Jeanne Cavelos reviews*Wind from a Foreign Sky: Book 1 of the Tielmaran Chronicles* by Katya Reiman. In the Movie/TV column, Dan Perez discusses horror writers on *The X-Files*. In the Folkroots column, Terri Windling discusses the road that has no end: tales of the traveling people. In the Artists Gallery, Kristine Kathryn Rusch discusses the art of Bob Eggleton. And in the Games column, Mark Sumner reviews *Master of Orion 2* for the PC and *King's Field II* for the Playstation.

Moving on to the fiction ...

First up is "The Church at Monte Saturno" by Robert Silverberg, which marks his second appearance in the magazine. As with his first story in Realms ("Diana of the Hundred Breasts"), this piece has a bit of an archaeological slant. Taking place in Sicily, this story draws heavily on the milieu and Christian mythology as an art professor discovers a lost Byzantine mosaic in a remote church ...only to learn the mosaic is possessed, with its pictures shifting from angelic to demonic portrayals. Writers can really take a lesson from Silverberg about how to make a story come alive through details. He's a master at this. Art to this one was provided by Ken Graning, which marks his sixth illustration in the magazine.

Next up is "The Right Sort of Flea" by Richard Parks, his second story in the magazine. Thus begins Richard's impressive and unending streak of subsequent fiction sales to RoF, setting him on the road to becoming Realms' most published author. "The Right Sort of Flea" draws upon one of the more famous pieces of Anglo-Saxon literature, this being the tale of Beowulf. The timing of reading this piece was perfect for me, because back in November '07 I had read the original tale in anticipation of the IMAX 3D movie, which I watched the day after reading the tale. Thus I was able to put Richard's tale into better perspective because of these recent readings/viewings. He picks things up near the end of the traditional tale, from when Beowulf fights the dragon. He adds some clever twists to the traditional telling, humanizing the story a little bit more as a result and making it more accessible to modern readers. Art to this was one was provided by Doug Andersen, which marks his second illustration in the magazine.

The third story is "Blessing the Last Family" by Batya Swift Yasgur & Barry N. Malzberg. This piece draws heavily on Judaism, as it explores the idea of each person having a Good Angel and a Bad Angel. The idea is based on an adapted passage from the Tractate Sabbath, and this passage is provided at the very beginning of the story to put the idea and story in context. What I found clever about this piece is that it's basically a Jewish spin on the old story of the Devil on one shoulder and an angel on the other, and rather than show things through the perspective of the guy with the shoulders, the authors opt for one of the angels instead. Art to this one was provided by Annie Lunsford, which marks her fourth illustration in the magazine.

The fourth story is "Stormchild" by Susan Wade, her second appearance in the magazine, and her first solo piece. This was a ghost story about a woman's spirit that leaves her body and delivers her child before she dies. Along the way, it explores such themes such as the power of the human spirit and how love conquers all. Art to this one was provided by Janet Aulisio, which marks her sixth illustration in the magazine.

Then we have "Lawnmower Moe" by William R. Eakin, his second appearance in RoF. Like his first story in the magazine, this story takes place in Redgunk, Mississippi. I have to give a tip of the literary cap to William on this one. At the beginning of the story, I found myself of the opinion that this particular story wasn't for me. But the more I read the more he drew me in, until he achieved a bizarre but compelling and completely fulfilling climax. He was quite the mad chef with this tale, combining a wide range of elements that shouldn't fit together but absolutely do. I never thought I'd buy into a story about a fat drunk guy mowing the lawn having a powerful and convincing connection to the ancient druids, but I did. Art to this one was provided by David Martin, which marks his third illustration in the magazine.

Finally we have a tale equally (if not more) bizarre, this being "The House" by Anne Harris. It is a tale about a strange house and its stranger inhabitants. Shawna sums up this quite well in her editorial header: "This is a story about a haunted house and some of its terrible inhabitants. But it's not really a fantasy at all. You'll see." You may be scratching your head here, wondering why in the world it would be in *Realms of Fantasy* if our editor didn't consider it fantasy. Good question. My best guess/answer is this: this story made me think of Kafka. "Metamorphosis"–his most famous story–isn't necessarily a fantasy story (others would argue otherwise, which is neither here nor there), but if you were to read this tale in a fantasy anthology (reprint, obviously) it wouldn't strike you as the strangest thing in the world to see it included. It's so off-the-wall bizarre that you can safely group it with fantasy, whether you consider it as such or not. So it is with "The House," I think. Art to this one was provided by J.K. Potter, which marks his second illustration in the magazine.

So that wraps up this issue. And my favorite tale? "Lawnmower Moe" by William R. Eakin. And my favorite illustration? Don Maitz's cover illustration.

*A few years after I wrote this retrospective, the editorial column was resurrected on the magazine's website and much to my delight I was afforded the chance to write a number of them, but alas, I never had the chance to write one that appeared *in* the magazine.

Originally posted on douglascohen.livejournal.com on January 9th, 2008

Part seventeen in my comprehensive retrospective as I read the fiction in *Realms of Fantasy* and offer my thoughts. This time around I'll be discussing the June 1997 issue.

The cover to this one is by Sanjulian, which marks the artist's second illustration in the magazine. It was originally the cover to *The Oathbound Wizard* by Christopher Stasheff.

A look in the masthead reveals that Stephen Vann is no longer the Art Director. His successor is Pamela Norman.

A rundown of this issue's nonfiction is as follows:

In the Books column, Gahan Wilson reviews *The Family Tree* by Sheri S. Tepper, *The Woman Who Lives in the Earth* by Swain Wolfe, *The Xothic Legend: The Selected Fiction of Lin Carter*, edited by Robert Price, and Jeanne Cavelos reviews *Wicked: The Life and Times of the Wicked Witch of the West* by Gregory Maguire. In the Movie/TV column, Dan Perez reviews the movie, *Warriors of Virtue*. In the Folkroots column, Terri Windling writes about trickster tales. In the Artists Gallery, Richard S. Meyers writes about the art of James C. Christensen. And in the Games column, Mark Sumner reviews the computer RPG, *Diablo* and *Tomb Raider* for the Playstation.

On to the fiction ...

The first story is "Bad Medicine" by Martha Wells, which marks her second appearance in the magazine. This one is an urban fantasy tale dealing with some folks who use a certain brand of folklore magic to protect mankind against gate wizards and witches and such. Very descriptive and fast-paced. It's also worth noting that this is the first story in RoF that featured an African-American protagonist. The illustration to this one was provided by Alan Pollack.

Next up is a high fantasy tale by Kristen M. Corby called "The Horse From the Sea." I enjoyed this story, but it becomes all the more impressive if you take the time to read her bio (I always read the author bios as I go through the issues), which notes that this is the first story she ever wrote (though not her first sale). The story itself explores some fairly familiar ground, as a people who worship a god of the sea are conquered by a people who worship a god of the desert. She puts her own brand on the story though, as we see how these two religious peoples manage to reconcile their differences. Artwork to this one was provided by Carol Heyer, which marks her sixth illustration in the magazine.

The third story is "Riders of the Rainbow Ridge" by Diana L. Paxon. This story features a rather unusual mix of elements, taking place in the Rocky Mountains of Colorado during the time of the Wild West, and blending in a number of tidbits from Norse mythology. And making an artist the protagonist in a tale about Ragnorak was also a surprising choice. Art to this one was provided by Ken Tunell.

Next up is a middle grade fantasy by Jane Yolen called "Fallen Angel." It marks her second story in the magazine, and the best word to describe this tale is charming. An angel is cast out of Heaven, and basically loses its wings in the process. Three very bright children stumble upon the angel and take it home. Mom and Dad can't see the angel and the children help the angel get some new wings in a way that leaves you smiling come the end. Artwork to this one was provided by Steven Adler.

Last up is "A Dark Fire, Burning From Within" by Leslie What, which marks her third story in the magazine. The fantasy element is slight in this one, and it has sort of a science fantasy vibe to it. The tale focuses on finding the courage to struggle on when all hope seems lost—a familiar theme to epic fantasy fans—as a pregnant woman finds the courage to struggle to freedom after her lover is captured. Art to this one was provided by David Beck, which marks his seventh illustration in the magazine.

So that wraps up this issue. And my favorite story? "Fallen Angel" by Jane Yolen. And my favorite artwork? Alan Pollack's illustration to "Bad Medicine" by Martha Wells.

Originally posted on douglascohen.livejournal.com on January 10th, 2008

Part eighteen in my comprehensive retrospective as I read the fiction in *Realms of Fantasy* and offer my thoughts. This time around I'll be dissecting the August 1997 issue.

As it happens, I have a special attachment to this issue. The August 1997 issue is the first issue of *Realms of Fantasy* I ever bought. At the time, it was the current issue on the newsstands, so we're talking about about a little more than ten years ago from the time I'm writing this. I'm fairly certain I'd heard of the magazine before, but until this point I'd never been tempted to buy an issue. And I'd never heard the name Shawna McCarthy. I was mostly a fan of those bricks known as epic fantasies (I still enjoy them, when I can actually find one that's worthwhile), and when I wasn't reading epic fantasy, my interest resided with sword & sorcery.

It was this latter interest that led me to *Realms of Fantasy*. To those unaware, I started reading fantasy because of Robert E. Howard, the creator of Conan and several other fine S&S creations. At this point in my young reading career, Howard's fantasies were the only short fiction I was interested in. And considering that Howard had been dead for sixty-one years at this point, I basically knew absolute squat about the speculative short story market. And I was fine with that. But I decided to buy this particular issue, not for the fiction, but because of the caption of Kevin Sorbo on the cover. And no, this didn't have anything to do with Hercules, a show I was never able to get into (or Xena, for that matter). This particular caption was depicting Sorbo in the soon-to-be-released Kull movie, Kull being another one of the fine sword & sorcery creations of Robert E. Howard (Kull actually predated Conan by about three years). So it was the film section of *Realms of Fantasy* that snagged me, because I was still a rabid REH fan at the time (and I remain a great admirer of his storytelling abilities).

Anyway, I read the article (btw, the movie was nothing short of awful), thought about reading the short fiction, looked at the next epic fantasy waiting in my piles, and promptly forgot about my copy of RoF. I didn't read it until three years later, after I attended the Odyssey Fantasy & Science Fiction Writing Workshop. And speaking of Odyssey, here's another coincidence pertaining to the issue in question: Odyssey is run by Jeanne Cavelos, and she's also its main teacher throughout its six weeks. And who do you think it was that happened to write what happened to be a guest editorial in this issue? Yup. None other than the great Jeanne Cavelos, the person whose teachings imparted to me the skills to eventually tackle the assistant editor gig at *Realms of Fantasy*.

Ah, symmetry.

Moving on ...

The cover to this one depicts another important figure in the sword & sorcery genre, this being Michael Moorcock's Elric of Melniboné. The illustration is by Michael Whelan, which marks his fifth illustration in the magazine and was originally the cover to *Stormbringer*. I mus admit this was also a bit of a selling point with me when I bought the magazine, since I was also a fan of Elric.

A rundown of this issue's nonfiction is as follows:

In the Books column, Gahan Wilson reviews *Silicon Karma* by Thomas A. Easton, *Kar Kalim* by Deborah Christian, *Giant Bones* by Peter S. Beagle, and the aforementioned Jeanne Cavelos reviews *Children of the Vampire: The Diaries of the Family Dracul*. In the Movie/TV column, Dan Perez covers the aforementioned *Kull the Conqueror*. In Folkroots, Terri Windling writes about myth, mysticism, and magic: the Pre-Raphaelites and fantasy. In the Artists Gallery, Terri Windling provides further coverage of the Pre-Raphaelites and the Romantic Tradition. And in the Games column, Mark Sumner reviews the PC game, *Heroes of Might and Magic II*, and the video game, *Krush Kill 'N Destroy*.

On to the fiction ...

The opening story is "The Chapter of the Hawk of Gold" by Noreen Doyle, which marks her second appearance in the magazine. The first story was also a "Chapter" story, this being "The Chapter of Bringing a Boat Into Heaven," back in the February '96 issue. Like the first "Chapter" story, this one draws on Egyptian mythology. Unlike the first story, this one is set in the modern day, dealing with a museum curtator who gets her desires fulfilled in a most unusual way. Artwork to this one was provided Janet Aulisio, which marks her seventh illustration in the magazine.

Next up is "Balkan Siege," by Russell William Asplund, a topical ghost story taking place in Sarajevo, depicting a teenage girl's daily struggles to survive in a city torn apart by war. A quick perusal of previous stories in

RoF (I'm keeping a detailed story log as I read along) shows that this was the first truly topical fantasy story run in the magazine. Art to this one was provided by David Beck, which marks his eighth illustration in the magazine.

The third story is "The Spiral Garden" by Louise Cooper, a high fantasy piece that marks her second appearance in the magazine. As with her other piece ("His True and Only Wife"), the story has a decidedly dark slant. A queen is married to an insane king. The only time he consummates with her is to have children. To date, she's given him nineteen children, but each time the king has had the child killed, because it doesn't have his bright red hair, and so there is always a shadow of a doubt in his twisted mind that maybe the child isn't his. Chilling. How the queen addresses this nightmare is quite ...appropriate. Art to this one was provided by Tom Canty, which marks his second illustration in the magazine.

The fourth story was "Fade Out" by Marnie Winston-Macauley, and it has the honor of being the 100th story published in RoF. This was an odd little urban fantasy tale about a screenwriter writing a soap operah script that is becoming a little too real. Art to this one was provided by Greg Carter.

Finally we have "Teeth" by David Phalen, a darkly humorous fairy tale, which presents a decidedly twisted (but entertaining) depiction of the tooth fairy. If any of you have kids that still believe in the tooth fairy and they happen to read RoF and have access to back issues, (an unlikely combination, but you never know), steer them clear of this story. Art to this one was provided by Thomas Fleming.

So that wraps up this issue. And my favorite story? "The Spiral Garden" by Louise Cooper. And my favorite artwork? Tom Canty's accompanying illustration to the same story.

Originally posted on douglascohen.livejournal on January 11th, 2008

Part nineteen in my comprehensive retrospective as I read the fiction in *Realms of Fantasy* and offer my thoughts. This time around I'll be dissecting the October 1997 issue, which marks the magazine's third anniversary.

The cover to this one is by Luis Royo, which marks his second illustration in the magazine. It is the second of the magazine's infamous "chicks in chainmail covers." The first chick in chainmail cover (June '96) was somewhat revealing, but this one takes things a healthy eyeful further. The distinction is worth noting just because I know some people have taken issue with these covers over the years. But the last one was somewhat more ...unassuming. So this might be the first chick in chainmail cover that some people took legitimate issue with. The illustration originally appeared on the cover of issue twelve of *Magnum Magazine*.

Also worth noting is that on the cover you'll see the words: LOUISE COOPER: NEW FICTION! Only there is no fiction by Louise Cooper in this issue. She had a story in the last issue (with the same blurb on the cover, and another story in the issue I'm currently reading (February '98), but not in this issue. Whoops! Someone dropped the ball on that one!

Moving on ...

This issue features a guest editorial by none other than Jane Yolen, as she discusses the use of different narrative voices in fantasy literature. Since Yolen continues this essay the following issue, it marks the first time the magazine ran a two-part editorial.

A rundown of the issue's nonfiction is as follows:

In the Books column, Gahan Wilson reviews *Dogland* by Will Shetterly, *The Ignored* by Bentley Little, *Return to Lankhmar* by Fritz Leiber, and Jeanne Cavelos reviews *Winter Rose* by Patricia A. McKillip. In the Folkroots column, Terri Windling writes about legends of water lore. In the Movie/TV column, Dan Perez laments the lack of fantasy movies (I'd say this has changed dramatically in the last 10+ years). In the Artists Gallery, Jane Frank writes about the art of Ian Miller. And in the Games column, Mark Sumner reviews *Creatures* for the PC and the RPG, *Deadlands*.

On to the fiction ...

The opening story is "Drowned Love" by C.W. Johnson, a dark fantasy tale that also marks the first time a mermaid has made its way into our pages (I think). It's a pretty engaging tale, about a man with a tortured past that is part of a deep-sea salvage team. Since this takes place before the days of modern scuba gear, the protagonist relies on the air pockets captured in a large bell when he goes into the depths, going back and forth between the bell and the wreckage for as long as possible before returning to the surface. Pretty cool. Art to this one was provided by Alan Pollack, which marks his second illustration in the magazine.

Next up is "And Horses Are Born With Eagle's Wings" by Sherwood Smith. This is a story that every fan of fantasy should read at least once. Solid characterizations and smooth writing, as it deals with an elementary school music teacher whose music is just a little too magical ...at least for some. I say that every fantasy fan should read this story because it deals with something that raises my hackles whenever it's mentioned, i.e. Christian fundamentalists that denounce fantasy works as evil/witchcraft/Satanic/etc. I don't have a problem with fundies (as they're called in the story) regarding their religious beliefs, but denouncing works of fantasy because you're afraid of what they'll do to your kids is more than just a little overboard. I mean really. And Smith doesn't attack these people with her story. She addresses this issue, and handles it in a manner I greatly admired. So kudos to Sherwood, and thank you to Shawna for having the guts to publish this. Art to this one was provided by Ken Graning, which marks his seventh illustration in the magazine.

Then we have "The Lady of Shalott House" by Tanith Lee, which marks her fifth appearance in the magazine. This one is a pretty standard ghostly love story, dealing with a painter who meets the ghost of a brokenhearted woman and helps reunite her with the ghost of her lover who killed himself. But as Tanith excels at doing, she uses her language to cast a mood and raise the level of the reading experience. Art to this one was provided Mary O'Keefe Young, which marks her ninth illustration in the magazine.

Then we have "Leningrad Blues" by E.A. Johnson. This one was an urban fairy tale set in a recently disbanded Soviet Union. The level of detail is quite strong (and quite engaging, as I learned a number of interesting tidbits regarding this land), and the story as a whole kept me happily turning pages. A man who is part of an underground music group catches a golden fish that grants him a wish in exchange for its freedom. The man wishes for the woman of his dreams, and she's everything he could want. And she'll be his forever, so long as he loves her above all else. Without a doubt one of the stronger urban fantasy tales I've read to date. Art to this one was provided by Broeck Steadman, which marks his third illustration in the magazine.

Following this was "The Wolf Man's Wife" by Peni R. Griffin, which marks her second appearance in the magazine. This one follows some familiar patterns, but is quite engaging as it tells the tale of a woman who marries a man, and everything is perfect, except she must promise him to never go outside at night. And to provide a bit of a spoiler here, this story also marks our first werewolf tale in the magazine. Art to this one was provided by Janet Aulisio, which marks her eighth illustration in the magazine.

Last up we have "Meadow Song" by William R. Eakin, which marks his third appearance in the magazine. For the third time he visits the town of Redgunk, Mississippi, this time with a tale of recaptured love, as an old man is reunited with his dead love, only she's as young as she was back in the sixties. How I saw the ending coming in this one, I have no idea. I shouldn't have. But I did. Art to this was provided by Annie Lunsford, which marks her fifth illustration in the magazine.

So that wraps up this issue. And my favorite story? A number of good ones, but I have to go with "Leningrad Blues" by E.A. Johnson. And my favorite artwork? Alan Pollack's illustration to "Drowned Love" by C.W. Johnson.

Originally posted on douglascohen.livejournal.com on January 15th, 2008

Part twenty in my comprehensive retrospective as I read the fiction in *Realms of Fantasy* and offer my thoughts. This time around I'll be wrapping up the 1997 publishing season by discussing its December issue.

The cover to this one should be familiar to a lot of epic fantasy fans, as it was the original cover art by Doug Beekman to *Wizard's First Rule* by Terry Goodkind, book one in *The Sword of Truth* series.

A rundown of this issue's nonfiction is as follows:

In the Books column, Gahan Wilson reviews *How Few Remain* by Harry Turtledove, *American Goliath* by Harvey Jacobs, *Bring the Jubilee* by Ward Moore, *The Encyclopedia of Fantasy* by John Clute and John Grant, and Jeanne Cavelos reviews *The Annotated Lovecraft*, edited by S.T. Joshi. In the Folkroots column, Terri Windling writes about banshees and boggarts, spriggans and sprites: the legends of our "Good Neighbors." In the Movie/TV column, after lamenting the lack of fantasy movies last issue, Dan Perez discusses fantasy's success on TV. In the Artists Gallery, Jane Frank covers the artwork of Sanjulian, and in the Games column, Mark Sumner reviews the PC game, *Dungeon Keeper*, a card game based on Clive Barker's *Imajica*, and the PC game, *Age of Empires*.

On to the fiction ...

The first story is "The One Act" by A.M. Dellamonica, which marks her second appearance in the magazine. This tale was a big old stew with a little of everything, as the ghost of a woman's twin sister shares her body, making her seem schizophrenic. Art to this one was provided by Michael Gibbs, which marks his third illustration in the magazine.

Next up is "Lord Madoc and the Red Knight" by Richard Parks, which marks his third appearance in the magazine. The interesting twist on this type of story is that it isn't "Sir" Madoc. Normally it is the knight on the chivalrous quest in these types of tales. Often he must combat other knights, but here the other knights are the enemy only. Parks draws heavily on Welsh lore in this story, and like the best of these sorts of tales do, he succeeds in turning a clever reinvention. Art to this one was provided by Doug Andersen, which marks his third illustration in the magazine.

Then we have "Kaleidoscope" by Kate Daniel, a powerful tale about a woman who learns some difficult truths about her father after he dies. When she comes across the old kaleidoscope her father had given her as a child, she uses it to try and reinvent her past. Art to this one was provided Janet Aulisio, which marks her ninth illustration in the magazine.

After this we have "In the Land of the Bears" by K.D. Wentworth. This was a very powerful story, drawing heavily on American history's Trail of Tears and the sadness it inflicted on so many generations of oppressed Native Americans. In the end, she turns the tale into something very resonant and beautiful, which gave me some nice goosebumps on my arms. Art to this one was provided by David Martin, which marks his fourth illustration in the magazine.

Next up is "Walter's Christmas Night Musik" by Susan J. Kroupa, which marks her second appearance in the magazine. This one is a heartfelt Christmas miracle tale about an older man in a music store being visited by the ghosts of Motzart, Beethoven, Bach, and others. Art to this one was provided by Charles Demorat, which marks his third illustration in the magazine.

The final story is "Silver Apples" by Beverly Suarez-Beard, which marks her second appearance in the magazine. This high fantasy tale was right up my alley, about a woman cursed to be the guardian of the silver apples, which have mystical healing properties. She's an enchantress sort, and whatever man comes along is doomed to fall in love with her and die. But everything and then some goes out the window when a woman comes seeking the silver apples instead. Clever plotting, good world-building, nice characterizations, and loads of imagery. Art to this one was provided by Steven Adler, which marks his second illustration in the magazine.

So that wraps up this issue. And my favorite story? Well, you could probably flip a coin between "In the Land of the Bears" and "Silver Apples," because I enjoyed both of them that much. But I'll give the nod to "Silver Apples" by Beverly Suarez-Beard, because as I said, this story is right up my alley. And my favorite artwork? Steven Adler's accompanying illustration to "Silver Apples."

Originally posted on douglascohen.livejournal.com on January 17th, 2008

Part twenty-one in my comprehensive retrospective as I read the fiction in *Realms of Fantasy* and offer my thoughts. This time around I'll be tackling the February 1998 issue.

The cover to this one is by Stephen Youll. It was originally the cover to *Exile's Children* by Angus Wells.

A quick glance at the masthead reveals that Pamela Norman's brief run as Art Director has drawn to a close. There is no one in her place listed as Art Director, but the previous Assistant Art Director, Christina Krug, is now the Graphic Designer.

A rundown of this issue's nonfiction is as follows:

In the Books column, Gahan Wilson reviews *Son of Rosemary* by Ira Levin, *Gate of Ivory, Gate of Horn* by Robert Holdstock, *The Subtle Knife* by Phillip Pullman, and Jeanne Cavelos reviews *The Conjurer Princess* by Vivian Vande Velde. In the Movie/TV column, Dan Perez covers Conan on the small screen. In the Folkroots column, Terri Windling writes about the golden arrows of Eros: mythic tales of passion and desire. In the Artists Gallery, Jane Frank discusses the art of Richard Bober. And in the Games column, Mark Sumner reviews *Final Fantasy VII* for the Playstation, and the card game, *Portal*, from Wizards of the Coast.

On to the fiction ...

This is a very important issue in the magazine's history and evolution, and the reason behind this can be found in the lead story, "Lost Girls" by Jane Yolen. "Lost Girls" marks Yolen's third story in the magazine. It also marks the first original story printed in *Realms of Fantasy* to receive a Nebula nomination. In fact, Yolen's story takes things a step further by winning this award in 1999 for Best Novelette. It marks the first major award the magazine ever won, and to this day it remains the sole Nebula Award winner to be printed in the magazine (a crying shame if you ask me, but I digress).* As to the story itself, "Lost Girls" is a complete reinvention of the Peter Pan mythology, as Peter and the Lost Boys force multiple "Wendys" into service (i.e. girls with different names, but all "Wendys" to provide the same function as the original), but when they have to do all the work they end up going on strike. This in turn leads to some revelations about who the true villains are in Neverneverland, something that is often hinted at in the orignal book upon careful reading. Art to this one was provided by Annie Lunsford, which marks her sixth illustration in the magazine.

Then we have "Lustman" by Pat York, which marks her second appearance in the magazine. In her editorial byline for this story, Shawna wrote the following: "Yes, there's a hologram in this story, and it's set in the future, too. But if you don't think it's a fantasy, then you've never been in love." And that pretty much sums it up. If you discount the love factor in this story as a fantastical element, it's straight science fiction. But if you look at it the way Shawna did, then this is indeed a fantasy story, about the fantasies we create in our minds and hearts when we're completely and head over heels in love. Art to this one was provided by Mary O'Keefe Young, which marks her tenth illustration in the magazine. This makes her the first artist with ten illustrations in the magazine.

Then we have "Tithing Night" by Louise Cooper, which marks her third appearance in the magazine. This was a high fantasy tale relying on mood and tension. A family waits in their home with a stranger for the tithing night, which comes around once every seven years, when a mysterious presence comes to the village and exacts its price in the form of one person it takes away. In return, the village receives the force's protection and blessing. As is the usual with Cooper in RoF, the tale is rather dark. Art to this one was provided by John Monteleone.

Batting clean-up we have "Fata" by Peni R. Griffin, which marks her fourth appearance in the magazine. This was a rather short tale, only about a page, dealing with a fey-type creature that is having an affair with a mortal man. All seems well and fine in this easygoing tale ...until the man's mortal lover shows up on the scene. Art to this one was provided by J.K. Potter, which marks his third illustration in the magazine.

The last story is the "Queen of Yesterday" by Sally McBride. This was a dark tale about a woman trying to learn her strange and mysterious origins from her vampiric-like mother in the hopes this will enable her to come to terms with her life. Art to this one was provided by Alan Pollack, which marks his third illustration in the magazine.

And that wraps up this issue. And my favorite story? No surprises here. I'm going with "Lost Girls" by Jane Yolen. And my favorite illustration? Stephen Youll's cover.

*While true at the time this retrospective was written, the magazine's short fiction subsequently won another Nebula Award for Best Short Fiction for "How Interesting: A Tiny Man" by Harlan Ellison, published in our February 2010 issue.

Originally posted on douglascohen.livejournal.com on January 22nd, 2008

Part twenty-two in my comprehensive retrospective as I read the fiction in *Realms of Fantasy* and offer my thoughts. This time around I'll be discussing the April 1998 issue.

The cover to this is another chicks in chain mail cover. It's by Luis Royo, which marks his third illustration in the magazine. It was originally the cover to issue thirty-two of *Magnum Magazine*.

A rundown of this issue's nonfiction is as follows:

In the Books column, Gahan Wilson reviews *One Day Closer to Death* by Bradley Denton, *The Wild Road* by Gabriel King, and Jeanne Cavelos reviews *The Gratitude of Kings* by Marion Zimmer Bradley. In the Movie/TV column, Dan Perez writes about actress, Hudson Leick in *Xena: Warrior Princess*. In the Folkroots column, Terri Windling writes about stories of winter lore. In the Artists Gallery, Terri Windling covers the art of Alan Lee. And in the Games column, Mark Sumner reviews *Total Annihilation* for the PC, *Uprising* for the PC, *Dark Reign* for the PC, and *Myth: The Fallen Lords* for the PC.

On to the fiction ...

The lead story this issue is "Unicorn Stew" by William Eakin, which marks his fourth appearance in the magazine, and also his fourth Redgunk, Mississippi tale. This story struck me as particularly poignant, and as Eakin did with his mummy tale, he deals with unicorns in a rather untraditional way. A unicorn sacrifices itself in place of a young boy and everyone believes the boy to be dead, and years later the boy returns to meet his sister. This is a story about tragedy, sacrifice, love, and second chances. Art to this one was provided by Joel Naprstek, which marks his second illustration in the magazine.

Next up is "Egyptian Motherlode" by David Sandner and Jacob Weisman. This tale featured a rather wild mix of elements, as a rap group goes on tour with the band Egyptian Motherlode, only to learn they're part of a deeper psychadelic and spiritual journey that delves into Egyptian mythology. Art to this one was provided by Michael Gibbs, which marks his fourth illustration in the magazine.

Then we have "Juanito, the Magic Beans, and the Giant" by Carrie Richerson, which marks her second appearance in RoF. This story was really entertaining, featuring a mix of Aztec mythology (something I see a fair amount of in the slush, by the way), alternate history, and a reinvention of Jack and the Beanstalk. It sounds a bit absurd, I'm sure, but I assure you it's a seamless blend, replete with excellent world-building, smooth pacing, and a satisfying ending. Art to this one was provided by Web Bryant, which marks his seventh illustration in the magazine.

Following this we have "Miss'ippi Snow" by Deborah Therese D'Onofrio, a surrealistic tale about a nurse who falls in love with soldiers she's tending, but then Death takes them away. Ultimately, this causes her to fear falling in love. I won't give away the ending, but if you don't pay attention in this one you'll miss the fantastical element. Art to this one was provided Janet Aulisio, which marks her tenth illustration in the magazine.

Finally we have "Tiger, Tiger" by Severna Park. This one features a really cool premise, as we see a policewoman in India hunting after a reincarnated serial killer who used to be a tiger. It draws on the characters' pasts and steeps you in the milieu to really bring this one together. Featuring a lot of extremely short scenes, it moves at a very fast clip. Many of the stories in this issue strike me as particularly ambitious, and this one is no exception. Others must have thought so too, because "Tiger, Tiger" was Long Listed for the Locus Award for Best Short Story in 1999. Art to this one was provided by Charles Demorat, which marks his fourth illustration in the magazine.

So that wraps up this issue. And my favorite story? Lots of good ones to choose from, but I'm going with "Juanito, the Magic Beans, and the Giant" by Carrie Richerson. And my favorite artwork? Luis Royo's cover illustration.

Originally posted on dcuglascohen.livejournal.com on January 24th, 2008

Part twenty-three in my comprehensive retrospective as I read the fiction in *Realms of Fantasy* and offer my thoughts. This time around I'll be discussing the June 1998 issue.

The cover illustration to this one is by Ken Kelly. It was originally the cover to *Barbarians*, edited by Robert Adams, Martin H. Greenberg, and Charles Waugh. It features the male equivalent of the chick in chainmail cover, i.e. the bare-chested barbarian raising his axe in triumph. I suppose you could call it boys in beefcake.

A quick glance at the masthead reveals the return of Steven Vann as Art Director. Christina Krug, who was for a time the Assistant Art Director and then had her title changed to Graphic Designer, remains in the masthead under this latter title.

A rundown of this issue's nonfiction is as follows:

In the Books column, Gahan Wilson reviews *Paris in the Twentieth Century* by Jules Verne, *Dawn Song* by Michael Marano, *Old Man's Beast* by H. Russell Wakefield, and Jeanne Cavelos reviews a new volume that collects two of J.R.R. Tolkien's novellas, *Smith of Wooton Major* and *Farmer Giles of Ham*. In the Movie/TV column, Dan Perez covers *Tarzan and the Lost City*. In the Folkroots column, Terri Windling covers feline tales in mythology. In the Artists Gallery, Karen Haber covers the art of Jim Burns. And in the Games column, Mark Sumner reviews the computer games, *USCF Chess*, *Chessmaster 5500*, *Combat Chess*, and *Power Chess*.

I should also note that with Karen Haber handling the Artists Gallery this issue, it marks a little bit of the changing of the guard, as the columnists in this section were a rotating cast of contributors. There would still be different columnists going forward, but Karen would come the closest to being the column's regular contributor. It should also be noted this issue marks Mark Sumner's last issue as the games columnist. He was the first and only columnist for this section until this point, with a very respectable run from October 1994-June 1998.

Moving on to the fiction ...

The lead story is "Meeting the Messenger" by Don Webb, which marks his third appearance in the magazine. This marks the first piece of Cthulhu fiction (a creation of H.P. Lovecraft's, to anyone not in the know) to appear in the magazine. I rarely see Cthulhu submissions to the magazine, which is probably for the best, since Shawna once told me she's not the biggest fan of this subgenre. But it would seem this one tickled her fancy, in which a man's attempts to translate a portion of ancient text leads him to come into contact with something from the Lovecraftian great beyond. Art to this one was provided by John Snyder.

Then we have "Kin to Crows" by Christopher Rowe, a dark fantasy tale dealing with a charming young man whose hubris leads to his seeming undoing, only to lead to an unusual sort of rebirth. This one was all about character and milieu (deep country South), and it leads to a rather abrupt but appropriate ending. Art to this one was provided by David Martin, which marks his fifth illustration in the magazine.

Third is "I Bring You Forever" by Tanith Lee, which marks her sixth appearance in the magazine. This high fantasy tale is set in the same universe as her Flat World novels, and it deals with a queen who wishes to achieve immortality, only to have her wish granted in a most unusual way. As is the usual case with Lee, the story is rich in language and milieu. Art to this one was provided by Carol Heyer, which marks her seventh illustration in the magazine.

Next we have "Moments of Truth" by Alan Smale, a heartfelt tale about an old woman with a certain power. On the surface, it seems like she has telepathy. But it isn't quite this. Instead, when moments of silence descend upon conversations, she has the unique gift of being able to read information from that silence, to glean the innermost truths of the speakers with a fairly high accuracy. Lots of subtext in this one, and it's handled very skillfully. Art to this one was provided by John Berkey, which marks his third illustration in the magazine.

Following this we have "Protocols of Consumption" by Robert Charles Wilson, which marks his second appearance in the magazine. Like his previous tale in RoF ("The Perseids"), this one features a lot of paranoia, mixed with a lot of thought-provoking ideas. The underlying premise that he plays is that information is exchanged on a chemical level, so what happens when all these manmade chemicals are dumped into the earth? What sorts of messages are relayed, and how are they distorted? Wild stuff. Art to this one was provided by Eric Dinyer.

Finally we have "Steel Penny" by Janni Lee Simner, which marks her second appearance in the magazine. Like her other story in RoF ("Sarah's Window"), this is a middle grade fantasy that deals with the fey. But Simner isn't just recycling the same old story. This is a very touching tale about a young girl babysitting her baby sister. When the baby is stolen by the fey, it becomes a story of sacrifice, revolving around promises and love, which ultimately leads to a clever and touching solution. Art to this one was provided by Janet Aulisio, which marks her eleventh illustration in the magazine.

So that wraps up this issue. And my favorite story? "Steel Penny" by Janni Lee Simner. And my favorite artwork? Carol Heyer's illustration to "I Bring You Forever" by Tanith Lee.

Originally posted on douglascohen.livejournal.com on January 26th, 2008

Part twenty-four in my comprehensive retrospective as I read the fiction in *Realms of Fantasy* and offer my thoughts. This time around I'll be discussing the August 1998 issue.

This issue marks a first in terms of covers. The cover features Lucy Lawless in her role as Xena Warrior Princess from the defunct TV show. This is the first issue of *Realms of Fantasy* to feature a fantasy star from television, as opposed to reprint or original fantasy artwork. Given that Xena is wearing her standard attire, I suppose you could arguably lump this into the same vein as the chicks in chain mail cover, but I choose to think of this one as one of RoF's media covers. Also, a look at the price shows that it's increased from $3.50 to $3.99. There would not be another price increase until the August 2009 issue.

Something in the Letters Page also caught my attention. There is a letter from Deborah Therese D'Onofrio, whose story, "Miss'ippi Snow,' appeared in the April 1998 issue. This is the first time a fiction contributor had a letter appear in the Letters Page. Basically, it expresses her appreciation for being published in RoF, and her admiration for the artwork. Speaking as an editor, I always find these sorts of letters extremely gratifying.

A rundown of this issue's nonfiction is as follows:

In the Books column, Gahan Wilson reviews *Irrational Fears* by Williams Browning Spencer, *The Great War: The American Front* by Harry Turtledove, *Roverandom* by J.R.R. Tolkien, and Jeanne Cavelos reviews *Dragon's Winter* by Elizabeth A. Lynn. In the Movie/TV column, newcomer Stephen Lynch discusses the various animated fantasy movies of filmmaker, Ray Harryhausen. In the Folkroots column, Terri Windling discusses how dusk, dawn, and the days of the dead provide doorways into other worlds. In the Artists Gallery, Karen Haber discusses the artwork of Brom. And in the Games column, newcomer Eric T. Baker reviews the Xena trading card game, the 2.0 version of the gaming tool, Web RPG, *Tales form the Infinite Staircase: An Advanced Supplement for the Planetscape Product Line*, and *Dragonlance: Fifth Age: A Saga Companion*.

On to the fiction ...

The lead story is "Flower Kiss" by Constance Ash, which was nominated for a Nebula in 2000 for Best Short Story. It marks the third story in

Realms to be nominated for the Nebula, and with good reason. Taking place in modern West Africa, this folk tale features a particularly exotic (to me) and engaging milieu, as it tells the story of a young woman who struggles to keep the traditions of her family while her oppressive and wicked step-family who seek to steal everything she has. Quite unlike anything that's been published in RoF before. Art to this one was provided by Web Bryant, which marks his eighth illustration in the magazine.

Next up is "And Now Abideth These Three" by Sherwood Smith, which marks her second appearance in the magazine. This middle grade fantasy is about a preteen girl living among the rich of Hollywood and Malibu and such, only she's an outcast among her classmates because she's not rich like they are. At a classmate's birthday party there is a pond with little fairies that this girl can see, but most others can't. This is an honest and believable tale that teaches a valuable lesson about making assumptions. Art to this one was provided by Steven Adler, which marks his third illustration in the magazine.

Then we have another romp through Hollywood in the form of "Dr. Rumpole" by S.P. Somtow. Basically, this story is Hollywood meets Rumplestiltskin. Only instead of spinning straw overnight, our Rumplestiltskin-like character turns unsalvageable scripts into Oscar-winning masterpieces ...overnight. And like the original fairy tale, there is a price to be exacted for his services. The story has a nice current of humor throughout, and when you factor in the seedy underbelly of Hollywood into the mix, it makes for a fun read. Art to this one was provided by David Beck, which marks his ninth illustration in the magazine.

Next up is "Happy Ending" by James Van Pelt. This modern-day story has a metafictional flavor to it, and the author draws on his extensive experience as both writer and writing teacher to spin a fascinating tale about a high school teacher (and writer) and a troubled student of his. I don't want to ruin the ending, even though the "ending" isn't really the ending. By this, I mean the author tells the story out of sequence, so what would be the end to a traditional story isn't quite the end here (nor should it be). I would imagine this was a tough story to write, but the author pulls it off brilliantly. Fans of the movie *Memento* should like this one. Art to this one was provided by Greg Carter, which marks his second illustration in the magazine.

Finally we have "Greed" by J. Michael Matuszewicz, a high fantasy tale about a barmaid and a wizard on a quest. Like "And Now Abideth These Three," this story plays with expectations, because all is far from what it seems, though this doesn't become apparent until close to the end. Art to this one was provided by John Monteleone, which marks his second illustration in the magazine.

So that wraps up this issue. And my favorite story? Part of me feels guilty for not choosing "Flower Kiss." I mean, it was nominated for a Nebula for crying out loud. But I can't deny what the geek centers of my brain are telling me. So the honor must go to "Happy Ending" by James Van Pelt. Just a riveting tale from "beginning" to "end." And my favorite artwork? I declare our first tie in this area, between David Beck's illustration to "Dr. Rumpole" by S.P. Somtow, and Greg Carter's illustration to "Happy Ending" by James Van Pelt.

Originally posted on douglascohen.livejournal.com on January 29th, 2008

October 1998 (Issue 25)

Part twenty-five in my comprehensive retrospective as I read the fiction in *Realms of Fantasy* and offer my thoughts. This time around I'll be discussing the October 1998 issue.

The cover to this one is by Luis Royo, which marks his fourth illustration in the magazine. Attempts to determine the origin of this illustration were unsuccessful.

There are a couple of noteworthy happenings in the masthead. Christina Krug's title has changed from Graphic Designer back to Assistant Art Director. Also, under Copy Editors, Laura Cleveland is listed for the first time. I make mention of this because these days Laura has a bigger role at RoF, that of Managing Editor. There was a stretch of time after Laura had earned her current role that she left the magazine (reasons unknown), but when she returned, I remember Shawna mentioning how glad she was to have Laura back as Managing Editor. I'm not arguing either. She seems really organized, and ever since Laura returned to take over as Managing Editor, the amount of free copies I receive with each issue has increased, and they always find their way to me earlier than ever before. Cheers, Laura.

A rundown of this issue's nonfiction is as follows:

In the Books column, Gahan Wilson reviews *The Complete Pegana–All the Tales Pertaining to the Fabulous Realm of Pegana*, edited by S.T. Joshi, *The Encyclopedia Cthuluiana–Expanded and Revised Second Edition* by Daniel Harms, *The R'lyeh Text*, "researched, transcribed and annotated" by Robert Tuner (meant to be a followup to *The Necronomicon*), and Jeanne Cavelos reviews *Flanders* by Patricia Anthony. In the Movie/TV column, Dan Perez covers *John Carpenter's Vampires*. In the Folkroots column, Terri Windling writes about the magical lore of birds. In the Artists Gallery, Karen Haber covers the art of James Warhola. And in the Games column, Eric T. Baker reviews the PC game, *Might and Magic VI: The Mandate of Heaven*, the RPG, *City of Lies: A Campaign Setting for Legend of the Five Rings*, the RPGs *Hercules: The Legendary Journeys & Xena: Warrior Princess*, *Return to the Tomb of Horrors: An Advanced Dungeons and Dragons Adventure*, and the RPG *Mage: The Sorcerers Crusade* from White Wolf Publishing.

On to the fiction ...

The lead story this issue is "Armageddon's Rose" by Christopher Mowbray. Just about everyone knows that one of the most clichéd story ideas one can visit in fantasy is that of Adam and Eve/the Garden of Eden. But as everyone also knows, even what is seemingly the most clichéd idea is worth reading about if the author can bring a worthwhile spin to the story. Mowbray does just that in this Garden of Eden tale in which one final bit of Eden still exists, only the old man tending it is not an angel but the Serpent. Art to this one was provided by Patrick Arrasmith.

Then we have "I Met a Traveler From an Antique Land" by David Sandner, which marks his second appearance in the magazine, and his first solo work. This one is a piece of dark fantasy that has a bit of a psychadelic quality to it. It's a twisted and sad love story, wherein a man comes back to life and cannot return to the dead until he lets go of the love he has toward his wife. While the author refers to the creature in the story as a vampire (a fair labeling), the front cover uses a teaser of "Zombie Love" in reference to this tale. It really does contain a lot of zombie qualities too, so this strikes me as a rather fair label as well. And if you consider it a zombie tale, it would mark the first zombie tale to appear in RoF. Art to this one was provided by Eric Dinyer, which marks his second illustration in the magazine.

Next up is "The Secret in the Chest" by Fiona Kelleghan, which marks her first fiction tale. This one is a fairy tale about a damsel in distress, and features some clever plotting as the author decides to take on many of the traditional conventions found in these sorts of stories as a knight must overcome all the usual sterotypes in order to win the damsel over. Art to this one was provided by Steven Adler, which marks his fourth illustration in the magazine.

Then we have "Alice" by Peni R. Griffin, which marks her fourth appearance in the magazine. This modern-day piece deals with the everyday mysteries that surround us, the ones we take for granted or fail to notice at all, and the prices we must pay to unravel them. Art to this one was provided by Mary O'Keefe Young, which marks her eleventh illustration in the magazine.

Following this is "The Inner Inner City" by Robert Charles Wilson, which marks his third appearance in the magazine. This story is a reprint, and was originally published in *Northern Fright 4* from Mosaic Press in

September 1997. As was the case with his other two stories in RoF, this one is loaded with thoughtful material, mixed with healthy doses of paranoia. Wilson's stories are refreshing in a way I don't encounter too often in fantasy. I read lots of stuff that is fun (and even more stuff that isn't). I read some stuff that challenges your Emotional Quotient, or EQ. But it's rare that I encounter fantasy stories that challenge your IQ. Science fiction does this plenty, but not so much with fantasy (braces for a series of posts seeking to prove me wrong). This time Wilson takes on religion, presenting a scenario where a group of academics make a cash bet where each one must come up with his/her own religion. Where it goes from here is pretty wild. This story was nominated for the 1998 World Fantasy Award for Best Short Fiction. Art to this one was provided by Jeff Potter.

Finally we have a young adult story by Jim Van Pelt called "Home." The illustration features an adolescent boy running for dear life from a giant robot. Readers of speculative literature often equate robots to science fiction. Usually this is accurate, but there are exceptions. This is one of them, in which a boy who has never belonged anywhere is approached by a robot only he can see. We don't know the story behind the robot or the things it can do, so the explanations could easily be fantastical instead of scientific. And without explanations, the arguments for fantasy become that much stronger. Art to this one was provided by Walter Velez.

So that wraps up this issue. And my favorite story? "I Met a Traveler From an Antique Land" by David Sandner. And my favorite artwork? Luis Royo's cover illustration.

Originally posted on douglascohen.livejournal.com on February 7th, 2008

Part twenty-six in my comprehensive retrospective as I read the fiction in *Realms of Fantasy* and offer my thoughts. This time around I'll be slicing and dicing the December 1998 issue.

The cover to this one is by Michael Whelan, which marks his sixth illustration in the magazine. It depicts Michael Moorcock's albino prince, Elric of Melnibone, lifting his vampiric blade, Stormbringer, in triumph. This is the second cover to feature the albino prince, and the first one was also by Michael Whelan. The artwork is nice enough, although Elric is somewhat more muscular than I'm used to picturing. I'll attribute this to Stormbringer providing him some particularly powerful soul-energy to feed upon.

A rundown of this issue's nonfiction is as follows:

In the Books column, Gahan Wilson reviews *Exorcisms and Ecstasies* by Karl Edward Wagner, edited by Stephen Jones, *Death Stalks the Night* by Hugh B. Cave, edited by Karl Edward Wagner, *The Door Below* by Hugh B. Cave, and Jeanne Cavelos reviews *Heartfire* by Orson Scott Card. In the Movie/TV column, Dan Perez covers the *Highlander* TV series. In the Folkroots column, Terri Windling writes about how artist, Brian Froud, brings folklore to life. In the Artists Gallery, Karen Haber covers the art of Doug Beekman. And in the Games column, Eric T. Baker reviews the RPG *Night of 1,000 Screams*, the trading card game *Hercules: The Legendary Journeys*, *Get Medieval* for the CD-Rom, the RPG *City O' Gloom: A Campaign Setting for Deadlands*, *Advanced Dungeons & Dragons Core Rules Version 2.0*, and the RPG *Epiphany: The Legends of Hyperborea*. It should also be noted that this marks Dan Perez's last issue on the Movie/TV column. His run lasted from the February 1996 issue through the December 1998 issue, with him handling this column most of these issues.

On to the fiction ...

Leading things off is "The Pliable Child" by Michael Libling. This is an interesting little tale about a young child who becomes whatever people want, like a piece of clay that molds to one's desires. Given the girl's power, I can't say I was surprised that there was a decided religious angle to the story. Art to this one was provided by Charles Demorat, which marks his fifth illustration in the magazine.

Next up is "Wotan's Pass" by David Hoing. This is another religious story, dealing with piousness, envy, and the old ways vs. the new. One tidbit I found very interesting in this piece was the idea of converting the god as opposed to his follower(s). Art to this one was provided by Web Bryant, which marks his ninth illustration in the magazine.

Third in the batting order is "Innamorata" by Lisa R. Cohen, which marks her second appearance in the magazine. This tale deals with a man who is inhabited by and ultimately shares a rather symbiotic relationship with an alien presence he stumbles upon in a forest. The connection between the protagonist and the alien presence is so personal that it resembles something very close to love, and in some ways transcends it (at least as we mere humans understand the idea). Personally, I considered this piece science fiction, which begs the question as to why Shawna considered it fantasy, and hence suitable to RoF. And I think I have the answer. To date, I've read four pieces (including this one) in various issues of *Realms of Fantasy* that I consider science fiction, and another one that sort of walks the line. Four of these stories have explored a common theme in one way or another: love. So. Ever hear the expression the magic of love? Love ...magic ...fantasy. Simply put, I'd say there are certain speculative stories that Shawna feels are fantasies due to how the love element is handled, regardless of what the supporting elements in the tale might be. I'm not arguing with this stance either. Love isn't logical, but there's a certain elemental logic to the simple breakdown I provided above. Does that mean every speculative story dealing with love qualifies as fantasy? Certainly not. But some are, even if they don't seem like fantasy at first blush. It all depends on what your definition of fantasy is. All you have to do is read the Letters Page each issue to see how widely such a definition can vary. Art to this one was provided by Jon Foster, which marks his third illustration in the magazine.

The next story is "The Mongols Among the Stars" by Martha Bayless. Of course, if you look at the tables of contents page, it would have you believe this story was written by regular fiction contributor, Peni R. Griffin. This calls for a "D'oh!" The story itself feels like a Far Eastern folktale, as Chinggis Khan and his army climb into the very sky itself, with the intent of conquering the moon and stars and planets. Art to this one was provided by Janet Aulisio, which marks her twelfth illustration in the magazine.

Then we have "Going Vampire" by Leslie What, which marks her fourth appearance in the magazine. This one combines Hollywood and vampires to explore, of all possible things, love. More specifically, a vampire learns he is still able to fall in love. Art to this one was provided by John Hanley.

Finally we have "Old Times" by James Sallis. This one is a short-short, in which a man tries to glean inside information regarding which flights will crash. This story lacked artwork, making it the first story published in the magazine without an illustration.

So that wraps up this issue, and also wraps up 1998. And my favorite story? Well, science fiction or not, the story was very compelling, so I'm going with "Innamorata" by Lisa R. Cohen. And my favorite artwork? Janet Aulisio's illustration to "The Mongol Among the Stars" by Martha Bayless.

Originally posted on douglascohen.livejournal.com on February 22nd, 2008

Part twenty-seven in my comprehensive retrospective as I read the fiction in *Realms of Fantasy* and offer my thoughts. This time I'll be kicking off the 1999 publishing year by discussing the February issue.

The cover to this one features Robert E. Howard's iconic barbarian, Conan. The art is by Boris Vallejo, and I recognize the cover as a reprint, because it once graced one of those old Conan pastiche paperbacks from Tor Books that I read rather voraciously when I was twelve. This one was for *Conan the Triumphant*, which was written by Robert Jordan back before he achieved mega-success with his *Wheel of Time* novels.

There are a couple of things worth noting in the masthead. Christina Krug's run as Assistant Art Director (and other positions) has drawn to a close. The new Assistant Art Director is Ronald Stevens, which strikes me as a bit odd since he was the magazine's original Art Director. Go figure.

In the Letters Page, there are two separate letters in here from previous contributors to the magazine, these being Fiona Kelleghan and Christopher Rowe. Both authors landed their first sale with RoF, although I was unaware it was Christopher's first sale until I read his letter. He also mentions in his letter that "Kin to Crows" received an Honorable Mention in the Year's Best Fantasy & Horror anthology, edited (at that time) by Ellen Datlow (who's still at the helm) and Terri Windling (who has moved on). I would mention other authors whose stories received Honorable Mentions in these retrospectives, but unless you have a copy of the anthology, this information is a lot harder to track down than it is for stories that were reprinted. My point? You never what you'll learn from reading the Letters Page.

A rundown of this issue's nonfiction is as follows:

In the Books column, Gahan Wilson reviews *The Avram Davidson Treasury*, edited by Robert Silverberg and Grania Davis, *Crypt Orchids* by David J. Schow, *In the Shadow of the Gargoyle*, edited by Nancy Kilpatrick and Thomas S. Roche, *Hoka! Hoka! Hoka!* by Gordon R. Dickson, and Jeanne Cavelos reviews a trade paperback edition of *The Lion, the Witch, and the Wardrobe* by C.S. Lewis. In the Movie/TV column, newcomer

Thomasina Gibson covers *The Crow* TV show. In Folkroots, newcomer Joseph Monti* writes about Charles de Lint's approach to fantasy, mythology, and consensual reality. In the Artists Gallery, Terri Windling covers the art of Mark Wagner. And in the Games column, Eric T. Baker reviews *Campaign Cartographer 2* for the PC, the RPG *The Ways of the Clans: Book Five: The Way of the Scorpion, A Supplement for the Legend of the Five Ring, Die by the Sword* for the PC, and *A Paladin in Hell: An Advanced Dungeons & Dragons Adventure*.

On to the fiction ...

The lead story is "Dragons and Other Extinctions" by Patrick Weekes. Unless I missed something, this marks the first story to appear in Realms that has elves, as well as dwarfs and centuars. To those of you trying to claw your way out of our slush pile, please take note of this. The long wait for a centaur to appear in the magazine is something I chalk up to happenstance. Elves and dwarfs are another matter. Their importance to the genre cannot be overlooked, but in my opinion these races have become rather cliche. Shawna must think so too if it took this long for her to publish something in this vein. Trust me when I tell you that I see plenty of stories with elves and dwarfs in the slush. The problem with these stories is that whole cliche thing. This story gets around that quite nicely. It's still high fantasy, but it turns a lot of the conventions right on its head, as we are presented with a future where humans and magic have died off and technology and the world are evolving. The author provides some other clever touches, which is why Shawna took this one. And without having read all the fiction yet, I'll guarantee that if there are other stories in Realms with elves and dwarfs, the stories will present a decidedly new slant. If it proves otherwise, I shall eat my words. It should also be noted that the author's bio indicates that this is his first sale. Art to this one was provided by Alan Pollack, which marks his fourth illustration in the magazine.

Next up is "Bitter Chivalry" by Darrell Schweitzer, who for many years was the coeditor of *Weird Tales*. This was an Arthurian tale that deals with one of the knights left behind during the Grail Quest. So King Arthur gives the knight a different sort of quest: to bring someone comfort. The author nails this one perfectly, capturing the heroic simplicity some of these solo Arthurian adventures often featured. Art to this one was provided by Todd Lockwood, which marks his fourth illustration in the magazine.

Then we have "Dragon of Conspiracy" by William R. Eakin, which marks his fifth appearance in the magazine. It also marks his fifth Redgunk, Mississippi tale to appear in RoF. In some of his other Redgunk tales, he tackles traditional creatures in unusual ways, such as mummies and unicorns. This time he's at it again, with, you guessed it, dragons. But as seems to be the case with all his Redgunk tales, regardless of the beasties involved, the story always comes back to the characters. In this piece, a prostitute's newborn son is infected with her herpes while her father's emotion creates a dragon that lives in the pipes of Redgunk, but this dragon comes to care about their fates. I should also note that I'm fairly certain this is the first issue of RoF to have two separate stories that deal with dragons. Art to this one was provided by Joel Napstrek, which marks his third illustration in the magazine.

Then we have "Northwest Passage" by Derryl Murphy. This marks the 150th story to be published in RoF. This one takes place in the Arctic, and the strength of this piece is definitely the milieu. I absolutely believed everything was freezing cold as a man goes to the Arctic to unlock the secrets of his grandfather and has a run-in with his ghost. Art to this one was provided by Ken Graning, which marks his eighth illustration in the magazine.

Finally we have "A Ghost of a Chance" by David Bischoff. This one deals with a man's guardian angel coming to him while he's playing blackjack in Las Vegas. I've never been to Vegas (unless you include a brief stopover for a connecting flight to Los Angeles), but I've been to Atlantic City a number of times. So I can say with some authority that the author absolutely captures the manic energy that comes with gambling in a casino. And plunking an angel down in the middle of that frenetic energy ...just a lot of fun. Art to this one was provided by Patrick Arrasmith, which marks his second illustration in the magazine.

So that wraps up this issue. And my favorite story? Well, I think I have a bit of bias here, because last month I won 500 dollars playing blackjack (had I stopped gambling sooner I would've made 1100), which fills me with good feelings toward this game of chance. So I'll have to go with "A Ghost of Chance" by David Bischoff. And my favorite artwork? Todd Lockwood's illustration to "Bitter Chivalry" by Darrell Schweitzer.

*In going back to edit these retrospectives for book form, every so often I am given new reminders about what a small world this is. Seeing Joe Monti's name is one more example of this. Several months after RoF closed for the final time, Joe Monti was the literary agent who sold the *Oz Reimagined* anthology, which I co-edited with John Joseph Adams. I am also involved or in discussion with Joe about a couple of other projects that I'm not at liberty to discuss at the time I'm writing this.

Originally posted on douglascohen.livejournal.com on February 25th, 2008

Part twenty-eight in my comprehensive retrospective as I read the fiction in *Realms of Fantasy* and offer my thoughts. This time around I'll be performing exploratory surgery on the April 1999 issue.

The cover is by Keith Parkinson, which marks his third illustration in the magazine. The artwork was originally a personal project of his.

In the masthead, in addition to Art Director, Stephen Vann, and Assistant Art Director, Ronald Stevens, this issue also lists Dawn M. Stein as the Graphic Artist. I believe this is the first time all three positions were listed in the masthead. I don't know exactly how the art duties were divvied up during this time, but as I've noted in the past, the art is such an important part of RoF, so I feel I should mention this addition to the Realms staff.

Next up is the Letters Page. There is another letter from a contributor, this time James Sallis. For whatever reason, I always like to note when the authors write us.

A rundown of this issue's nonfiction is as follows:

In the Books column, Gahan Wilson reviews Avram Davidson's short story collection, *The Boss in the Wall*, *Climb the Wind* by Pamela Sargent, *The Riven Codex* by David and Leigh Eddings, and Jeanne Cavelos reviews *Black Butterflies* by John Shirley. In the Movie/TV column, newcomer Mary Baumann discusses good and bad witches. In the Folkroots column, Heinz Insu Fenkl discusses Korean folkore. In the Artists Gallery, Karen Haber covers the art of Stephen Youll. And in the Games column, Eric T. Baker reviews *Redguard* for the PC, the RPG *Code of Bushido: An Adventure of Honor and Duty*, the RPG *The Mythic Seas*, *Redjack: Revenge of the Brethren* for the PC and Mac, and the RPG *Legacy: War of the Ages*.

On to the fiction ...

The lead story is "Jordan's Waterhammer" by Joe Mastroianni. This tale deals with men that are grown on a "farm" and are used to mine ore beneath the surface. They are given simple rewards for performing their duties well, and while it was the Morlocks in *The Time Machine* by H.G. Wells who dwelled in the underworld, the sheer innocence of these men reminded me of the Eloi. The story revolves around the revered teachings of one of these men who once went to the surface and brought back strange notions, such as love. These teachings have been secretly passed along, and when the story begins things are about to reach a boiling point. This is another one of those pieces that I consider science fiction. As to why Shawna bought it, I'll point you to her editorial caption for the story: "This story might feel like science fiction, but its heart–the power of myth, language, and love to transform–is pure fantasy." Notice how she mentioned love? Two issues earlier, Lisa R. Cohen had a story published called "Innamorata" that I also considered science fiction. I then went on a bit of a tangent, offering a possible explanation as to why the stories I've seen in Realms I've considered to be science fiction were accepted by Shawna for publication. I pinpointed the idea of love, how four out of five of these stories dealt with love in one way or another. You can now make that five out of six. Seems I was on to something. Some years later I brought this story to the attention of my friend and editorial colleague John Joseph Adams, and it was reprinted in *Wastelands: Stories of the Apocalypse*. Art to this one in RoF was provided by John Berkey, which marks his fourth illustration in the magazine.

Next up is "Arthur's Wishes" by Tim Myers. This piece of Arthuriana deals with a young Arthur who accidentally ensnares his cousin Morganna into granting him three wishes. The author deals with the old wish theme in some very inventive ways, and I very much appreciated that while the story was self-contained, very casual hints were dropped about the tragic union that would ensue between these two characters at some unknown future date. Art to this one was provided by Gary Lippincott, which marks his fourth illustration in the magazine.

Then we have "Baptism on Bittersweet Creek" by Christopher Rowe, which marks his second appearance in the magazine. This is an odd tale about golden-skinned youth that is stumbled upon by some of the town boys. The golden-skinned youth doesn't speak, but he manages to impact the songs of the local congregation in some unusual ways. Art to this one was provided by Web Bryant, which marks his tenth illustration in the magazine.

Following this we have "Take a Long Step" by Richard Parks, which marks his fourth appearance in the magazine. This tale is rather quirky, as it deals with a god on the great Wheel who has come back, and the reader is left to decide whether his little adventures are fate or coincidence.

Having now read four of Richard's stories for these retrospectives (and a good number more since I've been at RoF), I'm struck by his willingness to tackle a wide spectrum of fantasy stories. And given how many sales he has with the magazine, he does so quite successfully. No pigeonholing here! Art to this one was provided by Michael Gibbs, which marks his fifth illustration in the magazine.

Finally we have "How We Play the Game in Salt Lake" by M. Shayne Bell. This contemporary fantasy deals with an AIDS victim who attends a minor league baseball game and witnesses a young girl have her tooth extracted with a pair of pliers in order to help a player on the field get a hit so he might go on to a career in the major leagues. I can only describe this story as bizarrely compelling. Art to this one was provided by Janet Aulisio, which marks her thirteenth illustration in the magazine.

So that wraps up this issue. And my favorite story? Once again I'm giving the nod to the "miscreant" work of science fiction in our beloved fantasy magazine, because "Jordan's Waterhammer" was a very powerful tale. And my favorite artwork? Gary Lippincott's illustration to "Arthur's Wishes" by Tim Myers.

Originally posted on douglascohen.livejournal.com on February 27th, 2008

Part twenty-nine in my ongoing retrospective as I read the fiction in *Realms of Fantasy* and offer my thoughts. This time I'll be discussing the June 1999 issue.

The cover art to this one is by Brom. It is a reprint of some artwork he did for TSR—probably for their Dark Sun campaign—though I was unable to track down the exact details. The winged demon in this one is giving off a serious dominatrix vibe, but given the overall attire I think this one can also be safely lumped in with the infamous chicks in chainmail covers.

There are more changes to the masthead with this issue. Ronald Stevens, once the Art Director, then briefly back as the Assistant Art Director, seems to have moved on. The new Assistant Art Director is Scott Crawford. There's certainly been a lot of activity in the art department over the last twelve or so issues.

I've noted how several covers have featured Michael Moorcock's Elric of Melnibone. Well, Elric isn't on the cover this time, but Michael Moorcock *is* in the Letters Page. Moorcock was one of my formative authors in the genre of fantasy, so seeing a letter from him that is quite generous with its praise of the fiction in RoF is something I absolutely wanted to note.

A rundown of this issue's nonfiction is as follows:

In the Books column, Gahan Wilson reviews *Sirens and other Daemon Lovers*, edited by Ellen Datlow & Terri Windling, *The Tooth Fairy* by Graham Joyce, *The Complete Silence* by Algernon Blackwood, *Barlowe's Inferno*, written and illustrated by Wayne Barlowe, while Jeanne Cavelos reviews *Extremities* by Kathe Koja, and Brian Murphy from the Sovereign Media office reviews *Enchantment* by Orson Scott Card. In the Movie/TV column, newcomer Resa Nelson covers the movie, *The Mummy*. In the Folkroots column, Heinz Insu Fenkl writes about Korean ghosts and demons. In the Artists Gallery, Karen Haber covers the artwork of Kinuko Y. Craft. And in the Games column, Eric Baker reviews *Baldur's Gate*, a computer game based on the paper-and-dice RPG, *Advanced Dungeons & Dragons*, the RPG *Vampire: The Masquerade* from White Wolf Publishing, and the PC game, *Thief: the Dark Project*.

This issue could be considered one of the more important ones in *Realms of Fantasy*'s publication history. Why? Simply put: respect. Three of the five stories herein were singled out for excellence in one form or another, and sometimes by more than one venue. What's more, this issue would mark the beginning of an impressive run over the next four or so issues, with stories earning recognition and awards from various venues. Clearly, *Realms of Fantasy* has established itself at this point among the other genre magazines, both on a commercial level and a literary one.

On to the fiction ...

The lead story is "The Grammarian's Five Daughters" by Eleanor Arnason. This one skirts the line between metafiction and fairy tale, and I rather enjoyed it. Each of the grammarian's daughters strike out to earn their fortune during the course of the story, and to aid them along their way, mom gives each of them various parts of the human language: nouns, verbs, adjectives, adverbs, and prepositions. Really clever and very skillfully told. This one earned a lot of notice. First, it was nominated for the 2000 World Fantasy Award for Best Short Story. It is the only original story published in RoF to be nominated for a World Fantasy Award. I've said it before and I'm sure I'll say it again. That's bloody ridiculous. But complaining about the various awards systems within our genre isn't the point of these retrospectives, so I'll save the in-depth rant for another time. In addition to being nominated for a World Fantasy Award, this story was also reprinted in the 13th edition of *Year's Best Fantasy & Horror*, edited by Ellen Datlow & Terri Windling. And in addition to this, "The Grammarian's Five Daughters" was later reprinted on the *Strange Horizons* website. *Strange Horizons* keeps all its fiction archived, so if you're curious what all the hubub was about for this particular story, you can visit the website and read it for free. Art to this one was provided by Steven Adler, which marks his fifth illustration in the magazine.

Next up is "Sailing the Painted Ocean" by Denise Lee. This one deals with a ship lost at sea that becomes caught in a rather bizarre and surreal voyage during WWII. Like the first story, this one was selected for inclusion in the 13th edition of *Year's Best Fantasy & Horror*, edited by Ellen Datlow & Terri Windling. Art to this one was provided by Janet Aulisio, which marks her fourteenth illustration in the magazine.

And so long as we're discussing decorated stories, let's go for the trifecta. Next up is "Fortitide" by Andy Duncan. The main character in this one is General George Patton. In this tale, the general is unstuck in time, finding himself repeating situations in history he's encountered before. And of course he tries to change certain outcomes here and there, but Time has ideas of its own. This is the longest story I've read in the magazine. It was also nominated for the 2001 Nebula Award for Best Novella, so that may explain why Shawna was compelled to take this one when its word length is so much longer than the magazine's stated guidelines. Art to this one was provided by John Berkey, which marks his fifth illustration in the magazine.

Following this comes another tale dealing with a specific period in history, this being "Stalin's Candy" by William Shunn. This one does a solid job of depicting the oppression of Communist Russia, how the country did everything in its power to grind the people under its heel, until they were frightened sheep that didn't dare stand up to their government. But even in times such as these one can find hope, as this story shows us. Although this tale was published years before I met him, I'll note that Bill and I were once part of the same critique group, the now defunct 8th of February. Art to this one was provided Charles Demorat, which marks his fifth illustration in the magazine.

Finally we have "Mausturm" by Kate Reidel. This one deals with a rat infestation in the house of a man who has commited horrible crimes. Gradually, this infestation builds to supernatural levels. Hints are dropped throughout the tale, but we don't learn the reason for this situation until the story is almost over. But even then it's left to the reader to decide exactly why this infestation took pace. Art to this one was provided by David Beck, which marks his tenth illustration in the magazine.

So that wraps up this issue. And my favorite story? I'll have to go with "The Grammarian's Five Daughters" by Eleanor Arnason. And my favorite artwork? Brom's cover illustration is racy but well done.

Originally posted on douglascohen.livejournal.com on February 29th, 2008

Part thirty in my comprehensive retrospective as I read the fiction in *Realms of Fantasy* and offer my thoughts. This time around I'll be discussing the August 1999 issue.

The cover to this one is by Greg Hildebrandt, part of the famed Hildebrandt Brothers artist duo. It was originally a cover for a Simon & Schuster book, though I was unable to discover which one. This cover was also nominated for a 2000 Chesley Award for Cover Illustration.

Let's hop over the Table of Contents page. The editorial caption beneath "Rozsa-Neni and Farkas Asszony" reads as follows: "If you're a reader, a writer, or an editor, you'll love this story. If you're not, you'll love it anyway." No offense intended to the author, but this caption doesn't belong with this story. Why? Because this exact editorial caption was used in the previous issue for "The Grammarian's Daughter." D'oh!

Over in the Letters Page, another fiction contributor wrote in (Darrell Schweitzer), this time in response to Assistant Editor Rebecca McCabe's guest editorial. I believe this is the first time a contributor wrote a response to one of the editorials.

A rundown of this issue's nonfiction is as follows:

In the Books column, Gahan Wilson reviews *Dark Sister* by Graham Joyce, *Dark Cities Underground* by Lisa Goldstein, *The Savage Tales of Solomon Kane* by Robert E. Howard, illustrated by Gary Gianni, *The Year's Best Fantasy and Horror, Twelfth Annual Edition*, edited by Ellen Datlow & Terri Windling, and Jeanne Cavelos reviews *Santa Steps Out: A Fairy Tale for Grown-Ups* by Robert Devereaux. In the Movie/TV column, Resa Nelson covers Hollywood's remake of *The Haunting*. In the Folkroots column, Heinz Insu Fenkl explores family dysfunction in the myths of various cultures. In the Artists Gallery, Karen Haber covers the aforementioned Brothers Hildebrandt. And in the Games column, Eric Baker reviews *Birthright Campaign Setting* for *Advanced Dungeons & Dragons*, the White Wolf campaign guides, *Guide to the Camarilla* and *Guide to the Sabat*, the RPG, *The Dragon and the Bear: The Novgorod Tribunal*, *Heretic 2* for the PC, the PC and Mac game, *Quest for Glory: Dragon Fire*, and the card game, *Fortune Teller Collectibles*.

On to the fiction ...

The lead story is the aforementioned "Rozsa-Neni and Farkas Asszony" by Deborah Therese D'Onofrio, which marks her second appearance in the magazine. This one deals with an old childless woman whose husband dies. She then finds contentment by putting on a wolf pelt that allows her to become a werewold and taking care of those who comes to her. By drawing on Hungarian lore, it explores this old trope in some unusual ways. Art to this one was provided by Patrick Arrasmith, which marks his third illustration in the magazine.

Next up is "The Girl Who Loved Fire" by K.D. Wentworth, which marks her second appearance in the magazine. No, the girl who loved fire isn't a pyromaniac. She can talk to fires, and the characterizations and language do an excellent job of exploring this idea. Art to this one was provided by Broeck Steadman, which marks his fourth illustration in the magazine.

Following this we have "How the Highland People Came to Be" by Bruce Holland Rogers. This high fantasy piece was nominated for the 2001 Nebula Award for Best Novelette. The plotting and worldbuilding in this one are both clever and outside-the-box, as the story explores how lies can sometimes become truth in the most unexpected of ways. Art to this one was provided by Jacques Bredy, and it was selected for inclusion in *Spectrum 10: The Year's Best in Contemporary Fantastic Art*.

Then we have "A Brother Grimm" by Sten Westgard. This one is sort of a metafictional fairy tale, dealing with the authors of Grimm's Fairy Tales, as the creatures of their tales strike back at them. The story is decidely dark, so I guess you can say the author is taking a page out of Grimm's Fairy Tales. Art to this one was provided by Stephen Johnson.

Following this we have "The Hounds of Winter" by Brian A. Hopkins and James Van Pelt. For James, this marks his third appearance in the magazine. I suppose you could term this piece as science fantasy. Centuries ago a colony ship crashed on the cold, forbidding world of Jotunheim. The colonists remain stranded here, but they've lost most of their advanced technology, and each day is a struggle for survival against the planet's vicious animals. The animals are of a familiar sort, such as bears or wolves, but the rules of nature are different here, and here we diverge into fantasy. Zach's wife is bitten by a wolf and becomes one herself. Zach kills a wolf and eats its heart to be reunited with his wife in wolf form. The story overflows with tension, and the level of detail does a wonderful job of sucking you in. Art to this one was provided by John Hanely, which marks his second illustration in the magazine.

Rounding out this group of six we have "Wailer" by Bruce Glassco. This is a funny fantasy told through a series of letters, and it marks the first appearance of a banshee in the pages of *Realms of Fantasy*. Art to this one was provided by Tony Diterlizzi.

So that wraps up this issue. And my favorite story? As always, I feel guilty when I don't select a Nebula nominee. I also feel guilty for not selecting Wentworth's story, because I really enjoyed it and last time I really enjoyed her story but ended up selecting another one as my favorite. But the winner is "The Hounds of Winter" by Brian A. Hopkins and James Van Pelt. This one really got its hooks into me ...about as much as the protagonist Zach got that hook into that wolf. And building on my established logic, since the cover was nominated for a Chesley Award, I suppose I should feel guilty for it not being my favorite. But I'm afraid I'm going with Patrick Arrasmith's illustration to "Rozsa-Neni and Farkas Asszony" by Deborah Therese D'Onofrio.

Originally posted on douglascohen.livejournal.com on March 5th, 2008

Part thirty-one in my comprehensive retrospective as I read the fiction in *Realms of Fantasy* and offer my thoughts. This time around I'll be offering some thoughts about the October 1999 issue.

Anytime we reach October, it marks another publishing year for *Realms of Fantasy*. October 1999 marks year number five. I'd have to say that in its first five years, RoF did an excellent job establishing itself. The publishers, editors, art staff, writers (fiction & nonfiction), and artists should all be commended. But enough praise ...

Let's talk about the cover. I recognize this one too. It's another Boris Vallejo cover (his style is rather distinctive), featuring Conan. This marks the second RoF cover with Conan. Like the other one, it was originally one of the old Conan pastiche paperbacks from Tor Books. Once again it's one of the pastiches that Robert Jordan wrote: *Conan the Magnificent*.

A rundown of this issue's nonfiction is as follows:

In the Books column, Gahan Wilson reviews *The Descent* by Jeff Long, *The Marriage of Sticks* by Jonathan Carroll, *More Annotated H.P. Lovecraft*, edited and annotated S.T. Joshi and Peter Cannon, Jeanne Cavelos reviews *Night Tales* by John Maclay, and Brian Murphy reviews *The Ultimate Encyclopedia of Fantasy*, edited by David Pringle. In the Movie/TV column, Resa Nelson covers the movie, *The 13th Warrior*. In the Folkroots section, Midori Snyder discusses Sleeping Beauty. In the Artists Gallery, Jane Frank covers the art of Daniel Horne. And in the Games section, Eric Baker reviews the RPG, *Legend of the Five Rings GM's Survival Guide*, the RPG, *GURPS: Discworld*, *Advanced Dungeons and Dragons Tomes: Axe of the Dwarvish Lords*, the RPG, *Furry Prates: Swashbuckling Adventures in the Furry Age of Piracy*, and the CRPG, *Majesty: Sovereign of Ardania*.

On to the fiction ...

The lead story is "Raney's Hounds" by Jessica Wynn Reisman. The protagonist's "profession" in this one is rather interesting, because he's a hobo. He quickly finds himself entangled with another a mysterious stranger, and the two of them spend most of the story fleeing a trio of hellhounds. Art to this one was provided by Ken Graning, which marks his ninth illustration in the magazine.

Then we have "The Damsel in Distress" by E.A. Johnson, which marks his second appearance in the magazine. This one is a fairy tale, featuring the damsel held prisoner by the dragon, with shining knights in armor seeking to come to her rescue. The twist? What do you do when the monsters are all in the damsel's mind? Art to this one was provided by John Monteleone, which marks his third illustration in the magazine.

Next up is "Chenting, in the Land of the Dead" by Kij Johnson. This one has the feel of a far eastern folk tale. A man and a woman go to different versions of the same afterlife, because each one envisions it differently. This piece is on the short side, but it still manages a solid twist at the end. Art to this one was provided by Patrick Arrasmith, which marks his fourth illustration in the magazine.

After this we have "Sally Harpe" by Christopher Rowe, which marks his third appearance in the magazine. Like his other two stories, this one takes place in the Deep South, and it has a decidedly dark bent as it explores the dangers of breaking promises as a girl's refusal to keep her promise causes her to be reanimated. What I liked about this idea is that the person breaking the promise isn't the one who made it. Art to this one was provided by J.K. Potter, which marks his fourth illustration in the magazine.

Following this is "Dusi" by Devon Monk. This piece deals with Greek mythology, and as best I can remember it marks the first appearance of Medusa within RoF. So imagine my surprise when her first appearance plunks her in the middle of modern-day Seattle. Art to this one was provided by Chuck Demorat, which marks seventh illustration in the magazine.

Finally we have "The Voyage to the Moon" by Derryl Murphy, which marks his second appearance in the magazine. This one is what you might call a science fiction fairy tale, as it cleverly combines the first moon landing with the story of Jack and the Beanstalk. And while it may be a science fiction fairy tale, if it's a fairy tale I still consider it fantasy. Figure that one out. Art to this one was provided by Walter Velez, which marks his second illustration in the magazine.

So that wraps up this issue. And my favorite story? "Sally Harpe" by Christopher Rowe. And my favorite artwork? J.K. Potter's accompanying illustration to "Sally Harpe."

Originally posted on douglascohen.livejournal.com on March 6th, 2008

Part thirty-two in my comprehensive retrospective as I read the fiction in *Realms of Fantasy* and offer my thoughts. This time around I'll be putting a cap on the 1990's by discussing the December 1999 issue.

The cover to this one is by Luis Royo, which marks his seventh illustration in the magazine. It was originally the cover to the November 1991 issue of *Heavy Metal Magazine*.

The Letters Page this issue is mysteriously absent.

A rundown of this issue's nonfiction is as follows:

In the Books column, Gahan Wilson reviews a reissue of *The King of Elfland's Daughter* by Lord Dunsany, *Jack of Kinrowan* by Charles de Lint, *White of the Moon, New Tales of Madness and Dread*, edited by Stephen Jones, and Jeanne Cavelos reviews *Harry Potter and the Sorcerer's Stone* by J.K. Rowling, and Brian Murphy reviews *Dragon Weather* by Lawrence Watt-Evans. In the Folkroots column, Terri Windling writes about rites-of-passage in fantasy. In the Movie/TV column, Scott Edelman covers Tim Burton's *Sleepy Hollow*. In the Artists Gallery, Karen Haber covers the art of Rowena Morrill. And in the Games column, Eric T. Baker reviews *Dungeon Keeper 2* for the PC, a reissue of the *Feng Shui* card game and a supplement to it called *Blood of the Valiant*, and *Jerusalem by Night: A City Sourcebook for Vampire: The Dark Ages* from White Wolf. I should note that this issue marks the last one for Jeanne Cavelos as a reviewer. She had a very respectable run, from the August 1995 issue through the December 1999 issue. It's also interesting to note that Scott Edelman, who handled the Movie/TV column for this issue, was also the editor for *Science Fiction Age*, the now defunct sibling magazine to *Realms of Fantasy*.

On to the fiction ...

Given my tastes, overall this issue strikes me as one of the strongest I've read so far in terms of its fiction. The lead story is "Aftershock" by F. Paul Wilson. While I've heard him do a reading (for a Repairman Jack story), this marks the first time I've read his fiction. Honestly, this story blew me away. I absolutely understand why it won the Bram Stoker Award in 2000 for Best Short Fiction. The basic premise deals with a man and woman whose lives become entangled in a big way when it's revealed that being struck by lightning allows them to see their dead children. Really powerful characterizations, strong imagery, and excellent pacing. I can't recommend this one enough. Art to this one was provided by John Hanley, which marks his third illustration in the magazine.

For those of you who are unaware, my favorite author is George R. R. Martin. This happened back in 1996 when I read *A Game of Thrones*, the first volume in his epic fantasy series. I absolutely loved the novel, and lost a lot of sleep to finish it (and the subsequent ones). After it was done, I naturally tried to read something else. It fell flat. Very flat. In fact, a good month must have passed before I could bring myself to enjoy another novel. My point? I felt bad for the next story. Surely it would fall flat for me after such a kick-ass tale as "Aftershock." How could I possibly give this story a fair read?

I could've waited to read it, but you may have noticed, these days I tend to do these retrospectives in bunches. When I have the time to read these back issues, I need to make use of it. So I started reading the next story, "The Queen in the Hill" by Kage Baker ...and it held its own. The "Queen in the Hill" is a Company story. Baker has written other short stories in this universe, as well as novels in this universe published by Tor. This had a science fantasy feel to it. It reminded me of Frank Herbert's *Dune*, and also Dan Simmons' duology a few years ago, of *Ilium* and *Olympos*. But the story and world were entirely Baker's own. This one draws on Greek milieus, featuring some godlike beings that are using humans for their breeding projects. Very skillfully told, and the whole premise intrigued me enough that at some point I'm going to try the first novel in this universe. Art to this one was provided by Michael Whelan, which marks his seventh illustration in the magazine.

Following this we have "Glamour" by Bruce Glassco, which marks his second appearance in the magazine. This is another story that deals with the Faerie, something I see a lot of, both in the slush and the magazine. What was refreshing about this tale was that instead of focusing on the Faerie, it focuses on the humans whose lives were impacted by the meddling of the fey folk. I can be a rather tough sell with fey stories, but this one I liked. Art to this one was provided by Mary O'Keefe Young, which marks her twelfth illustration in the magazine.

After this comes "The Giant's Tooth" by Bruce Coville. This one is a lighthearted fairy tale about a man who almost gets eaten by a giant. At the last second, an old woman saves him ...inside the giant's mouth. Escape is impossible, and so we see the man settle down in the giant's mouth and make a life for himself. I can also be a tough sell with lighthearted stuff, but this was fun. Art to this one was provided by Joel Napstrek, which marks his fourth illustration in the magazine.

Finally we have "The Witch's Child" by Lisa Goldstein. This marks her second appearance in the magazine, but it's her first original work to appear in RoF. This story was a retelling of the fairy tale of Rapunzel. What I liked was how much Goldstein humanized this tale. That's no easy thing to do, because when you think about it the story itself is pretty ridiculous. Art to this one was provided by Broeck Steadman, which marks his fifth illustration in the magazine.

So that wraps up this issue, as well as the 1990's. And my favorite story? Almost any other issue I'd go with "The Queen in the Hill' by Kage Baker, but with this issue the honor must go to "Aftershock" by F. Paul Wilson. Great, great stuff. And my favorite artwork? Luis Royo's cover illustration.

Originally posted on douglascohen.livejournal.com on March 7th, 2008

Part thirty-three in my comprehensive retrospective as I read the fiction in *Realms of Fantasy* and offer my thoughts. This time around I'll be kicking off the millenium with the February 2000 issue.

The cover to this one is by Michael Whelan, which marks his eighth illustration in the magazine. My research failed to uncover the origins of this piece.

In the masthead, we learn that Scott Crawford's brief run as Assistant Art Director seems to have reached its end. Taking his place is Dawn Stein (listed as Graphic Artist in earlier issues) with the the title of Associate Art Director.

Next I'll note that after a mysterious disappearance of one issue, the Letters Page has returned.

A rundown of this issue's nonfiction is as follows:

In the Books column, Gahan Wilson reviews *Mr. X* by Peter Straub, *Harry Potter and Chamber of Secrets* as well as *Harry Potter and the Prisoner of Azkaban*, both by J.K. Rowling, and *The Annotated Dragonlance Chronicles* by Margaret Weis & Tracy Hickman. In the Movie/TV column, Resa Nelson covers the TV series, *Angel*. In the Folkroots column, Heinz Insu Fenkl discusses aliens and angels. In the Artists Gallery, Karen Haber covers the artwork of John Jude Palencar. And in the Games column, Eric T. Baker reviews *Darkstone* for the PC, the RPG, *Forge: Out of Chaos*, *The Forgotten Realms Interactive Atlas*, the RPG, *7th Sea*, and *Nocturne* for the PC.

Onto the fiction ...

This issue kicks off with "The Troops" by Peni R. Griffin, which marks her fifth appearance in the magazine. This is an odd tale about a little girl's toys coming to life to do battle with a threat from beyond. I remember Shawna once telling me that most of what I pass along to her she considers publishable, and that most of the stuff she passes on she's seen already in one form or another. I bring this up because reading this reminded me of a story I once slushed that I thought for sure Shawna would take. Only she didn't. Sure enough, this story also dealt with a child's toys coming to life and going to battle. So I wouldn't be surprised if at least part of the reason

Shawna rejected that other story was because she'd "seen this before." I'd like to think I'm pretty good at what I do, but Shawna has been at this a lot longer than I have. She's read more, and has probably forgotten more stories than I remember. Perhaps one day some brash young editor will say as much about me. Art to this one was provided by Web Bryant, which marks his eleventh illustration in the magazine.

The next story is "Burial Detail" by Kristine Kathryn Rusch, which marks her second appearance in the magazine. This one takes place soon after the American Civil War, and focuses on a recently freed slave. In order to feed his family, the man works on a burial detail. A grim hard job to begin with, but it becomes much worse when you have the Sight, and you see the past of every corpse you touch. Art to this one was provided by Patrick Arrasmith, which marks his fifth illustration in the magazine.

Next up is "The Chapter of Coming Forth by Night" by Noreen Doyle and Lois Tilton, and this definitely marks one of the longer stories we've run in Realms. For Noreen, it marks her third appearance in the magazine. This is also the third of her Chapter tales to be printed in RoF. Like the previous two, this one has a decided mythological bent, as an obsessed American on an archaeological dig threatens to unearth secrets from Egypt's ancient past. The story gradually becomes a clash of new vs. old, progress vs. tradition, and technology vs. mysticism as a goddess from Egypt's past attempts to preserve her secrets. Art to this one was provided by John Berkey, which marks his sixth illustration in the magazine.

Following this we have "How Konti Scrounged the World" by Richard Parks. Like Peni, this marks Richard's fifth appearance in the magazine. Let me take a moment to say hats off to both of these authors. To this point, only four authors have appeared five or more times in the magazine with their fiction (the other two being Tanith Lee and William R. Eakin). These two are definitely part of the Realms stable of authors. They still are, as both continue to appear in the magazine on a fairly regular basis. As to Richard's tale, this one is a creation myth (African, I would say). Interestingly enough, it deals with the most unimpressive god in the pantheon, and it demonstrates how he manages to create the best of all worlds. Never underestimate the little guy! Art to this one was provided by Michael Gibbs, which marks his sixth illustration in the magazine.

Finally we have "Laurel Wood" by Anna Kirwan. This one is a fairy tale dealing with a man who must emply nothing but a single stick to accomplish a seemingly impossible mission. Quite impressive what one can manage with clever plotting. Art to this one was provided by Steven Adler, which marks his sixth illustration in the magazine.

So that wraps up this issue. And my favorite story? "How Konti Scrounged the World" by Richard Parks. And my favorite artwork? Steven Adler's illustration to "Laurel Wood" by Anna Kirwan.

Originally posted on douglascohen.livejournal.com on March 26th, 2008

Part thirty-four in my comprehensive retrospective as I read the fiction in *Realms of Fantasy* and offer my thoughts. This time around I'll be discussing the April 2000 issue.

The cover to this one is a Boris Vallejo illustration, his third such to grace the magazine. It was originally published in his *Mythical Creatures Calendar* (year unknown).

I'll also note the mysterious disappearance of the bio page in this issue.

A rundown of this issue's nonfiction is as follows:

In the Books column, Gahan Wilson reviews *Dark Detectives–Adventures of the Supernatural Sleuths*, edited by Stephen Jones, *The Talisman* by Jonathan Aycliffe, *The Fox Woman* by Kij Johnson, and newcomer Paul di Filippo reviews *The Artist of the Missing* by Paul LaFarge, *Tamsin* by Peter S. Beagle, *The Fantasies of Robert Heinlein*, edited by David Hartwell, and Brian Murphy reviews *Sea Dragon Heir* by Storm Constantine. In the Movie/TV column, Marty Baumann discusses social commentary in vampire films. In the Folkroots column, Terri Windling discusses the Green Man, The Green Woman, and the Mythic Forest. In the Artists Gallery, Terri Windling covers the art of Charles Vess. And in the Games column, Eric T. Baker reviews *Asheron's Call* for PC-Windows CD-ROM, *Age of Wonders* for the PC-Windows CD-ROM, and *Magic: The Gathering Interactive Encyclopedia* for the PC-Windows CD-ROM.

Onto the fiction ...

The lead story in this issue is a rare reprint, this being "The Dead Boy at Your Window" by Bruce Holland Rogers. I say rare because before this issue the last time RoF ran a reprint was with "The Frog Prince" by Gahan Wilson back in the August 1995 issue, which was still part of RoF's first publishing year. This story first appeared in the Nov/Dec 1998 issue of *The North American Review*, and it marks Bruce's second appearance in the magazine. The story is rather short, probably weighing in under 1000 words, but it packs a very strong punch in so short a span. Basically, a mother ends up delivering a stillborn child, but her love is so strong it brings the babe back to life, and he exists among the living, not quite dead or alive. After six years, he ends up becoming a human kite and floats off to the Land of the Dead, where he goes on to become a shephard, running letters back between the worlds of the living and the dead. Powerful stuff. Others thought so as well, because this story won the 1998 Stoker Award for Best Short Fiction, and also the 1999 Pushcart Prize. Art to this one was provided Janey Aulisio, which marks her fifteenth illustration in the magazine.

Next up we have "The Woman in Scarlet" by Tanith Lee, which marks her seventh appearance in the magazine. This high fantasy piece features a really cool premise: an elite warrior brotherhood bonds with their sentient swords, just about all of which feature female personalities. The swords are not just the only weapons these warriors use, but they're also the men's lovers, because the weapons reward their wielders unimaginable pleasure in their dreams. In return, the warriors remain celibate in the waking world. This premise only becomes more intriguing when the protagonist's sword ends up betraying his love. Art to this one was provided by Luis Royo, which marks his sixth illustration in the magazine.

Following this is "The Gift of the Winter King" by Naomi Kritzer. As best I can remember, this is only the second post-apocalyptic tale to appear in RoF. The premise is an interesting one, as we see a Christian missionary trying to spread the word of God after the apocalypse. Shawna's editorial caption for this story sums it up best: "The message received is not always the same as the message sent. Sometimes this can make a huge difference in the final Word." Art to this one was provided by John Monteleone, which marks his fourth illustration in the magazine.

Then we have "When Beasts Eat Roses" by Bruce Glassco, which marks his third appearance in the magazine. This one has a metafictional flare to it, as it features Mary Shelly's Frankenstein coming to life ...off the page, that is, and interacting with the other creator, i.e. Mary Shelly herself. Some might call this metafictional horror, but others consider *Frankenstein* to be science fiction, so some might argue this is metafictional science fiction. Regardless, the whole premise is fantastical enough that the story hardly seems out of place in RoF. Art to this one was provided by Brom, which marks his second illustration in the magazine.

Lastly we have "Wilderness Living" by Kate Riedel, which marks her second appearance in the magazine. This one offers a spin on the fox-tale from Chinese mythology, as we see a man take a fox-woman for a lover in modern-day times. Art to this one was provided by Eric Dinyer, which marks his third illustration in the magazine.

So that wraps up this issue. And my favorite story? "The Dead Boy at Your Window" by Bruce Holland Rogers. And my favorite story original to the pages of *Realms of Fantasy*? "The Woman in Scarlet" by Tanith Lee. And my favorite illustration? Brom's illustration to "When Beasts Eat Roses" by Bruce Glassco.

Originally posted on douglascohen.livejournal.com on April 11th, 2008

June 2000 (Issue 35)

Part thirty-five in my comprehensive retrospective as I read the fiction in *Realms of Fantasy* and offer my thoughts, right up to the present. This time around I'll be discussing the June 2000 issue.

The cover to this one is by Gary Ruddell. I was unable to determine the origins of this illustration.

The bio page has returned with this issue. Also, while the letters page is in this issue, strangely it's in the middle as opposed to its usual spot near the beginning.

A rundown of this issue's nonfiction is as follows:

In the Movie/TV column, Resa Nelson covers Disney's *Dinosaur*. In the Books column, Gahan Wilson reviews *Prospero's Children* by Jan Siegel, *Knight of the Demon Queen* by Barbara Hambly, *The Ultimate Triumph*, a collection of tales by Robert E. Howard, illustrated by Frank Frazetta, and Paul Di Filippo reviews *The False House* by James Stoddard, *Dark Sister* by Graham Joyce, *The Merlin of St. Gilles' Well* by Ann Chamberlin, and *Dragonholder* by Todd McCaffrey, and Brian Murphy reviews *Etruscans: Beloved of the Gods* by Morgan Llywelyn and Michael Scott. In the Folkroots column, Heinz Insu Fenkl discusses the Binary Serpent. In the Artists Gallery, Karen Haber discusses the art of Diane and Leo Dillon. And in the Games column, Eric T. Baker reviews *King of Dragon Pass: Adventure and Heroism on a Magical Frontier* for Windows or Macintosh, *Mage the Ascension, 2nd Edition* from White Wolf Publishing, and the RPG, *The Montaigne Nations Book*.

On to the fiction ...

The lead story this issue is "The Seventh Sleeper" by Kate Reidel, which marks her third appearance in the magazine. This story marks a couple of firsts for the magazine. First, Kate's story, "Wilderness Living," was the last story in the previous issue. So this marks the first time an author has had back to back stories published in RoF. Second, "The Seventh Sleeper" is the first story in ROF to deal with the legendary Charlemagne. In particular, it tells how Charlemagne's magician surives through the centuries, into post World War II Germany. Art to this one was provided by J.K. Potter, which marks his fifth illustration in the magazine.

Next up is "The Road to Candarei" by M. Shayne Bell, which marks his second appearance in the magazine. This one is a pretty straightforward tale about a knight seeking to deliver a message on behalf of his king, only to become caught in a repeating loop of being in the same place. I liked the vehicle that was relied on to cause this repeating cycle. Art to this one was provided by Don Maitz, which marks his fourth illustration in the magazine.

Then we have "Enchanted Ground" by David Sandner, which marks his third appearance in the magazine. This contemporary fantasy deals with a man who lost almost everything, and this great emptiness causes him to discover a tiny pocket of emptiness in an alley, a place where he can be invisible and do as he pleases. It's a very honest piece, as the author depicts a number of shocking things the protagonist does with this great privacy. Art to this one was provided by Michael Dubisch, which marks his fourth illustration in the magazine.

Following this we have "A Troll Story: Lessons in What Matters, No. 1" by Nicola Griffith. This one relies on Norweigan mythology to tell the tale of a troll haunting the landscape and how it was finally overcome. It was also reprinted in *Year's Best Fantasy*, edited by David Hartwell & Kathryn Cramer. Art to this one was provided by Web Bryant, which marks his twelfth illustration in the magazine.

The next story is "Princess Fat Grits: Lesson in What Matters, No. 7" by Nicola Griffith. Obviously this is part of a series of stories by the same author. This one is a funny fairy tale about a fat princess who takes it upon herself to deal with a dragon, with some unusual results. The whole "Lessons in What Matters Aspect" is that both stories begin with a strange and dangerous voice talking to a child, trying to drive a lesson home, and telling a story to illustrate this point. This marks the first time an author has has had two stories in the same issue, and also the first time an author had back to back stories in the same issue. Art to this one was provided by Annie Lunsford, which marks her seventh illustration in the magazine.

Next up is Libby Thomas' Chemistry Set: Lesson in What Matters, No. 4" by Nicola Griffith. Obviously this is part of the same series as well, and it also marks the first time an author has had three stories in a single issue, as well as back to back to back stories. This one is a short short, and is kind of difficult to describe without giving away every last detail, but I'll relay an interesting aside about this tale. Sometimes I read the stories in an issue out of order. I'll only have limited time available, so I'll look for the shortest tale in an issue in the hopes of finishing it in time. So I read this story before the other two by this author, only to notice the author's name wasn't listed for this tale. I checked the ToC, and there was no sign of this story either (or "Princess Fat Grits," and no mention of "Lessons in What Matters" for "Troll Story"). So then I checked the bio page. I saw bios for both Richard Parks and Cory Doctorow, and since neither of them seemed to have other stories in this issue, I figured at least one of them must be responsible for *this* story. I don't know Cory, but I know Richard, so I dropped him an email and explained things in an attempt to get to the bottom of this mystery. Richard must have read this issue, because he emailed me back, saying how Nicola Grifftith wrote this. Some flipping through the pages confirmed Richard's statement. So a big thanks to Richard for taking the time to respond. And as to why Richard and Cory were in the bio page ...both of them have stories in the following issue. D'oh! Also, this story has no accompanying illustration, which marks the second story in the magazine without an illustration.

Finally we have "A Ghost of an Affair" by Jane Yolen, which marks her fourth appearance in the magazine. This one seems to fall somewhere between ghost story and magic realism as it depicts a love story that transcends time itself ...at least for a little while. Art to this one was provided by Steve Adler, which marks his seventh illustration in the magazine.

So that wraps up this issue. And my favorite story? I'll give the nod to "Princess Fat Grits: Lessons in What Matters, No. 7" by Nicola Griffith. I usually don't go for silly, but this tickled me just right, and it had some thoughtful touches and solid writing to boot. And my favorite artwork? Gary Ruddell's cover illustration.

Originally posted on douglascohen.livejournal.com on April 18th, 2008

Part thirty-six in my comprehensive retrospective as I read the fiction in *Realms of Fantasy* and offer my thoughts, right up to the present. This time the lucky contestant is the August 2000 issue.

When I met with Shawna back in 2005 to discuss the position of assistant editor, one of the first things she asked was if I had read any of the issues of the magazine. "A couple," I told her. It was the truth, too. I had read exactly *two* issues. One of them I've already done my retrospective on, this being the August 1997 issue. I purchased that issue because I wanted to read about the then-upcoming Kull movie. The reason I purchased *this* issue is quite simple. I had just finished the Odyssey Fantasy & Science Fiction Writing Workshop, and armed with a much stronger understanding of the short fiction market, I went out and bought the latest issues to a bunch of the bigger magazines, in the hopes of gleaning some idea of the editors' tastes. August 2000 just happened to be the issue of RoF out at the time.

As to the issue itself ...

The cover to this one is by Scott Gustafson. It features Merlin entertaining a young Arthur with a display of butterflies. This was originally made into a canvas print by the Greenwich Workshop.

One thing I'd like to note concerning the editorial this issue is that Shawna bids a fond farewell to *Science Fiction Age*, which had just ceased publication. To those of you unaware, *Science Fiction Age* was the sister magazine to Realms. I've actually never read an issue of SFA, but in terms of format and presentation, it's my understanding that it was basically the science fiction equivalent of *Realms of Fantasy*. *Science Fiction Age* actually preceded Realms by about two years, so it had an eight-year run before reaching its end. With its next issue, Realms would be a frisky six years of age. It's a shame *Science Fiction Age* is no longer publishing, but I suppose this an unfortunate sign of the times for short fiction.*

There's also another change in the masthead in this issue. Stephen Vann's run as Art Director has once again drawn to a close. In his place is former Art Director, Ronald (in this issue Ron) Stevens. Not to make light of the situation, but what is it with these two guys? It seems as if every few issues they take each other's place.

A rundown of this issue's nonfiction is as follows:

In the Books column, Gahan Wilson reviews *The Terror in the Night* by E.F. Benson, edited by Jack Adrian, *Phantom Perfumes and Other Shades–Memories of Ghost Stories Magazine*, edited by Mike Ashely, *The Night Wind Howls* by Frederick Cowles, *Lady Ferry and Other Uncanny People* by Sarah Orne Jewett, and Paul Di Filippo reviews *The Burning City* by Larry Niven & Jerry Pournelle, *Mollie Peer* by Van Reid, *Bloodrights* by N. Lee Wood, and Brian Murphy reviews *Dragons of a Fallen Sun* by Margaret Weis & Tracy Hickman, the belated book four in the *Dragonlance Chronicles*. In the Movie/TV column, Resa Nelson covers *The Hollow Man*. In the Folkroots column, Terri Windling discusses the story of Snow White. In the Artists Gallery, Karen Haber covers the artwork of Barry Windsor-Smith. And in the Games column, Eric T. Baker reviews the CRPG, *Planescape: Torment*, the RPG, *Call of Cthulhu*, the RPG supplement, *Post Modern Magick*, the AD&D supplement, *Reverse Dungeon*, and the RPG supplement, *Nights of Prophecy* from White Wolf Publishing for their *Vampire: The Masquerade Campaign*.

On to the fiction ...

Given that it's been eight years since the last time I read these stories, I decided to reread them all, even the ones I thought I remembered quite clearly. My reactions to some of these stories the second time around left me quite surprised.

The lead story in this issue is "Cactus Land" by Kate Orman. This is one of the stranger stories I've read in RoF, which isn't necessarily a bad thing. Orman has a rather compelling blend of elements in this tale. It's what you might term a pre-apocalyptic tale. The year is 2027, and bit by bit the world is falling apart. This really isn't the focus of the story, but the author cues the reader in by slipping several elements normally encountered in post-apocalyptic literature. And while all this is going on, the continent of Australia (the story's setting) is undergoing a strange transformation as Aztec culture seems to be inexplicably experiencing a revival here. Really strange, but I bought into it. I distinctly remember not enjoying this story when I read it back in 2000. Obviously my feelings have changed. I attribute this to several factors, but this biggest reasons come from working for *Realms of Fantasy*. It isn't because this is a *Realms of Fantasy* story that

I liked it, but rather three years on this job–reading slush, reading back issues, working with authors on rewrites, swapping emails with Shawna and seeing her at work–has really expanded my definitions of what constitutes good fantastical short fiction. I can say with real confidence that I'm a better editor now than when I started. If this story was in the slush at the beginning of my reign of terror, there's a chance I would've rejected it. That would've been a mistake. Now I'd know better. Experience counts. Art to this one was provided by John Picacio.

The second story is "Mousers" by Peni R. Griffin, which marks her sixth appearance in the magazine. Every editor has types of stories that are tough sells with them. Some of my "tough sells" are elves, dwarves, and the fey. One of Shawna's tough sells is cat stories. Shawna must've really liked "Mousers," because this one is *all* about cats. Actually, it's a ghost tale about cats, and a cute one at that, as a kitten is raised to hunt mice, along with the help of its ghostly predecessor. Art to this one was provided by Laurie Hardin, which marks her fourth illustration in the magazine.

Followng this we have "The 4th Law of Power" by Richard Parks, which also marks his sixth appearance in the magazine. This one is a high fantasy tale about a woman's quest to hunt down the magical Laws of Power. Seeing this title might make one ask, "Hey, where are the stories about the first three Laws of Power?" I'm afraid I don't have these answers.** I don't even know if there are earlier Laws of Power stories (they haven't appeared in RoF to this point) but I can tell you that this tale holds up quite well on its own. Art to this one was provided by John Monteleone, which marks his fifth illustration in the magazine.

Next up is "Return to Pleasure Island" by Cory Doctorow. This is another tale I remember having a lot of difficulty with when I first read it. But once again, I found myself far more interested reading it all these years later. This one is decidedly dark (and the more you think about it, the darker it is). It revisits Pleasure Island from the classic Pinoccio tale, but does so with a modern-day spin. And here's something interesting, as I stumbled across this background for the story over at the author's website:

This is the story of the ogres who run the concession stands on Pleasure Island, where Pinnocchio's friend Lampwick turned into a donkey. Like much of my stuff, this has a tie-in with Walt Disney World; the idea came to me on the Pinnocchio ride in the Magic Kingdom, in 1993. I went back and reviewed the original novel, in two translations, and found that Pleasure Island was a scary,

scary place. During this time, I spent a lot of time listening to the creepy voiceover on "High-Diddle Dee-Dee" on Stay Awake, a wonderful Disney tribute album. The result is what you see below. Like many of my recent stories, "Return" deals with self-indulgence, discipline, and attenuated attention-spans.

Art to this one was provided by David Beck, which marks his eleventh illustration in the magazine.

Following this we have "Mom and Dad at the Homefront" by Sherwood Smith, which marks her third appearance in the magazine. This is a really touching YA tale in the tradition of Narnia and other universes where the children use closets and such as portals to secret fantasy worlds. What's really clever about this one is that it explores this idea from the perspective of the parents. Ever wonder what they're going through while their children are off adventuring? This is the 200th story to be published in Realms *of Fantasy*. It's a milestone number, and Shawna & crew managed it with style, because not only was this story reprinted in *Year's Best Fantasy*, edited by David Hartwell & Kathryn Cramer, but it was also nominated for the 2002 Nebula Award for Best Short Story. Pretty sweet. Art to this one was provided by Mahendra Singh.

The final story is "Playing in the Dark" by David Phalen, which marks his second appearance in the magazine. This one is real short, and it deals with some children who play with shadows each night come bedtime. This story did not have illustration, the third such in the magazine's run.

So that wraps up this issue. It's certainly one of the longest retrospectives I've done to date. And my favorite story? "Mom and Dad at the Homefront" by Sherwood Smith. And my favorite artwork? Scott Gustafson's cover illustration.

Originally posted on douglascohen.livejournal.com on April 22ⁿᵈ, 2008

*I suppose I was a bit prescient with this comment at the time, because less than a year RoF would cease publication for the first time.

**When I made the original post on my LiveJournal account, Richard Parks actually responded, solving the mystery in the comments section: "The first two in the 'Laws of Power' series appeared in Dragon Magazine about five years earlier. 'The First Law of Power' wasn't written until after 'The Fourth law of Power,' and it appeared in RoF in 2001."

Part thirty-seven in my comprehensive retrospective as I read the fiction in *Realms of Fantasy* and offer my thoughts. This time around I'll be discussing the October 2000 issue, which marks the sixth anniversary for the magazine.

The cover to this one is by Luis Royo, which marks his seventh illustration in the magazine. It features a sexy babe in skimpy (perhaps kinky is the better word) strips of leather and steel. The artwork itself is very detailed and I'm actually a fan of the work of Luis Royo, but I'd have to say that along with the demon dominatrix cover some issues back, this must be among the most controversial covers to grace the magazine. This illustration was originally the cover to the November 1995 issue of *Heavy Metal Magazine*.

Moving on, there has been another change in the masthead. Ron Stevens' one issue return as Art Director has come to an abrupt end. His replacement is, for a change, not Steven Vann. Instead, the new Art Director is Samantha Detulleo.

A rundown of this issue's nonfiction is as follows:

In the Books column, Gahan Wilson reviews *A Wolf at the Door and Other Retold Fairy Tales*, edited by Ellen Datlow & Terri Windling, *Chimera* by Will Shetterly, *Shadows Bend* by David Barbour and Richard Raleigh, *Man of Two Worlds, My Life in Science Fiction and Comics* by Julius Schwartz, and Paul Di Filippo reviews *A Trip to the Stars* by Nicholas Christopher, *Jim Morrison's Adventures in the Afterlife* by Mick Farren, *Antarktos* by Robert Price, *The Snow Queen* by Eileen Kernaghan, and *At the Foot of the Story Tree* by Bill Sheehan. In the Movie/TV column, Resa Nelson provides a preview for the fall 2000 genre TV circuit. In the Folkroots column, Heinz Insu Fenkl explores the deeper meaning of the caduceus. In the Artists Gallery, Brian Sibley discusses the art of John Howe. And in the Games column, Eric T. Baker reviews the third edition of *Dungeons & Dragons*, a *Forgotten Realms* supplement based on R.A. Salvatore's *Icewind Dale Trilogy*, and the RPG supplement, *Croatan Song*, for *Werewolf: The Apocalypse* from White Wolf Publishing.

On to the fiction ...

The lead story is "Luther and the Demon" by Franklin Thatcher. This one deals with the Martin Luther responsible for the groundbreaking split in Christianity back in the 16th century (as opposed to the other famous Martin Luther, who was pretty groundbreaking in his own right). In this piece a bit of a mystical element is introduced as Luther tries to reconcile his faith with his past. Art to this one was provided by Ken Graning, which marks his tenth illustration in the magazine.

Following this we have "River Woman" by Devon Monk, which marks her second appearance in the magazine. In this one we witness the depths of a mother's love as she attemps to find her son who was lost two days earlier to a flooding river. The magical element is introduced when we meet the River Woman, a mysterious water spirit who helps the protagonist reach a critical crossroads and decision regarding her son. Art to this one was provided by Patrick Arrasmith, which marks his sixth illustration in the magazine.

Then we have "The Children of his Old Age" by Tanith Lee, which marks her eighth appearance in the magazine. This one is a high fantasy that deals with a familiar theme, that being dragons and dragon hunters. But as she excels at doing, Lee takes an old idea and breathes new life into it, by having the the dragon and his hunter break with tradition by not fighting each other. Art to this one was provided by Janny Wurts, who happens to be an accomplished high fantasy author herself.

Next up is "Hey Hey Something Something" by Jan Lars Jensen. This one takes a rather fascinating premise, as we learn about a game that only children can truly play or understand. As children pass into adulthood, the rules of the game become lost on them, and they can no longer understand the words when the children are playing what has been classified as Hey Hey Something Something. If an adult witnesses it, they tend to become disoriented and look through it, as if the game didn't exist. On a sociological level, this one was fascinating, because the whole time it feels like there is a disturbing kernel of truth to this logic. Art to this one was provided by John Picacio, which marks his second illustration in the magazine.

Then we have "Judgment Day" by Richard Parks, which marks his seventh appearance in the magazine. Richard's story marks a couple of firsts in the magazine. One is that while there have been a few apocalypse stories this one marks our first Armageddon story. It also marks the first story told from the viewpoint of God, in which God learns the true reason behind Armegeddon, and an interesting twist at the end is thrown in for good measure. Art to this one was provided by Charles Demorat, which marks his eighth illustration in the magazine.

Next up is "Spirit Stone" by Naomi Kritzer, which marks her second appearance in the magazine. This one is a high fantasy piece that deals with a young woman who was trained to be a midwife. When she is married off to her new husband, she quickly realizes that he has no interest in her, except to be the midwife to his other fourteen wives. But when Sarai realizes her necklace actually houses a spirit that can grant her wishes, she finds herself presented with choices she never thought she had. Where it goes from here is quite different than your standard wishing tale. Art to this one was provided by Steven Adler, which marks his eighth illustration in the magazine.

Finally we have "Saving the Skychildren" by Mindy L. Klasky. This high fantasy plays with a rather fascinating premise. Imagine a world where astrology is king, and people's signs are broken into a caste system of swan, owl, lion, and sun. Each class has its rank tattooed upon its face, and has its own special skill set where they are prevalent. In this particular story, a mad king is bent on conquering a land across the sea, but there is nothing left to conscript to his armies but children, those that are swans and lions in particular. In this tale, a woman is caring for orphaned children, attempting to shield them from the mad king's armies, but because of their classifications, these children have a say in what happens, especially since the woman bears the lowest rank of sun. This one really provided an interesting look at a rather outside-the-box culture. Art to this one was provided by Robert Grabb.

So that wraps up this issue. And my favorite story? "Saving the Skychildren" by Mindy L. Klasky. And my favorite artwork? Well, as I said about the cover, it's rather racy, but I'm a fan of Royo's work. So I'll go with the cover.

Originally posted on douglascohen.livejournal.com on April 28th, 2008

Part thirty-eight in my comprehensive retrospective as I read the fiction in *Realms of Fantasy* and offer my thoughts. This time around I'll be examining the December 2000 issue.

The cover to this one is by Michael Whelan, which marks his ninth illustration in the magazine. It's another Elric cover, which marks the third time the albino prince has graced the cover of ROF. It was originally the cover to a special hardcover edition of *The Vanishing Tower*.

An interesting tidbit on the Letter Page stems from something that happened in the previous issue. The last few lines from "Luther and the Dragon"—the lead story from the October 2000 issue—were cut off at the end of the story, so they're added here. Thankfully I was aware of this, so when I reached the last sentence in the last issue, I turned right to the Letters Page of this issue. But I sympathize with readers who had their reading experience cut off at such a critical moment, not to mention the author!

A rundown of this issue's nonfiction is as follows:

In the Books column, Gahan Wilson reviews *Reunion at Dawn and Other Uncollected Ghost Stories* by H.R. Wakefield, *Smoke and Mirrors* by Neil Gaiman, *Magic Terror* by Peter Straub, and Paul Di Filippo reviews *Damned If You Do* by Steve Aylett, Jeff Noon, and Will Self, *The White Bone* by Barbara Gowdy, *The Grand Tour* by Jody Lynn Nye, and reissues of *Tales of the Dying Earth* by Jack Vance and *Time and the Gods* by Lord Dunsany. In the Movie/TV column, Resa Nelson covers the movie, *Shadow of the Vampire*. In the Folkroots column, Terri Windling discusses the literary fairy tales of France. In the Artists Gallery, Karen Haber covers the art of Rick Berry. And in the Games column, Eric T. Baker reviews *Vampire the Masquerade: Redemption* for the PC, the RPG, *Everway: Visionary Roleplaying*, and the RPG, *Deluxe Hero Wars: Epic Role-Playing in Mythic Glorantha*.

On to the fiction ...

This marks the first time that *Realms of Fantasy* has run stories by five previous contributors in a single issue. Since this issue contains six stories, the one first-timer is the lead story, "Rare Firsts" by Paul Di Filippo. This one deals with a rare books dealer who schemes, scams, and nickel and dimes his way to the greatest possible profit. But when he stumbles upon an extraordinary collection of rare volumes, he rediscovers his love of books. The magic in this story is the magic of reading. I'm sure it's the kind of story that certain fantasy fans would have a very difficult time accepting as fantasy, but I have to say I enjoyed it. This is one for hardcore readers, not to mention writers and editors. Art to this one was provided by Greg Carter, which marks his third illustration in the magazine.

Next up is "Conceiving Kings" by Dave Smeds, which marks his third appearance in the magazine. This one is a piece of Arthuriana, though you don't learn that for certain until late in the story. Rather than Arthur or his court, the focus is on the Iceni several hundred years before the days of Arthur in which we are provided an alternate look at the origins of Britain's most famous king, with the groundwork for his coming laid out centuries in advance among the Picts. Art to this one was provided by John Monteleone, which marks his sixth illustration in the magazine.

Following this we have "The Golem" by Naomi Kritzer, which marks her third appearance in the magazine. This one takes an interesting premise as the golem from Jewish mythology is brought to life to protect the Jews in Prague during WWII. But when the golem discovers it has free will, it's anyone's guess what will happen. Powerful stuff, which ended up being reprinted in *Year's Best Fantasy 2*, edited by David Hartwell & Kathryn Cramer. Art to this one was provided by Web Bryant, which marks his thirteenth illustration in the magazine.

Then we have "Thrushbeard" by Bruce Glassco, which marks his fourth appearance in the magazine. This one is a fairy tale that in some ways reminded me of Shakespeare's *Taming of the Shrew*, as we witness a king trying to bring an extremely strong-willed princess to heel. Where it goes however, is quite different from old Bill's tale. Art to this one was provided by Broeck Steadman, which marks his sixth illustration in the magazine.

After this is "The Man For the Job" by Lawrence Watt-Evans, which marks his second appearance in the magazine. This one is a light piece about a group of siblings—four brothers and one sister—that go in quest of a magical helmet to help them overcome a dragon that is terrorizing a village. The twist? One of the helmet's great powers is that it changes the sex of the wearer while it's being worn. As one might expect, silliness (not to mention discomfort) ensues. Art to this one was provided by Joel Naprstek, which marks his fifth illustration in the magazine.

Finally we have "Things Don't Always Turn Out Like We Plan" by Leslie What, which marks her fifth appearance in the magazine. In this one we meet a middle-aged wife who has always had the ability to have visions. The visions are slight though, tenuous. But when she and her husband are in a near-fatal crash on New Year's Eve, her abilities begin to manifest while they're in the hospital. Gradually it's revealed these abilities are tied to Death, which is interesting since it also represents an unexpected crossroads in her life. Art to this one was provided by Greg Carter, which marks his fourth illustration in the magazine. This also makes Greg the first artist to have two interior illustrations in the same issue.

So that wraps up this issue, as well as the publishing year for 2000. And my favorite story? "Rare Firsts" by Paul Di Filippo. And my favorite artwork? Michael Whelan's cover.

Originally posted on douglascohen.livejournal.com on May 5th, 2008

Part thirty-nine in my comprehensive retrospective as I read the fiction in *Realms of Fantasy* and offer my thoughts. This time around I'll be breaking in 2001 by discussing the February 2001 issue.

The cover to this one is by Luis Royo, which marks his eighth illustration in the magazine. I was unable to determine the origins of this piece.

A rundown of this issue's nonfiction is as follows:

In the Movie/TV column, Marty Baumann discusses bringing Stephen King novels to the big screen. In the Books column, Gahan Wilson reviews *The Yellow Sign and Other Stories* by Robert W. Chambers, edited by S.T. Joshi, *The Complete Weird Tales of Robert W. Chambers*, edited by S.T. Joshi, *Out of the Dark, Volume One: Origins* by Robert W. Chambers, edited by Hugh Lamb, *Out of the Dark, Volume Two: Diversions* by Robert W. Chambers, edited by Hugh Lamb, *The Lust Lizard of Melancholy Cove* by Christopher Moore, *In the Dark* by Edith Nesbit, edited by Hugh Lamb, *My Favorite Horror Story*, edited by Mike Baker and Martin H. Greenberg, and Paul Di Filippo reviews *The A'Rak* by Michael Shea, *A Wizard in the Way* by Christopher Stasheff, and *Wheel of the Infinite* by Martha Wells. In the Folkroots column, Heinz Insu Fenkl discusses how Australian Aboriginal art and American television share a mystic bond. In the Artists Gallery, Karen Haber discusses the art of Terese Nielsen. And in the Games column, Eric T. Baker reviews *Baldur's Gate II* for the PC, *Heavy Metal: F.A.K.K.2* for the PC, *Rail Empires: Iron Dragon* for the PC, the RPG, *Three Days to Kill*, and the RPG, *Lesser of Two Evils* for the *Legend of the 5 Rings* game.

There is one point of interest I'd like to note before I start dissecting the fiction. In the previous issue, I noted it was the first time the magazine had run stories by as many as five previous contributors. This issue also has stories by five previous contributors. The difference is that last issue had a total of six stories. This issue has a total of five. In other words, this marks the first issue wherein the fiction all came from previous contributors. Just one more example of how Realms had been building up a stable of authors over the years, but that the previous thirty-eight issues always had at least one new voice contributing fiction is just as significant. Generally speaking, I think the best speculative magazines achieve a nice blend of repeat offenders and new voices. I have no hesitation in saying that Realms has managed this just fine since I've come aboard, but clearly this wasn't a new development brought on by yours truly ...well, *maybe* we have a few more stories coming out of the slush than we used to.

On to the fiction itself ...

The lead story in this issue is "The Trickster's Wife" by Richard Parks, which marks his eighth appearance in the magazine. This is a short piece steeped in Norse mythology. It deals with Ragnarok, and as Richard often seems to do in his Realms stories (and I'd imagine in other venues as well), he explores it in an unexpected way, telling how Ragnarok did not come to be just yet. Art to this one was provided by Mahendra Singh, which marks his second illustration in the magazine.

Following this we have "The Darbies" by Kate Riedel, which marks her fourth appearance in the magazine. This one deals with a mother and her troubled teenage daughter. After her daughter has a run-in with the law, mom moves them into the woods, where she hopes to bond with her daughter and get her back on the right track. Things seem to be slowly changing for the better, but along the way mysterious hints are dropped about the Darbies, who own this area, as well as some local folklore about some fairies that supposedly inhabit the forest. Gradually these three ideas come together, and it's demonstrated to the reader that it's one thing to set your child along the right path and quite another to believe they're walking it. Art to this one was provided by J.K. Potter, which marks his sixth illustration in the magazine.

The middle story is "The Man Who Stole the Moon: A Story of the Flat Earth" by Tanith Lee, which marks her ninth appearance in the magazine. This one deals with a master thief whose arrogance and carefree ways finally lead to his capture. When he meets the king, he is given the impossible task of stealing the moon or his life will be forfeit thanks to some spells cast upon him by the court wizards. The thief has a year to manage this task, though it hardly seems like enough time. But when he strikes a bargain with a minor demon, it leads to layer upon layer of deception, until it finally catches the attention of the head honcho among demonkind. It's a very rich, otherworldly tale, and it was selected for inclusion in *Year's Best Fantasy 2*, edited by David Hartwell & Kathryn

Cramer. Art to this one was provided by Carol Heyer, which marks her eighth illustration in the magazine.

Then we have "Breaking Spells" by M. Shayne Bell, which marks his third appearance in the magazine. This one is a young adult piece with an ambiguous fantastical nature. Dad is having an affair and Mom has become a mess as a result. Brother and sister suspect the mistress of being a witch who has placed an enchantment on Dad. They resort to various methods to break the spell, but in the end they resort to love lure him back. It's left to the reader to decide whether love conquers all, even magic, or whether the resolution is the more mundane home is where the heart is, and the "spell" was nothing more than lust. I chose to believe the mundane in this one (I usually go the other way in such stories), but as I mentioned this one is ambiguous, so I don't view it as any less of a fantasy piece. Art to this one was provided by John Picacio, which marks his third illustration in the magazine.

Finally we have "Night Sweats" by James Van Pelt, which marks his fourth appearance in the magazine. I guess the best way to describe this one is a post-apocalyptic ghost story. It involves a woman who moves into a house that turns out to be haunted. This woman's grandfather was among the native population in Japan subjected to the horrors of the atom bomb. Meanwhile, back in America, there was a teenage couple. At the precise moment the bomb was dropped, the boyfriend was on his way to meet his girlfriend for what would be their first time giving themselves to each other, shortly before he left town. On the way he tragically loses his life in an accident with a milk truck ...and this happens at the precise moment the Bomb is dropped. This unfortunate chap would be the ghost mentioned above. As you might imagine, he's got some unresolved issues. As to the hauntee (i.e. the woman living in the house), when you combine her past with the fact that she's also a thirty-something virgin with issues of her own regarding sex and sexuality, we're left with a powerful combination of elements with some deep characterizations. James recently mentioned to me that there was actually a whole subplot he took out of this piece before submitting it to RoF, though I can't imagine what it is. The story feels quite complete. Art to this one was provided by Michael Gibbs, which marks his seventh illustration in the magazine.

So that wraps up this issue. And my favorite story? "Night Sweats" by James Van Pelt. And my favorite artwork? Carol Heyer's illustration to

"The Man Who Stole the Moon: A Story of the Flat Earth" by Tanith Lee.

Originally posted on douglascohen.livejournal.com on May 14th, 2008

Part forty in my comprehensive retrospective as I read the fiction in *Realms of Fantasy* and offer my thoughts. This time around I'll be focusing on the April 2001 issue.

The cover features the iconic Conan, which marks the third time he has graced an RoF cover. The artwork is by Doug Beekman, which marks his second illustration in the magazine. It was originally the cover to issue 232 of *The Savage Sword of Conan*. I'd say Frank Frazetta's classic Conan paintings influenced this piece quite heavily.

In the masthead, I'll note that Laura Cleveland, our current Managing Editor, has been promoted from Copy Editor to Associate Editor.

A rundown of this issue's nonfiction is as follows:

In the Movie/TV column, Resa Nelson writes about strong women fantasy characters in TV other than Xena. In the Folkroots column, Terri Windling discusses how Victorian fantasies represented England's Golden Age of fairy art, literature, and drama. In the Books column, Gahan Wilson reviews *Come Twilight, A Novel of Saint-Germain* by Chelsea Quinn Yarbro, *The Wooden Sea* by Jonathan Carroll, *The Face in the Frost* by John Bellairs, *The Bottoms* by Joe R. Lansdale, and Paul Di Filippo reviews *When the King Comes Home* by Caroline Stevermer, *Shadows Bend* by David Barbour and Richard Raleigh, *The Life of Sir Aglovale de Gallis* by Clemence Housman, and *The Vampire Master and Other Tales of Horror* by Edmond Hamilton. In the Artists Gallery, Terri Windling keeps her Victorian theme intact by exploring Victorian fairy paintings. And in the Games column, Eric T. Baker reviews *Rune* for the PC, the RPG, *The Sights of Freiburg*, the computer RPG, *Sea Dogs*, the RPG supplement, *Ars Magica for The Mysteries: The Mind of the Magus*, and the RPG supplement, *The Creature Collection* for the *Sword and Sorcery* brand name from White Wolf Publishing.

On to the fiction ...

The lead story is "Redmond's Private Screening" by Kevin J. Anderson. This one relies on the rather interesting setting of 1911 Hollywood. Basically, a samurai and his parents have fallen on hard times. The samurai agrees to commit ritual suicide in front of the camera to raise money to send his parents back to Japan. It leads to a ghostly tale of vengeance, and along the way it is demonstrates that even during its earliest days Hollywood was quite corrupt. This story can also be found as podcast 013 on the *Pseudopod* website.* Art to this one in RoF was provided by Jon Foster, which marks his fourth illustration in the magazine.

Next up we have "Messages" by Rob Vagle, which according to his bio is his first published short story. In this one we meet two young boys who are the best of friends. One of them is slowly dying, from what I believe is cancer. They're out playing one day when the dying boy comes across a bottle in the water. The bottle speaks to him in a message his friend can't hear. He speaks a message back into the bottle, seals it, and throws it back into the water. The next day the bottle is back, with a new message. The dying boy comes to trust the bottle, as he thinks it's trying to help him, but his friend remains suspicious. Everything reaches a climax when a fight breaks out over the bottle, and the other friend finally hears the voice in the bottle. What is said and how it ends is for you to find out by reading this piece. Art to this one was provided by Laurie Harden, which marks her fifth illustration in the magazine.

Following this we have "Otherling" by Juilet Marillier. I have to admit that this is the sort of story that turned me into a fantasy fan. It also feels like it's the sort of story that was always there, just waiting for someone to pluck it from the writerly ether and set it to paper, sort of like Ursula K. Le Guin's *A Wizard of Earthsea*. What we have here is a high fantasy tale that deals with a tribe of people who rely on the magical powers of Bard to use his or her gifts to lead the tribe down the right path. Bard always picks his successor ...to an extent. Once each generaton, twins are born to the tribe. Bard chooses which of the twins to make his apprentice. It then falls to him to kill the other twin. The other twin becomes "the Otherling," a spirit that flows into his or her sibling, providing the necessary power to one day become Bard. The Otherling can offer guidance to Bard, and its initial sacrifice also provides a measure of balance that is demanded (i.e. it is the way of things). This particular tale focuses on one woman's rise and reign as Bard, and her existence as teacher to her eventual replacement when the twins are born to the tribe and she must make her choice about who lives and who dies. I think Shawna sums this one up quite nicely in her editorial byline for this one: "When we choose with our hearts, sometimes the choices we make are flawed. When we choose with our heads, they almost always are." I figured out much of the ending to this one early on, but I didn't care. If it ended any other way, I would've been disappointed. But the author delivered, and I was quite pleased. This piece was originally published in *Voyager 5: Collector's Edition*. Art to this one was provided by Paul Lee.

Next up is "Harden Times" by Susan J. Kroupa, which marks her third appearance in the magazine. This one is a post-apocalyptic tale that takes place in Utah. Something known as the Death has swept through many parts of the country, leaving few survivors in its wake. We're introduced to a woman who survived but lost her family, and a young Navajo, trying to return to his reservation in the desperate hope that he'll find his family is still alive. The two of them end up bonding through a horse, which each of them desires for different reasons. If there is a fantastical element in this piece, I'd point to the horse, although the fantasy element is intentionally slight and intentionally ambiguous. I think this another piece where Shawna is pushing/expanding the boundaries of what she considers fantasy by taking it for the magazine.

For those of you who are unaware, through these years I've noticed an ongoing debate in the Letters Page that pops up every so often. You have the traditionalists who write in complaining that just about any story not set in a secondary world isn't fantasy and therefore has no business in RoF. "Harden Times" would have them up in arms (and perhaps it will in the Letters Pages of the next couple of issues). Then you have the other camp, which says you shouldn't put constraints/limitations on the genre. Let the magic/fantasy occur where it will. Clearly Shawna falls into the latter camp, but she very fairly gives both parties their say in the Letters Pages. As for me, I must confess that in my heart of hearts I harbor a preference for secondary world fantasies, but *I am by no means a traditionalist*. I am open to *all* sorts of fantasy. Of my nineteen slush survivors (to date) only six of them are set in secondary worlds. That should tell you everything you need to know. Art to this one was provided by David Robyn Seeley.

After this we have "Sop Doll" by Milbre Burch. This is a sort of indirect sequel to Jack and the Beanstalk. It definitely has a fairy tale feel to it, and it's told in a true storytelling voice as Jack finds himself stuck in the middle of a game of cat-and-mouse between a pack of enchanted cats and another one of enchanted hounds. The fairy tale aspect worked really well for the queen of fairy tales herself, one Terri Windling, because she selected it for inclusion in the 15th editon of the *Year's Best Fantasy & Horror*, edited by herself and Ellen Datlow. Art to this one was provided by Tony Di Terlizzi, which marks his second illustration in the magazine.

Lastly we have "The Premature Burials" by Andy Duncan, which marks his second appearance in the magazine. This is a darkly humorous tale about a stunning woman who refuses to marry any man, unless he agrees that the moment she dies, he will be buried next to her, be he alive or dead. She in turn would return the favor, if he should die first. Growing up, I rather enjoyed watching *Tales from the Crypt* on HBO, and while the language in this story carries a sophistication that far exceeds the show in question, in terms of content I could totally envision this story being adapted for an episode of this show. I'm uncertain about the author's feelings toward said show, but this is meant as a compliment. Art to this one was provided by Stephen Johnson, which marks his second illustration in the magazine.

So that wraps up this issue. And my favorite story? "Otherling" by Juliet Marillier. Quite the beautiful tale. And my favorite story original to RoF? "Redmond's Private Screening" by Kevin J. Anderson. And my favorite artwork? Doug Beekman's cover.

*In checking something about this piece on the *Pseudopod* website for the book edition of these retrospectives, I also happened to just notice that the reader for this piece back in 2006 was Scott Sigler, who has since gone on to a very successful career as a bestselling author in the speculative genres. I find this extra interesting since Scott has contributed a story to an unannounced anthology that I'll be editing, due out in 2016. Just one more example of how small the speculative fiction world is.

Originally posted on douglascohen.livejournal.com on May 23rd, 2008

Part forty-one in my comprehensive retrospective as I read the fiction in *Realms of Fantasy* and offer my thoughts. This time around I'll be documenting the June 2001 issue.

The cover to this one is by Scott Grimando. I was unable to track down the origins of this illustration.

A rundown of this issue's nonfiction is as follows:

In the Folkroots column, Heinz Insu Fenkl explores the origins of the words "Heaven" and "Hell-o." In the Movie/TV column, Resa Nelson covers *The Forsaken* and *The Mummy Returns*. In the Books column, Gahan Wilson reviews *The Amber Spyglass* by Phillip Pullman, *Declare* by Tim Powers, *The Whisperer and Other Voices* by Brian Lumley, *Dark Terrors 5: The Gollancz Book of Horror*, edited by Stephen Jones and David Sutton, and Paul Di Filippo reviews *Moonlight* by Susan Dexter, *Nasty Stories* by Brian McNaughton, *Tagging the Moon* by S.P. Somtow, and *St. Patrick's Gargoyle* by Katherine Kurtz. In the Artists Gallery, Karen Haber covers the art of Janny Wurts. And in the Games column, Eric T. Baker reviews the RTS game, *Kingdom Under Fire*, the second edition of RPG, *Lord of the Five Rings*, and the RPG, *Unknown Armies*.

On to the fiction ...

The lead story is "What the Tyger Told Her" by Kage Baker, which marks her second appearance in the magazine. In this one, the story unfolds through the perspective of a yong girl. The reader is forced to connect some dots, as the child doesn't understand everything she witnesses. Of course, any confusion is cleared up by the pet tyger her rich family keeps locked away in a cage, because the tyger starts talking to her, and it has a preturnatural understanding of what is going on. And what is going on? The child's father has passed away. Her mother is considered a lowborn woman, but because the child has younger baby brothers, this branch of the family stands to inherit a rather significant fortune. Enter the sleazy and depraved uncle, and a rather fascinating tale unfolds that was selected for inclusion in *Years Best Fantasy 2*, edited by David Hartwell & Kathryn Cramer. Art to this one was provided by Mark Harrison, which marks his second illustration in the magazine.

Next up is "The First Law of Power" by Richard Parks, which marks his ninth appearance in the magazine. It also marks his second "Power" story to appear in the magazine. In this high fantasy piece, we witness how the quest for the Seven Laws of Power started, and meet a couple of familiar characters along the way. As with "The Third Law of Power" (his other "Power" story in Realms), we learn that discovering a Law of Power is not so simple as reading it in a book or having it recited to you. Of course, the irony here is that to learn what the Law of Power is, we the readers are reading to learn what it is! Art to this one is a rare interior reprint. It is by Stephen Youll, which marks his second illustration in the magazine.

Following this is the baseball fantasy "If I Never Get Back" by Bruce Glassco, which marks his fifth appearance in the magazine. This one draws on the lyrics of that familiar song, "Take Me Out to the Ballgame," as it weaves a post-WWII tale about the ghosts of a baseball team doomed to repeat the same game over and over ...until a war veteran comes along that happened to do a little umpiring once upon a time. A couple of thoughtful twists on the nature of ghosts prevent this one from falling into the realm of cliché. Art to this one was provided by John Berkey, which marks his seventh illustration in the magazine.

Then we have "In Sorrow Bring Forth the Children" by Franklin Thatcher, which marks his second appearance in the magazine. In this one, an older gentleman witnesses his wife wasting away from cancer. Since they don't have children, it's all the more painful for him to lose her. The only time she doesn't seem to be suffering is when she's creating these detailed toles, but the toles end up being horrible creatures in miniature, such as gremlins, goblins, etc. In effect, these toles are representations of her malignant suffering. After she dies, the man finds himself surrounded by hundreds of these little buggers. As you might expect, they start coming to life, but there is one tole that is unfinished, and it falls to the husband to finish it so that everything might be set to rights. Art to this one was provided by Lori Koefed.

After this is "The Panther and the Lamb" by Donna Farley. This one is a tale about a scholar who summons a female jinn, or a jinniyah. Something about those first few paragraphs gave me an idea for a story, and I thought to myself, "Wow, if I had a female jinn in front of me, a real clever wish might be to make her fall in love with me." And wouldn't you know it this is exactly what the author did! There goes my story idea!

Anyway, in those brief moments I thought I had myself a story idea I figured this would lead to some free wishes for the wisher, and this is exactly what happened, as the wisher receives all sorts of freebies, with the jinniyah anxious to please her loved one in every possible way. Everything seems to be going according to plan, until we learn how just as you can't buy love neither can you wish for it. Fun tale, but you can't really be surprised I'd say this. After all, this was "my idea." Art to this one was provided by Mahendra Singh, which marks his third illustration in the magazine.

Finally we have "Between the River and the Road" by Jonathan L. Howard, which according to his bio marks the author's first published story. This takes place in modern-day times in the city of York in merry old England. The author does an excellent job of capturing the local flavor through descriptions and dialect, and the opening tirade by one of the characters against the evils of various candy corporations is downright hilarious. Apparently, York is one of the most haunted places in the world, and the author provides us an example as two friends investigate an odd church that you see when you're walking toward it, but it's completely invisible when you start walking toward it from the opposite direction. As you might expect, the results of this little venture are fairly disastrous. Art to this one was provided by Chuck Demorat, which marks his ninth illustration in the magazine.

So that wraps up this issue. And my favorite story? "What the Tyger Her" by Kage Baker. And my favorite illustration? Stephen Youll's reprint that accompanied "The First Law of Power" by Richard Parks.

Originally posted on douglascohen.livejournal.com on May 31st, 2008

Part forty-two in my comprehensive retrospective as I read the fiction in *Realms of Fantasy* and offer my thoughts. This time around I'll be offering my two cents concerning the August 2001 issue.

The cover here represents another first for *Realms of Fantasy*, as this marks the first time it has featured a scene from a TV miniseries. The cover features Julianna Marguilies from *The Mists of Avalon* miniseries from TNT. The less said about this miniseries the better, I think, as I considered it a steaming pile of garbage. The one point in its favor is that I read the novel by Marion Zimmer Bradley in anticipation of the miniseries, and quite enjoyed it. (Confession: I've never read the sequel and never will. Why? The cover! As I mentioned all the way back in my second retrospective, when this book was reviewed in the Books column, something about that woman's hands on the cover and the arch of her neck gives me a serious case of the heebie-jeebies. I can't explain it, as no other cover or artwork of any kind has ever done this to me).

A rundown of this issue's nonfiction is as follows:

In the Movie/TV column, Resa Nelson covers the aforementioned *The Mists of Avalon* miniseries. In the Folkroots column, Gregory Frost writes about the Thousand and One Nights. In the Books column, Gahan Wilson reviews *Horror of the Century: An Illustrated History*, edited by Robert Weinberg, *Dreamside* by Graham Joyce, *The Ash Tree Press Annual Macabre 2000*, edited by Jack Adrian, and Paul Di Filippo reviews *The Treasury of the Fantastic*, edited by David Sandner & Jacob Weisman, *Talking in the Dark* by Dennis Etchison, *The Dragon and the Fair Maid of Kent* by Gordon Dickson, and *Warrior Fantastic*, edited by Martin Greenberg & John Helfers. In the Artists Gallery, Laura Cleveland discusses the art of Camelot (no doubt a thematic decision for the magazine, given the cover and the Movie/TV column's subject). And in the Games column, Eric T. Baker reviews White Wolf Publishing's RPG, *Mummy: The Resurrection*, *Realm Overseer 3D* for the PC, and the 3rd edition D&D supplement, *Sword and Fist: A Guidebook to Fighters and Monks*.

On to the fiction ...

The lead story is "Giants and Ogres and Trolls" by Lois Tilton, which marks her second appearance in the magazine, and her first solo appearance (her previous story in RoF was co-authored with Noreen Doyle). If you read this title aloud and pay attention to its cadences you might be able to guess where the author is drawing her inspiration for this story. If not, the first sentence clues you in: "'Oh my!' said Dorothy." Yup. It's a remix of L. Frank Baum's *The Wonderful Wizard of Oz**, the first reimagining of this classic milieu to appear in RoF. It's a fairly amusing tale, and the author does a superb job of capturing the wacky feel of Oz and the charming innocence of Dorothy. It's a somewhat darker Oz we encounter, though certainly familiar, and there is a dark undercurrent of humor that carries you right up to the end. Art to this one was provided by Gary Lippincott, which marks his fifth illustration in the magazine.

Next up we have "Incognita, Inc." by Harlan Ellison. This story was originally published a few months earlier, in the January 2001 issue of *Hemisphere Magazine*. In addition to its reprint in RoF, it was also reprinted in the 14th edition of *Year's Best Fantasy & Horror*, edited by Ellen Datlow & Terri Windling. It was also Short Listed for the 2002 Locus Award for Best Short Story. Once you learn the premise, it becomes abundantly obvious as to why so many editors bought this one. How many fantasy stories have you read where there is a map to a lost land? But ...have you ever wondered who in the hell is drawing these maps? Ellison answers this unasked question in very clever fashion, as we learn about who draws the maps to the Isle of King Kong and Ur and Zothique (yes, he mentions all of these places, and I give him props for the shout-out to Zothique), and many others. Well worth the read and quite charming. Art to this one was provided by Patrick Arrasmith & Allen Douglas. It is the first appearance in the magazine for Douglas, but the seventh for Arrasmith. This also marks the first co-illustrated piece to appear in the magazine.

Following this we have "Wait-a-While" by Allan Dean Foster, which marks his second appearance in the magazine. In this one, a disillusioned writer takes a vacation to Australia in the hopes of finding some inspiration, so he might write something fresh and new instead of the shclock he's been churning out. Then he learns about a naked woman and her naked daughter inhabiting the nearby forests and decides to investigate. In the process, he discovers more than he bargained for, about himself and the world at large. Art to this one was provided by Scott Grimando, which marks his second illustration in the magazine.

After this is "The Butterfly Man" by Steven Popkes. In this one, there is a doctor with a presence inside him that he terms "the butterfly man." The butterfly man allows him to see babies inside the fetus, and to see their defects. One day the doctor's life becomes entangled with a pregnant prostitute whose child is going to be born without a brain. Powerful stuff. Art to this one was provided by Paul Lee, which marks his second illustration in the magazine.

Then we have "The Slayers" by David Lee Summers. It's real simple to summarize this one: Moby Dick, but with dragons instead of whales. Fun, clever stuff. Art to this one was provided by Mark Harrison, which marks his second illustration in the magazine.

Finally we have "The Stars Underfoot" by James Van Pelt, which marks his fifth appearance in the magazine. In this young adult tale, an adolescent experiences a somewhat surreal adventure when the ice he's standing on breaks. Only ...it seems that the ice on the "other side" is breaking too, so that while the protagonist is falling into the water, someone else is simultaneously falling out of the water and into the protagonist's world. Heady stuff. Art to this one was provided by David Beck, which marks his twelfth illustration in the magazine.

So that wraps up this issue. And my favorite story? "Incognita, Inc." by Harlan Ellison. And my favorite story that is original to *Realms of Fantasy*? "The Butterfly Man" by Steven Popkes. And my favorite artwork? Gary Lippincott's illustration to "Giants and Ogres and Trolls" by Lois Tilton.

*Something I know quite a bit about, as a few years after reading this story I coedited my first anthology, *Oz Reimagined: New Tales from the Emerald City and Beyond*, published by 47North.

Orignally posted on douglascohen.livejournal.com on June 17th, 2008

Part forty-three in my comprehensive retrospective as I read the fiction in *Realms of Fantasy* and offer my thoughts. This time around I'll be delving into the October 2001 issue, which marks the seventh anniversary of the magazine.

The cover to this one is by Luis Royo, which marks his ninth illustration in the magazine. I was unable to determine the origins of this piece.

I will note the editorial in this issue has gone missing again.

A rundown of this issue's nonfiction is as follows:

In the Movie/TV column, Resa Nelson covers the TV show, *Witchblade*, and also discusses Edgar Allen Poe movies of years past. In the Books column, Gahan Wilson reviews *City of Saints & Madmen: The Book of Ambergris* by Jeff VanderMeer, *The Exchange* by Jeff VanderMeer (as Nicholas Sporlender), illustrated by Louis Verden), *American Gods* by Neil Gaiman, *Bran Mak Morn, The Last King* by Robert E. Howard, *The Conan Chronicles, Volume 1* and *Volume 2* by Robert E. Howard, and Paul Di Filippo reviews *Everybody Has Somebody in Heaven* by Avram Davidson, *Artemis Fowl* by Eoin Colfer, *Issola* by Steven Brust, and *The Arthurian Companion* by Phyllis Ann Karr. In the Artists Gallery, Karen Haber covers the artwork of Michael Whelan. And in the Gaming column, Eric T. Baker reviews *Gauntlet: Dark Legacy* for the PlayStation 2, *Defenders of the Faith: A Guidebook to Clerics and Paladins* for third edition *Dungeons & Dragons*, *The Dying Earth Roleplaying Game* based on Jack Vance's novels of the same name, and the RPG, *Rune*, and newcomer Jim Sturz reviews the RPG, *Faded Suns*. There is no Folkroots column in this issue.

On to the fiction ...

The lead story is "Big City Littles" by Charles de Lint, which marks his third appearance in the magazine. This one is a reprint, and it originally appeared in a complimentary limited edition chapbook published by Triskell Press in 2000. In this piece, de Lint tells an entertaining urban fantasy tale about the Littles, a tiny race of beings that once had wings but lost them a long time ago. When they read about their own story in a book by a children's author, they seek out the author in the hopes that she can help them reclaim their wings. Unfortunately, the author learned the story from her grandfather and has no special knowledge about how they can reclaim their wings, so she's forced to think outside the box to solve this problem. This story ended up being reprinted in *Year's Best Fantasy 2*, edited by David Hartwell & Kathryn Cramer. Art to this one was provided by Web Bryant, which marks his fourteenth illustration in the magazine.

Next up we have "Limnery in Cursive" by Terry McGarry. This high fantasy tale is set in the same universe as her novel, *Illumination*. It depicts a rather interesting society, where mages are forbidden to use their magic without being ordered to do so by the aristocracy. In order to recognize a mage, it is standard practice to brand them. Unsurprisingly, this one is a tale about fleeing persecution ...only here it is the mages who are oppressed by the everyday man. Art to this one was provided by David Anderson.

After this one is "The Sea of Time and Space" by Liz Williams. This one is a dark fantasy tale about a haunted soul who has been alive for many ages, and due to an ancient curse it craves human blood. Many aspects of this one had a Lovecraftian feel to it. Art to this one was provided by J.K. Potter, which marks his seventh illustration in the magazine.

Then we have "Once" by Jack Slay Jr. This one is a southern gothic tale about a man who has the somewhat innocuous ability to glimpse small mundane moments in the near future. But everything is thrown into question when after years of just going about his business when he's confronted with the dangerous choice of actually using his power to make a difference. Art to this one was provided by Toran Kotter.

Following this we have "Patterns" by Mary Soon Lee. This one has suggestions of being a post-apocalyptic tale, though there's no way to be certain. Basically, the weather patterns throughout the world have stopped changing, so wherever it's snowing it continues to snow, etc. In this world, the author weaves a brief tale of family by telling quick tales from their interlinked lives. As you might imagine, not everyone is in the same weather pattern area at the start of things. Art to this one was provided by Melissa Ferrreira.

Finally we have "A Hole in Her Head" by Maya Kaathryn Bohnhoff. In this one, we are introduced to an artist whose work used to be somewhat mediocre ...until some sort of portal to another realm started opening in her mind. This portal allows her to create paintings that have become the latest rage, and every critic and buyer considers her an absolute genius. The problem? Tapping into this realm gives her tremendous debilitating headaches that ultimately lead to seizures and a tumor. She is faced with the choice of removing the tumor and losing her gift or leaving it in and risking losing her life. This one takes a powerful look at the sacrifces creative people will go to create a works of art that matter. Art to this one was provided by Michael Kerr.

So that wraps up this issue. And my favorite story? "A Hcle in Her Head" by Maya Kaathryn Bohnhoff. And my favorite artwork? Web Bryant's illustration to "Big City Littles" by Charles de Lint.

Originally posted on douglascohen.livejournal.com on June 24th, 2008

Part forty-four in my comprehensive retrospective as I read the fiction in *Realms of Fantasy* and offer my thoughts. This time around I'll be going on about the December 2001 issue.

There's a lot to talk about with this issue. As always, though, I'll start with the cover, which is by John Monteleone, marking his seventh illustration in the magazine. I was unable to determine the origins of this illustration.

Until this point, the magazine's lone assistant editor has been Rebecca McCabe. If you check the masthead, she's still listed as such. Now here's where things get interesting. Follow with me. Yes, this is the December issue, but this issue was released in October. It's always like this, i.e. we release the magazine at the beginning of when it hits the newsstands (in this case October), but on the cover the publication date is the month it comes off the newsstands. Now, Rebecca's successor was Carina Gonzalez, who you won't find in the masthead in this issue (No surprise here, as when I came aboard RoF it took some months before my own name appeared in the masthead). However, according to Carina's old website, she accepted her position at *Realms of Fantasy* on–of all possible days–September 11, 2001. So she came aboard shortly before this issue was released, and probably too far along into the process to add her name to the masthead. As to whether Rebecca was still working with the magazine too, I don't know for certain. I would guess yes. She was there since the beginning (or close to it), and until this point she was the only assistant editor. She was pretty entrenched. I'd imagine a bit of transition was in order. Either way, this point in RoF's history marks an important changing of the guard in the editorial department (or at least the beginning of such), which is worth noting.

And since I'm discussing the masthead, I'll also mention that Dawn M. Stein's run as Graphic Designer is over. In her place we get to welcome Ryan Costa. As to other preliminaries, after going AWOL last issue, the editorial page makes its return, as Shawna discusses her time teaching at Clarion over the summer.

Whew. Breath. On to a rundown of this issue's nonfiction:

In the Movie/TV column, Resa Nelson provides a rundown of the fall 2001 speculative lineup on TV. The Folkroots column is back this issue,

and Gregory Frost discusses the fairy tales that came out of French salons.
In the Books column, Gahan Wilson reviews *Wicked* by Gregory Mcguire,
From the Dust Returned by Ray Bradbury, and Paul Di Filippo reviews *The
Devil is Not Mocked and Other Warnings* by Manly Wade Wellman, *The
Crow: Hellbound* by A.A. Attanasio, *The Treachery of Kings* by Neal
Barrett, *Similar Monsters* by Steve Savile, and *Will World* by J.M. DeMateis.
In the Artists Gallery, semi-regular columnist Jane Frank covers the
artwork of Richard Powers. And in the Games column, Eric T. Baker
reviews *Max Payne* for the PC, the RPG *Exalted*, from White Wolf
Publishing, the *Dungeons & Dragons* module, *Return to the Temple of
Elemental Evil*, and the comic RPG, *HackMaster's Player Handbook*.

On to the fiction ...

The lead story is "If on a Moonlit Night" by M. Shayne Bell, which
marks his fourth appearance in the magazine. This one is an urban fantasy
tale that catches your attention because of the various elements the author
incorporates into the tale. Ready? Our protagonist is a gay man with AIDS,
taking medicine for it that causes side effects, while also facing the daily
challenges of maintaining this lifestyle ...as well as those that come with
being a werewolf. I haven't read that many werewolf tales, but I feel pretty
confident in saying that this is an unusual blend of story elements. And
clearly the author was doing something right with this mix, because the
story was nominated for the 2002 Gaylactic Spectrum Award for Best
Short Fiction. Art to this one was provided by Lori Koefed, which marks
her second illustration in the magazine.

Next up we have "As Sweet" by Daniel Abraham. This one also relies
on an unusual mix of elements. Ready (again)? Our protagonist is
experiencing a midlife crisis and is seriously considering having an affair
with the father of one of her students in her English class. Concurrently,
she's being visited by the ghost of Rosalind, Romeo's "other love" from the
story of Romeo and Juliet, and in a tale that manages to span the ages we
learn how Rosalind is none other than Leonardo Da Vince's Mona Lisa.
Sorry, I can't explain it any better than this. You'll have to read it. Art to
this one was provided by Paul Lee, which marks his third illustration in the
magazine.

Following this we have "The Innocent and the Piper" by Eric T. Baker.
I should take a moment to mention that Eric has been (and is at the time
I write this) the longtime fantasy games reviewer at RoF. Board games,

video games, RPGs, you name it and he plays it and reviews it. I've never really gone into much depth on this aspect of the magazine, as I'm not really a gamer. I played some AD&D in high school, and a few years ago I went through a *Magic: the Gathering* phase, but that's about it. I don't really play video games or anything else, so I don't feel particularly qualified to comment on Eric's columns. That said there are lots of people who enjoy fantasy games, so Eric's columns are certainly an important part of the magazine.

As to the story itself, this one had a sort of urban gothic feel to it, with a rather interesting take on vampires. Imagine if you would that the vamps invented a drug that is highly addictive to humans. Now imagine that the reason they created this drug is because it makes human blood tastier. Now imagine that the two main characters in the story are a human hooked on the drug and a vampire who hates being a vampire and still remembers what it was like to be human ...and the two of them are in search of a cure for vampirism. Of course, the human could use something of a cure herself for her addiction. Like I said, an interesting take. Art to this one was provided by David Seeley, which marks his second illustration in the magazine.

Then we have "Queen" by Gene Wolfe. Now, anyone who knows anything about Wolfe's writing knows that much of his fiction can be quite intelligent, and it often challenges the reader to figure out what is going on. "Queen" is no exception. I'm not ashamed to admit that while I consider myself a pretty savvy reader, in my time I've read some Wolfe material that has left me scratching my head. But I'm happy to say that I understood what was happening in "Queen." There were several different levels to this piece, but essentially this is a story concerning Jesus Christ's mother and her ascension to Heaven after his death to witness his coronation as the King of Heaven. "Queen" was selected for inclusion in the fourteenth edition *Year's Best Fantasy & Horror*, edited by Ellen Datlow & Terri Windling. It was also selected for inclusion in *Year's Best Fantasy 2*, edited by David Hartwell & Kathryn Cramer. Lastly, it was long listed for the 2002 Locus Award for Best Short Story. Art to this one was provided by Mahendra Singh, which marks his fourth illustration in the magazine.

After this we have "A Respectful Silence" by Richard Parks, which marks his tenth appearance in the magazine. It should also be noted that with this story, he moves into sole possession of the title of RoF's most published fiction author, a title he would never relinquish for the rest of the magazine's run. It should also be noted that with this publication, Richard becomes the first author to reach double digits in terms of fiction publications with the magazine. As to the story itself, Richard once again demonstrates his versatility in fantasy as he introduces us to an alternate universe where the existence of ghosts is accepted by everyone. And in such a universe, it's only natural that the FBI would have paranormal agents who are more than part of some obscure department, ala *The X-Files*. From here, he does a very convincing job of postulating how such agents would conduct their investigations, as our FBI protagonist looks into the case of a ghost of a female figher pilot from WWII. Art to this one was provided by John Berkey, which marks his eighth illustration in the magazine.

Next up we have "Artie's Angels" by Catherine Wells. I don't for a moment consider this a fantasy. It's post-apocalyptic sf. Why, you ask? Well, picture a world where the radiation levels are so high that if you don't take shelter in special city-sheltering spheres, you and your children become horribly deformed. Even in these spheres, there are extremely lawless and dangerous areas, and there is the threat of mauraders from outside the spheres breaking in and wreaking havoc. There are occasional shuttles that leave Earth behind for a better world, but unless you're rich it's impossible to book passage on one. If you're not one of the wealthy waiting your turn on the shuttle, those in the spheres are left to carve whatever semblance of a life they can manage. For many of them it's a rather hopeless existence. That's post-apocalyptic sf if I've ever encoutered it. And yet, if I had been the fiction editor instead of Shawna and I came across this story, I would've taken it for RoF in a heartbeat. Why? Well, besides being a really strong story, there is a strong King Arthur analogy that is woven throughout the tale with considerable skill. Artie=Arthur and his Angels=the Knights of the Round Table. Blending post-apocalyptic sf with Arthuriana is a rather unusual choice, but it works rather well here, which is why I'm glad Shawna took this one. Of course, if you need further proof that this is in fact post-apocalyptic sf, I will point you to *Wastelands: Stories of the Apocalypse*, edited by John Joseph Adams. This one was released within the past year, and it's a reprint anthology that assembles what Adams considers the best post-apocalyptic literature released in recent times. "Artie's Angels" was among his choices. Art to this one was provided by Scott Grimando, which marks his third illustration in the magazine.

Finally we have "Last Tour of Duty" by Devon Monk, which marks her third appearance in the magazine. It also marks the 250th story to be published in *Realms of Fantasy*. We've published a number of war stories in the magazine, but I'm fairly certain this is the first one that takes place during the Vietnam War. In this piece, we're exposed to the war through the perspective of an overwhelmed doctor. Among his unit, there is an intern who is considered the ultimate good luck charm, because every solider he's treated for injuries has lived. So our protagonist goes on an unauthorized mission to recruit this intern from another unit to help with the mounting injuries ...and that's where everything takes a sharp left turn as we witness strong examples of duty, loyalty, and sacrifice, three of the more noble results that emerge from the horrors of war. Art to this one was provided by John Picacio, which marks his fourth illustration in the magazine.

So that wraps up this issue, as well as the 2001 publishing year. And my favorite story this issue? "Artie's Angels" by Catherine Wells. And my favorite illustration? John Picacio's illustration to "Lasy Tour of Duty" by Devon Monk.

Originally posted on douglascohen.livejournal.com on June 26th, 2008

Part forty-five in my comprehensive retrospective as I read the fiction in *Realms of Fantasy* and offer my thoughts. This time around I'll be delving into the February 2002 issue.

We have another first with the cover. There have been media covers before; in the past the magazine has featured TV programs and miniseries as covers, but this marks the first time it's depicted a movie. And which movie is it? Just one of the most commercially successful movies–fantasy or otherwise–of all time: *Lord of the Rings: the Fellowship of the Ring*.

Inside, Shawna offers a rather poignant editorial, as she writes about 9/11. So while this is the February 2002 issue, it would've hit newstands in December 2001. No doubt she had already handed in her editorial for the December 2001 issue, which hit the stands in September 2001. So I'd imagine this issue marked her first chance to write about the events in question.

A rundown of this issue's nonfiction is as follows: In the Movie/TV column, Resa Nelson covers *Lord of the Rings: The Fellowship of the Ring*. In the Folkroots column, Heinz Insu Fenkl discusses the origins of the literary vampire. In the Books column, Gahan Wilson reviews *A Pleasing Terror, The Complete Supernatural Writings* by M.R. James with Christopher & Barbara Roden as general editors, *Mrs. Amworth* by E.F. Benson, *Shadows and Silence*, edited by Barbara & Christopher Roden, *The Golden Gong and Other Nightpieces*, edited by Jessica Amanda Salmonson, *The Haunted Grange of Goresthorpe*, which is the first publication of the first ghost story ever written by Sir Arthur Conan Doyle, and Paul Di Filippo reviews *The Beasts of Barakhai* by Mickey Zucker Reichert, *The Bone Doll's Twin* by Lynn Flewelling, *The Rundelstone of Oz* by Eloise McGraw, and *Discovering H.P. Lovecraft* by Darrell Schweitzer. In the Artists Gallery, Karen Haber covers the work of Donato Giancola. And in the Games column, Eric T. Baker covers the role-playing video games *Art of Magic: Magic and Mayhem* and *Throne of Darkness*, the paper-and-dice RPG supplemental pack, *Weep*, to the RPG game, *Unknown Armies*, the RPG and collectible card game, *7th Sea*, *The Forgotten Realms* campaign for 3rd edition *Dungeons and Dragons*, the *Ravenloft* campaign, reintroduced under White Wolf

Publishing (formerly published by TSR), the RPG, *Temple of the Troll God* from Fast Forward Entertainment, and the RPG, *Coin's End* for Kenzer and Company's *Kingdoms of Kalamar* setting.

On to the fiction ...

The lead story is "Fable For Savior and Reptile" by Steven Popkes, which marks his second appearance in the magazine. As the title suggests, this story is a fable. It examines the relationship between that of Jesus and a turtle that talks to him. Such a description may make this sound like a silly story, but I assure this isn't the case. It starts with the two of them meeting when Jesus is a young boy and it takes us through Jesus's life, up through his crucifixion, with the "savior" and the "reptile" meeting again and again. The entire tale is told from the point of view of the turtle, and offers a unique spin on the tale of the Christ. Others must have thought so too, as it ended up being reprinted in *Year's Best Fantasy 3*, edited by David Hartwell & Kathryn Cramer. Art to this was provided by Michael Gibbs, which marks his eighth illustration in the magazine.

Next up we have "The Burning Man" by Paul Melko. This one is a high fantasy tale about a man who dares to sleep with a wizard's wife. In retaliation, the wizard curses the man to burn for a thousand years. Nothing can put the fires out, and the man is left screaming day and night. In addition, the wizard also curses his wife, leaving her frozen in their bedchamber, forcing her to listen to her lover's constant screams outside their castle for the duration of the curse. From here, Melko tells several different stories as a thousand years pass and what happens around the burning man during this time. It's worth noting that the burning man committed adultery, and yet the author manages to paint him as a sympathetic character. The last sentence in this one is cut off due to a printing error (as is the last sentence of Brian Plante's "Magic 101") and you have to wait until the Letters Page of the following issue to read it. Thankfully, I was aware of this and had the subsequent issue on hand, allowing me to read the last line (and that of "Magic 101") without missing a beat. Art to this one was provided by Kyle Anderson.

After this we have "Dark Seed, Dark Stone" by Jane Yolen, which marks her fifth appearance in the magazine. The fantasy element in this one shows up late, as it tells the tale of two warring tribes through the eyes of a young woman. Toward the end, the ghost of the young woman's father comes to her, demanding she kill the son of one of his enemies from the other tribe. In standard fantasy fare, this is the sort of request that the character honors. But Yolen is hardly your standard author, and so she takes this request in a rather different direction. Art to this one was provided by Scott Grimando, which marks his fourth illustration in the magazine.

Then we have "The Muse" by Lillian Stewart Carl. This one takes place in modern times, and it depicts a middle-aged woman on vacation in Scotland. The magical element in this builds slowly, as the protagonist finds herself drawn into a bizarre entanglement with a local fey. We've run a lot of fey stories over the years, and I'd say a big reason why is that the authors always manage to find ways to bring new twists to these stories. This story is no exception. We've all heard about the human that stays too long in the world of the fey, but how about the fey that stays too long in the world of Man? Look no further than this story. Art to this one was provided by Eric Dinyer, which marks his fourth illustration in the magazine.

Following this we have "The Sea-Maid" by Catherine Wells, which marks her second appearance in the magazine. This one takes the tale of the Little Mermaid and plunks it firmly in modern times. What's interesting is that our first person narrator is aware of this story, and remarks on it several times as he tells us his story. It's sort of like "This can't be happening, but is," as he finds himself pulled along in an inevitable tide. There are some nice characterizations in this one, with the modern day touches inventive enough that I found it a worthwhile retelling. Art to this one was provided by Web Bryant, which marks his fifteenth illustration in the magazine.

Finally we have "Magic 101" by Brian Plante. This one is wacky. Here we have a college student who is working a nightshift at the local radio station, playing songs from the sixties. He's more of a modern rock n' roll guy and is part of a band, but the gig means money. Meanwhile, he's given an assignment in psychology class to design, conduct, and write up an original experiment. The easiest way to explain what our protagonist comes up with is this passage from the story: "'I'm trying to demonstrate what's known as False Memory Syndrome.' That's like when you tell a kid that some teacher molested him when he was in kindergarten, and then he grows up thinking he remembers stuff that never really happened." With this idea in mind, the protagonist convinces the other members of his band to help him record a song that sounds like it was from the 60s. They name it "Crying Shame" and call the pretend band the Poppycocks. Then our protagonist plays it on the radio station during his DJ gig. Soon people start calling in, requesting the song. He even goes so far as to ask people about their memories from the 60s concerning this song. And sure enough, False Memory Syndrome kicks into gear. Soon enough, "Crying Shame" is the most popular song at the station. Then one weekend it's "Twin Spin Weekend" at the station, which meant you have to play two songs in a row by each artist. So the protagonist and his buddies compose a second song by the Poppycocks: "I'll Give You a Ring." Things go on like this, building and building, until there is supposed to be a live concert, featuring various oldies bands. And wouldn't you know it the Poppycocks are scheduled to be a part of it ...and they actually show up. Art to this one was provided by Chuck Demorat, which marks his tenth illustration in the magazine.

So that wraps up this issue. And my favorite story? "Magic 101" by Brian Plante. And my favorite artwork? Web Bryant's illustration to "The Sea-Maid" by Catherine Wells.

Originally posted on douglascohen.livejournal.com on June 28th, 2008

Part forty-six in my comprehensive retrospective as I read the fiction in *Realms of Fantasy* and offer my thoughts. This time around I'll be discussing the April 2002 issue.

The cover to this one is by Scott Grimando, which marks his fifth illustration in the magazine. I was unable to determine the origins to this artwork.

This retrospective marks one of those milestone issues for the magazine, as we have a couple of firsts, along with a couple of lasts that are worth mentioning. Let's start with the lasts. This issue marks the last editorial we ran.* It also marks the last issue Rebecca McCabe appears in the masthead as Assistant Editor. Fittingly then, the last editorial is written by none other Rebecca McCabe, which was her third editorial in the magazine. In it, she addresses the rumors of missing manuscripts that had been directed toward her, and defends herself and her work over the course of almost eight years as assistant editor. I found this goodbye to be both thoughtful and eloquent.

Now let's talk about the firsts. This marks the first issue that my direct predecessor, Carina Gonzalez, appears in the masthead. While she took over for Rebecca, and I in turn took over for Carina, Rebecca and I were and are listed as Assistant Editors (Rebecca started off as Editorial Assistant before being given the sexier title of Assistant Editor), while Carina is listed as Editorial Intern. Why this is, I don't know, but her responsibilities were similar to ours. Either way, this issue marks an official passing of the torch. What it also marks is the first time there has been a significant change in the editorial department.

To me, this is very important, which is why I feel compelled to go on at some length. Shawna is the editor, and since the fiction is arguably the most important feature of the magazine, this magazine is a reflection of her tastes more than anyone else's. But let's not forget that it was and is her tireless assistants who wade through the slush, and what we pass along from the slush is a reflection of our tastes. What Shawna takes from our selections for publication isn't only what she considers worthy of the magazine, it's also where her tastes and ours intersect.

Those intersections can be viewed as glimpses into the tastes of her assistants. And since no two people share the exact same tastes, the kinds of stories we've passed (and will pass) along to Shawna will sometimes differ. I couldn't tell you all of Rebecca's slush survivors, but if I read an author bio and it mentions this is the author's first publication, or that before this publication the author only had small press credits, it's quite likely these authors were slush survivors. Same thing goes for authors from Carina's era, and I've read a number of her slush survivor tales before I started these retrospectives. And having read these tales, I can tell both Rebecca and Carina's tastes are somewhat different than my own. Not better or worse, just different. What this means (to me anyway) is that when these editorial changes take place, while the vision of the magazine remains Shawna's, subtle shifts in some of the fiction we publish will take place.

How can they not? If Rebecca, Carina, and I all have somewhat different tastes, it stands to reason that Shawna's tastes will intersect with ours in different ways. This in turn will lead to some different types of slush survivors being published, which will lead to a slight shift in the flavor of the magazine. Let me reiterate that these changes would be subtle. Everything remains a story that Shawna likes, but a different assistant editor means that sometimes a different kind of story is being brought to her attention.

Let me be very clear here, as what I'm discussing can be a touchy subject if misinterpreted. I'm not talking about the abilities of the various editors, nor am I talking about the merits of the various stories we've passed along to Shawna that have been published. I'm just talking about how different stories will ring the bells of different readers, and how this could influence the personality of a magazine. It's certainly so for editors, so I don't see why it wouldn't be the case to a lesser extent regarding assistant editors. As to who is better at their job and who pulled out the best slush survivors, well, you may feel free to debate such things among yourselves, but for the purposes of these retrospectives I have no interest in going down that road. The last tidbit I'll mention before moving on (finally!) is that any subtle shifts in the magazine's personality probably wouldn't show up for some issues yet, since we always have stuff in inventory.

One other change I'll note is that in the masthead, Ryan Costa's brief run as Graphic Designer is over. Replacing him is Jennifer Schneider.

A rundown of this issue's nonfiction is as follows:

In the Folkroots column, Ari Berk writes about the alphabets of the northern world. In the Movie/TV column, Resa Nelson writes about the top ten high fantasy movies. In the Books column, Gahan Wilson reviews *American Empire: Blood & Iron* by Harry Turtledove, *Nightmare at 20,000 Feet* by Richard Matheson, *The Zippy Annual* by Bill Griffith, *Algernon Blackwood, An Extraordinary Life* by Mike Ashley, and Paul Di Filippo reviews *Fantasy of the 20th Century* by Randy Broecker, *Book of the Dead* by E. Hoffman Price, *Ill Met By Moonlight* by Sarah Hoyt, and *The Crow Maiden* by Sarah Singleton. In the Artists Gallery, Terri Windling discusses the art of Kay Nielsen. And in the Games column, Eric T. Baker reviews the RPG, *Sorcecer*, the RPG, *Swashbuckler, Tangled Strands*, an adventure module for the RPG, *7th Sea*, and the RPG book, *Hackmaster GM Guide*, which is part of the *Hackmaster* RPG game that is a parody of *Dungeons & Dragons*, the RPG, *The Wheel of Time*, based on the NY Times Bestselling series of novels, *New York by Night*, a City Source Book for the RPG, *Vampire: The Masquerade*, the multi-player online RPG, *Fighting Legends*, and the real-time strategy game, *Battle Realms* for Ubi Soft.

Now, on to the fiction ...

The lead story is "Kallisti" by Richard Parks, which marks his eleventh appearance in the magazine. This one is a piece of Greek mythology that deals with some of the key events leading up to the Trojan War revolving most notably around Paris, Eris, and the Apple of Discord. We also witness a chunk of the fallout based on Richard's ideas, and it leads to a twist ending that left me nodding my head. I was expecting it, but was pleased nonetheless, since it struck me as the best possible ending and I was hoping the author would go here. Art to this one was provided by David Seeley, which marks his third illustration in the magazine.

Following this we have "Hubris" by James Patrick Kelly. This also deals with Greek mythology and at the same time is a cross with metafiction, as it becomes a cross between modern literature and a man's encounter with the Greek Muse. Art to this one was provided by Patrick Arrasmith, which marks his ninth illustration in the magazine.

After this we have "Honeysuckle Flowers" by Katya Reimann, a high fantasy tale set in the same universe as her trilogy of novels known as the Tielmaran Chronicles. This one revolves around the tale of two lovers, and the woman is a witch. The princess of their homeland is going to be married soon, and the lovers' lives are thrown into chaos by the arrival of her husband-to-be, who foolishly wishes to hunt in the Changing Lands, a magical land where no one returns from. And his appointed guide into these lands is the witch's lover. Things are made even more complicated by the fact that the witch has been summoned to attend the princess, which would force her to leave her lover. Everything finally comes to a head in the Changing Lands in unexpected fashion. Art to this one was provided by Scott Grimando, which marks his sixth illustration in the magazine. And while we've had an artist with two interior illustrations in the same issue (Greg Carter, December 2000), this is the first issue where an artist had his work appear both on the cover and as an interior illustration.

Then we have "The Rose in Twelve Petals" by Theodora Goss. I actually attended the Odyssey Writing Workshop the same year as Theodora (or Dora, as I and many others call her), back in 2000. I believe that she is the first Odyssean to crack the pages of *Realms of Fantasy*. There have been a ton of Clarionites (Clarioners?) published in the magazine, but the Clarion workshop is far older than Odyssey. So this is kind of cool for Odyssey, as it was less than ten years old at the time. Of course, you deserve the whole story behind this one. Dora did indeed attend Odyssey, but she also attended Clarion in 2001. In fact, if memory serves correctly, Shawna actually discovered this story while teaching at Clarion that summer. She read Dora's story and liked it so much she decided to take it for the magazine. This was her first published story, so it's a pretty good way to break in! But it gets better. "The Rose in Twelve Petals" was also selected for inclusion in *Year's Best Fantasy & Horror 16*, edited by Ellen Datlow & Terri Windling. Dora has certainly been one of the magazine's biggest discoveries, as she's since gone on to publish a host of short stories, and she's been nominated for both the Nebula and World Fantasy Award. As to the story itself (he said, treating it like an afterthought!), it's a very unusual retelling of Sleeping Beauty. As you might expect, it's told in twelve parts, and the rose naturally plays an important part. Art to this one was provided by Stephen Johnson, which marks his third illustration in the magazine.

Next up we have "Field of Angels" by Lauren Halkon, a bizarre high fantasy tale that deals with warring factions striving for the possession of various angels. It's a tough one to describe beyond that, so I'll simply steal

Shawna's editorial caption for this one: "Is it a fair trade–the food of the spirit for the hunger of the soul?" Art to this one was provided by Lauren Halkon.

Now we turn our attention to "The Djinn Who Lives Between Night and Day" by Bruce Holland Rogers, which marks his third appearance in the magazine. This one is a short tale, and there isn't much to say about it except that it deals with a djinn whose actions are so ambiguous he might be evil, or he might be good. It's really left to the reader to decide. Art to this one was provided by Mahendra Singh, which marks his fifth illustration in the magazine.

Finally we have "The Veil Beyond the Veil" by William Shunn, which marks his second appearance in the magazine. This one takes an unusual look at the afterlife, as a woman finds herself being reincarnated again and again. But usually the greatest change is that she keeps coming to life in different worlds. Wild stuff. Art to this one was provided by Greg Carter, which marks his fifth illustration in the magazine.

So that wraps up this issue. And my favorite story? I'm a big fan of Homer's *Illiad*, so I'm going with "Kallisti" by Richard Parks. And my favorite artwork? Stephen Johnson's illustration to "The Rose in Twelve Petals" by Theodora Goss.

*This was true at the time I wrote this retrospective, but we subsequently published an editorial in the August 2009 issue, after the magazine was rescued from extinction, and again in the June 2011 issue, which celebrated the magazine's 100th issue. Following the August 2009 issue, we also ran a number of editorials on the magazine's website.

Originally posted on douglascohen.livejournal.com on July 3rd, 2008

Part forty-seven in my comprehensive retrospective, as I read the fiction in *Realms of Fantasy* and offer my thoughts. This time around we're getting into the June 2002 issue.

The cover to this one is by Todd Lockwood, which marks his fifth illustration in the magazine. It was originally the cover to issue 258 of *Dragon Magazine*.

I noted last issue that the editorials reached their (unfortunate) end, so this marks the first issue without them. In the masthead, since Rebecca McCabe has now officially moved on, this is the first issue without her name appearing in the masthead as either editorial assistant or assistant editor since April 1995, the magazine's fourth issue. The Carina Gonzalez era is now well underway. Also, I'll note that Laura Cleveland's title has changed from Associate Editor to Managing Editor in the masthead.

A rundown of this issue's nonfiction is as follows:

In the Movie/TV column, Resa Nelson covers the *Dinotopia* miniseries. In the Books column, Gahan Wilson reviews *Demons* by John Shirley, *Crouching at the Door*, edited by Jack Adrian, *Beneath the Moors and Darker Places* by Brian Lumley, *Islandia* by Austin Tappan Wright, and Paul Di Filippo reviews *Haussmann, or the Distinction* by Paul LaFarge, *Coup de Grace and Other Stories* by Jack Vance, and *Fluid Mosaic* by Michael Arnzen. In the Folkroots column, Helen Pilinovsky writes about the reality of fairy tales. In the Artists Gallery, Karen Haber covers the artwork of Todd Lockwood. And in the Games column, Eric T. Baker reviews *Final Fantasy X* for the Playstation 2, *Gorasul: The Legend of the Dragon* for the PC, the RPG, *Sorcerer and Sword*, the boxed set, *The Lord of the Rings Roleplaying Adventure Game*, the *Dungeons and Dragons* adventure source book, *Deathright*, for the *Kingdoms of Kalamar* supplement, and the adventure source book, *Time of Tumult* for White Wolf's *Exalted* world. Also introduced in this issue is a short-lived nonfiction feature called What I'm Reading, in which a popular fantasy author writes about s/he is currently reading. In this issue, the featured author is Charles de Lint.

Now to the fiction ...

The lead story is "Boulder Country" by Steven Popkes, which marks his third appearance in the magazine. In this one, Popkes takes the political figure Janet Reno–most visible during the Bill Clinton era–and posits an alternate reality wherein she was never part of Bill Clinton's cabinet, and was instead a judge. From here, he takes this version of Janet Reno and through a surreal adventure through a rather strange world. Pretty out there. Art to this one was provided by Allen Douglas, which marks his second illustration in the magazine and his first solo illustration.

Following this we have "The Run of the Fiery Horse" by Hilary Moon Murphy, a Far Eastern tale about a young girl born under the sign of the Fiery Horse, which according to the astrological charts will make her very difficult to rear. As you might expect from a Fiery Horse, the girl has a strong will and she enjoys running, which means she doesn't want to have her feet wrapped in the ancient Chinese tradition, which keeps the feet of the girl forever small and dainty, but also seriously impairs the ability to walk. Enter the soul-eating serpent that gobbles people's souls through their dreams. The Fiery Horse is a particularly tasty soul, and the serpent is eager to taste it. It proposes a deal to the young girl, which she accepts, this being she will go seven years without having her feet wrapped, but at the end of this time he gets to eat her soul. Seven years is a long time to a little girl of seven (eight?), and so she accepts. A fun read, if I do say so myself. This one also appeared as podcast number 003 on the *PodCastle* website. Art in the magazine was provided by Web Bryant, which marks his sixteenth illustration in the magazine.

Next up we have "Into the Dark" by Patrice Sarath. This one is another fey tale, something I've seen a lot of in RoF's pages. I like the angle the author takes though. We've all heard about the human baby that is stolen by the fey and replaced with a changeling. This story takes that idea a step further, exploring what would happen if the parents raised the changeling as if he were their own flesh and blood. The story starts when the changeling is about thirteen or so, and while it looks like a human, we soon realize something isn't quite right. From here, revelations and characters being put through the proverbial emotional ringer follow, leading up to an ending that takes no prisoners. If I could use one word to describe this one it would be unflinching. Art to this one was provided by Toran Kotter, which marks his second illustration in the magazine.

After this we have "Leeward to the Sky" by Devon Monk, which marks her fourth appearance in the magazine. In this one, Devon takes a stab at high fantasy, which is something different from her previous publications in the magazine. Here we meet an old woman who is too broken down to weave her magic anymore. Yet she also weaves the sails for the ships that sail from port, and does it so skillfully that the townspeople see a kind of magic in this. She is feared but also revered, an essential part of the community but not exactly the kind of person invited over to dinner. But everything about who she is and what she'll do is put into question when a mountain man comes into town and does what no one else will: looks upon her as a woman. Not the sort of high fantasy I encounter too often, but it successfully achieves its aim at challenging assumptions. Art to this one was provided by Laurie Harden, which marks her sixth illustration in the magazine.

Then we have "Lindeman's Life" by Eric M. Witchey. Lindeman is a building. Yes, a building. The whole story is told through Lindeman's perspective, right from when he was first constructed, to replace the "old-timer" next to him. Eventually Lindeman become the old-timer, as a new building is built to replace him. Somehow, this tale manages to avoid being preposterous, and also becomes rather powerful in the bargain. Art to this one was provided by Chuck Demorat, which marks his eleventh illustration in the magazine.

Finally we have "Even Small Prayers" by Kathryn J. Brown. This one is an urban fantasy tale that interweaves the stories of a goddess who borders on forgotten with that of three friends. The goddess feeds on prayers, and is desperate for a mere crumb, let alone a temple of worshipers. Meanwhile the three friends find themselves in a heap of trouble from being intertangled with the world of sex, drugs, and music. In the end, one man's willingness to believe proves the difference as to whether or not the goddess and all three friends will be saved. Art to this one was provided by Mike Kerr.

So that wraps up this issue. And my favorite story? "Lindeman's Life" by Eric M. Witchey. And my favorite artwork? Todd Lockwood's cover.

Originally posted on douglascohen.livejournal.com on July 13th, 2008

Part forty-eight in my comprehensive retrospective as I read the fiction in *Realms of Fantasy* and offer my thoughts, right up to the present. This time around I'll be tackling the August 2002 issue.

The cover to this one is a reprint by Stephen Youll, which marks his third illustration in the magazine. It was originally the cover to *Star Stone* by Christopher Stasheff.

A rundown of this issue's nonfiction is as follows:

In the Movie/TV column, Resa Nelson covers the movie, *Reign of Fire*. In the Folkroots column, Heinz Insu Fenkl writes about the connection between man and clay in creation myths. In the Books column, Gahan Wilson reviews *The Invisible Eye* by Erckmann-Chatrian, *The Floating Cafe* by Margery Lawrence, *Brushfire: Illuminations from the Inferno* by Wayne Barlowe, and Paul Di Filippo reviews *Expecting Beowulf* by Tom Holt, *Ombria in Shadow* by Patricia McKillip, and *Fire Bringer* by David Clement-Davies. In the Artists Gallery, Karen Haber covers the artwork of Frank Frazetta. And in the Games column, Eric T. Baker reviews the RPG, *The Sorcerer's Soul*, the RPG source book, *Exalted: The Dragon Blooded* from White Wolf Publishing, the RPG, *The Ebon Mirror*, from the *Penumbra* line of *Dungeons & Dragons* products, *The Elder Scrolls III: Morrowind and Grandia II* for the PC and Xbox, and *Circus Maximus* for the Xbox.

On to the fiction ...

The lead story is "The Fence at the End of the World" by Melissa Mia Hall. This one is an unusual tale about a pair of young sisters who live in a house that is on the edge of existence. The mother has passed on, but her spirit remains among them, issuing constant warnings to not go beyond the fence. But being cooped up can get to us all, and when one of the sisters decides to ignore Mom's advice, all bets are off. Art to this one was provided by Laurie Harden, which marks her seventh illustration in the magazine.

Next up is "Where Angels Fear to Lunch" by Fraser Sherman. This one features the classic dick from the detective tales, with a customer coming into his office with an unusual case at the beginning of the story. The catch? This particular private eye is also the Wandering Jew. And his client? An angel, of course, claiming someone is out to kill him. Of course, as with any mystery, it turns out to be somewhat more complicated than that, and mysteries, theologies, and betrayals combine for a most unusual climax. Art to this one was provided by Hugo Martin.

Following this we have "The Librarian's Daughter" by Carrie Vaughn. This one is a high fantasy tale about a girl who wears the skin of a horse that once belonged to an evil wizard. She was very close to the horse before its death, and wearing the skin allows her to tell prophecies. But while keeping this connection to the horse is wonderful, it also sets her apart from everyone else. For a young woman, this can be difficult, and everything is thrown into question when she encounters a charming thief who stirs up feelings that make her consider what it might be like to lead an ordinary life so she might be with him. Yet walking away from who she is can be hard ...about as hard as it is for a young thief to stop stealing. Yet there is a compromise of sorts, or more accurately, an inevitable ending that doesn't become known until the last dark sentence. Of course, I like dark, so this didn't bother me. Art to this one was provided by Mark Harrison, which marks his fourth illustration in the magazine.

Then we have "The Witch's Bicycle" by Tim Pratt. This one is a zany young adult tale about a witch who tries to maintain her youth by manipulating some modern-day teenagers to her will. Simply put, Awkward Boy likes Girl. Awkward Boy is also being bullied, and Bully happens to like Girl as well. Girl likes Awkward Boy over Bully, and Bully is intent on making life even more miserable for Awkward Boy. Witch uses her magic to stoke the fires of the classic love triangle, so that it unfolds in the classic manner of centuries ago, wherein the combatants do lethal battle for the heart of the girl. Such combat and its results allow the witch to maintain her beauty. All very logical, yet it leads to a rather surprising conclusion. The word I would use to describe it is ...real. Very very unexpected. Art to this one was provided by Michael Kerr, which marks his second illustration in the magazine.

After this we have "Woewater" by Liz Williams, which marks her second appearance in the magazine. In this dark fantasy tale, a man must spend the night in a manor he believes to be haunted by a were-creature. This one is all about playing with reader expectations. Art to this one was provided by Lori Koefoed, which marks her third illustration in the magazine.

Next up we have "How it Ended" by Darrell Schweitzer, which marks his second appearance in the magazine. In this one we meet a knight who has taken part in the Crusades, but is now entering the latter years of his life. As to what it's about beyond this, I'll steal Shawna's editorial byline: "If your death is a waste and your life is a dream and a sin, how can you ever achieve redemption?" Obviously this story attempts to answer that, and in so doing it was selected for inclusion in *Year's Best Fantasy 3*, edited by David Hartwell & Kathryn Cramer. Art to this one was provided by Paul Lee, which marks his fourth illustration in the magazine.

Finally we have "A Taste of Damsel" by Tom Gerencer. In this one, we're provided a lighthearted read about a dragon that has been asleep for centuries and awakens in modern times. He happens to be a talking dragon, and rather than going on a rampage of flames and feasting, he decides to engage the first guy he sees in conversation, trying to undestand what the hell has happened. Silliness ensues, along with some silly results. Art to this one was provided by Christopher Schenck.

So that wraps up this issue. And my favorite story? "The Witch's Bicycle" by Tim Pratt. And my favorite artwork? Stephen Youll's cover.

Originally posted on douglascohen.livejournal.com on July 28th, 2008

Part forty-nine in my comprehensive retrospective as I read the fiction in *Realms of Fantasy* and offer my thoughts. This time around I'll be ruminating upon the October 2002 issue, which means RoF has reached its eighth year of publication.

The cover to this one is by Donato Giancola and was originally the cover to *A Secret History: The Book of Ash* by Mary Gentle.

A rundown of this issue's nonfiction is as follows:

In the Movie/TV column, Resa Nelson covers M. Night Shymalan's *Signs*. In the Books column, Gahan Wilson reviews *The Blues Ain't Nothin'* by Tina L. Jens, *Dark Universe* by William F. Nolan, *The Emperor of Dreams: The Lost Worlds of Clark Ashton Smith*, edited by Stephen Jones, and Paul Di Filippo reviews *Once ...* by James Herbert, *Face* by Tim Lebbon, and *Knight Fantastic*, edited by Martin Greenberg and John Helfers. In the Folkroots column, Terri Windling writes about the many interpretations of the tale of Bluebeard. In the Artists Gallery, Karen Haber covers the artwork of Omar Rayyan. And in the Games column, Eric T. Baker reviews *Dungeon Siege* from Microsoft, the *Exalted* RPG supplement, *Savage Seas* from White Wolf Publishing, the RPG, *Mechanical Dream*, the *Hackmaster* RPG supplement, *Little Keep on the Borderlands*, and the *7th Sea* RPG supplement, *Mightier than the Sword*. It's also worth noting that this is Paul Di Filippo's last issue as a book reviewer for RoF. He had a respectable stint, from April 2000 issue through October 2002, a run of sixteen issues.

On to the fiction ...

The lead story is "Action Figures" by Mark Bourne. This one is a superhero piece dealing with Superman. Superman is never mentioned by name, and neither are any of his arch-enemies, nor Metropolis, the Daily Planet, Lois Lane, Jimmy Olson, or any other name or place associated with Supes. Yet whenever Superman is being discussed, we know it's him, and we know we're in Metropolis. Credit the author with some clever touches that make it abundantly clear to the reader very early on. So while this is a piece about Superman, it only deals with him peripherally. Instead, we're introduced to some of the everyday citizens of Metropolis.

We see how their lives intertwine, and while none of them have a personal relationship with the Big S, the author uses these people to demonstrate how Superman impacts the lives of everyone in Metropolis. It's an interesting read, i.e. reading a story about the most iconic superhero of all time when the story isn't really about him. Art to this one was provided by David Seeley, which marks his fourth illustration in the magazine.

Next up is "In the Witch's Garden" by Naomi Kritzer, which marks her fourth appearance in the magazine. This one is a science fantasy retelling of Hans Christian Anderson's classic fairy tale, "The Snow Queen." It's been so long since I've been exposed to the original story that I'm afraid I don't remember how this version is different. I can take some educated guesses, but I can't be certain. Art to this one was provided by Web Bryant, which marks his seventh illustration in the magazine.

Following this we have "Half of the Empire" by Bruce Holland Rogers, which marks his fourth appearance in the magazine. This tale features a Far Eastern flavor, telling of a man in search of simple pleasures who finds himself presented with opportunities to gain so much more than he ever imagined. It's a rather short tale, and as is Rogers' M.O. with such stories in RoF, there are some rather logical if unexpected plot twists that go into this one. Art to this one was provided by Mahendra Singh, which marks his sixth illustration in the magazine.

Then we have "Honeydark" by Liz Williams, which marks her third appearance in the magazine. In this one we're introduced to a man of power fleeing Constantinople for political reasons. He takes lodging with an unusual family, particularly their daughter who has a strange power over bees. This story was reprinted in *Year's Best Fantasy 3*, edited by David Hartwell & Kathryn Cramer, and artwork was provided by Melissa Ferreira, which marks her second illustration in the magazine.

After this we have "The Pond in 3-D" by Bruce Glassco, which marks his sixth appearance in the magazine. I can think of no way to describe this one but a modern-day take on *The Creature from the Black Lagoon*. Art to this one was provided by Laurie Harden, which marks her eighth illustration in the magazine.

Finally we "East of the Sun, West of the Moon" by Elizabeth Counihan. This one mixes a lot of different elements into the proverbial stew. At first it feels like a fairy tale. Then it feels like high fantasy. Then some science fictional elements are introduced that make me call this science fantasy.

It's a rather bizarre tale about a princess who is married to a strange creature that is a beast by day and a man by night. She is horrified by one and quite attracted to the other. (One guess as to which is which!) Eventually she becomes pregnant with her husband's child and is separated from him. What follows is a wild tale of her quest to be reunited with him, as she journeys through space and time. Art to this one was provided by Scott Grimando, which marks his seventh illustration in the magazine.

So that wraps up this issue. And my favorite story? "Action Figures" by Mark Bourne. And my favorite artwork? Scott Grimando's illustration to "East of the Sun, West of the Moon" by Elizabeth Counihan.

Originally posted on douglascohen.livejournal.com on August 5th, 2008

Part fifty in my comprehensive retrospect.ve as I read the fiction in *Realms of Fantasy* and offer my thoughts. This time around I'll share some thoughts regarding issue the December 2002 issue. Wow. Fifty issues (not to mention fifty retrospectives). Definitely one of those milestones achievements for a magazine.

Good stuff. The cover to this issue is by Luis Royo, which marks his tenth illustration in the magazine. I was unable to determine the origins of this illustration.

A rundown of this issue's nonfiction is as follows:

In the Movie/TV column, Resa Nelson discusses how the fantasy miniseries experienced a rebirth in the 90s that's still ongoing. In the Books column, Gahan Wilson reviews *The Selected Stories of Manly Wade Wellman*, *The Center Cannot Hold* by Harry Turtledove, *The Circus of Dr. Lao* by Charles G. Finney, *In the Garden of Poisonous Flowers* by Caitlin R. Kiernan, and *A Walking Tour of the Shambles* by Gene Wolfe and Neil Gaiman, illustrations by Randy Broecker and Earl Geier, cover by Gahan Wilson (i.e. the reviewer). The other half of the book reviews are handled my Paul Witcover, which marks his first issue as one of RoF's book reviewers, a position he still holds as I write this. The first books Paul reviewed are *The Translator* by John Crowley, *A Scattering of Jades* by Alexander C. Irvine, and *Sir Apropos of Nothing* by Peter David. In the Folkroots column, Ari Berk and William Spytma write about the Wild Hunt. In the Artists Gallery, Julie E. Czerneda writes about the art of Luis Royo. And in the Games column, Eric T. Baker reviews *Children of the Sun: A Dieselpunk Roleplaying Game*, the real-time strategy game, *Warcraft III*, *Shinobi* for PlayStation 2, *The Book of Challenges for Dungeons & Dragons*, and *Dramatis Personae: Campaign Ready NPCs*.

On to the fiction ...

The lead story in this issue is "Vida" by Leigh Kennedy. In this one, a girl's mother is murdered by her stepfather right at the beginning of the tale. The incident is so traumatic that the girl's mind ends up retreating into a strange dream realm to cope with what has happened. As you might imagine, it becomes a story about whether she can mentally, emotionally, and spiritually recover from this brutal event. Art to this one was provided by John Picacio, which marks his fifth illustration in the magazine. His artwork was also selected for inclusion in the Editorial section of *Spectrum 10: The Best in Contemporary Fantastic Art.*

Following this we have "Seven Brothers, Cruel" by my good buddy, David Barr Kirtley (although this was published some years before we knew each other). This one is a high fantasy story that has a young adult feel to it. At the story's onset, it deals with a subject rather familiar to high fantasy fans: the oppressed damsel, seeking a brave knight to take her away from her cruel family. Further familiarity is provided by the introduction of the brave, strong, and handsome knight who wishes to make his mark on the world and seeks to do the noble thing by taking his newfound love away from this horrible situation. Anyone familiar with RoF's fiction should realize Shawna isn't a big fan of clichéd fiction. Neither am I for that matter. Attacking clichés is another matter. Personally, I love it when an author takes a genre cliché and turns it on its head. Not only does it mock the cliché, but when done right it provides the reader with something at once familiar but fresh. If I were to point to one reason why Shawna bought this piece (and why I would have in her place), I'd say it's precisely what I'm discussing, because this tale takes several unusual but believable deviations from the usual route. The fantastical element in this one is somewhat brief and with a few minor alterations this story could have taken place back in the medieval times of our own world. *But* the idea that he reinvents is one so ingrained (or should I say "so clichéd") in the fundamental fabric of traditional high fantasy that this story *can only* be told as a fantasy tale to achieve the proper level of effectiveness. And given how how the author goes about deconstructing this cliché, additional fantastical elements probably would have detracted from this story instead of adding to it, as our knight gradually comes to realize this princess is hardly what he dreamed of. Art to this one was provided by Kyle Anderson & Myunghee Lee. For Kyle, it marks his second illustration in the magazine; for Myunghee, it marks his first.

Next up is "Moira" Lois Tilton, which marks her third appearance in the magazine. This is the second tale I've seen in the magazine that provides a remix of the Trojan War, the first being Richard Parks's "Kallisti." The similarities end there however, as "Kallisti" explores a lot of the events leading up to the war, while "Moira" explores a lot of the events following the war. In this case, we're introduced to several children from some of the war's notable heroes. This strikes me as a big risk on the part of the author, but all is well since I'd say she pulls this off just fine. Art to this one was provided by Gary Lippincott, which marks his sixth illustration in the magazine.

Then we have "Strife Lingers in Memory" by Carrie Vaughn, which marks her second appearance in the magazine. Like Kirtley's piece, this one is high fantasy that attacks some of conventions of the genre, and like Tilton's piece the bulk of this piece takes place after a war. Assume for a moment that the Big Epic Fantasy Tale has reached its conclusion. The evil has been vanquished at great cost. The hero and his love can now rule the kingdom in piece. This is basically where Vaughn's story starts, i.e. where the rest of these tales normally end. This is possible because Vaughn explores the cost. Not the cost of lives lost in the war or the cost to the royal coffers. No, instead she explores the personal cost, the emotional toll the heroes must pay for such decisive and storied victory. Because really, if you must fight to overcome such overwhelming evil, doesn't it stand to reason that happily ever after must come with *cost*? Vaughn proves it does. Art to this one was provided by Paul Lee, which marks his fifth illustration in the magazine.

Then we have "Dawn, by the Light of a Barrow Fire" by Patrick Samphire, which marks his first publication. In this one, an archaeological team uncovers the bones of a prehistoric child. Based on the damage to the child's skull, it seems clear it died in some unfortunate accident. Even more unfortunately, one of the people on the dig has recently lost his own child in an accident and he's on the verge of an emotional breakdown. Finding these bones only serves to compound matters. What follows is a mystical encounter that transcends the barrier of time itself as two men from *vastly* different eras meet and find they share a common bond. Art to this one was provided by Eric Westbrook.

Finally we have "It Comes and Goes" by Robert Silverberg, which marks his third appearance in the magazine. This one is a reprint, and was originally published in the January 1992 issue of *Playboy*. It was reprinted in *Year's Best Fantasy & Horror 6*, edited by Ellen Datlow & Terri Windling. The story itself is pretty straightforward and absolutely compelling. Tom is a recovering alcoholic. One day he's walking by a house and glimpses a naked and stunningly beautiful woman in the doorway. Things get progressively stranger as sometimes the house isn't even there, while other times he witnesses animals being lured inside the house and never coming out. Doors open and close by themselves. An occupied tricycle disappears into the house as well. And every so often the beautiful woman is there, beckoning him to enter. All this threatens to drive poor Tom back to his drinking, as it seems like the only safe solution to his unhinging mind. Poor guy ...but a great story. Art to this one was provided by Web Bryant, which marks his eighteenth illustration in the magazine.

So that wraps up this issue, as well as 2002. And my favorite story? "It Comes and Goes" by Robert Silverberg. And my favorite story original to Realms of Fantasy? "Strife Lingers in Memory" by Carrie Vaughn. And my favorite artwork? Gary Lippincott's illustration to "Moira" by Lois Tilton.

Originally posted on douglascohen.livejournal.com on August 7ᵗʰ, 2008

Part fifty-one in my comprehensive retrospective as I read the fiction in *Realms of Fantasy* and offer my thoughts. This time around I'll be discussing the February 2003 issue.

The cover to this issue features another photograph from the Lord of the Rings movies, the second cover to do so. It also marks the fourth media cover RoF has used.

A rundown of this issue's nonfiction is as follows:

In the Movie/TV column, Resa Nelson covers *Lord of the Rings: The Two Towers*. In the Folkroots column, Heinz Insu Fenkl writes about fortune cookies. In the Books column, Gahan Wilson reviews *Hauntings* by Vernon Lee, assembled by David G. Rowlands, *Things That Never Happen* by M. John Harrison, *Blood Song: A Silent Ballad* by Eric Drooker, and Paul Witcover reviews *The Lady of the Sorrows* by Cecila Dart-Thornton and *The Scar* by China Mieville. In the Artists Gallery, Karen Haber writes about the art of Darrel Anderson. And in the Games column, Eric T. Baker reviews *The Buffy the Vampire Slayer Roleplaying Game*, *The Lord of the Rings Roleplaying Game* from Decipher Games, *Icewind Dale II* for the PC, *Kingdom Hearts* for PlayStation 2, and *The Mark of Kri* for the PlayStaton 2.

On to the fiction ...

The lead story is "Fable from a Cage" by Tim Pratt, which marks his second appearance in the magazine. As the title notes, this one is a fable, though far from a traditional one (something that is noted in the story). There are really two stories taking place in this one. There is the story of a thief who becomes ensnared by a fey to help her complete her ancient mission. There is also a secondary story–told in quick scenes–that features the man telling the primary story. How these stories intersect is rather interesting, and leads to a dark and satisfying conclusion. Others must have thought so too, since it was selected for inclusion in *Year's Best Fantasy 4*, edited by David Hartwell & Kathryn Cramer. It also appeared as podcast 208 on the *Podcastle* website. Art to this one in RoF was provided by Lori Koefoed, which marks her fourth illustration in the magazine. This artwork was also selected for inclusion in the Editorial section of *Spectrum 10: The Best in Contemporary Fantastic Art*.

Next up we have "Stegosaurus Boy" by Steven Popkes, which marks his fourth appearance in the magazine. This tale combines a number of different elements into what can only be termed as a literary stew. Picture a white boy of thirteen, just entering the throes of adolescence. This boy has a major fascination with dinosaurs, Stegosaurus being his favorite extinct beastie. Now let's set the story in Alabama in the 1960s, right in the throes of the Civil Rights movement. Our protagonist is at that age where he starts thinking for himself about weighty subjects, race among them. His mother is gone, so with just one parent his father's views and opinions hold all the more weight. And his father's views are complex. He walks the fine and tricky line of racism, sometimes seeming to sympathize with black people while other times seeming quite content with the status quo. One of their cousins is a member of the KKK, and when the boy asks his father why he never joined the KKK, his basic response is "I was never asked." But we're shown it's really more complicated than this; refusing such a request can be dangerous to one's health. As if all this isn't complicated enough, let's factor in that each year there is family reunion, and one branch of the family is black, a result of some slavemasters raping their slaves back in the days of slavery.

But wait, there's more. The boy wakes up one night during the full moon and discovers that he's a stegosaurus. It turns out this is a special form of lycanthropy that runs through the entire family, as in *all* the branches. The change manifests itself during adolescence, and each person in the family will change into whatever animal s/he took a special liking to during his/her formative years. Dad is an allosaurus, for example, and their cousin in the KKK (who was also at the family reunion) is a wolf. This is a story about change and acceptance, of right vs. wrong, of family loyalties and the many shades of black and white (no pun intended) during times of social upheaval. It's also one hell of a juggling act on the part of the author. Art to this one was provided by Chris Cocozza.

Following this we have "A Hunter's Ode to His Bait" by Carrie Vaughn, which marks her third appearance in the magazine. I must admit that ever since I started this retrospective project, I've been anticipating reading this one. You see, this piece has a bit of a reputation ...an infamous one. Long before I started working at RoF, I knew about this story. At first I knew about it because Carrie and I are both graduates of the Odyssey Fantasy & Science Fiction Writing Workshop, so I learned something of the tale's content through these channels. But then I heard about this story again ...and again ...and yet again. I actually knew the ending to this one in advance, as over the years I've been exposed to a number of conversations about this very tale, in particular the ending. Let's just say that if you don't know the ending going in, it might shock you. I've spoken to some who like this ending (and for the record I'm among them), and others who found the ending so offensive they stopped reading the magazine. And no, I'm not just making this up. Given this, even though I still have a few issues left to read in this project before I've read everything at least once (eight issues and change), I have no qualms over awarding this tale the unofficial title of "*Realms of Fantasy*'s Most Controversial Story."

Considering the content of the previous story, I also find this tremendously ironic. As to the story itself, it takes place in medieval Britain but gives off a high fantasy vibe. A unicorn hunter purchases a young virginal girl from her mother and proceeds to use the child as bait to lure unicorns out of hiding. (To those unfamiliar with traditional unicorn mythology, female virgins attract unicorns.) The operation proves a smashing success, as the hunter amasses bundles of loot, killing unicorn after trusting unicorn. Years pass, and as the virginal girl grows older she starts attracting older and more illustrious unicorns, which are far more valuable. Along the way, she's also become quite fetching. And the hunter becomes conflicted, battling between his love of the hunt and his growing attraction toward this unblemished beauty. I'll stop right here before I risk giving away that controversial ending.

And don't worry, even if you think you've figured it out, you haven't! Instead, I'll share with you what Shawna said to me when I mentioned to her that this story has a bit of an infamous reputation and raised some reading hackles: "That's one of the things I loved about it—the unicorn is the sacred cow of fantasy." I guess it wasn't too sacred for *Podcastle* either, because it appeared on their site as their 164th podcast. Art to this one in RoF was provided by Stephen Johnson, which marks his fourth illustration in the magazine. This artwork was also selected for inclusion in the Editorial section of *Spectrum 11: The Best in Contemporary Fantastic Art*.

Then we have "Return Stores" by Karen Traviss. This one delves into an area you don't read much about in fantasy: dockyards. In this piece we're introduced to a young man whose grandfather had been a welder in the Navy dockyards. It turns out he was fired for stealing from the dockyards, but until his dying day he proclaimed his innocence. When the young man finds his grandfather's old bugle and several other items from his Navy days, it prompts him to seek out his grandfather's surviving friends. This in turn leads to an investigation to learn the truth about his grandad's thefts, and in the bargain he learns about an old legend and a mysterious song on the bugle that, if played, could reveal the truth about his grandfather. One problem: no one seems to know how the song goes. Art to this one was provided by John Berkey, which marks his ninth illustration in the magazine.

Last but not least we have "Here After Life" by Devon Monk, which marks her fifth appearance in the magazine. In this one we meet a man on the verge of death. Or to put it more accurately, we meet several versions of the man. While Jim clings to comatose life in a hospital bed, we're introduced to five projections of himself of varying age, from newborn infant right up to his current thirty-eight years. These various projections hold a bit of discourse about how to proceed, and being as Jim has changed quite a bit over the years, he has quite a bit of difficulty agreeing with himself (himselves?). But an agreement must be reached while Jim's body is still alive, and time is running out. Of course, given the story's content, it begs the question of whether this is truly a fantastical tale. After all, this could just be dream, right? It's a fair argument if this occurs to you as you're reading this, but come the end of the tale the author answers this possible question in resounding fashion. Art to this one was provided by Patrick Arrasmith, which marks his tenth illustration in the magazine.

So that wraps up this issue. And my favorite story? I had to give this one more thought than usual (many worthy candidates!), but in the end I'm going with "Stegosaurus Boy" by Stephen Popkes. And my favorite artwork? Lori Koefoed's illustration to "Fable from a Cage" by Tim Pratt.

Originally posted on douglascohen.livejournal.com on August 15ᵗʰ, 2008

Part fifty-two in my comprehensive retrospective as I read the fiction in *Realms of Fantasy* and offer my thoughts, right up to the present. This time around I'll be discussing the April 2003 issue.

The cover to this one is by Donato Giancola, which marks his second illustration in the magazine. It was originally the cover to *Walls of Air* by Barbara Hambly.

April 2003 marks another end of an era for the magazine. This time I refer to fact this was the last issue to include the Letters Page.* Karen M. Keen therefore holds the honor of being the last person to have a letter published in ROF. Also worth noting is that at the end of each Letters Page, the following note was included: *Your letters are welcome. Send them to: [address]. Or better yet, email to: [email address].* This issue is no exception, which means the note was included by accident or the decision to discontinue the Letters Page was reached between issues.

A rundown of this issue's nonfiction is as follows:

A new column is introduced with this issue called Past Lives, written by Emma Bull. As Bull explains in this first column, the editors at RoF approached her about writing a column about Renaissance fairs, and she expanded upon this idea, so that she could take readers back to past lives of other milieus. Much of the inaugural column focuses on the Society for Creative Anachronism, or the SCA, a society dedicated to recreating life in the Middle Ages ...but with indoor plumbing. As to the rest of the nonfiction, in Folkroots, Terri Windling writes about changelings. In the Books column, Gahan Wilson reviews *The Year's Best Fantasy and Horror 15*, edited by Ellen Datlow & Terri Windling, *The Mammoth Book of Horror 13*, edited by Stephen Jones, *Dark Terrors 6*, edited by Stephen Jones & David Sutton, *Keep Out the Night: 12 Stories Weird and Grim*, edited by Stephen Jones, *Beware!* edited by R.L. Stine, and Paul Witcover reviews *Summerland* by Michael Chabon, *Dragonstar* by Barbara Hambly, and *The Alchemist's Door* by Lisa Goldstein. In the Artists Gallery, Karen Haber covers the art of William Kaluta. And in the Games column, Eric T. Baker reviews *Legia 2* for the PS2, *Arx Fatalis*, an RPG for the PC, *Dragon's Lair 3D* for the Xbox, the RPG supplement, *Buffy the Vampire*

Slayer: Director's Screen, The Elder Scrolls III: Tribunal, a Morrowind Expansion for the PC, and *Campaign Cartographer 2 Pro* for the PC. There is no Movie/TV column this issue.

On to the fiction ...

The lead story this issue is "The Ice is Singing" by James Patrick Kelly, which marks his second appearance in the magazine. As it happens, last night I attended the monthly KGB Fantastic Fiction Reading Series, held the third Wednesday of each month in the KGB Bar in NYC. One of the two readers there was James Patrick Kelly, who read two shorter works. One of them was "The Ice is Singing." Go figure. Anyway, "The Ice is Singing" is a rare horror piece in RoF. It starts out with a man doing some innocent iceskating, when underneath the ice of the lake he notices a dead man, face and hands pressed against the ice. If that isn't strange enough, he's the only one who seems to notice this figure. From here, things grow more eerie as the realization of what is happening slowly dawns on the protagonist. Art to this one was provided by Laurie Harden, which marks her ninth illustration in the magazine.

Next up is "Blink" by Thomas Seay. Like the previous work, this one is a short piece about a dying man (hint hint about that last piece) whose life is flashing before his eyes. The problem is the flash seems to be caught in a repeating loop of sorts. Art to this one was provided by Michael Gibbs, which marks his ninth illustration in the magazine. This illustration also won the Spectrum Gold Award in the Editorial Category in *Spectrum 11: The Best in Contemporary Fantastic Art*. It is the first RoF illustration to snag this award.

Then we have "Lost Men" by Billie Aul. This one is an urban fantasy tale dealing with a post-Flood world that has caused all the magical races–dwarves, elves, gnomes, vampires,etc.–to come out of hiding from underground. In this particular tale, we're introduced a supernatural detective who is hired to investigate the case of some disappearing lovers. As you might imagine, the supernatural beasties figure into this one rather heavily. Art to this one was provided by Hugo Martin, which marks his second illustration in the magazine.

Following this is "Moonblind" by Tanith Lee, which marks her tenth appearance in the magazine. This makes Tanith the second person to reach this milestone, Richard Parks being the first. So far, this is my favorite story of hers to appear in the magazine. This one features a rare werewolf tale. More specifically, it focuses on the hunters of these werewolves, dangerous men who live for the Hunt and are greatly revered. The protagonist is a gifted hunter who is perhaps a little too in love with the Hunt, as he grows to realize there is nothing in life that he loves *but* the Hunt–not his wife, not his friends, not his mount nor his hunting hounds. Only the Hunt, which is rather perverse since the one source of his love is attached to the creatures he lives to kill. Everything is truly thrown into question when he comes upon a baby werewolf ...in human form. As Lee so often does, she keeps it about the characters and manages to avoid predictability in her endings. In the bargain, she achieves something powerful. Others thought so too, since this piece was selected for inclusion in *Year's Best Fantasy* 4, edited by David Hartwell & Kathryn Cramer. Art to this one was provided by Paul Lee, which marks his sixth illustration in the magazine.

After this is "Captain Fantasy and the Secret Masters" by Tim Pratt, which marks his third appearance in the magazine. This one is a piece of superhero fiction that does an excellent job of deconstructing the genre. Early on we're introduced to the protagonist who is a metamorph (i.e. shape changer). He used to work for a secret agency in the government, and early on he is brought back into the fold, because his abilities are needed; basically there is a super-villainess on the loose, and she's got the suits worried. To stop her, they want to counter her with the greatest superhero ever, none other than Captain Fantasy. The problem is that Captain Fantasy is suffering from acute short-term memory loss; whatever new memories he forms are forgotten five minutes later. But the suits believe that with a metamorph impersonating Captain Fantasy's dead sidekick, it will rouse Captain Fantasy into action (medical cases are cited to back this claim). From here, the story takes off with a lot of fast action, complex characterization, and clever plotting. But as I touched on before, the true appeal of this piece is the way Tim deconstructs the superhero genre. He takes apart the campiness and silliness that sometimes plagues this genre, and provides thoughtful explanations as to why these superheroes behave as they do. Come the end of the story, he's really turned the superhero genre on its ear while still managing to tell a story that fits right into it. This one appeared on the *PodCastle* website as PodCastle Giant 4, a designation reserved for longer pieces. Art to this one in RoF was provided by Joel F. Naprstek, which marks his sixth illustration in the magazine.

Finally we have "Dusi's Wings" by Maya Lassiter (not to be confused with an earlier RoF story called "Dusi" by Devon Monk). I actually have an unusual connection to this story: in 2001, I attended the inaugural Orson Scott Card's Literary Boot Camp with this author. She wrote this story during that week of class and the whole class (along with OSC) critiqued it. The rest as they say is history. As to the story itself, it deals with a young woman living on the streets and making a living off her music, as well as a fallen angel who seeks to feed off her soul. To do this, the angel seeks to seduce her by pretending to an attractive human male around her age and using memories of her past that she has buried for years. It seems to be working too, in fact the angels knows it is ...but all that careful planning becomes threatened what he starts to care about more than a good feeding. Art to this one was provided by Michael Kerr, which marks his third illustration in the magazine.

So that wraps up this issue. And my favorite story? "Captain Fantasy and the Secret Masters" by Tim Pratt. And my favorite artwork? Michael Gibbs' illustration to "Blink" by Thomas Seay.

*It was true at the time I wrote this, but we changed that trend for one issue, bringing it back in style in RoF 100.

Originally posted on douglascohen.livejournal.com on August 21st, 2008

Part fifty-three in my comprehensive retrospective as I read the fiction in *Realms of Fantasy* and offer my thoughts, right up to the present. This time around I'll be discussing the June 2003 issue.

The cover to this one is by Kinuko Y. Craft. It was an image from her then-forthcoming calendar from 2004. In this piece, it depicts Eleanor of Aquitaine on horseback.

This marks our first post-Letters Page issue. When I joined the magazine this feature was already defunct, but I'll miss reading the letters in the back issues. Another change this issue is that the Contributors Page has moved from the back of the magazine to the front. Also, I'll note that Carina Gonzalez's name is mysteriously absent from the masthead.

A rundown of this issue's nonfiction is as follows:

In the Folkroots column, Ari Berk writes about the mythical white stag. In the Past Lives column, Emma Bull discusses time travel etiquette at Renaissance festivals and such. In the Books column, Gahan Wilson reviews *J.R.R. Tolkien: Author of the Century* by Tom Shippey, *Mysteries of Time and Spirit: The Letters of H.P. Lovecraft and Donald Waldrei*, arranged and annotated by S.T. Joshi and David E. Schultz, *Schalken the Painter and Others* by J. Sheridan Le Fanu, assembled and commented upon by Jim Rockhill, *Tales of the Lovecraft Mythos*, edited by Robert M. Price, and Paul Witcover reviews *White Apples* by Jonathan Carroll, *Leviathan 3*, edited by Jeff VanderMeer and Forrest Aguirre, and *Meditations on Middle-Earth*, edited by Karen Haber. In the Artists Gallery, Jane Frank discusses the Haggard Project, in which today's leading illustrators capture the spirit of H. Rider Haggard's novels in a gallery of cover paintings. And in the Games column, Eric T. Baker reviews *Dark Cloud 2* for the PS2, *Buffy the Vampire Slayer: Player's Handbook* for the BTVS Roleplaying Game, the dungeon module *Necropolis* from Necromancer Games, an imprint of White Wolf, and *The Lord of the Rings Roleplaying Adventure Game: The Two Towers*. There is no Movie/TV column this issue.

The lead story is "Seeds-for-Brains" by David Barr Kirtley, which marks his second appearance in the magazine. It also marks the 300th story to be published in the magazine. This one is a rather fun retelling of the

Headless Horseman story, told from the perspective of the Headline Horseman. Over the years *Realms of Fantasy* has published a quite a number of retellings of fairy tales and legends, but this is the first time the magazine published a retelling of the Headless Horseman. Art to this one was provided by Scott Groto.

Next up we have "The Man Who Did Nothing" by Karen Traviss, which marks her second appearance in the magazine. This one is a rather rare horror tale to appear in RoF's pages, and much of the theme can be gathered from the title. Basically, it's about what happens when good men do nothing while the world goes to pieces around us. In a nutshell, the people in a city are starting to riot because they want a middle-aged man to be evicted. Why? Because they're convinced he's the anti-Christ. As you might expect, the local politicians hardly take this claim seriously, even when things start turning violent. A rather chilling tale, one that was selected for inclusion in *Year's Best Fantasy & Horror 17*, edited by Ellen Datlow & Kelly Link and Gavin Grant. Art to this one was provided by Michael Gibbs, which marks his tenth illustration in the magazine. The illustration was selected for inclusion in the Editorial section of *Spectrum 11: The Best in Contemporary Fantastic Art*.

Following this we have "Crossing Into the Empire" by Robert Silverberg, which marks his fourth appearance in the magazine. It also marks the second tale of his to be reprinted in the magazine. It was originally published in David Copperfield's anthology, *Beyond Imagination*, in 1996. This one is an odd but engaging tale about a medieval city that periodically comes unstuck in time and forms a sort of gateway to modern Chicago. Merchants from Chicago then enter the portal with everyday items such as cans of Coke and compasses and trade them for precious jewels, rare volumes, etc. Each side is getting a wonderfully unique item, so both parties are happy. Of course, only a very few people ever go through the portal, because you must be properly prepared to go into this city, meaning you must know the language, the customs, etc. Also, these Chicago merchants are believed to be sorcerers, and so some quarters fear them. Top this off with the fact the portal tends to close after a couple of days, and this trading expedition is every bit as dangerous as it is lucrative. Now imagine you're one of the merchants and a monkey wrench is thrown into this situation, and you'll get an idea of where this story goes. Art to this one was provided by Todd Lockwood, which marks his sixth illustration in the magazine. This illustration won the 2004 Chesley Award for Interior Illustration. It is the second illustration in RoF to win this award, and both times Todd Lockwood was the artist. The illustration was also selected for inclusion in the Editorial section of *Spectrum 11: The Best in Contemporary Fantastic Art*.

After this we have "Pinioned" by Gabriel Edson. This one is a contemporary fantasy about a woman who can transform back and forth between a swan and a human woman through the use of her fabulous feathered cloak. Years back her husband captured her by capturing the cloak and keeping it locked away so she couldn't escape. They've since had a child and have been happily married for years ...or have they? This one is a sad tale about love and obsession can become so easily confused. Art to this one was provided by Gabriel Edson.

Then we have "Alephestra" by Bruce Holland Rogers, which marks his fifth appearance in the magazine. As with many of Rogers' tales in RoF, this one is on the short side. Basically, it's the tale of a goddess who was forgotten because she disappeared among the world of the mortals. Not so much living among the mortals, mind you, but the *world*. What threw me for a quick loop early was the choice to follow the path of Roman mythology as opposed to Greek mythology. I didn't have a problem with it, I just didn't expect it. Art to this one was provided by Sheila Rayyan. This illustration was nominated for the 2004 Chesley Award for Interior Illustration. (To learn the winner, see a couple of paragraphs above.)

The penultimate story in this is "A Fault Against the Dead" by Nina Kiriki Hoffman. This one is an urban fantasy tale about a young woman able to talk to ghosts. But the constant company has her at the breaking point, and everything threatens to blow up when a stalker starts pursuing her ...while the ghost of one of his victims is keeping her company. Art to this one was provided by Web Bryant, which marks his nineteenth illustration in the magazine.

Finally we have "The Drowned Mermaid" by Christopher Barzak. This one is a powerful contemporary fantasy tale about a world where the mermaids have returned and are enticing the humans "back to the sea where they belong." Enter a married couple whose daughter has run away. One possibility is that she's joined the mermaids, although there's no way to know for certain. At the beginning of this story, the mother comes upon an unconscious mermaid that has washed ashore. Although there are procedures for this sort of thing, Mom chooses to take the memaid back to her beach house and take care of it. Dad doesn't exactly approve, and this becomes a source of friction between them. Anyway, as Mom takes care of the mermaid we gradually come to understand how fragile she is both emotionally and mentally since the loss of her daughter, and the mermaid, although a different species represents a chance to be Mom again. It's a rather sad and tragic tale, something Chis has a knack for. (Chris knows me well enough to know that's a compliment!) Art to this one was provided by Chris Cococzza, which marks his second illustration in the magazine.

I'll also take this opportunity to give a shoutout to Chris for his role in this retrospective series. I doubt Chris is even aware of this, but an innocent comment on his blog has extended this whole retrospective series by quite a bit. You see, when I first started these retrospectives, it was my intention to do this series up until the April 2005 issue, or the last issue before I came aboard.* But early on during this retrospective series I happened to be reading Chris's blog one day, and he mentioned my RoF Retrospectives ...except he mentioned that I was blogging about each issue right up to the present. When I read that I stopped and thought to myself, "That's a good idea. I don't know why I didn't decide to do that from the beginning." So I picked up his innocent mistake and ran with it. So if it wasn't for Chis, these retrospectives would be over in another eleven issues. Instead, there are still another thirty-two retrospectives remaining (and counting). So those of you enjoying these retrospectives should thank Chris for extending this series for quite some time yet. I, however, curse the day Mr. Barzak was born, because these retrospectives, while interesting to write, are time-consuming and my own personal albatross. Damn you, Chris!

So that does wrap up this issue. And my favorite story? *Grumble, grumble* "The Drowned Mermaid" by Christopher Barzak. And my favorite artwork? Todd Lockwood's illustration to "Crossing into the Empire" by Robert Silverberg.

*You'll notice that every issue from the first one calls this a "comprehensive retrospective." Obviously this wasn't the idea from day one. But while editing these retrospectives for book form, I made some tweaks to provide better scope/understanding of the project as a whole now that it's complete. It's hardly a secret, as I document when and where each and every retrospective was originally posted, and these original postings remain unaltered and accessible for free for anyone curious enough to investigate.

Originally posted on douglascohen.livejournal.com on August 25th, 2008

Part fifty-four in my comprehensive retrospective as I read the fiction in *Realms of Fantasy* and offer my thoughts. This time around I'll be slicing and dicing the August 2003 issue.

The cover to this is by RoF's longtime book reviewer, Gahan Wilson. It was nominated for a 2004 Chesley Award for Cover Illustration. This is the first issue to feature as many as eight separate works of fiction ...even though the cover notes there being "7 new stories." Doh! A look at the masthead also reveals that Carina Gonzalez's name is once again mysteriously absent.

A rundown of this issue's nonfiction is as follows:

The Movie/TV column makes its return, as Resa Nelson covers the movie, *The League of Extraordinary Gentlemen*. In the Folkroots column, Kristen McDermott discusses Shakespeare's folklore and the English holiday cycle. In the Books column, the aforementioned Gahan Wilson discusses the success story of Harry Potter, while Paul Witcover reviews *Fitcher's Brides* by Gregory Frost, *Tapping the Dream Tree* by Charles de Lint, *The Ogre's Wife* by Richard Parks, and *Hobbits, Elves, and Wizards: Exploring the Wonders and Worlds of J.R.R. Tolkien's Lord of the Rings* by Michael N. Stanton. In the Artists Gallery, Jane Frank covers the art of John Berkey. In the Past Lives column, Emma Bull provides a list of suggestions for the forthcoming summer for those interested renaissance fairs, civil war reenactments, and so on. And in the Games column, Eric T. Baker reviews *Indiana Jones and the Emperor's Tomb* for the Xbox, *Kung Fu Chaos* for the Xbox, *Skies of Arcadia Legends* for the Gamecube, *Tenchu 3: Wrath of Heaven* for the PS2, *Gladius* for the PS2, *Winds of War* for the PC, an expansion of the real-time strategy game, *Heroes of Might and Magic*, *The Arms and Equipment Guide* for *Dungeons & Dragons*, and *Amplitude* for the PS2.

On to the fiction ...

The lead story is "Worshipping Small Gods" by Richard Parks, which marks his twelfth appearance in the magazine. This one is a short tale about a saint that seeks to serve the will of the Buddha by bending a god to his will so that the god will build a bridge from one mountain to the next. Of course, the god has other ideas and a battle of wills and patience ensues. It's also worth noting that in 2007, Richard put out a short story collection through Prime Books called *Worshipping Small Gods,* which obviously includes the story in question. Art to this one was provided by Laurie Harden, which marks her tenth illustration in the magazine.

Next up is "Kristen With Caprice" by Alan Smale, which marks his second appearance in the magazine. This one is another shorter tale (when eight stories have to share space in RoF you shouldn't expect too many long ones). Basically, a couple has broken up and when the ex swings by the apartment to pick up the last of his stuff, he finds his former girlfriend has a pair of rather small goats. But these goats are more than they seem, and are they perhaps enough to mend a relationship seemingly broken beyond repair? This story also appeared on the *PodCastle* website, as podcast 101. Art to this in RoF one was provided by Mary LaRue Wells.

Following this we have "Does He Take Blood?" by Karen Traviss, which marks her third appearance in the magazine. This one is a light piece taking place on an Earth where humans and demons are living side by side. This particular piece focuses on a demon too old to fly who has been put in a retirement home. The conflict in this one stems from the fact that retirement homes are human concepts, and no self-respecting demon would want to spend its last days in such a manner. Art to this one was provided by Toran Kotter, which marks his third illustration in the magazine.

Then we have "The Ghost Girls of Rumney Mill" by Sandra McDonald. This one deals with the ghosts of children who for one reason or another have yet to move on from this world. The ghost girls have their place where they dwell, the ghost boys have theirs. With children, this is how it should be. But everything is thrown into question one day when a ghost boy wearing a dress shows up to Rumney Mill, wanting to stay with the girls. Why? Because he honestly believes he was meant to be a girl. What follows is a powerful story of tolerance concerning gender and sexuality, a theme that doesn't seem to be explored too often in speculative literature through children. It should also be noted that this short was on the short list for the 2004 James Tiptree Jr. Award, and was reprinted in *The James Tiptree Award Anthology 1: Sex, the Future, and Chocolate Chips Cookies,* edited by Karen Joy Fowler, Pat Murphy, Debbie Notkin, and Jeffrey D. Smith. It was also the first story published in Realms to make the shortlist for this award. Art to this was provided by Melissa Ferreira, which marks her third illustration in the magazine.

After this we have "Down With the Lizards and the Bees" by Tim Pratt, which marks his fourth appearance in the magazine. This delves into Greek mythology by taking the tale of Orpheus and Eurydice and twisting it around utterly, placing it in today's world, and depicting a gay man who travels into the underworld to bring back his lover. There are other clever tweaks of the tale along the way, clever enough that this tale was nominated for the 2004 Gaylactic Spectrum Award for Best Short Fiction. Art to this one was provided by Scott Goto, which marks his second illustration in the magazine.

This story is followed by "The Brician Saint" by Kage Baker, which marks her third appearance in the magazine. In this one we have a trio of soldiers who following a recent battle have stolen a small but valuable holy statue. As the story unfolds, we are given suggestions that the statue may be more than it seems, and perhaps the god this holy statue depicts is taking vengeance on these man for their outrageous audacity ...or perhaps not. Some men can be skeptical, even to their graves. The story wraps up with a rather nice twist. Art to this one was provided by Dave Leri.

The penultimate tale in this one is "Seamstress" by Sarah Prineas. According to Carina Gonzalez's old slush site, this is one of her slush survivors. Going by the list here (and I don't know if it's comprehensive), it may be her first slush survivor, since I'm uncertain if "Lindeman's Life" was pulled from the slush by Carina or her predecessor, Rebecca McCabe. As to the story itself, this one is a rather clever look at what goes on behind the fairy tales. To be more specific, have you ever wondered how the Fairy Godmother comes up with these different items that the characters in these tales need? What if instead of that wonderful wave of her wand that just makes everything appear out of thin air, the items were produced in what is basically a sweat shop? I'll stick in an observation that is just occurring to me now, as I'm realizing that a lot of the stories this issue excel at turning conventions on their heads. This tale is no exception. Art to this one was provided by Lori Koefoed, which marks her fifth illustration in the magazine. It was also selected for inclusion in the Editorial section of *Spectrum 11: The Best in Contemporary Fantastic Art*.

Finally we "Turnings" by Laura Ann Gilman. This one is the shortest tale of the issue. It deals with a woman with sorcerous connections to the earth and a man with sorcerous connections to the air falling in love, and how this love is as two ships passing in the night. Art to this one was provided by Sheila Rayyan, which marks her second illustration in the magazine.

So that wraps up this issue. And my favorite story? "The Ghost Girls of Rumney Mill" by Sandra McDonald. And my favorite artwork? Dave Leri's illustration to "The Brician Saint" by Kage Baker.

Originally posted on douglascohen.livejournal.com on August 29th, 2008

Part fifty-five in my comprehensive retrospective as I read the fiction in *Realms of Fantasy* and offer my thoughts. This time around I'll be discussing the October 2003 issue.

This issue puts RoF in its ninth year of publication. The cover to this one is by Luis Royo, which marks his eleventh illustration to appear in the magazine. It's another one of the now infamous RoF chicks in chain mail covers, and the illustration was originally a Prism Chase Card, which were a series of Luis Royo images published by Comic Images. In the masthead, Carina Gonzalez's name has returned.

A rundown of this issue's nonfiction is as follows:

In the Movie/TV column, Resa Nelson covers the movie, *Underworld*. In the Past Lives column, Emma Bull discusses how to dress for fairs on a budget. In the Folkroots column, Heniz Insu Fenkl discusses mermaid lore. In the Books column, Gahan Wilson reviews *The Light Ages* by Ian R. MacLeod, *The Etched City* by K.J. Bishop, *Kissing Carrion* by Gemma Files, and Paul Witcover reviews *Celtika: Book One of the Merlin Codex* by Robert Holdstock, *Lords of Rainbow* by Vera Nazarian, and *The Witch Queen* by Jan Siegel. In the Artists Gallery, Karen Haber covers the art of Jeffrey Jones. And in the Games column, Eric T. Baker reviews *Arc the Lad: Twilight of the Spirits* for the PS2, *Final Fantasy: Origins* for the PS2, *X2: Wolverine's Revenge* for the PS2, Xbox, and PC, *Run Like Hell* for the Xbox, Wizard of the Coast's *Urban Arcana Campaign*, and *Monster Smackdown* for the *Buffy the Vampire Slayer* RPG line.

On to the fiction ...

The lead story is "Okra, Sorghum, and Yam" by Bruce Holland Rogers, which marks his sixth appearance in the magazine. This story is a rare African folk tale about a princess who is sent by her father to spend the summer with an old man in order to learn wisdom. As you might expect, there is a twist. This one was the Miniature 20 podcast on the *PodCastle* website, which I imagine is for stories that are vignettes. Art to this one in RoF was provided by Mona Caron.

Next up we have "In the Forest of Forgetting" by Theodora Goss, which marks her second appearance in the magazine. This one is a story about a surreal journey through the forests of one's woman mind as she is dying from cancer. In the last issue, I mentioned that Richard Parks had a story called "Worshipping Small Gods," and that he released a short story collection through Prime Books with the same title. So what a coincidence that one issue later I'll be telling you that Theodora released a short story collection through Prime Books called *In the Forest of Forgetting*. Art to this one was provided by Lori Koefoed, which marks her sixth illustration in the magazine.

Following this we have "The Doorman Gunner" by Michael Bishop. This one is a rare zombie tale in RoF. I haven't read much in this area, but I love the concept behind this one. It deals with an American soldier who dies in service during the Vietnam War but comes back and continues serving. He keeps his intelligence and memories, and his views are morbid to say the least. Much of the tale is about this doomed soul trying to find his final release, and it's told through the perspective of a medley of characters, including soldiers, a pilot, a priest, and a prostitute. Art to this one was provided by Dave Leri, which marks his second illustration in the magazine.

Then we have "The Day Pietro Coppino Spoke to the Mountain" by William Shunn, which marks his third appearance in the magazine. This one takes place in Italy during the 1800s. The story deals with an eccentric master sculptor who is on the verge of creating his greatest masterpiece, scultped from the purest block of marble he's ever beheld. The sculpture itself is of Pluto from Roman mythology spiriting Persephone away to the underworld. But at the beginning of the story, something is terribly wrong with the sculpture. Persephone's fingers have started to droop. We go on to learn Pietro lost his wife some twenty years earlier in a cave-in at one of the quarries where the marble comes from. Shortly afterward, Pietro and his son took the time to speak to the king mountain, because in this world there is a bit of holy connection between the sculptors and the mountains that provide the marble to sculpt with. But Pietro has continued to bear a grudge about his wife's death, and this is causing the Persephone to wilt. When Pietro's son learns of his father's defiance, he takes him to speak to the mountain once more. There is a story of love vs. forgiveness, or as Shawna interprets it in her editorial byline, honor vs. glory. Art to this one was provided by Paul Lee, which marks his seventh illustration in the magazine.

After this we have "Runesmith" by Harlan Ellison and Theodore Sturgeon. This marks Ellison's second appearance in the magazine, both of them reprints. For Sturgeon, it marks his first, although it's posthumous, since he passed away in 1985. It should also be noted that this story is dedicated to the memory of Cordwainer Smith and was originally published in the May 1970 issue of *The Magazine of Fantasy & Science Ficton.*As to the story itself, this one is a post-apocaylptic tale about a man who was duped into using black magic to bring about the end of civilization, and now the creatures who tricked him are trying to use him to bring their dark masters into the world. To date, this is the last story to be reprinted in RoF.* To date, it's also the oldest story to be reprinted in the magazine. Art to this one was provided by Patrick Arrasmith, which marks his eleventh illustration in the magazine. The illustration was also selected for inclusion in the Editorial section of *Spectrum 11: The Best in Contemporary Fantastic Art.*

After this we have "Deep in the Woods of Grammarie" by Michael Swanwick. This one features seven short-short fairy tales, some of them retellings, such as Jack and the Beanstalk and Little Red Riding Hood. Each story has its own little illustration, and I believe this is the first story to have multiple illustrations. The series of illustrations were provided to this one by Mona Caron, making it the second story she illustrated for the magazine.

Finally we have "Strings" by Karen Traviss, which marks her fourth appearance in the magazine. This one delves into Greek mythology, as is a retelling of the story Orpheus and Eurydice. In this version, however, when Eurydice is bitten by the snake, instead of killing her it causes her to go deaf. The deafness renders her immune to the charms of Orpheus's lyre, which allows her to see him for the monster he is. When she eventually dies and goes to the underworld, Orpheus once again goes after her. But this time, instead of a rescue mission its tone is more of an attempted kidnapping. Art to this one was provided by Stephen Johnson, which marks his fifth illustration in the magazine.

So that wraps up this issue. And my favorite story? "The Day Pietro Coppino Spoke to the Mountain" by William Shunn. And my favorite artwork? Dave Leri's illustration to "The Doorman Gunner" by Michael Bishop.

*And having now read the entirety of the fiction in *Realms of Fantasy*, I can tell you it is in fact the last fiction reprint to ever appear in the magazine.

Originally posted on douglascohen.livejournal.com on August 30th 2008

Part fifty-six in my comprehensive retrospective as I read the fiction in *Realms of Fantasy* and offer my thoughts. This time around I'll be discussing the December 2003 issue.

The cover to this one is another *Lord of the Rings* movie cover, which is our third one and our fifth media cover.

A couple of tidbits about the masthead. Until this issue, Mark Hintz was always listed as the publisher. Starting with this issue, he's now listed as Chief Executive Officer. Also, near the bottom of the masthead, Joe Varda was listed as Vice President and Advertising Director. In this issue, he's still listed as such and in the same place. But near the top of the masthead, right underneath Mark's name, he's also listed as the Publisher.

A rundown of this issue's nonfiction is as follows: in the Movie/TV column, Resa Nelson provides an overview of the fall movies. In the Folkroots column, Terri Windling discusses how Hans Christian Anderson is the father of the modern fairy tale. In the Books column, Gahan Wilson reviews *Mortal Engines* by Phillip Reeves, *Spring-Heeled Jack* by Phillip Pullman, *The Wolves in the Walls* by Neil Gaiman and Dave McKean, and Paul Witcover reviews *The Anvil of the World* by Kage Baker, *The Battle of Evernight* by Cecilia Dart-Thornton, and *Eragon, Book One of the Inheritance Trilogy* by Christopher Paolini. In the Past Lives column, Emma Bull picks up where she left off last column, discussing how to attend Renaissance fairs and such on a budget. In the Artists Gallery, Ari Berk discusses the illustrated book by himself and Brian Froud, *The Runes of Elfland*. And in the Gaming column, Eric T. Baker reviews *Pirates of the Caribbean* for the Xbox and the PC, *Rachet and Clank Go Commando* for the PS2, *Unlimited Saga* for the PS2, *The Magic Box*, the latest supplement for the *Buffy the Vampire Slayer Roleplaying Game*, and *Ghostwalk*, a *Dungeons & Dragons* supplement.

On to the fiction ...

The lead story is "Dancing Day" by Liz Williams, which marks her fourth appearance in the magazine. This one takes the old story of a human possessed by a demon and turns it on its head by telling the story from the demon's perspective and invoking some sympathy in the process. Art to this one was provided by Lori Koefoed, which marks her seventh illustration in the magazine.

Following this we have "Of Soil & Climate" by Gene Wolfe, which marks his second appearance in the magazine. Wolfe is known for writing challenging fiction, and this one is no exception. It's mostly told from the perspective of a modern-day psychiatrist who ends up switching bodies with a warrior in a seconday fantasy world. On the surface, it sounds simple enough, but Wolfe makes this piece complex, because he tells us the bulk of the story from the analytical mind of the psychiatrist and because the reader is expected to figure a lot on his own. This one ended up being selected for inclusion in *Year's Best Fantasy 4*, edited by David Hartwell & Kathryn Cramer. Art to this one was provided by Andy B. Clarkson.

Next up we have "Divided By Time" by William Shunn, which marks his fourth appearance in the magazine. In this one, a man enters a magic shop and ends up exchanging one of his great character weaknesses for a device that allows him to travel with a time-bubble surrounding him. The time-bubble allows him to live an entire life of experiences as he journeys across the earth to Jerusalem to find the woman he loves. Art to this one was provided by Eric Fortune and it was selected for inclusion in the Editorial section of *Spectrum 11: The Best in Contemporary Fantastic Art*.

Then we have "Romanticore" by Tim Pratt, which marks his fifth appearance in the magazine. This piece is hard to sum up because there's so much going on. This one is a love story, but it explores the concepts and meaning of love in very unusual ways, reaching as far back as mankind's primal and mythic roots. A man on the rebound becomes involved with a woman, knowing that it will only last a few months, because that's when her longtime partner returns. Along the way, both of them fall in love. And the whole time the man is having strange dreams about being a lion. When the woman's partner returns, even though she has grown to love the protagonist and he hopes they can still see each other, she tells him it's time to end things. From here, things get really weird. It turns out the lion dreams stem back to ancient times, when one of the man's ancestors slept with a lion god. The onset of dreams is happening because of the woman and particularly her partner, whose mythic roots are with the manticore, an ancient enemy to the lion. Obviously they're on a collision course. There are some similarities here to animal totems, but to call it such wouldn't be accurate. I think the real power behind this one is the collision of primal attractions and urges vs. the more modern development of love. Art to this one was provided by Scott Grimando, which marks his eighth illustration in the magazine.

Finally we have "Yamabushi" by Richard Parks, which marks his thirteenth appearance in the magazine. This one is a Far Eastern fantasy about a man seeking enlightenment who crosses paths with a goblin known as a tengu. Tengus exist to trick and tempt holy men from the path of true righteousness. The tengue takes our protagonist to be a yamabushi monk and starts plaguing him. The man claims he is no monk and seeks to strike a deal with tengu. The tengu agrees to the man's proposal, but all is not as it seems ...or is it? As Shawna wrote in the editorial caption for this one: "We live in a world of illusion, and things are not always as they seem. But sometimes they are." Art to this one was provided by Paul Lee, which marks his eighth illustration in the magazine.

So that wraps up this issue, as well as 2003. And my favorite story? "Romanticore" by Tim Pratt. And my favorite artwork? Scott Grimando's illustration to the same story.

Originally posted on douglascohen.livejournal.com on September 6th, 2008

Part fifty-seven in my comprehensive retrospective as I read the fiction in *Realms of Fantasy* and offer my thoughts. This time around the February 2004 issue steps up to the plate.

The cover to this one is another *Lord of the Rings* movie cover. This is the fourth Lord of the Rings movie cover, the fourth movie cover overall, and the sixth media cover.

A rundown of this issue's nonfiction is as follows:

In the Movie/TV column, Resa Nelson covers the final *Lord of the Rings* movie, *The Return of the King*. In the Folkroots column, Ari Berk discusses various facets of northern European folklore, particularly *Kalevala*. In the Past Lives column, Emma Bull discusses finding your niche if you want to be a part of Renaissance fairs and such. In the Books column, Gahan Wilson reviews five volumes that collect much of Manly Wade Wellman's work, these being, *The Third Cry to Legba and Other Invocations*, *The Devil is Not Mocked and Other Warnings*, *Fearful Warnings*, *Fearful Sin's Doorway and Other Ominous Entrances*, and *Owls Hoot in the Daytime and Other Omens*, as well as *The Boats of the "Glen Carrig" and other Nautical Adventures* by William Hope Hodgson, *Midnight Sun*, which gathers all the short fiction and poems about Karl Edward Wagner's Kane, *A Choir of Ill Children* by Tom Piccirilli, *Veniss Underground* by Jeff VanderMeer, and Paul Witcover reviews *Fudoki* by Kij Johnson, *Tooth and Claw* by Jo Walton, and *Mortal Suns* by Tanith Lee. In the Artists Gallery, Karen Haber covers the artwork of Greg Spalenka. And in the Gaming column, Eric T. Baker reviews *Final Fantasy XI* for the PC, *Disgaea: Hour of Darkness* for the PS2, *Otogi: Myth of Demons* for the Xbox, and the RPG, *Orpheus*, from White Wolf Publishing.

On to the fiction ...

The lead story is "The One Who Conquers" by Bruce Holland Rogers, which marks his seventh appearance in the magazine. This is a dark fairy tale about a tribe of trolls who are visited by a strange voice that goads them to attack the humans on the surface, so that they might take over the humans' towns and have all the comforts they do. The voice provides them all sorts of advice and protection, and everything goes accorrding to plan when the trolls do as their new god tells them. Unfortunately for these trolls, everything is also going according to plan for the voice. Art to this one was provided by Laurie Harden, which marks her eleventh illustration in the magazine.

The next story is "Still Man" by William R. Eakin, which marks his sixth appearance in the magazine. Like his five previous tales in RoF, this one takes place in the town of Redgunk, Mississippi. In this one, there are stories that circulate among the folk of Redgunk about a man they call the Still Man, part of the reason being the special brand of moonshine he makes in his stills. Still Man also happens to be experimenting with AI. For the most part, people give him a wide berth, because of some of the darker rumors surrounding him. But all that changes when a young woman from social services comes to his home, looking for his daughter. When the social worker drinks this special moonshine, primal truths are unlocked in the bargain. Art to this one was provided by Brian Horton, and it was selected for inclusion in the Editorial section of *Spectrum 11: The Best in Contemporary Fantastic Art*.

Then we have "Tiny Flowers & Rotten Lace" by Jay Lake. The protagonist in this one is a young boy, but to me this one feels less like middle grade fantasy and more like horror. Our protagonist has a mother who's gone insane and a cruel father who keeps her locked in the bedroom at all hours. At the beginning of the story, the protagonist is being pursued by a mysterious brick monster. Given his family situation and how he gets picked on at school, he doesn't really have anyone to turn to. But although he's scared and isolated, gradually he manages to uncover the dark secrets of his family. In the bargain, he learns who the true monster is. Art to this one was provided by Lori Koefoed, which marks her eighth illustration in the magazine.

After this we have "Rattler" by Gene Wolfe & Brian Hopkins. For Wolfe, it marks his third appearance in the magazine. For Hopkins, I can only assume this is the same Brian Hopkins who co-wrote "The Hounds of Winter" with James Van Pelt back in the August 1999 issue of RoF. That would make this his second appearance in the magazine. This would also make him the first author to co-write stories with two different authors, both of them previously published in the magazine. As to the story itself, it's about a car that's inhabited by the spirit of a man's dead dog. Not much more I can say, since this one is all in the telling. Art to this one was provided by Joel F. Naprstek, which marks his seventh illustration in the magazine.

Following this we have "The Flowers of Tekheli" by Liz Williams, which marks her fifth appearance in the magazine. This one takes place in the nation of Kazekhstan. In it, a young woman is in a car accident with her brother and his friends. Her brother's friends are killed, but the woman's brother mysteriously disappears. Eventually it's discovered that he's being held captive by the ancient and vengeful spirit of a young woman. In life, this spirit was a poet, but some young men did something terrible to her, costing her the ability to use her voice. Since she didn't know how to write, she could no longer perform her poetry. Hence the whole vengeful spirit angle toward young men. It falls to the young woman to rescue her brother while appeasing a spirit that seems inconsolable. Art to this one was provided by Allen Douglas, which marks his third illustration in the magazine.

Next up is "Power Sources" by Julia H. West. Depending on how you look at this one, it could be termed science fiction or fantasy. A modern-day storyteller has traveled to another planet to learn their methods of storytelling, which involves using living fibers (such as a sample of someone's hair), which in turn draws on the planet's "energies." We're never really told what these energies are, which is fine. But because it remains nebulous, it falls to the reader decide whether these energies are magical, of if there is a more scientific explanation. The protagonist in this one considers it magic, so that could sway some readers to argue this is fantasy. Personally, this read like unexplained science fiction to me, but not to the degree that I'll argue the relevance of it belonging in a fantasy magazine. Art to this one was provided by Michael Kerr, which marks his fourth illustration in the magazine.

Finally we have "Heart's Desires" by Nina Kiriki Hoffman, which marks her second appearance in the magazine. This one takes place during Halloween. I haven't been keeping track of this particular fact, but it may be our first Halloween story. Anyway, this is a short piece about some trick-or-treaters who visit the house of what turns out to be a witch. When one of the boys has an attack because of his sickness, we're shown how you needn't always fear what you don't understand. Art to this one was provided by Laurie Harden, which marks her twelfth illustration in the magazine.

So that wraps up this issue. And my favorite story? "The One Who Conquers" by Bruce Holland Rogers. And my favorite artwork? Brian Horton's illustration to "Still Man" by William R. Eakin.

Originally posted on douglascohen.livejournal.com on September 13th, 2008

Part fifty-eight in my comprehensive retrospective as I read the fiction in *Realms of Fantasy* and offer my thoughts, right up to the present. This time around I'm be yakking about the April 2004 issue.

I've read this issue before. When I interviewed with Shawna back in 2005 for the position of Assistant Editor, one of her questions was whether I had read any issues of the magazine. I had read two and have covered both of them in previous retrospectives (August 1997 and August 2000). But when Shawna decided to take me on for a trial period, she also wanted me to familiarize myself with some of the more recent issues. So she grabbed the two closest issues and told me to read the fiction in them. One of these issues was April 2004, which means I first read this one back in May 2005. That's well over three years ago, so I took the time to read all of these stories again.

But before we get into this fiction ...

The cover to this one is by Gordon Crabb, and was originally the cover to *Guardian of the Promise* by Irene Radford.

A rundown of this issue's nonfiction is as follows:

In the Movie/TV column, Resa Nelson discusses fantasy time travel movies. In the Folkroots column, Helen Pilinovsky discusses how the Russian fairy tale character Baba Yaga has a place in contemporary fiction. In the Books column, Gahan Wilson reviews *Lost Boy Lost Girl* by Peter Straub, *The Complete Tolkien Companion* by J.E.A. Tyler, *The Lord of the Rings and Philosophy: One Book To Rule Them All*, edited by Gregory Bassham and Eric Bronson, *Zippy Annual*, drawn and written by Bill Griffith, and Paul Witcover reviews *The Knight* by Gene Wolfe, *Conqueror's Moon: Book One in the The Boreal Moon Tale* by Julian May, and *The Thackery T. Lambshead Pocket Guide to Eccentric & Discredited Diseases*, edited Dr. Jeff Vandermeer & Dr. Mark Roberts (I will assume this is tongue in cheek). In the Artists Gallery, Jane Frank covers the art of Lisa Snellings. And in the Games column, Eric T. Baker reviews *Draconomicon* (an obvious riff on H.P. Lovecraft's *Necronomicon*) for the *Dungeons & Dragons* line, *The Player's Guide to Low Clans*, a supplement from White Wolf for the *Dark Ages: Vampire* line, the RPG, *Viking Age*,

Hunter the Reckoning: Redeemer, the third in the series and second for the Xbox, the RPG, *Crimson Skies: High Road to Revenge*, and *Crouching Tiger, Hidden Dragon* for the PS2. There is no Past Lives column this issue.

On to the fiction ...

The lead story is "In a Tower High" by Pamela D. Lloyd. I guess the best way to describe this one is an anti-fairy tale. It takes place in modern times, and depicts a working woman in the city. At every turn in the story (which is basically a depiction of her life at the moment), we are introduced to the fairy tale equivalent, or rather the anti-fairy tale equivalent, which goes on to demonstrate why this woman's life is no fairy tale. I should add that I don't mean to make it sound like this is a sad tale, or that the protagonist is miserable. Far from it. Her life is just utterly devoid of fairy tale sensibilities. Art to this one was provided by Laurie Harden, which marks her thirteenth illustration in the magazine.

Next up is "Israbel" by Tanith Lee, which marks her eleventh appearance in the magazine. This time Tanith takes on vampires, setting the story in Paris. One of the common traits in vampires is that they can't see their reflection. So in this one a beautiful vampire hires an artist to paint her portrait, so that she can finally look at herself once more. It's a clever twist, and things only become more twisted when the matter of payment is discussed and the artist wishes to become a vampire. A human wishing to become a vampire isn't exactly knew, but how humans become vampires in this one—

along with what happens after he makes his request—are both elements that help make this one a worthwhile addition to this crowded area of fantasy/horror. Art to this one was provided by Patrick Arrasmith, which marks his twelfth illustration in the magazine. This illustration was also selected for inclusion in the Editorial section of *Spectrum 11: The Best in Contemporary Fantastic Art.*

After this we have "The King's Snow" by Josh Rountree. According to her old (and now defunct) slush site, Josh is one of Carina Gonzalez's slush survivors. As to his story, this one is a high fantasy tale taking place in a world whose inhabitants wish to avoid being subjected to the King's Snow, which from what I gathered is a terrible winter storm. In order to avoid this fate, the king periodically selects a Daggerbearer, basically his chosen champion to once more do battle with and slay the mysterious creature known as the Turion. Each time, the Daggerbearer is accompanied by the

Witness, the lone person who accompanies the Daggerbearer on his journey from beginning to end. In this one, the Daggerbearer turns out to be an unwilling hero, a farmer and devoted father who wants nothing to do with the glory of being a Daggerbearer. Yet he's intent on doing his duty to king and providing his son a future, something that can't happen if he doesn't slay the Turion. Of course, as every high fantasy fan knows traits such as these help make the protagonist even more of a hero. Art to this one was provided by Eric Fortune, which marks his second illustration in the magazine.

Then we have "The Tao of Flynn" by Eric M. Witchey, which marks his second appearance in the magazine. This one deals with insurance salesmen. Richard is the best salesman in the office ...until Flynn comes along. Every time Flynn visits a potential customer, he gets the sale. Every. Single. Time. No one sells every single time out. Cooper the boss gets suspicious, so he orders Richard to spend the day with Flynn, to make sure that Flynn is with the program, a set of guidelines Cooper expects everyone to follow when seeking a sale. So Richard spends the day with Flynn ...and there's something about this guy. Charming as can be, almost too charming. Almost as if there's something magical about him. Everyone is anxious to hear what Flynn has to say, wants to be his friend, wants to talk to him. And so on. And yet there's nothing sinister going on. Not one bit. Flynn is a good guy, which is why Richard takes to *his* program (and really, you would too). Cooper doesn't like this one bit, which is why he puts a plan into action to take both Flynn and Richard down. But that Flynn ...oh he's tricky. Art to this one was provided by Andy B. Clarkson, which marks his second illustration in the magazine.

Following this we have "Portrait of an Unidentified Angel" by Wendy A. Shaffer. This one takes place during the Renaissance and features a painter named Michelangelo (but not *the* Michelangelo) who is gravely ill. He is also in hiding for some of his past crimes, and there are those who dearly love to help rush along the end of his life. But all this is pushed to the side when Michaelangelo is visited by a mysterious angel who wishes him to paint its portrait. Given that he's too weak to travel, flat broke, and the artist in him would love nothing more than to paint this fine specimen, he agrees. But the angel refuses to reveal its identity. Instead, it wishes Michelangelo to guess, promising that if he fails to guess properly, then it will reveal its identity when the portrait is finished. Details about

Italy and painting are in abundance in this one, and while I knew what was coming this time around, I still remember the pleasant surprise I encountered the first time I read this one come the story's end. Art to this one was provided by Dave Leri, which marks his third illustration in the magazine.

Finally we have "Calamity Warp" by Gene Wolfe, which marks his fourth appearance in the magazine. This one is a short but odd tale about the new pet dog that is able to move through space-time. That creates some serious problems when the dog starts fetching things out of space-time. Eventually she brings back a new shadow to her master ...and the shadow decides to stay. Art to this one was provided by Laurie Harden, which marks her fourteenth illustration in the magazine. I believe this also makes her the first artist to have two illustrations in back to back issues.

So that wraps up this issue. And my favorite story? "The Tao of Flynn" by Eric M. Witchey. And my favorite artwork? Dave Leri's illustration to "Portrait of an Unidentified Angel" by Wendy A. Shaffer.

Originally posted on douglascohen.livejournal.com on September 18th, 2008

Part fifty-nine in my comprehensive retrospective as I read the fiction in *Realms of Fantasy* and offer my thoughts. This time around I'll be discussing the June 2004 issue.

The cover to this one is by Matt Hughes. It was originally a European cover to Matt's first book, though I was unable to track down the title.

A look at this issue's masthead reveals that Jennifer Schneider's considerable run as Graphic Designer is over. Taking her place is Jesse Guay.

A rundown of this issue's nonfiction is as follows:

In the Movie/TV column, Resa Nelson provides a roundup of the spring movies. In the Folkroots column, Terri Windling discusses animal brides and bridegrooms in folklore and fantasy. In the Books column, Gahan Wilson reviews *In the Land of Time and Other Fantasy Tales*, edited with an introduction and notes by S.T. Joshi, *The Collected Jorkens* by Lord Dunsany, introduced and edited by S.T. Joshi, *Tales of War*, edited by Darrell Schweitzer, *The Double Shadow and Other Fantasies* by Clark Ashton Smith, *Songs and Sonnets Atlantean, the Second Series* by Clark Ashton Smith, *Graphic Classics Mark Twain*, edited and published by Tom Pomplun, and Paul Witcover reviews *Alphabet of Thorn* by Patricia A. McKillip and *The Tyrant* by Michael Cisco. In the Artists Gallery, Ari Berk discusses the Ancient Spirit, Modern Voice: The Mythic Journeys Art Exhibition. And in the Games column, Eric T. Baker reviews *Sex and Sorcery*, a supplement to the RPG, *Sorcerer*, *Jet Li: Rose of Honor* for the PS2, *Drakengard* for the PS2, *Wrath Unleashed* for the PS2 and the Xbox, *The Diamond Throne*, a sourcebook for the *Arcana Unearthed Campaign in Dungeons & Dragons*, and the *War of the Worlds Sourcebook*. There is no Past Lives column this issue.

On to the fiction ...

The lead story is "Singing Innocence & Experience" by Sonya Taafe. This one takes place in modern times and revolves around a unicorn that looks like a man. Where the horn should be there is a mark cn his forehead. This unicorn has become bonded to a woman in her twenties who is still a virgin. Throughout the story there is a delicate balance between the woman, the unicorn (who has become a roomate of sorts), and the woman's human love interest. At the same time, she finds the unicorn heartbreakingly beautiful. I rather enjoyed the concept of the unicorn in human form. Art to this one was provided by Brian Horton, which marks his second illustration in the magazine.

Following this we have "Tiny Bells" by Bruce Holland Rogers, which marks his eighth appearance in the magazine. As with most of his RoF tales, this one is a short-short. These are always the hardest sorts of stories to describe without giving away everything, because they're over in a blink. So I'll leave this one as being about displaced dreams seeking a home and let your imagination do the rest. Art to this one was provided by Laurie Harden, which marks her fifteenth illustration in the magazine.

Next up we have "Stalking the Leopard" by Tanith Lee, which marks her twelfth appearance in the magazine. This one takes place in a futuristic city at the height of decadence that mixes in just a touch of noir flavor. It focuses around a woman of high society who has become bored with life. All that changes when a rare fire breaks out in the city. When the protagonist and her friends go to investigate, she spots a striking man walking out of the fire unharmed. Avly (the protogonist) becomes quite attracted to him and takes to following him over the ensuing days. And when she discovers that this man is an assassin, it only heightens her attraction at it all builds toward the climax. Art to this one was provided by John Berkey, which marks his tenth illustration in the magazine.

Then we have "On Windhover Down" by Liz Williams, which marks her sixth appearance in the magazine. This one takes place near an alternate London, where strange and decadent gods are worshipped. When a young girl delivers a head to the worshippers of these gods, she becomes embroiled in far more than she bargained for and must turn to ancient and forgotten forces to save her. Art to this one was provided by Allen Douglas, which marks his fourth illustration in the magazine.

After this we have "Country Life" by Karen D. Fishler. Instead of London, we move to outside of Paris during the time Louis XVII, as a tax collector visits an unmapped county that appears to have never paid its taxes. However, he's not on official business, and plans to earn himself a small fortune through his "collecting." But as such stories go, the collector becomes embroiled in far more than he expected, as he meets the beautiful daughter of the imposing countess he hopes to scam, must deal with the beautiful woman's highly protective brother, unravel the mystery of where this county's gold comes from, and all the while there is some strange and monstrous creature eating the local cows at night. Art to this one was provided by Lori Koefoed, which marks her ninth illustration in the magazine.

Then we have "The Archer" by Ian Donald Keeling. This one also features a female protagonist who happens to be a virgin, this one at age thirty. This one has never even been on a date. But everything changes when she meets a gorgeous man who turns out to be Cupid from Greek mythology. And of course he fires his love arrow and our loveless protagonist feels love at last. But all is not as it seems. It turns out that once upon a time Cupid defied Zeus and took a mortal woman for his lover that Zeus desired for himself. In his wrath, Zeus decreed that their child would never know love. And Cupid has honored that decree ...until now. Art to this one was provided by Michael Kerr, which marks his fifth illustration in the magazine.

Finally we have "Charlie the Purple Giraffe Was Acting Strangely" by David D. Levine. According to Carina Gonzalez's old (and now defunct) slush site, David is a slush survivor. I have to admit that I'm a little puzzled by this. According to David's bio in this issue, he attended the Clarion West Workshop in 2000. My understanding from multiple sources (including Shawna) is that back during Carina's tenure (and before this as well, I believe), graduates from any of the Clarion workshops were automatic passes to Shawna. This practice was discontinued after I took over as assistant editor, although every so often I still encounter the occasional Clarion student under the impression that his or her story should be passed along to Shawna. Regardless, I have no idea how David both attended Clarion but is also considered to be a slush survivor. As to the story itself, it features comic characters, the principle being Charlie the Purple Giraffe. And the reason Charlie has been acting strangely? Quite simply, he has become aware that there are readers. Of course, none of his fellow comic characters believe him. Most of the characters react to him as you might expect, and while everything unfolds inside your mind like a lighthearted cartoon, there is a disturbing undercurrent that grows stronger as the story moves along. This undercurrent manages to strike a nerve, and perhaps others thought so as well, because this piece was reprinted in *Year's Best Fantasy 5*, edited by David Hartwell & Kathryn Cramer, as well as *The*

Mammoth Book of Extreme Fantasy, edited by Mike Ashely. Art to this one was provided by Dirk and Lieve Michaels.

So that wraps up this issue. And my favorite story? The possible slush survivor, "Charlie the Purple Giraffe Was Acting Strangely" by David D. Levine. And my favorite illustration? Allen Douglas's illustration to "On Windohover Down" by Liz Williams.

Originally posted on douglascohen.livejournal.com on September 25th, 2008

Part sixty in my comprehensive retrospective as I read the fiction in *Realms of Fantasy* and offer my thoughts. This time around I'll be discussing the August 2004 issue.

The cover to this one is another movie cover, which marks the magazine's fifth movie cover and the seventh media cover. It features Keira Knightley in her role as Guinevere in the movie, *King Arthur*. Concerning this movie, while I thought some of the actors gave strong performances overall I found this movie rather weak, adding little worthwhile material to the Arthurian mythos.

A rundown of this issue's nonfiction is as follows:

In the Movie/TV column, Resa Nelson covers the aforementioned *King Arthur*. In the Folkroots column, Terri Windling discusses the lore of Little Red Riding Hood. In the books column, Gahan Wilson reviews *Gathering the Bones*, edited by Jack Dann, Ramsey Campbell, and Dennis Etchison, *All Hallows: The Journal of the Ghost Story Society*, edited by Barbara Roden, *Selected Letters of Clark Ashton Smith*, edited by David E. Shultz and Scott Connors, *Gates of Empire and Other Tales of the Crusades* by Robert E. Howard, edited by Paul Herman, and Paul Witcover reviews *Monument* by Ian Graham and *The Fourth Circle* by Zoran Zivkovic. The Past Lives column makes a return this issue, as Anastasiya Samusenska discusses the historical reconstruction of knighthood in the White Castle Festival in Belarus. In the Artists Gallery, Jane Frank discusses the artwork of LesEdwards/Edward Miller. And in the Games column, Eric T. Baker reviews *Ninja Gaiden* for the Xbox, the RPG, *Riddle of Steel*, *Champions of Norrath* for the PS2, *Nightshade* for the PS2, *Blood and Salt* from White Wolf's *Exalted* line, and *Unearthed Arcana*, a supplement to *Dungeons & Dragons*.

On to the fiction ...

The lead story is "The Angel's Daughter" by Jay Lake, which marks his second appearance in the magazine. This one is a short-short that delves into Arabian mythology about a brave lad of the desert who manages to capture the heart of an angel's daughter. This piece would be right at home among the tales of Scheherazade's *One Thousand and One Nights*. Art to this one was provided by Maral Agnerian.

Following this we have "The Smell of Magic" by Mike Lewis. This one is a high fantasy tale about a young man who has been apprenticed to sniff out the magic dwelling in shapeshifters who live among the humans. When I say "sniff" I mean that quite literally. He has an extraordinary sense of smell. If you've ever seen the movie, *Perfume*, it approaches that level. There is a test to sniff out the shapeshifters involving the teenagers in a given village who have come "of age," presumambly because the smell can now be detected. In this particular tale, the protagonist has returned to his village after a couple of years away, and is reuinited with family, friends, and the requisite village love. The writing is nice enough, but everything struck me as rather predicactable and ho-hum ...or so I thought until I reached the end. That made reading this one entirely worthwhile. Art to this one was provided by Heather Hudson.

Then we have "The Water Castle" by Jay Lake, which marks his third appearance in the magazine and his second story in this issue. Back in the June 2000 issue, Nicola Griffith actually had three stories in one issue. However, those stories were loosely connected, and in that respect it was no surprise to see them all published in the same issue. In Jay's case, "The Water Castle" & "The Angel's Daughter" are not connected at all, except through the author. So this would make Jay the first author to have two completely unrelated stories in one issue of RoF.

As to the story itself, it's rather rich in detail. We're introduced to a world where humans were once served by small furry creatures called the Pleasant People. However, concerning this servitude, let's just say it wasn't all gumdrops and lollipops. So eventually, when humans gave birth, the Pleasant People developed a method of creating twins of the newborn babies from the afterbirth. These twins became known as the Poison People, and their presence eventually sparked a war that, come the beginning of the story, has left mankind struggling for its survival. The story itself focuses around a woman, starting in childhood with the death of her father, and it follows her through the years as she becomes mankind's greatest hope for survival. Thanks to her father's experiments before his death, the girl knows how to use a crude form of science to tell the Poison People from the real people. This one skirts the line between high fantasy and science fantasy as the girl rallies humankind through the years. And all the while, she seeks to learn her ultimate destiny, which is somehow connected to a glass egg her father gave to her at his death. I'm leaving lots of juicy details out here, but that's because Jay packed enough into this world to return here and write a novel if he wants to. Art to this one was provided by Scott Grimando, which marks his ninth illustration in the magazine.

Next up is "Words & Music" by Kate Riedel, which marks her fifth appearance in the magazine. It is also the 350th story to be published in *Realms of Fantasy*. This piece features a teenage runaway in need of work. She walks into a bookstore, hoping to sell some textbooks, and ends up accepting a job, complete with a room upstairs. Seems ordinary enough, accept that soon she notices that the bookstore has a habit of having whatever the customer asks for, even if it wasn't on the shelf a moment ago. And of course it makes absolutely no difference if the text has been erased from the face of the earth. There is something cosmic about this bookshop but it's never explained in full. This didn't really bother me, which is a testament to the author as this sort of stuff often drives me nuts. But the people are vehicles to the cosmic function of the bookshop. Those who come looking for these books are meant to find them. Yet while the people serve the will of the bookshop, the employees of the shop seem to pick whom they wish to hire to continue serving. It's all very fascinating, and there's a strong religious undercurrent throughout that kicks this one into another level of thoughtfulness. Art to this one was provided by Chris Cocozza, which marks his third illustration in the magazine.

Then we have "The Right God" by Richard Parks, which marks his fourteenth appearance in the magazine. This one takes a somewhat lighter approach to religion than the previous story, presenting a world where traditional religion has broken down. Instead, new gods seem to be popping up everywhere. Enter Don Lang, an average divorced guy in his forties ...average except for the god called Rockball that has taken up residence in his mirror and has informed Don that his new vocation is to be Rockbottom's prophet. The problem (if this isn't enough) is that Rockbottom has no idea what he is a god *of*. Things are further complicated when Don meets a woman named Amelia who's basically in the same situation he is, only her god is named Stonemother. Thanks to the meddling of their gods, both of them find themselves out of work. With all this time on their hands, they end up joining forces to figure out what the deal is with these mysterious gods, and all the while there is a possible attraction developing between them, complicated by the presence of their gods. Art to this one was provided by Hugo Martin, which marks his third illustration in the magazine.

Following this we have "Elfrither's Ghost" by Kij Johnson, which marks her second appearance in the magazine. This one is a short-short ghost story that takes place in some ancient Roman ruins. I'll steal Shawna's editorial caption to describe this one: "Ghosts are not made of flesh and blood, but they are often made by flesh and blood." Art to this one was provided by Laurie Harden, which marks her sixteenth illustration in the magazine.

The penultimate tale in this issue is "The Laily Worm" by Nina Kiriki Hoffman, which marks her third appearance in the magazine. This story is adapted from the story, "The Laily Worm and the Machrel of the Sea," from *The Child's Ballads*. I had never heard of *The Child's Ballads*, so here is the explanation I stole from Wikipedia: "*The Child Ballads* are a collection of 305 ballads from England and Scotland, and their American variants, collected by Francis James Child in the late 19th century. The collection was published as *The English and Scottish Popular Ballads* between 1882 and 1898 by Houghton Mifflin in ten volumes."

As to the story itself, it deals with a pair of siblings with royal blood. Along with their father and stepmother, they're exiled to an isolated castle in the north that guards against raids from the Norsemen. Everything seems to be going well enough, until the stepmother becomes pregant. Suddenly the children she'd forged such wonderful relationships with have become obstructions to advancing her own blood. So she casts a spell on both children, changing them into their inherent animal forms. The brother becomes a dragon, the sister a macherel. The sister is tossed into the sea and the stepmother forces the brother to guard a mysterious oak tree. The brother is in danger of losing his humanity, until he's visited by his sister, who's learned how to change into human form once each week. When she's there, she cleans her brother and brushes his hair (yup, this dragon has hair), and it brings back memories of his childhood and helps him maintain a semblance of his humanity. The characterization of the dragon is particularly interesting, and everything unfolds rather logically. I've never read the original story, but I get the feeling that Hoffman remained rather true to it, because there's a lot of resonance in this one that strikes the mythic cord deep inside the reader. Art to this one was provided by Peter Ferguson

Finally we have "Falling With Wings" by Devon Monk, which marks her sixth appearance in the magazine. This one has an interesting premise. Winged beings toss their children from the sky when they're still babies or young children and let them fall into the mud around Mount Discard when the children are still wingless. It's believed there is something in the soil that is essential to the children growing their wings when they're older so they can take their place in the sky. There is a tribe of sorts at the base of the mountain, featuring everything from babies to adolescents on the verge of adulthood. Most if not all of them were retrieved from the mud by a man named Setham, who is wingless and helps raise the children until they grow their wings and are ready to jump from Mount Discard and put their wings to use. One of the oldest of the tribe is Dawn, who narrates the story. The time is drawing close when Dawn will seek to take her place in the sky. Only she is rather attracted to Setham. That poses a problem since Sethem is wingless and long past the age of sprouting wings. But there is also more to him than meets the eye. But is it enough for love between the two of them to take wing? Art to this one was provided by Matt Hughes, which marks his second illustration in the magazine.

So that wraps up this issue. And my favorite story? Many worthy candidates, but I must give the honors to "The Laily Worm" by Nina Kiriki Hoffman. And my favorite artwork? Matt Hughes' illustration to "Falling with Wings" by Devon Monk.

Originally posted on douglascohen.livejournal.com on September 30th, 2008

Part sixty-one in my comprehensive retrospective as I read the fiction in *Realms of Fantasy* and offer my thoughts. This time around I'll be slicing and dicing the October 2004 issue, which puts the magazine in its tenth year of publication. In this day and age for speculative fiction in print magazines, ten years is quite the accomplishment.

The cover to this one is by Luis Royo, which marks his twelfth illustration in the magazine. The original illustration was a jigsaw puzzle of 1000 pieces.

There are some tidbits worth noting in this issue's masthead. First, Joe Varda's run as Publisher has drawn to its close. There is no one taking his place in the masthead for this position. Mark Hintz was the publisher before him, and when Joe Varda took over this title, Mark became the Chief Executive Officer. Mark is still the CEO in this issue, and the title of Publisher has been dropped from the masthead. Also, Laura Cleveland's long run as Managing Editor has drawn to a close. Taking her place is Christopher D'Amore. For whatever reason, he's listed as the Assistant Editor, but his duties are those of the Managing Editor. And we're not quite done. Samantha DeTulleo is no longer listed as the Art Director. Strangely, no one else is either. That title is also absent from the masthead. These days, Samantha is listed in the masthead in the exact position in question. So I'm uncertain whether she left and later came back to this position, or if she was here all along and title just got dropped from the masthead for a while.

A rundown of this issue's nonfiction is as follows:

In the Movie/TV column, Resa Nelson coves the movie, *Sky Captain and the World of Tomorrow*. In the Folkroots column, Ari Berk writes about the Dance of the Labyrinth. In the Books column, Gahan Wilson reviews *Gaspard de la Nuit* by Aloysius Bertran (translated and introduced with an introduction and afterword by Donald Sidney-Fryer and forward by by T.E.D. Klein), *Swiftly* by Adam Roberts, *Dead Lines* by Greg Bear, *The Day I Swapped My Dad for Two Goldfish* by Neil Gaiman and illustrated by Dave McKean, and Paul Witcover reviews *Gardens of the Moon* by Steven Erickson, *The Darkness that Comes Before* by R. Scott Bakker, *Novelties &*

Souvenirs by John Crowley, and *Another Green World* by Henry Wessells. In the Artists Gallery, Karen Haber covers the artwork of Daniel Horne. And in the Games column, Eric T. Baker reviews the RPG, *Adventure!*, the video game version of the movie, *Van Helsing*, for the Xbox and PS2, *Shrek 2* for the PC, Xbox, PS2, and GC, *La Pucelle: Tactics* for the PS2, and *Thief: Deadly Shadows* for the PC and Xbox. There is no Past Lives column this issue.

On to the fiction ...

The lead story is "Almost (But Not Quite) Heaven" by Tom Gerencer, which marks his second appearance in the magazine. This one is a humorous tale about a man who's visited by a host of different zany gods that you wouldn't expect to be gods, like the god of hors d'oevres and the god of sushi. It's all one big party until the god of agnosticism arrives. The whole scenario feels rather Lewis Carollesque. Art to this one was provided by Craig McKay.

After this we have "Embers" by Rudi Dornemann. This one marks the first steampunk tale to appear in RoF. The story starts out when a young woman and her father come across a clockwork man in their courtyard in a steam town in a nineteenth America that is starting to develop its railroad systems. Until this point, steam-powered machines have been the prevalent sources of energy and transporation, with things like dirigibles already in existence. The emerging railways are also experimenting with steam, and using the fire of dragons to power many of their devices. The presence of the dragons keeps this one from veering too much into the realm of science fiction. Anyway, the clockwork man they discover isn't on, but the woman and her father manage to wake him by placing in a fire and heating his ceramic skin. Of course, this causes quite the brouhaha in town, since the clockwork man is a product of the rail companies, and the emerging railroads are threatening the business done by steam towns. To complicte matters, the young woman feels an emerging attraction toward the well-spoken and charming clockwork man. Eventually an angry mob shows up, fearing what the clockwork man represents. Mind you, it isn't the theat of machines, but the threat to their livelihood. It all leads up to a poignant climax and ending that deals with the end of childhood, love, loss, and dreams. Art to this one was provided by Lori Koefoed, which marks her tenth illustration in the magazine.

Next up we have "There Are Girls, Green Girls" by Ian McDowell. This one is a YA tale about an adolescent Jewish girl growing up in redneck country (this term being how the narrator desribes this region). She is something of an outcast here, even among the other outcasts. Then she makes friends with the new Chinese girl in town, who is also an outcast. Things take a sharp turn when she learns that her new friend's mother was actually a Chinese forest spirit, and the mother wishes to bring her daughter back to the forest. The catch is that so long as she wishes to stay among the humans, she can. But the call is growing ever stronger. Things come to a head when the two friends (and the hot new boyfriend) go to a nighttime party on a secluded hill ...surrounded by the forest. Art to to this one was provided by Dave Leri, which marks his fourth illustration in the magazine.

Then we have "The Old Woman and the Moon" by Stephen Popkes, which marks his fifth appearance in the magazine. This one draws on Native American mythology. It starts by telling the tale of a magician who falls in love with the moon and devises a spell to bring her down to him so he might take her for his wife. Time passes, so much in fact that the world has forgotten about the moon. A woman eeking out a harsh existence finds herself thrust into the task of returning the moon to her rightful place in the sky, but there is a price to be paid to restore the world to its proper balance, a price that might be too steep to ask of any one person, or as Shawna puts it in her editorial caption: "Sometimes a sacrifice requires you to dig into yourself, but sometimes you have to dig deep into another." Art to this one one was provided by Jesse Guay, presumably the same Jesse Guay listed in the masthead as Graphic Designer.

Following this we have "King Orfeigh" by Ruth Nestvold. This one is based on the medieval tale of Sir Orfeo, a mixture of the Greek myth of Orpheus and Celtic folklore. In this one, the King of the Sidhe has charmed away the human king's wife and is taking her back to his kingdom. But the man is in pursuit, hoping to bring her back to him. But all he can rely on to win her heart back is his music. And surely this isn't enough to overcome the many charms of the King of the Sidhe ...surely? Art to this one was provided by Paul Lee, which marks his ninth illustration in the magazine.

Then we have "The Beast" by Bruce Holland Rogers, which marks his ninth appearance in the magazine. This one is another short-short from

Rogers, about a man who captures a strange beast whose saliva has great curative properties. But the only way to get the Beast to give up its saliva is to make it suffer. Once again I'll steal Shawna's editorial caption to sum this one up: "What would you pay for the health–for the life–of your children and family? Is there any price too high?" Art to this one was provided by Matt Tisdale.*

Finally we have "In a Glass Casket" by Tim Pratt, which marks his sixth appearance in the magazine. This one is a horror piece about a young boy who comes across a glass casket in an alley. Locked inside in the glass casket is a teenage girl, but he can't tell whether she's alive ...until he sees the tears leaking from her closed eyes. Uncertain what to do, he leaves the girl and hurries home before he's late. Ever since Billy's father left, the boy's mom likes him to be home where she can keep an eye on him. But when Billy gets home, there is a strange man over, asking his mother questions about a girl that he's looking for. His mother is acting strangely, as if unaware of what's going on. The man asks Billy about the girl, but Billy lies, saying he doesn't know anything. Later, he sneaks out to rescue the girl, using the tools from his father's toolbox. When he finally frees her, we learn the man looking for her is her father. Her father is overly possessive refusing to let the girl go, going so far as to use his magic to cause his daughter pain to keep her from escaping. But his daughter has magic of her own to evade him, and the chase has been going on for quite some time. It all leads up to a rather horrifying conclusion, between the girl and her father ...as well as Billy and his own mother. Art to this one was provided by Patrick Arrasmith, which marks his thirteenth illustration in the magazine. It was also selected for inclusion in the Editorial section of *Spectrum 12: The Best in Contemporary Fantastic Art.*

So that wraps up this issue. And my favorite story? It was a tough choice, but I have to give the honors to "In a Glass Casket" by Tim Pratt. The ending sent a serious shudder down my spine. And my favorite artwork? Dave Leri's illustration to "There are Girls, Green Girls" by Ian McDowell.

*A little side-story for you that I never included in the original retrospective: while this story was published before I started working with the magazine, one day very early into my tenure with RoF, while going through the slush (yes, I speak of those prehistoric years when editors dealt with paper submissions), I came across a fan letter addressed to Bruce Holland Rogers, addressing this story. There was no email address, so I emailed Shawna, asking what I should do. She basically left up to me, so I emailed Bruce Holland Rogers, explained the situation to him, and typed up the entire letter for his benefit. I always did my best to go the extra mile for RoF authors.

Originally posted on douglascohen.livejournal.com on October 8th, 2008

Part sixty-two in my comprehensive retrospective as I read the fiction in *Realms of Fantasy* and offer my thoughts. This time around it's all about the December 2004 issue.

The cover is another movie cover for Lord of the Rings, our fourth such cover (Elijah Wood is looking mighty anguished). It is the magazine's sixth movie cover and its eighth media cover.

On to the fiction ...

A rundown of this issue's nonfiction is as follows:

In the Movie/TV column, Resa Nelson covers The Lord of the Rings Exhibition. In the Books column, Gahan Wilson reviews *The Faery Reel: Tales From the Twilight Realm*, edited by Ellen Datlow & Terri Windling, *The Captain of the 'Pole Star'* by Arthur Conan Doyle, *I Am Alive and You Are Dead: A Journey into the Mind of Phillip K. Dick* by Emmanuel Carrere, *The Bloody Crown of Conan* by Robert E. Howard, *Year's Best Fantasy 4*, edited by David G. Hartwell & Kathryn Cramer, and Paul Witcover reviews *Iron Council* by China Mieville. In the Folkroots column, Gregory Frost (with Helen Pilinovsky) writes about the inaugural Mythic Journeys Conference in Atlanta, GA, which took place from June 2-6, 2004. The Past Lives column makes its return again as Emma Bull writes about the importance of clothes at historical reenactments. In the Artists Gallery, Ari Berk writes about *Goblins! A Survival Guide and Fiasco in Four Parts* by himself and artist, Brian Froud. And in the Games column, Eric T. Baker reviews the RPG *DragonMech* from White Wolf Publishing, the RPG, *Deliria: Faerie Tales for a New Milennium*, *Front Mission 4* for the PS2, *Sly 2: Band of Thieves* for the PS2, and *Spider-man 2* for the PC. This issue marks the last appearance of the Past Lives column.

On to the fiction ...

The lead story in this one is "The Cardinal's Cats" by Cherith Baldry. This story takes an idea more common to the mystery genre, wherein the story is told through the point of view of the lovable feline whose pluckiness manages to save the day. Set in sixteenth century France, our feline heroine and company (the company being more cats), set out to thwart the machinations of the Cardinal's nephew and his evil witch lover. Considering that this is a fantasy magazine, I found the idea of telling this from the point of view of a cat to be surprisingly refreshing. Art to this one was provided by Craig McKay, which marks his second illustration in the magazine.

After this we have "Sonnets Made of Wood" by Leah Bobet. A glance at the accompanying artwork will bring to mind Robin Hobb's high fantasy trilogy, The Liveship Traders. And while there are indeed some superficial similarities between the two worlds, this story is entirely Leah's own. As to the story itself, the language carried a dark charm that sucked me right in. It tells the tale of a mermaid who has given up her tail to take a human king for a husband. This part is pretty much standard fare when it comes to many a mermaid tale, but the author takes this one in some rather unusual directions, including a reversal of the standard mythology of the mermaid seducing the unsuspecting human. The climax to this one is both horrific and heartbreaking, as it sheds light on a seemingly innocent riddle presented earlier in the tale. Coming back to the art on this one, it was provided by Matt Hughes, which marks his third illustration in the magazine.

Next up we have "The Chamber of Forgetting" by Sarah Prineas, which marks her second appearance in the magazine. This one is a high fantasy tale that starts off by introducing us to a man in excrutiating pain, and having no idea who he is. As the tale unfolds, we gradually learn that he is an assassin from an enemy nation, sent to the kill the king. These particular assassins are particularly deadly even among others of their profession. Their training begins when they're children and they kill their first victim before they turn ten. If they fail at their mission, they're expected to kill themselves. Only this particular assassin was taken prisoner. Besides undergoing some extreme questioning that has left him with scars and mangled fingers, he was also placed in the newly created chamber of forgetting. This chamber causes a loss of memory, and so when we meet the assassin, he's a very different person from the one who tried to kill the king. Instead, he's gentle and unassuming. When negotiations are opened with his home nation, his return is demanded. Everyone knows he'll be killed if he's returned for failing at his mission and not taking his life, and this in turn raises some serious ethical dilemmas: those who placed him in the chamber of forgetting caused this man to change into someone different, with no memories of what he'd done before. Given this, is it right to turn him over for crimes he has no recollection of and no intention of committing when they're the ones who changed him? Good stuff. Art to this one was provided by Hugo Martin, which marks his fourth illustration in the magazine.

Following this we have "The Wild Man" by Caitlin Matthews. This one dips into Arthuriana, but unlike the other tales to appear in this magazine, this one draws on the *Mabinogion*, which shares the stories of Arthur and his court from the Welsh perspective/interpretation. In this one, Arthur and his companions come upon a man more than half wild, haunted by painful memories form his past. Gradually we learn that the Wild Man was forced to watch various tortures inflicted upon his kin that either killed them or left them as rabid as wolves ...and their torturer was one of Arthur's kin. And so Arthur is forced to decide between family and justice. The author sheds some light on her idea in an afterword. To quote part of it: "This is one of the untold stories hidden with Culhwch and Olwen, that great compendium of lost British Celtic tales, one of the oldest stories in the Mabinogion." Art to this one was provided by Paul Lee, which marks his tenth illustration in the magazine.

Then we have "The Secret of Making Brains" by Joe Murphy. This one marks the first of Joe's popular Sprokly tales to appear in the pages of RoF. This is also the first continuing series I've come across that was still being published in our pages when I came aboard. In fact, our latest issue at the time I'm writing this (October 2008) includes a story called "The Horned Toad in the Hubcap," which is set in this universe. As to the story itself, as I've already made abundantly obvious, we're introduced to Sprokly and her family who live in an abandoned town. Grampser is the head of her family ...except this is no ordinary family. Grampser has learned the secrets of words and symbols and other strange powers, and combined with his amazing technical proficiency, he is able to create manikins and imbue them with life. He has created a number of mechanical animals that are more than just mechanical, including a rather unique species of horned toad. Grampser has taught/is teaching these secrets to other members of his family, including some of the created ones like Sprokly. In this tale, Sprokly is trying to figure out the secret of making brains. It takes place during her thirteenth birthday, which is made all the more interesting when they receive an unwanted human visitor who has come to study the horned toads. Sprokly is fascinated by him, as is her brother, who is a real human. And while Grampser wishes to keep this stranger off his property, he also doesn't want anyone leaving. So when Sprokly's brother tries to sneak off with the human visitor, it leads to Sprokly learning the secret of making brains. It also represents the beginning of the end to Sprokly's childhood, as she learns that the world in not entirely black and white. Art to this one was provided by Andrea Wicklund.

Finally we have "Talent" by Laura Ann Gilman, which marks her second appearance in the magazine. This one is a horror tale that takes place in what might be termed as *the* pool hall, because all the best people and all the up-and-comers frequent this spot. Among this group is someone named Eddie. Back in the day, Eddie was the best. But that was a long time ago. A long time ago. But Eddie refuses to acknowledge his time as king of the hill as past, so he clings to an unnatural life (if you can call it that), hardly uttering a word, sitting in the pool hall night after night, watching the pool players come in and out. And when a fourteen-year-old prodigy comes through those doors one night, well, suffice it to say that Eddie isn't pleased. Art to this one was provided by Michael Gibbs, which marks his eleventh illustration in the magazine.

And with these stories read and my write-up of each of them complete, I am happy to announce that I've now read every single story ever published in *Realms of Fantasy*. There are still a couple of issues to go before we reach my time, but I had these issues in my possession and had read the stories before I started these retrospectives. So yeah. I've conquered the mountain ...or part of it anyway. I mean, I still have twenty-three (and counting) retrospectives to go. But now that I've read all the stories, I feel like I can take a breath. I mean, it took me over a year to be able to say I've read everything, so it's been quite a project.

As to the rest of the retrospectives, while I've read everything, don't expect me to spit out the rest of these retrospectives in short order.* First, it takes a while to write these, and now that I've read all the stories I admit some of the fire has gone out of me to continue pumping out these retrospectives, though I do intend to finish the series regardless. I'm just going to be more laid back about it going forward. Second, while I may have read everything, for most of the remaining issues it's been somewhere between one to three years (plus change) since the last time I read their stories. So I'll want to reread all of them before writing the accompanying retrospective to each issue. Lastly—and this just happens to be some coincidental timing—in addition to my work at RoF I'm taking on some new and exciting responsibilities that won't allow me as much time for the retrospectives. So I think it's a safe bet that these retrospectives should continue for at least another half a year.**

So that wraps up this issue, as well as 2004. And my favorite story? "The Chamber of Forgetting" by Sarah Prineas. And my favorite illustration? Matt Hughes' illustration to "Sonnets Made of Wood" by Leah Bobet.

*Prophectic words indeed!

**Considering how long it took me to actually finish the series, this estimate is shall we say a little less prophetic.

Originally posted on douglascohen.livejournal.com on October 9th, 2008

Part sixty-three in my comprehensive retrospective as I read the fiction in *Realms of Fantasy* and offer my thoughts, right up to the present. This time around I'll be discussing the February 2005 issue.

I know it's been a while since the last time I posted one of these. As I mentioned in my last retrospective, after getting through last issue it meant I had read every story we've ever published, and I lost some of the fire to write the remaining retrospectives. But I do want to finish these retrospectives. I just needed to get away from them for a little while to recharge the batteries for this final stretch. Reading all the stories was a rewarding if sometimes exhausting experience, but there is work that still remains before this project is done.

And with that said ...

The cover to this one is by Matt Stewart. It's another Elric cover, the third of its kind. It was originally a private commission, but after RoF ran it as the cover it was nominated for a 2006 Chesley Award for Cover Illustration, Magazine.

A rundown of this issue's nonfiction is as follows:

In the Movie/TV column, Resa Nelson covers the *Elektra* movie. In the Folkroots column, Terri Windling discusses James M. Barrie. In the Books column, Gahan Wilson reviews *In the Night Room* by Peter Straub, *Sticks and Stones* by Peter Kuper, *The Fear Planet and Other Unusual Destinations (The Reader's Bloch, Volume One)*, volume one in a series collecting Robert Bloch stories, and Paul Witcover reviews *Jonathan Strange & Mr. Norrell* by Susanna Clark, *The Charnel Prince* by Greg Keyes, and *In Lands That Never Were: Tales of Sword and Sorcery* from *The Magazine of Fantasy & Science Fiction*, edited by Gordon Van Gelder. In the Artists Gallery, Ari Berk discusses the Duirwaigh Gallery. And in the Games column, Eric T. Baker reviews *Fable* for the Xbox, the board game, *Settlers of Catan*, *Star Wars Battlefront* for the PC, Xbox, and PS2, the *Dungeons & Dragons* campaign setting, *Eberron*, *Blood Will Tell* for the PS2, and *Gungrave: Overdrive* for the PS2.

On to the fiction ...

The lead story is "Returning My Sister's Face" by Eugie Foster. According to her old slush site (which is now defunct), this is one of Carina Gonzalez's slush survivors. As to the story, this one is an Asian fantasy dealing with a man whose family has little and is dependent on the kindness of a local lord while the protagonist himself serves as one of the lord's soldiers. Bad luck is associated with the family, leaving the protagonist's sister unmarried. However, a stroke of good fortune takes place in this regard, and the family's luck seems to be improving ...until their sickly mother takes a turn for the worse. On her deathbed, she makes her son give his word of honor to return the missing half of his sister's face. His sister's face is fine, but ultimately the two of them decide it will do no harm for him to give his word and let their mother die in some measure of peace. Given the title, I'm sure it comes as no surprise that the harmless promise proves to have great weight, as the protagonist finds his sister horrifically drowned in the river for adultery, her face so bloated and ruined that half of it seems to be missing. And so his promise comes into play as he seeks to unravel the mysterious circumstances surrounding her death. This piece also appeared as podcast 004 on the *Pseudopod* website. Art to this one in RoF was provided by Allen Douglas, which marks his fifth illustration in the magazine.

Following this we have "All Fish and Dracula" by Liz Williams, which marks her seventh appearance in the magazine. In this piece, it is the night of Samhain. As you might expect, people are out in force, many of them dressed in costumes. But on the night of Samhain there are dark forces about. Things can return from the dead ...from the depths ...including malevolent fish? Perhaps. Art to this one was provided by Michael Kerr, which marks his sixth illustration in the magazine.

Then we have "Fir Na Tine" by Sandra McDonald, which marks her second appearance in the magazine. This piece starts off with an adolescent girl on vacation with her family. While there, she runs into a boy her own age with the ability to create bits of flame. The boy—rakish lad that he is—sneaks a kiss from the protagonist before disappearing into the crowds. The sensation delivered by this fiery kiss is so overwhelming that the protagonist ends up spending a good deal of her life searching for this experience again. Her search yields mixed results, but the story did yield a reprint in *Best New Paranormal Romance*, edited by Paula Guran. I'd also like to take this opportunity to award this story the unofficial title of

"Realms of Fantasy's Steamiest Story Ever." Art to this one was provided by John Picacio, which marks his sixth illustration in the magazine.

After this we have "Crab Apple" by Patrick Samphire, which marks his second appearance in the magazine. This one is a young adult piece about a teenage boy whose father is dying from cancer. At the same time, he finds himself sucked into a strange adventure as he must rescue an odd girl who has eaten a cursed crab apple from a fey living inside a tree. It's quite a blend of the fantastic with grim reality, and it was selected for inclusion in *Year's Best Fantasy* 6, edited by David Hartwell & Kathryn Cramer. It was also appeared as podcast 056 on the *Pseudopod* website. Art to this one was provided by Melissa Ferreira, which marks her fourth illustration in the magazine.

Next up is "The Good Doctor" by Melissa Lee Shaw. This is a piece of horror fiction that deals with vampires in a rather unusual manner. It takes place in a village in Bolivia, where the lone doctor is a vampire ...and everyone knows it ...and everyone is fine with it. In exchange for medical treatment these people can only dream about, the doc merely requires what all vampires do: blood. It's a bargain these people are more than willing to make. But everything becomes threatened when a foreigner receives medical treatment and sees far more than she is supposed to. Art to this one was provided by Web Bryant, which marks his twentieth illustration in the magazine. This makes him the first artist to have twenty illustrations in the magazine.

Finally we have "Peas and Carrots" by Michael Canfield. This one skirts along the line of metafiction as a nameless character without lines in a play dares to want more when he falls in love the female lead. But to make such a dream come true, it involves going against the script. I haven't read too much fiction of this sort, although at times I was reminded of "Six Characters in Search of an Author." Art to this one was provided by Peter Ferguson, which marks his second illustration in the magazine.

So that wraps up this issue. And my favorite story? Some great choices, but I'm going with "Fir Na Tine." And not just because of the steaminess—it's a solid tale! And my favorite artwork? Matt Stewart's cover illustration.

Originally posted on douglascohen.livejournal.com on January 13th, 2009

Part sixty-four in my comprehensive retrospective as I read the fiction in *Realms of Fantasy* and offer my thoughts. This time around I'll be discussing the April 2005 issue.

This marks the first retrospective I've done since Sovereign Media announced that RoF was closing up shop. In my last retrospective, I'd mentioned that it had been a while since I'd done one and wanted to change that. This was indeed the plan. Then the news broke about RoF. Since then, I haven't really been in the mood to write one of these. But it's been over a month now, and almost two months since my last retrospective. So it's about time I do another. Even though the magazine has ceased publication, I do intend to finish this retrospective series. I've come this far, so why not? I'm not going to hold myself to any sort of timetable, though I'll *try* to do more than one every two months or so. And with that said, let's go to it.

The cover to this one is by Kinuko Craft, which marks her second illustration in the magazine. It depicts Eleanor of Aquitaine. My research suggests she put out some book or calendar featuring images of Eleanor of Aquitaine and that this is one of them, but I was unable to track down the particulars.

A rundown of this issue's nonfiction is as follows:

In the Movie/TV column, Resa Nelson covers the TV series, *Lost*. In the Folkroots column, Kristen McDermott discusses superstition in Western theater. In the Books column, Gahan Wilson reviews *The Book of Ballads*, illustrated by Charles Vess, *The Dry Salvages* by Caitlin R. Kiernan, *The Year's Best Fantasy and Horror, Seventeenth Annual Collected Edition*, edited by Ellen Datlow and Kelly Link & Gavin Grant, *Bad Magic* by Stephan Zielinski, and Paul Witcover reviews *The Wizard, Book Two of the Wizard Knight* by Gene Wolfe, and *Shadowmarch, Volume 1* by Tad Williams. In the Artists Gallery, Karen Haber covers the art of Gary Gianni. And in the Games section, Eric T. Baker reviews *Bloodlines* for the PC, *DOA Ultimate* for the Xbox, *Ghost in the Shell: Stand Alone Complex* for the the PS2, the MMORPG, *World of Warcraft*, the MMORPG, *Everquest II*, and the *Dungeons & Dragons Eberron* campaign source book *Sharn: City of Towers*.

On to the fiction ...

The lead story in this issue is "The Vampire Kiss" by Gene Wolfe, which marks his fifth appearance in the magazine. It should come as no surprise that Wolfe is bringing his own unique storytelling approach to this tale, meaning there is much that is left for the reader to puzzle out. This was a story I needed to reread, not just because the details had become rather fuzzy, but also because I didn't fully puzzle it out the first time I read it. I'm happy to say that this time I had a better handle on the tale. On the surface, someone is relating this tale as told to him by a recent orphan. Grief, sadness, and vampiric doings factor in. Seems simple enough. But the last two paragraphs put the story in a very different light (this would be the part I failed to notice the first time), because you come to realize that this is a story about vampires in the world of Oliver Twist. Art to this one was provided by J.K. Potter, which marks his eighth illustration in Realms.

Next up we have "The Wooden Baby" by Graham Edwards. This one marks the first of a number of tales Graham would publish with us concerning his supernatural detective. The background of the detective is rather mysterious (even his name isn't revealed). He has an office where people seem to find him accidentally, but the reality is that these people are finding him because these are the cases he's supposed to take. He has a medley of supernatural weapons on hand, and also a special coat he uses in this and his future tales; turning it inside out can change its material to suit his purposes. In this particular tale, the detective must solve the case of a human baby who has been replaced by a wooden one. The wooden baby doesn't move or cry or eat or anything else a typical baby does, but it is alive because it has a faint heartbeat and faint breath. Does the detective solve the mystery? Well, do you think Shawna would keep buying stories about a detective who screws up the case the first time she reads about him? Art to this one was provided by Michael Komarch.

Following this we have "Death, the Devil, and the Lady in White" by Richard Parks, which marks his fifteenth appearance in the magazine. The Lady in White in this one is a "beautiful and terrible spirit" who dwells in a pond near the underworld. Each year, she lures a number of unsuspecting men to their demise when they come too close to the pond. One man, John Alby, has fallen in love with the Lady, but he is more practical than most, and hence still alive. He'll approach the lake as close as he dares, hoping to catch a glimpse of his ladylove, resigned to the fact that this is what he'll have to settle for. But all this changes when John is approached by a man who claims he's Death. Death claims he has a way for John to win the love of the Lady in White. From here, what seems like one man's unusual quest for love actually ends up being a love triangle between Death, the Devil, and the Lady in White, with John Alby no more than a pawn in a game that has been going on for a very long time. Art to this one was provided by Scott Grimando, which marks his tenth illustration in the magazine.

Then we have "The Language of Moths" by Christopher Barzak, which marks his second appearance in the magazine. This one is a tale about adolescence, love, and the barriers and bridges of language. Eliot is an awkward adolescent who is being dragged off with his family to go camping, so that his entomologist father can search for a new species of moth that glows pink and orange. Also along for the ride is Eliot's older sister, Dawn, who is afflicted with a rather unique strain of autism. She never speaks, but when other talk she perceives the words as silvery bubbles. Some of these bubbles she pops for fun. Others she swallows. When the ones she swallows reach her stomach, it fills Dawn with music. Early on, we learn that Dawn believes if she swallows enough bubbles she'll be able to understand them one day. Dawn's isolation is rather obvious, but Eliot is also suffering his own brand of isolation, the sort brought on by an adolescence filled with resentment (much of it over having to constantly babysit his sister), uncertainy, and confusion. Over the course of the story, their two stories come to intersect. Eliot meets a boy in town named Roy and discovers his sexuality. Meanwhile, he notices that his sister displays an uncanny ability around insects, seemingly making them do simple tricks. In reality, Dawn is able to communicate with them through her gifts, but for much of the story Eliot is too involved with his feelings and needs to bother puzzling this out. Things continue building to a head, as Eliot discovers his crush on Roy is far from black and white, and Dawn uses her gift to communicate with the moth that her father is searching for. Along the way, these two siblings help bring each other out of their respective isolations. This story was longlisted for the 2006 Locus Award for Best Novelette. It was nominated for the 2007 Nebula Award for Best Novelette, and it was the winner of the 2007 Gaylactic Spectrum Award for Best Short Fiction, making it the first RoF story to win this award. Art to this one was provided by Eric Dinyer, which marks his fifth illustration in the magazine.

After this we have "Blackthorn and Nettles" by Liz Williams, which marks her eighth appearance in the magazine. This one is a dark tale, drawing on Welsh lore. Its main thrust is exploring the thin line between love and hate and demonstrating how shackled together these two emotions are. The story revolves around Creirwy, the narrator, her love interest Gwydion, and his sister Arian. While Arian is married, there is something deep and important developing between Creirwy and Gwydion, and Arian is none-to-pleased about their relationship. Gradually we learn that Gwyidion and Arian's relationship has an incestuous strain. A rather awkward relationship develops between Creirwy and Arian, one equal parts hate and love. The emotions these two feel toward each other run so deep that it ends up defying all probability by creating life, life not produced through consummation, but rather through the meeting and joining of love and hate. Art to this one was provided by Eric Deschamps.

Next up is "Dancing in the Light" by Jay Lake, which marks his fourth appearance in the magazine. This piece is a short-short about a young girl experiencing the magic of puberty, some of the everyday variety, but also a nice helping of the fantastical sort. Art to this one was provided by Matt Tisdale, which marks his second illustration in the magazine.

Finally we have "Christmas Apples" by Margaret Ronald. According to her old (and now defunct) slush site, this is one of Carina Gonzalez's slush survivors. This one is a contemporary Christmas tale about a woman who is part of a circle of magicians who has grown jaded toward Christmas. When she runs into a strange man who offers to pay her to drive him to a mysterious destination, she agrees. Along the way, we come to learn that her passenger has been seeking this destination for a very long time, and it falls to this woman to help him find it. In the process of doing this, she rediscovers the magic of Christmas. Art to this one was provided by Chris Cocozza, which marks his fourth illustration in the magazine.

So that wraps up this issue. And my favorite story? A lot of contenders, but I have to give the nod to "The Language of Moths" by Christopher Barzak. It's a beautiful tale. And my favorite artwork? Michael Komarch's illustration to "The Wooden Baby" by Graham Edwards.

Originally posted on douglascohen.livejournal.com on March 7ᵗʰ, 2009

Part sixty-five in my comprehensive retrospective as I read the fiction in *Realms of Fantasy* and offer my thoughts. This time around I'll be discussing the June 2005 issue.

This marks the first retrospective I'm doing since Warren Lapine bought the magazine and I subsequently received my promotions to nonfiction editor and art director. I suppose this is somewhat fitting, since it was while this issue was out that I joined the RoF team, back on May 10, 2005, which makes for a bit of symmetry at work here with these retrospectives. As you might expect, going forward I'll be able to offer more insights about the magazine.

Now before I get into the actual issue itself, this seems like the perfect time to discuss how I came to work at RoF. Those already familiar with this story should feel free to skip ahead, as I don't imagine I'll be sharing too much new information. But back in April of 2005 I was perusing Ralan.com to learn about the latest developments in the short fiction market. Under the *Realms of Fantasy* listing, I happened to notice that my predecessor, Carina Gonzalez, had stepped down from her position. There was no mention of a replacement. I believe a couple of days went by before I said to myself, "I should apply for that position. I can do that." At this time I was unpublished, and without previous editorial experience. I'd attended the Odyssey Writing Workshop, as well as Orson Scott Card's workshop, and that was pretty much it. But I figured I had nothing to lose, so I fired off an email to Shawna McCarthy that included a cover letter and resume. Imagine my surprise when I received an email from her just hours later about setting up an interview. So we swapped a few additional emails, set up the particulars, and when the day came around, I drove down to her house in NJ (the first and only time I've been there).

I'd say the interview lasted about forty-five minutes. Mostly we discussed the genre of fantasy, the magazine, and her expectations regarding the position. At the end of the interview Shawna decided to bring me aboard on a trial basis. She sent me home with about 100 manuscripts (ninety-seven to be exact) and some basic instructions to follow as I started slushing. I remember her telling me to be very picky about what I passed along because there was so much slush! When I asked her how long I had to get through everything, she laughed and said, "A month."

I should pause to add that I later learned that when I contacted Shawna, Carina was collecting resumes to pass along to her through the now-defunct Rumor Mill website. I had no idea about this at the time, so I guess I accidentally cut in line. When I asked Shawna about this some months later, she told me that she was waiting and waiting for those resumes and all the while the slush was piling up more and more. And then I emailed her, and she really needed someone, so she decided to bring me in for an interview. Gotta love timing. I later heard (I forget from who) that this pissed some people off (never learned who), but it was in complete innocence on my part. I wasn't visiting the Rumor Mill at that time. Although honestly? I'd do it all again.

But back to those ninety-seven manuscripts. Not wanting to leave anything to chance, I finished everything in two weeks. In that first batch, I didn't pluck anything I actually considered slush. I passed along a couple of pieces that these days I probably *would* consider slush, but at that time I was still figuring out what constituted an automatic pass. Anyway, Shawna must have been happy enough with the job I did, because the next time we met up, she gave me everything else she hadn't passed along last time (plus whatever had built up in the interim) for a grand total of 464 manuscripts. By far, it was the biggest batch I've ever had to deal with. And because I was still very new to my position at this time, my slushing process was much slower.

CONFESSION: I've never even told Shawna about this one. It was a lot of work to get through that batch, and I did it as fast as I could in the hopes of making my life easier going forward. At our next slush transfer, my spirit was almost broken. As Shawna passed along crate after crate of new slush, the thought running through my head over and over was "It's too much! It's *too* much!" To my untrained eye, it looked like the same amount of slush as before. A big part of me worried that I'd bitten off more than I could chew. But when I got home, much to my relief, I discovered that after I'd sorted and organized everything, this new batch was in fact 301 manuscripts, a difference of 160+. After that I was able to relax, and soon enough we were caught up in terms of our response times. And Shawna had been my boss ever since. Now, finally, let's discuss the June 2005 issue ...

A while back, I mentioned that during my interview with Shawna, she asked me if I'd read any issues of RoF. I said, "A couple," which was true. I'd read the August 1997 issue and the August 2000 issue. Shawna wanted me to read some more recent issues, so in addition to sending me off with my ninety-seven manuscripts of slush, she also sent me home with two issues of RoF. One was the April 2004 issue. This was the other issue, which again was the current issue at the time of my interview.

The cover to this one features Orlando Bloom, striking a pose in the movie, *Kingdom of Heaven* (thumbs down). This marks the magazine's seventh movie cover and its ninth media cover.

Although I came aboard to replace Carina, she was still a part of this issue when it came out and is appropriately still listed in the masthead.

A rundown of this issue's nonfiction is as follows:

The Folkroots column is by Ellen Steiber, dealing with the traditional lore behind gems and precious stones. Movie columnist Resa Nelson discusses *The Kingdom of Heaven* as well as the fine line between fantasy and horror movies. Book reviewer Gahan Wilson reviews the following books: *One for Sorrow, Two for Joy* by Clive Woodall, *Shadow Kingdoms: The Weird Works of Robert E. Howard, Volume 1*, and *Acquainted with the Night*, edited by Barbara and Christopher Roden, while Paul Witcover covers the following: *The Warrior Prophet*, Book Two in the in *The Prince of Nothing* series by R. Scott Bakker, *In the Palace of Repose* by Holly Phillips, and *Banewreaker*, Volume One of *The Sundering*, by Jacqueline Carey. In the Artists Gallery, columnist Karen Haber covers artist Tony DiTerlizzi. And in the Games Column, Eric T. Baker reviews a medley of games: *Star Wars: Knights of the Old Republic II: the Sith Lords, Half Life 2, Lord of the Rings: The Battle for Middle Earth, The Rise of the Kasai, Ars Magica*, and *The Masque of the Red Death: Adventures on Gothic Earth*.

On to the fiction ...

The lead story in this one is "The Storyteller's Wife" by Eugie Foster, which marks her second appearance in the magazine. According to Carina's old slush site (which is now defunct), this is one of her slush survivors. However, back in the February 2005 issue, I said "Returning my Sister's Face" by Eugie Foster was a slush survivor. Standard operating procedure at RoF is if your slush story is published in the magazine, you become an automatic pass the next time you submit something. So why is it different here? I don't know exactly. All I can think is that Shawna had both stories in her possession when she did a buying round. Eugie's quote on the site seems to indicate that Carina passed both along. I'm guessing Shawna has forgotten the details behind this one, so it seems only Eugie and Carina know the story behind these stories. Regardless, it seems Eugie is the only author to ever be published in RoF to have two separate slush tales.

As to the story itself, this one is about a woman whose parapalegic husband is abducted by the creatures of faerie so that he can spin tales for them to keep their kingdom thriving. Only in their kingdom, he has the use of his legs again. So when his wife follows him out of love in order to bring him home, it creates more dilemmas than she expected. Art to this one was provided by Heather Hudson, which marks her second illustration in the magazine.

Next up we have "Deliverance" by Jim C. Hines. Carina's old slush site indicates that this is another one of her slush survivors. I've now exhausted all of the slush survivors listed on her site, though I do know about another one we both share (I'll get into that in a future issue). So it seems that Carina left the magazine with a bang. As to Jim's story, this one is about a man who lost his wife a few years earlier. Only she's still around as a ghost. And as is the case with some ghosts in some stories, this ghost can touch him somewhat. Only Jim decided to take things a little further by making it possible for them to have ghost-sex (for lack of a better term). And at the beginning of the story, we learn that the man's ghost-wife is pregnant. Yikes! Or should I say boo! Art to this one was provided by Patrick Arrasmith, which marks his fourteenth illustration in the magazine.

Then we have "Foxtails" by Richard Parks, which marks his sixteenth appearance in the magazine. This also marks the first of Richard's popular Lord Yamada tales, a series of tales about a minor lordling named Yamada, who undertakes various strange assignments in medieval Japan. In this particular tale, Yamada is hired by an important nobleman to track down his runaway wife who actually turned out to be a fox-spirit in disguise. And while the lord still loves his fox-spirit wife, what he truly wants back is their son, whom she seems to have absconded with. But all is not as it seems, as Lord Yamada soon discovers. Art to this one was provided by Paul Lee, which marks his eleventh illustration in the magazine.

After this we have "Midnight Hunt" by Susan Yi. This one is about a young adolescent who is bullied by his older bigger half-brother. His older brother seems to take after their father, who is a stern man that is interested in his inhuman midnight hunts. Eventually the bully gets a dose of his own medicine, but whether this is for the best is a darker and much more disturbing question. Art to this one was provided by Ken Meyer Jr.

Next up is "Moments of Grace" by Aaron Shutz. This one is a touching tale about an old man and his Memory Book. This man has been alive a long time, and he uses pages from his Memory Book to help those in need. But each time he uses one of those pages, the memory is lost to him. But there is always one memory he has saved and treasured, and through it all he's managed not to use it. But it just might be that this time around he'll need to use that special memory to help those in need. But can he bring himself to do it? It's one of the more touching tales that's been published in RoF. Art to this one was provided by Joe Kovach.

Finally we have "Stones in Winter" by Karen D. Fishler, which marks her second appearance in the magazine. This one is a piece of Norse mythology, dealing with the valkyries who come and take the fallen heroes from the battlefield and bring them back to Valhalla. Only they only bring the fallen men back to Valhalla. In this piece, a woman dares defy the laws of the valkyries by following them to the halls of Valhalla to bring back her dead love that recently fallen in battle. Art to this one was provided by Eric Deschamps, which marks his second illustration in the magazine.

So that waps up this issue, and one of the lengthiest retrospectives to date.* And my favorite story? I must give the nod to "Moments of Grace" by Aaron Shutz. And my favorite artwork? I'll give the nod to the Heather Hudon's illustration to "The Storyteller's Wife" by Eugie Foster.

Originally posted on douglascohen.livejournal.com on April 19th, 2009

Part sixty-six in my comprehensive retrospective as I read the fiction in *Realms of Fantasy* and offer my thoughts. This time around I'll be slicing and dicing the August 2005 issue.

The cover to this one is by Luis Royo, which marks his thirteenth appearance in the magazine. I was unable to determine the origins of this illustration.

At the time I joined RoF the current issue was June 2005, but my predecessor, Carina Gonzalez, was listed in the masthead since that issue was already out. So while I've been with the magazine since May of '05, the August '05 issue is the first one to be released in which I was a part of the team (even if Carina is still listed in the masthead instead of yours truly).

A rundown of this issue's nonfiction is as follows:

In the Movie/TV column, Resa Nelson covers *War of the Worlds*, starring Tom Cruise, and a summer fantasy film preview is provided by Christopher D'Amore, a former managing editor at the magazine. Folkroots is handled by Heinz Insu Fenkl, who writes about fire in mythology. Gahan Wilson and Paul Witcover handle book reviews this issue, with Gahan covering *The Overnight* by Ramsey Campbell, *Black Blossom* by Boban Knezevic, *The Book of Dreams* by Catherynne M. Valente, and the hoax magazine, *Weird Trails*. Paul provides additional reviews of *The Dark Mirror, Book One of the Bridei Chronicles* by Juliet Marillier, *The White Mare, Book One of the Dalraida Trilogy* by Jules Watson, and *Three Hands for Scorpio* by Andre Norton. This issue's Artists Gallery features an article by Irene Gallo, Art Director of Tor Books, wherein she discusses how select pieces of art from *Spectrum*—an annual book collecting the best fantastical art—are on display at the Society of Illustrators. And in the Games column, Eric T. Baker reviews *Jade Empire* for the Xbox, *Untold Legends: Brotherhood of the Blade* for the Sony PSP, a pair of Japanese strategy RPGs in *Atelier Iris: Eternal Mana* and *Stella Deus: The Gate of Eternity*, the Whitewold RPG, *Werewolf of the Forsaken*, and the *Dungeons & Dragons* supplement, *Races of Destiny*.

Onto the fiction ...

The lead story is "The Penultimate Riddle" by Richard Parks, which marks his seventeenth appearance in the magazine. This one draws on Greek mythology as we are introduced to a poet who is seeking more out of life than merely to live. To achieve this goal he decides to court the deadly sphinx. Art to this one was provided by Randy Gallegos.

Next up we have "A Statement in the Case" by Theodora Goss, which marks her third appearance in the magazine. This story was reprinted in *Year's Best Fantasy & Horror 19*, edited by Ellen Datlow and Kelly Link & Gavin Grant. The story itself is set in modern times and draws heavily on Hungarian mythology, as a man tells his story to a detective about a friend of his from the old country and the strange creatures from his homeland that his friend's wife was selling. Art to this one was provided by Andrea Wicklund, which marks her second illustration in the magazine.

Then we have "The Queen's Wood" by Josh Rountree, which marks his second appearance in the magazine. This is a piece of high fantasy, and like Josh's first story in RoF ("The King's Wood"), it is a tale in the world of the creature known as the Turion. In this world, every so often the Turion must be slain to preserve the life of the king, which will allow the land to prosper. It is the Offered who must undertake this task, and afterward spill his own blood ...only this time the Offered is a woman, which has never happened before. As in "The King's Wood," we never actually see the battle with the Turion. Instead, we read about the Offered and the Witness (who always accompanies the Offered) passing through the Queen's Wood on their way to find the Turion. Inside, they must resist the lies and temptations offered by the wood's great enchantress before moving along to their final objective, and matters of faith and tradition are called into great question in the process. Art to this one was provided by Mike Kerr, which marks his eighth appearance in the magazine.

Following this we have "A Bedtime Tale for the Disenchanted" by Amy Beth Forbes. This piece is extremely short and does not have an accompanying illustration. As to the piece itself, it deals with a young woman who tries to manipulate and love to her advantage, only to learn it cannot be controlled.

After this we have "The Secret to Broken Tickers" by Joe Murphy, which marks his second appearance in the magazine. This is another one of Joe's Sprokly tales, which deals with a young wooden girl given life by her maker. There are certainly some Pinocchio overtones here, but Joe makes the characters and world his own, as evidenced by the fact that it was reprinted in *Year's Best Fantasy 2006*, edited by Rich Horton. Anywyay, in this piece Sprokly's real-life (i.e flesh and blood) brother brings a girl home who seems to love him and claims she can get help for Ma's ailing heart, but she is only interested in learning the family secrets, of which there are many (including Sprokly). Artwork is provided by Eric Dinyer, which marks his sixth illustration in the magazine.

Then we have "Countless Screaming Argonauts" by Chris Lawson. This is another piece drawing heavily on Greek mythology as well as history, as it takes the Colussus of Rhodes, constructed by the legendary architect Chares, the hero Jason of Golden Fleece fame, and the Cyclops, Polyphemus, blind for some years now thanks to Odysseus, and weaves all three of these seemingly disparate elements into a seamless tale of adventure and mythological heroism. Artwork to this one was provided by Allen Douglas, which marks his sixth appearance in the magazine.

Finally we have "When the Dragon Falls" by Patrick Samphire, which marks his third appearance in the magazine. This one is a short young adult piece about an adolescent whose parents are engaging in affairs, causing him to give up his childhood beliefs, and possibly much more in the bargain. Artwork to this one was provided by Josh Bradigan.

So that wraps up this issue. And my favorite story? I declare a tie, between "The Queen's Wood" by Josh Rountree and "Countless Screaming Argonauts" by Chris Lawson. And my favorite artwork? I'm going with the Luis Royo cover.

Originally posted on douglascohen.livejournal.com on June 12th, 2009

Part sixty-seven in my comprehensive retrospective as I read the fiction in *Realms of Fantasy* and offer my thoughts, right up to the present. This time around I'll be ruminating on the October 2005 issue, which puts the magazine in its eleventh year of publication.

The cover to this one is by Victoria Francés. While I was able to confirm this was a reprint, I was unable to determine the origins of this illustration.

There are a number of changes to the masthead this issue. First, while the June 2005 issue was the last one for Carina Gonzalez, her name was not removed from the masthead as Editorial Intern until this issue. Strangely enough, my name doesn't show up in her place. You would think it would have by now, not just because I'd been with the magazine three months at this point, but also because this issue Christopher D'Amore is listed as the Managing Editor. In the last issue, he was listed as the Assistant Editor. I remember asking Shawna about this, since it was agreed that Assistant Editor would be my title, and she was as puzzled about this as I was. So while they fixed his title this issue, I was left waiting. There are some other changes worth noting as well. Jesse Guay is no longer listed as Graphic Designer. Indeed, this title has been dropped entirely. But the title of Art Director makes its return this issue, in the form of Mae Ariola. Also, while I never listed Copy Editors in the past I'll note that with this issue the title of Copy Editor has also been eliminated from the masthead.

A rundown of this issue's nonfiction is as follows:

For the Movie/TV column, Resa Nelson covers *The Cave and The Corpse Bride*. Terri Windling handles the Folkroots column with an article about tricksters, messengers, and familiars. In the Books column, Gahan Wilson reviews *Four and Twenty Blackbirds* by Cherie Priest (I remember Cherie's editor, Liz Gorinsky, contacted me via email to track down an early review of this), *The Book of Renfield–the Gospel of Dracula* by Tim Lucas, and *Glass Soup* by Jonathan Carroll, while Paul Witcover reviews *Lord Byron's Novel: the Evening Land* by John Crowley, and *The Prodigal Troll* by Charles Coleman Finlay. In the Artists Gallery, Karen Haber covers artist Jon Foster. And in the Games column, Eric T. Baker reviews *Area 51* for the

PC, Xbox, and PS2, *Arc the Lad: End of Darkness* for the PS2, *Samurai Western* for the PS2, *Dungeon Master's Guide II* for *Dungeons & Dragons*, and *The Secret of Zir'An Core Gamebook* from Paragon Games via White Wolf.

On to the fiction ...

The lead story is "Robots and Falling Hearts" by Tim Pratt and Greg Van Eekhout. This marks Tim's seventh appearance in the magazine, and Greg's first. This one is a zany tale about robots, but it is most definitely a fantasy tale as opposed to science fiction. In this story, a young man who is seeking to unravel the riddle of the plague of robots afflicting mankind stumbles upon the cause of it all, a young woman who can shape reality with her thoughts. This story was reprinted in *Year's Best Fantasy 6*, edited by David Hartwell and Kathryn Cramer. It is also available for listening as podcast 031 on the *Escape Pod* website (which I'll note tends to podcast science fiction, so make of that what you will). Art to this one in RoF was provided by Peter Ferguson, which marks his third illustration in the magazine.

Next up we have "At the Queen's Hotel" by Kate Reidel, which marks her sixth appearance in the magazine. In this one, we meet a man who has come by a guitar under somewhat dark circumstances. Only this one is no ordinary guitar. It insists on being played, and it's very particular about the sorts of venues it wants to be played in. An interesting take on the old blues crossroads story. Art to this one was provided by Web Bryant, which marks his twenty-first illustration in the magazine.

Then we have "At the Top of the Black Stairs" by Darrell Schweitzer, which marks his third appearance in the magazine. This one reads like a story straight out of the golden age of *Weird Tales Magazine*, as a great king is brought back from the oblivion of death to carry out the wishes of Death and Time as the two engage in a cosmic game of chess. Who wins the game is another story entirely. Art to this one was provided by Paul Lee, which marks his twelfth illustration in the magazine.

Following this we have "Dead Wolf in a Hat" by Graham Edwards, which marks his second appearance in the magazine. And speaking of seconds, this story also marks the second appearance of Graham's long-running supernatural gumshoe detective tales in RoF. In this one, a wolf in a hat shows up dead on the detective's doorstep, and a dame from his past shows up a little later, and both of them are bringing nothing but trouble. That part is obvious to said detective. Figuring out just what in the world is going on is another matter entirely. Art to this one was provided by Ken Meyer, Jr., and marks his second illustration in the magazine.

After this we have "The Ecology of Fairie" by David Levine, which marks his second appearance in the magazine. In this one, a young teenager's mom is in the hospital fighting for her life due to a case of leukemia, but there are problems at home as well. The local ecology is being thrown out of whack as some evil fairies are killing the local frogs. The solution to this problem proves to be both elegant and logical. Art to this one was provided by Andrea Wicklund, which marks her third illustration in the magazine.

And finally we have "The Rain God" by Way Jeng. This one is a rather hilarious tale about a forgotten rain god in modern times who befriends the local Joe Schmo, and the god's somewhat maniac attempts to make a religious comeback by convincing his newfound friend to start worshipping him. Art to this one was provided by Joe Kovach, which marks his second illustration in the magazine.

So that wraps up this issue. And my favorite story? I'll give the nod to "The Rain God" by Way Jeng. And my favorite art? I'll give the nod to the cover by Victoria Francés.

Originally posted on douglascohen.livejournal.com on August 4th, 2009

Part sixty-eight in my comprehensive retrospective as I read the fiction in *Realms of Fantasy* and offer my thoughts. This time I around I'll be dissecting the December 2005 issue.

The cover to this one is an illustration by Joel Spector. I was unable to determine the origins of this illustration.

A rundown of this issues nonfiction is as follows:

In the Movie/TV column, Resa Nelson covers the movie version of *Harry Potter and the Goblet of Fire*. In Folkroots, Ari Berk writes about milk, honey, and bread in myth and legend. In the Books column, Gahan Wilson reviews *Harry Potter and the Half-Blood Prince* by J.K. Rowling, *Looking for Jake*, a short story collection by China Mieville, and *The Year's Best Fantasy & Horror, 18th Annual Collection*, edited by Ellen Datlow, Kelly Link, and Gavin Grant, while Paul Witcover reviews *Od Magic* by Patricia McKillip, *Dreadmaster, Book One of the Storm of Wings Trilogy* by Chris Bunch, and *The Hidden Family, Book Two of the Merchant Princes*, by Charles Stross. In the Artists Gallery, Ari Berk covers Brom and the art of the *Plucker*. And in the Games Column, Eric T. Baker reviews *Harry Potter and the Goblet of Fire* for the PC, Xbox, PS2, and Gamecube, the RPG *Serenity*, based on the movie, which was spawned from the TV show, *Firefly*, and also *D.I.C.E: DNA Integrated Cybernetic Enterprises*, a science fiction game for the PS2, *Shadow of the Colossus* for the PS2, Sega's *Spartan: Total Warrior*, *Painkiller: Hell Wars* for the Xbox, and *Rachet: Deadlocked* for the PS2.

On to the fiction ...

The lead story is "En Forest Noire" by Tanith Lee, which marks her thirteenth appearance in the magazine. It is also the 400th work of fiction to be published in the magazine. In this dark fantasy story, we are plunged into medieval France, where a rich tradesman's son is engaged to the daughter of an aristocratic family that has fallen on hard times. It seems like a good match, except the bride-to-be's brother has taken a distinct disliking toward this commoner that would marry his sister. Things progress to the point where he and his henchman drag off the groom-to-be in a haunted forest to leave him to die, but the ultimate results are somewhat unexpected ...for everyone. Art to this one was provided by Thomas Kidd.

Next up we have "Empty Places" by Richard Parks, which marks his eighteenth appearance in the magazine. In this high fantasy tale, a skilled thief is coerced into taking a job by an even more skilled and dangerous magician named Tymon the Black, who has a rather dark reputation that precedes him. Our good thief finds himself forced to break into a royal castle to carry out the magician's will, and he mistrusts the magician every step of the way. But as you might expect, all is not quite as it seems with this mission. This story was reprinted in *Fantasy: Best of the Year 2006*, edited by Rich Horton. It's also worth noting that Richard went on to publish a novel with Five Star Press called *The Long Look*, which featured the character of Tymon the Black. Art to this one was provided by Michael Komarck, which marks his second illustration in the magazine.

Then we have "Mortegarde" by Liz Williams, which marks her ninth appearance in the magazine. In this story of Norse mythology, a physician's quest to find Mortegarde in the World Tree leads to a confrontation with religious fanatics of another race as science, medicine, religion, and faith collide. Yet despite their many differences, the good doctor learns to his horror that his people and theirs are not as different as he first believed. I should add that this story ended up being reprinted in *Year's Best Fantasy 6*, edited by David Hartwell and Kathryn Cramer. Art to this one was provided by Dave Leri, which marks his fifth illustration in the magazine.

Following this we have "A Knot of Toads" by Jane Yolen, which marks her sixth appearance in the magazine. In this tale of dark fantasy, a learned woman comes back to her small island home after her father's passing and must confront the dark truth of his arcane dabblings with witchery that led to his death. Art to this one is provided by Eric Dinyer, which marks his seventh illustration in the magazine.

And finally we have "Lavender's Blue, Lavender's Green" by Patrick Samphire, which marks his fourth appearance in the magazine. In this young adult fantasy, a man and his daughter go searching for his missing wife, who all these years he believed is the Queen of the Fairies. Only his daughter believes otherwise, thinking Dad is gullible. Ultimately, poor old Dad is forced to confront a rather bitter truth, and almost as soon as he does, that bitterness turns into a surprise that turns his entire world inside out. It's also worth noting that this is the first story to be published in

Realms that was submitted to the magazine while I was Assistant Editor. Art to this one was provided by Melissa Ferreira, which marks her fifth illustration in the magazine.

So that wraps up this issue, as well as 2005. And my favorite story? "Lavender's Blue, Lavender's Green" by Patrick Samphire. And my favorite artwork? Thomas Kidd's illustration to "En Foret Noire" by Tanith Lee.

Originally posted on douglascohen.livejournal.com on August 16th, 2009

Part sixty-nine in my comprehensive retrospective as I read the fiction in *Realms of Fantasy* and offer my thoughts. This time around I'll be poking and prodding the February 2006 issue.

The cover to this one features an illustration by Donato Giancola. It depicts Arthur and Guinevere from the Arthurian legends and it was originally a private commission.

A rundown of this issue's nonfiction is as follows:

In the Books column, Gahan Wilson reviews *Screaming Science Fiction: Horrors from Outer Space*, edited by Brian Lumley, *To Charles Fort with Love* by Caitlin R. Kiernan, *Dark Delicacies*, edited by Del Howison and Jeff Gelb, and *Songs and Sonnets Atlantean, the Third Series* by Donald Sidney-Fryer, while Paul Witcover reviews *A Princess of Roumania* by Paul Park, and *The Girl in the Glass* by Jeffrey Ford. In Folkroots, Helen Pilinovsky discusses how goblin markets are the magical marketplaces of fantasy literature. In the Movie/TV column, Resa Nelson review's Peter Jackson's *King Kong*. In the Artists Gallery, Karen Haber discusses the art of Scott Gustafson. And in the Games column, Eric T. Baker reviews *MediEvil* for the Sony PSP, *Kingdom Under Fire: Heroes* for the Xbox, *Shin Megami Tensei: Digital Devil Saga 2* for the PS2, the real-time RPG, *Dragonsbard*, for the PC, *X-Men Legends 2: Rise of the Apocalypse* for the PC, PS2, Xbox, PSP, and Gamecube, and the James Bond game, *From Russia with Love*, for the PS2, Xbox, and Gamecube.

On to the fiction ...

The lead story in this one is "Messages" by Brett Alexander Savory. This story has the odd distinction of being the first story published in *Realms* to have a repeat title. Back in the April 2001 issue, the magazine published "Messages" by Rob Vagle. But that's where the similarities end. This one is a rather dark tale set in modern times. It deals with different secret parties, competing to obtain the writings from people who are "fugue writers." Fugue writers are people who are unknowingly channeling the words of a higher power. what might possibly be God. Any such writings are extremely valuable to the most powerful people in the world, as these folks wish to obtain such writings so they might carry out what they believe to be God's will. But here's the twist, and pardon me while I steal Shawna's editorial blurb to this one: "We humans think it's all about us. But what if it's not?" For those curious about this sort of thing, this story was submitted to the magazine after I joined the editorial ranks. It should also be noted that this story was reprinted in *Year's Best Fantasy & Horror 2007, 20th edition*, edited by Ellen Datlow, Kelly Link & Gavin Grant. Art to this one was provided by Michael Gibbs, which marks his twelfth illustration in the magazine.

Next up we have "Swansdown" by Deborah Roggie. This is a high fantasy tale about a wizard's young wife and her lover stealing the wizard's swanskins, donning them, becoming swans, and fleeing. The problem? The woman wants to stay in the swanskin, while the man wishes to resume his human form for a time. When a spinster on a farm happens to see him remove his swanskin and change back to a man, the lives of these three individuals becomes inextricably linked ...and even more so when the wizard comes looking for his wife. This is a tale of love, loss, and change. And for the curious, this one was in inventory before I joined up with the magazine. Art to this one was provided by Scott Grimando, which marks his eleventh illustration in the magazine.

Following this we have "The Road's End" by James Van Pelt, which marks his sixth appearance in the magazine. This one is a high fantasy tale about a man who returns home to settle down with his family after many years of traveling and adventure. He thinks that at last he is content, that he can rest after having seen and done so much. But the call of the world proves too strong to resist. This is another piece that was submitted to the magazine after I joined up. I can still remember my main comment to Shawna about this one; that this story's theme is one I haven't seen too often in secondary fantasies for short fiction (still don't). It brought to mind Robert E. Howard's poem, "Solomon Kane's Homecoming." Of course, that's a poem as opposed to prose, but I think it's still worth mentioning, since it was a poem that tells a story, and the bulk of Howard's tales about Solomon Kane were in fact prose. And being as I rather enjoyed Howard's poem, this comparison is also a compliment. Art to this one was provided by Craig Elliott.

Then we have "Uncle Vernon's Lie" by Patrick Samphire, which marks his fifth appearance in the magazine. This one was accepted by the magazine before I joined up. This is a middle grade fantasy about a young boy who's so scared of everything that it prevents him enjoying childhood as he should. So in an effort to cure him of his fears, the boy's father has him spend the summer with his Uncle Vernon. Before they part ways, his father issue's a warning, telling Benji that his uncle will tell one lie all summer. Seems simple enough. Except here a few of the things Uncle Vernon tells Benji during his stay: that there are little men living inside the black balls he uses as tea leaves, that there is a spring deep inside the earth that keeps it winding, that every time you shed a tear you're shedding an entire world and the people inside have until that tear hits the ground to live their entire lives, etc. So figuring out the one lie is not as easy as it seems. It's also not easy to figure out Uncle Vernon. He's an old man, but on the inside he has what you might call at least a partial Peter Pan complex. So while he's taking care of Benji for the summer, he also maintains the imagination of a child, which aids him in overcoming Beji's fears. This is a heartfelt and honest tale that drew me in the way few middle grade pieces can ...and I have to admit the following: when I read the ending, there was a lump in my throat. Kudos to the author. I've read and enjoyed quite a number of Realms stories, many of them sad, but off the top of my head I can think of two stories that made the sadness come bubbling up come the end. Goosebumps, sure. But actually leaving me sad for more than a heartbeat? Not too often, I'm afraid. I'm thick-skinned about this kind of stuff, so it's not a reflection on the authors or their stories. But this story broke through the proverbial wall (and I've yet to discuss the other), and I feel that's worth noting. Art to this one was provided by J.K. Potter, which marks his ninth illustration in the magazine.

Following this we have "Dead Letters" by Christopher Barzak, which marks his third appearance in the magazine. I'll also note that Chis writes that the story is "for Jenna Felice." Jenna Felice was an editor for Tor some years back (I can't remember her official title) who unexpectedly died at a young age. If I remember correctly, it was from an asthma attack. I met her once, at an Ursula K. Le Guin reading. Very nice person. As to the story, this was another one that was submitted to the magazine after I joined up. In this one, we are introduced to a character that used to be imaginary. She was the make-believe childhood friend of a girl named Sarah, and you can gather from the story that Sarah had a rather vivid imagination, and she believed in her friend more than most kids do with theirs. Eventually

Sarah moved on as she got older. You would think that would be the end of it. But when Sarah is murdered, her imaginary friend Alice comes to life, looking for Sarah, refusing to believe that she is truly dead. The bulk of the story is told through a series of letters that Alice mails to Sarah's old house. It's a rather surreal and emotional journey for the character, and while the premise may sound a bit far-fetched, the strong writing in this one makes you more than willing to believe what you're reading. Art to this one was provided by Chris Cocozza, which marks his fifth illustration in Realms.

Finally we have "The Land of Reeds" by Patrick Samphire, which marks his sixth appearance in the magazine, and his second story in this issue. This is another story that was submitted to the magazine after I joined up. Now, in the last issue, Patrick's "Lavender's Blue, Lavender's Green" marked the first story to be published in the magazine that was submitted for consideration after I joined up. In this issue, we've jumped to four out of six stories being submitted to the magazine after I joined up. So you can see that at this point Sovereign Media has burned through most of the inventory from the Carina Gonzalez era. As to the story itself, this one is a piece of Egyptian mythology. When Alexander the Great proclaims himself pharaoh of Egypt, the god Amon-Re stops walking through the underworld because Alexander's blood is that of an outsider. And so everything is put into doubt as to what will happen to future souls that seek the Land of Reeds, a place they go in the afterlife. This story was also podcast on the Pseudopod website as podcast 93. Art to this story in RoF was provided by Allen Douglas, which marks his seventh illustration in the magazine.

So that wraps up this issue. And my favorite story? Wow. I think this is one of the strongest issues I've read. In another issue, I would select just about any of these stories as my favorite in a heartbeat. But I've got to go with "Uncle Vernon's Lie" by Patrick Samphire for pulling on the old heartstrings. And my favorite artwork? I'll go with Allen Douglas' illustration to "The Land of Reeds" by Patrick Samphire.

Originally posted on douglascohen.livejournal.com on August 27ᵗʰ, 2009

Part seventy in my comprehensive retrospective as I read the fiction in *Realms of Fantasy* and offer my thoughts. This time around I'll be serving up the April 2006 issue.

The cover to this one is by Kinuko Craft, which marks her third illustration in the magazine. It was originally the cover to *The Hounds of Morrigan* by Pat O'Shea.

This issue holds some special meaning for me, for a couple of reasons. First is that in the masthead I am finally listed as Assistant Editor. We'll get to the other reason once I get to the fiction.

But first a rundown of the nonfiction:

In the Movie/TV column, Resa Nelson covers the video game adapted to the big screen, *Silent Hill*. In the Folkroots column, Kristen McDermott discussed the connection between fairies and English-speaking dramatic theater. In the Books column, Gahan Wilson reviews *Anansi Boys* by Neil Gaiman, *Platinum Pohl: The Collected Best Stories of Frederick Pohl*, and *The Coming of Conan the Cimmerian* (illustrated by Mark Shultz) and *The Conquering Sword of Conan* (illustrated by Gregory Manchess), both of which collect Robert E. Howard's original unexpurgated texts to his Conan tales, while Paul Witcover reviews *A Feast for Crows* by George R. R. Martin, *The Narrows* by Alex Irvine, and *Bear Daughter* by Judith Berman. In the Artists Gallery, Karen Haber covers the art of Tom Kidd. And in the Games column, Eric T. Baker reviews *The Movies* for the PC, *Quake 4* for the PC and Xbox 360, *Call of Cthulu: Dark Corners of the Earth* for the Xbox, *Soul Calibur III* for the PS2, *Lord of the Rings: Tactics* for the PSP, and the Whitewolf RPG *The Wurst of Grimtooth's Traps*. I should also mention that the Young Adult (YA) Books column makes its first appearance this issue. I'm assuming Michael Jones–the current YA book columnist–wrote this column, but for some strange reason the columnist isn't listed. Either way, the books reviewed were *The Inheritance Trilogy Book 2: Eldest* by Christopher Paolini, *The Sisters Grimm: The Fairy Tale Detectives* and *The Sister Grimm: The Unusual Suspects*, both by Michael Buckley, *The Lucy Chronicles: High School Bites* by Liza Conrad, *Rebel Angels* by Libba Bray, and *Wizards at War* by Diane Duane.

On to the fiction ...

The lead story is "Lady of Ashuelot" by Karen L. Abrahamson. This is the other reason this is a special issue for me, as this story marks my first slush survivor to appear in the magazine. I also take pride in the fact that it's the first piece of slush I ever pulled out from the submissions pile. I suppose it's only fitting that the first issue in which my name appears in the masthead is also the first issue in which one of my slush survivors appears. As to the story itself, this is a piece of Arthuriana that takes place in modern-day New Hampshire. Guinevere (or Gwen, as she's called in this version) is making a living as a blacksmith and taking care of the Lady of the Lake, who still has Excalibur. Enter Lancelot, who walks off the Greyhound bus, seeking Excalibur so that Arthur can be awakened from his mystical sleep so that the once and future king can walk again and return Britain to its glory. It sounds good in theory, but Lancelot is only thinking about himself and the love triangle (in this case between Gwen, Lance, and the Lady) complicates things further. This story has something of a feminist take on the mythos, and one of the things that grabbed my attention when reading was that Gwen was not dainty at all. Giving her a talent for blacksmithing goes so against expectations of the iconic princess, just as T.H. White went against expectations in *The Once and Future King* when he had the literary guts to make Lancelot ugly. When you can flip everything on its head in this subgenre, you're doing something interesting. Art to this one was provided by Michael Kerr, which marks his ninth illustration in the magazine.

Next up we have "Moon Viewing at Shijo Bridge" by Richard Parks, which marks his nineteenth appearance in the magazine. If memory serves me correctly, this piece was already in inventory when I joined the magazine. This is the second of Richard's Lord Yamada stories to appear in the magazine, and possibly the one to receive the most attention, as it received a number of positive reviews and was reprinted in *Fantasy: Best of the Year 2007*, edited by Rich Horton, and it was also podcast over on the *PodCastle* website as podcast 023. In this one, Lord Yamada is drawn back to his days at the Imperial Court in feudal Japan when the princess he used to know there sends for him. She is seeking his help as her son's claim to become the future emperor is in jeopardy. What follows is a labyrinthine story of twists and turns as Yamada and his companion seek the truth while providing aid, in what is probably the most politically dominated plot to ever appear in the magazine. At the same time, everything throughout remains completely character-driven, so there's some real nice balance here. Art to this one was provided by Paul Lee, which marks his thirteenth illustration in the magazine.

Then we have "Anywhere There's a Game" by Greg Van Eekhout, which marks his second appearance in the magazine, and his first solo appearance. This one was bought after I joined the magazine. Usually a sports story in fantasy turns out to be about baseball, but this one is a rare basketball fantasy, as a former professional basketball player relates to a reporter various supernatural encounters he's had during the course of his career. The story is really broken down into five shorter pieces, with each one focusing around his encounter with a different positional player, i.e. one supernatural story each for the center, power forward, small forward, shooting guard, and point guard. Art in the magazine was provided by Web Bryant, which marks his twenty second illustration in the magazine.

Following this we have "Ducks in a Row" by Devon Monk, which marks her seventh appearance in the magazine. Again, if memory serves me correctly, this one was accepted by the magazine before I joined up. This is a short piece about a boy at a carnival who has a somewhat supernatural connection to inanimate objects. And while this does factor into the story, it is not the point of this story. What is the point? Well, there is an underlying secret that's hinted at throughout the story, a dark one. It's easy to miss if you don't pay attention, and it pushes the story to an entirely new level once you realize what it is. No, I won't tell you. That would defeat the purpose. You must read it and decipher it for yourself. Art to this one was provided by Yuko Shimizu.

After this we have "Jane. A Story of Manners, Magic, and Romance" by Sarah Prineas, which marks her third appearance in the magazine. This one was submitted after I joined RoF and is a romantic fantasy piece with a heavy helping of Victorian flavor. In this one, scientists are warlocks dabbling with magic in this world, which is called "the element." Our protagonist Jane is extraordinarily irresistible to warlocks once they're around her, and just about all warlocks are men. All of this comes to a head when a group of warlocks endeavor to discover why her uncle's home seems to attract so many random storms containing "the element." As the title says, this is a story of manners, magic, and romance. Art to this one was provided by J.K. Potter, which marks his tenth illustration in the magazine.

Finally we have "Heart of Ice" by Jena Snyder. This one was submitted while I was with the magazine. With a few touches, this one could easily be high fantasy. As it is, it is a dark fantasy piece that takes place at an undetermined time in what I'm deducing to be somewhere in Quebec, Canada. In this piece the author draws on the mythology of the wendigo (or wittigo, as she calls it here), as we meet a woman who long ago was reduced to cannibalism and in a feverish state, she fed her dying child to her husband to save his life during a terrible winter. Only her husband killed himself when he learned what she had done, and she went mad, surviving in misery for countless years since then while maintaining her youthful beautiful appearance. Enter the requisite young man who is attracted to her. It sounds like you're being set up for the classic foolish man/Femme Fatale story, but this isn't the case. The author takes everything in some rather refreshing directions that makes reading this more than worthwhile. Art to this one was provided by Craig Elliott, which marks his second illustration in the magazine. This piece was selected for inclusion in the Editorial section of *Spectrum 13: The Best in Contemporary Fantastic Art.*

So that wraps up this issue. And my favorite story? Well, from here on out it gets trickier to maintain my objectivity whenever there's a slush survivor of mine in one of the issues, but I think I'm up to the task. So my pick this time around is "Anywhere There's a Game" by Greg Van Eekhout. And my favorite artwork? Web Bryant's accompanying illustration to "Anywhere There's a Game."

Originally posted on douglascohen.livejournal.com on September 4ᵗʰ, 2009

Part seventy-one in my comprehensive retrospective as I read the fiction in *Realms of Fantasy* and offer my thoughts. This time around I'll be dishing the goods on the June 2006 issue.

The cover to this one is by Luis Royo, which marks his fourteenth illustration in the magazine. It was originally a poster.

There is a change in the masthead worth noting. Christopher D'Amore's run as Managing Editor is over. His replacement is Catherine Sumner.

A rundown of the nonfiction is as follows:

In the Movie/TV column, Resa Nelson covers the Stephen King miniseries, *Nightmares and Dreamscapes*, based on the book of the same name. In the Folkroots column, Kit Whitfield discusses the werewolf in literature. In the Books column, Gahan Wilson reviews *The Plot Against America* by Philip Roth, the short story collection, *The Ocean and All Its Devices* by William Browning Spencer, *Weird Shadows Over Innsmouth*, edited by Stephen Jones, *The Complete Encyclopedia of Elves, Goblins, and Other Little Creatures* by Pierre Dubois, illustrated by Claudine and Roland Sabatier, and Paul Witcover reviews *The Thousandfold Thought, The Prince of Nothing, Book Three* by R. Scott Bakker, *His Majesty's Dragon* by Naomi Novik, and *A Shadow in Summer* by Daniel Abraham. In YA Books, Michael Jones is this time credited as the reviewer, and he reviews *Firebirds Rising*, edited by Sharyn November, *Tempting Fate* by Esther Friesner, *Skybreaker* by Kenneth Oppel, *When the Beast Ravens* by E. Rose Sabin, and *Young Warriors*, edited by Tamora Pierce and Josepha Sherman. In the Artists Gallery, Karen Haber covers the artwork of Rob Alexander. And in the Games Column, Eric T. Baker reviews *Dungeons and Dragons Online: Stormreach*, the miniature game, *Dream Blade*, *Kameo: Elements of Power* for the Xbox 360, *Dead or Alive 4* for the Xbox 360, *Perfect Dark Zero* for the Xbox 360, and the RPG, *World of Darkness Chicago*.

On to the fiction ...

The lead story is "Robin of the Green" by A.C. Wise. This is one of my slush survivors, so obviously it was bought after I joined the magazine. As you may expect based on the title, this story deals with Robin Hood. And the author turns a lot of the mythology inside out. For starters, Robin is a fey in this one. And the character of Guy—someone Robin is normally at odds with—has been friends with him since childhood. At the beginning of the story, Guy is engaged to be married to Maid Marion, and he exacts a promise from Robin that he will cause no problems. Robin agrees, and what follows is a rather interesting love triangle between these three characters, as Robin is unable to help himself when he looks upon Marion for the first time. Throughout the course of the story, there is also the subtle suggestion of another more intimate relationship between Robin and Guy that goes back years. However, being as I don't consider any of the tidbits the author drops to be conclusive on this front, I believe it is for the reader to decide whether any such relationship exists. I also find it interesting that this is the first piece of Robin Hood fiction RoF has ever published. This caught me a little bit by surprise when I learned this, and I admit I'm a little proud that twelve years into the magazine's run I was able to discover a story for the magazine that was a first. Art to this story was provided by Tom Kidd, which marks his second illustration in the magazine. This piece was selected for inclusion in the Editorial section of *Spectrum 14: The Best in Contemporary Fantastic Art.*

Next up we have "Pavel Petrovich" by Daniel Hood. This story was also accepted by the magazine after I joined up. This one is a dark fantasy tale about a man from the deepest wilds of the defunct Soviet Union, "beyond the beyond" as the author puts it. His tribe and his people are rather primitive, so when he is imprisoned, dealing with being locked up becomes something of an additional adjustment for one Pavel Petrovich. A definitive fantastical element in this one doesn't show up until later, but it's made clear rather early on that there's something off about Pavel, something different and strange, even in a prison. There are hints and suggestions of something stranger going on, and the character of Pavel Petrovich and the world of Soviet prisons are so interesting that it keeps you reading until the fantastical elements make themselves known. Art to this one was provided by Chris Cocozza, which marks his sixth illustration in the magazine.

The next story is "Undine" by Catherine Krahe. This one was also submitted to the magazine after I joined up. In this one, a gifted swimmer with a chance at the Olympics is getting over a serious injury that nearly cost her leg. Her swimming career is over, and her life has lost all direction. Enter the water-sprite that is trapped in the lake near her home that can offer her a chance to swim again like she used to if they trade places. The device in this story is an old standard, but the execution made this one fresh. Art to this one was provided by Eric Fortune, which marks his third illustration in the magazine. This piece was selected for inclusion in the Editorial section of *Spectrum 13: The Best in Contemporary Fantastic Art.**

Then we have "Sister of the Hedge" by Jim C. Hines, which marks his second story in the magazine. It's another story that was bought after I joined the magazine. This one was an interesting merger between Christianity and the old Sleeping Beauty tale. A girl is fleeing her dark past and comes to the Church of the Iron Cross where she takes up service with the others there in tending the Hedge. Inside this Hedge rests the sleeping princess (who, btw, is never referred to as Sleeping Beauty–I just picked up on the parallel). Also in this enchanted Hedge are the many princes over the years that have come seeking the sleeping princess, only to become trapped by the vines and impaled by their thorns, leaving them in living agony. It falls to the sisters and brothers of the Chruch of the Iron Cross to tend them in all things. Things take a dark turn when her father comes looking for her, and we learn that she fled from him because she's carrying twins that he impregnated her with. Art to this one was provided by Eric Deschamps, which marks his third illustration in the magazine.

After this we have "A Better Place" by Josh Rountree, which marks his third story in the magazine. This one was bought before I joined RoF. This one is a rather short piece about a young boy on a farm who has a chance to leave for "a better place," what sounds like every kid's wonderland. Art to this one was provided by Janet Hamlin.

Next up is "Schwarze Madonna and the Sandalwood Knight" by Jay Lake & Ruth Nestvold. This story was submitted before I joined the magazine, was caught in slush limbo for a while due to the change in assistant editors, and ended up being bought some months afterward. For Jay, it's his fifth appearance in the magazine. For Ruth, it's her second. It's also worth noting this is the first co-written story to appear in the magazine where both authors had previously been published in the magazine with just solo pieces. As to the story itself, this is a high fantasy tale. On the surface, it seems like something you might have heard about before, i.e. the farmer taking up the sword to confront the enemy. But the truth is that this story entirely deconstructs and reconstructs the high fantasy genre. Yes, a farmer takes up a sword, but he behaves as a farmer should and would under these circumstances, which impacts the entire tale on every single level. And the world is quite original to boot, dripping with details and atmosphere. Kudos to the authors for successfully tackling this one. It's a story of vengeance and especially love, and I'll steal Shawna's editorial tag for this one since it really captures the spirit of the piece, and trying to convey what's going on otherwise would fail to do this one justice: "Love can take many shapes and forms and lead lovers to many words and deeds. Some may ultimately be self-destructive, but in the end only time will tell." Art to this one was provided by Michael Komarck, which marks his third illustration in the magazine.

Finally we have "Ice" by Patrice E. Sarath, which marks her second appearance in the magazine. This was another piece that was submitted while I was with the magazine. In this one, an unnamed Canadian city is becoming buried in an endlessly falling snow. Everyone who didn't flee at the outset is now trapped in the city, including our professional hockey player protagonist. At the beginning of the story he is dealing with an injury just suffered in a game, but it's clear he's also dealing with some issues with his wife and a fellow teammate of his. All of these elements build toward a head when he receives a surprising invitation to the ballet and attends, at which point it becomes clear there is something sinister and strange at play. Art to this one was provided by Eric Dinyer, which marks his eighth illustration in the magazine.

So that wraps up this issue. And my favorite story? "Pavel Petrovich" by Daniel Hood. And my favorite artwork? Eric Fortune's illustration to "Undine" by Catherine Krahe.

*You may have noticed that occasionally pieces that appeared in *Spectrum* are listed out of order, or in strange orders. For example, we have pieces in this issue listed as appearing in both *Spectrum 13* and *14*. I assure you these aren't mistakes. Make of it what you will.

Originally posted on douglascohen.livejournal.com on September 18th, 2009

Part seventy-two in my ongoing retrospective as I read the fiction to the back issues of *Realms of Fantasy* and offer my thoughts, right up to the present. This time around I'll be revisiting the August 2006 issue.

This marks the first retrospective I've done since being promoted to Editor at RoF. It also marks the first retrospective I've done since we launched the new website, which in turn means it marks the first retrospective I've done since my retrospectives were added as content to the website. So before this point, I was just posting these retrospectives on my personal blog. Some people might have found them interesting to read since I work at RoF, but I had always done these in an unofficial capacity, i.e. I posted them on my blog because I wanted to, which was all the reason I needed. It's still all the reason I need, but now that they've been added to the magazine's website, I suppose these retrospectives are part of the official RoF canon. That's not something I ever expected, though it's certainly gratifying knowing that the magazine's publisher and webmaster believe these retrospectives should be included on the website.*

The cover to this one is by Charles Keegan and is original to the magazine.

A rundown of this issue's nonfiction is as follows:

In the Movie/TV column, Resa Nelson covers Bryan Singer's *Superman Returns* (one of my most hated superhero movies ever). In the Folkroots column, Midori Snyder discusses the journeys of the armless maiden. In the Books column, Gahan Wilson reviews *Star Changes, the Science Fiction of Clark Ashton Smith*, edited by Scott Connors & Ron Hilger, *ZIPPY/Type Z Personality* by Bill Griffith, *Alabaster* by Caitlin R. Kiernan, and Paul Witcover reviews *In the Eye of Heaven* by David Keck, *The Brief History of the Dead* by Kevin Brockmeier, *City of Saints and Madmen* by Jeff VanderMeer, and *In the Forest of Forgetting* by Theodora Goss. In YA Books, Michael Jones reviews *The Warrior Heir* by Cinda Williams Chima, *Uglies # 3: Specials* by Scott Westefeld, *Dreams and Visions*, edited by M. Jerry Weiss and Helen S. Weiss, *Midnighters # 3: Blue Noon* by Scott Westerfeld, *The Cronus Chronicles # 1: The Shadow Thieves* by Anne Ursu, *Grail Quest # 1: The Camelot Spell* by Laura Anne Gilman, and *Golden* by

Cameron Dokey. In the Artists Gallery, Karen Haber covers the art of John Picacio. And in the Games column, Eric T. Baker reviews *Oblivion* for the PC and Xbox 360, *Bone: the Great Cow Race* for the PC, *Auto Assault* for the PC, *Kingdom Hearts II* for the PS2, *Samurai Champloo* for the PS2, and the RPG *Forgotten Realms* supplement, *Power of Faerun*.

On to the fiction ...

This issue has a special place in my heart, as four of my slush survivors appear in this issue, which to this day remains a personal record for most slush survivors to appear in a single issue.** There are other reasons this issue is important to me, also having to do with the fiction. I'll get into that as I discuss the stories.

First up is "The Grand Mal Reaper" by Scott William Carter. This would be the first of the aforementioned slush survivors. This story has the rather interesting distinction of being the only one to ever get slushed by two different people at RoF before getting passed along to Shawna (unless a similar situation occurred before I joined the magazine). When my predecessor, Carina Gonzalez, left the magazine, there were still some stories in her possession. She finished reading them, selected those she wanted to pass along to Shawna, and eventually did just that, thus concluding her last official act with the magazine. Then Shawna turned around and gave me those stories, telling me to "re-slush" them. So in addition to my usual slush submissions, I sifted through Carina's final picks. Carina and I must have had fairly different tastes in fantasy, because I rejected all of these stories ...except one. The lone exception was "The Grand Mal Reaper" by one Scott William Carter. So I passed this one along to Shawna and she ultimately bought it for the magazine. So while I count Scott as one my slush survivors, credit should also go to Carina for first pulling that story out of the slush before I arrived. This would also mark her last slush survivor to appear in the magazine. So including Shawna, Scott's story went through three separate rounds of editorial consideration before finding its way into RoF. Truly, this story earned its way into our pages like no other has!

As to the story itself, this one is an unconventional superhero story. It deals with a young man afflicted with grand mal epilepsy, who also has the power to see people's deaths from far away. But he's come to view his power as a curse, as he can't see any way that such a power can help people. Given that he grew up a fan of comics and superheroes, it is a particularly bitter conclusion to come to. And so he does his best to suppress the visions, trying to float by on the edges of society as a normal person. But you know how it goes with superpowers ...you can't deny who you are. Sooner or later you must confront the truth about yourself in order to become a whole person. And sometimes the best ways to find truths are through love ...and heartache. Art to this one was provided by Andrea Wicklund, which marks her fourth illustration in the magazine. This illustration was selected for inclusion in the Editorial section of *Spectrum 14: The Best in Contemporary Fantastic Art.*

Next up we have "Of Metal Men and Scarlet Thread and Dancing with the Sunrise" by Ken Scholes. This is another one of my slush survivors. When I first came across this story in the slush, I recognized Ken's name from a writing forum I belonged to. I had never met him in person, but it did mark the first story I ever set aside where I knew the person in some capacity. This one is a science fantasy tale, and when I plucked it from the slush, I never imagined what would follow. Nor did the author for that matter. Those who have already read about Ken's successes that resulted from this tale should feel free to skip ahead. For everyone else, I will give you the short version: Doug finds story and decides it is most cool and "slush worthy." Doug passes story along to Shawna. Shawna decides to take story. Story is published. Story receives much critical praise. Ken writes a sequel and sends it to us. Shawna rejects it and suggests he write a novel in this world. At the same time, Ken's close friends and wife encourage him to finally sit down and write a novel. His good friend (and regular contributor to RoF), Jay Lake, tells Ken if he writes the novel then Jay will pass it along to his literary agent, Jennifer Jackson. Ken finally buckles and writes a novel. It is set in the same world as "Of Metal Men." It incorporates parts of this story and then expands upon it significantly. Critiques, etc. follow. When the novel is ready, Jay passes it along to Jennifer Jackson. Jennifer signs Ken as his client. Then she submits Ken's novel to Beth Meacham, an editor at Tor Books. Beth accepts the novel. Ken signs a deal for five books. Doug finally meets Ken in person at the 2007 World Fantasy Convention. Ken–a big man–gathers Doug in a monstrous bear hug that threatens to crack his spine. In case you'd like to read it, the first novel in the series is called *Lamentation* (in which Ken kindly included me in the acknowledgments page). The second was released not too long ago and is called *Canticle.**** Both of these have received good reviews as well. So this I suppose is a classic example of short story spawning the beginning of a writing career. I'm honored to have played a small part on it.

As to the story itself, at the beginning of the tale Rudolpho and his gypsy scouts come upon an impact crater that represents the smoking ruins of Windwir, once the city housing the greatest repository of knowledge in the world. In that crater, they find a sobbing robot, or "metal man." Rudolpho sets out to find the cause of the city's destruction, only to learn that the robot is the one responsible. But that shouldn't be possible. And so he sets out to uncover the truth behind this tragic destruction in a tale of sorcery, deceit, and love. Art to this one was provided Allen Douglas, which marks his eighth illustration in the magazine. It's also worth noting that Ken has stated on more than one occasion that when he saw Alan's artwork to his story, it resonated so deeply with him that he knew there were more tales to tell about this world and its characters. I would imagine this is one of the ultimate compliments a writer can pay his illustrator. And not to be left out of the festivities, it should be noted that Alan's illustration was selected for inclusion in the Editorial section of *Spectrum 14: The Best in Contemporary Fantastic Art.*

Next up we have "The Cold Drake" by Renee Bennett, another one of my slush survivors. This one is a high fantasy tale. Even better, it deals with dragons. As I've mentioned elsewhere in these retrospectives, I've always been a sucker for a well-told dragon tale. As to the story itself, the main character is the child of a human mother whose father was a high mage. The protagonist's father was an evil cold drake who raped the protagonist's mother, leaving her with a half-drake child.

I will always remember being drawn into this story based on how liquid smooth the prose was. This is worth mentioning because when I found this story I was trying to get the magazine caught up in its response times. I was doing pretty well on this front ...until I found a hidden cache of manuscripts. Suffice it to say this cache had been hidden from me far longer than it should have been. I was kind of buried in manuscripts when I first joined the magazine, and in my efforts to get caught up, somehow this stack of manuscripts got lost (the first and only time such a thing has ever happened to me). And once I found them and saw how old they were, I dived in like a madman, attempting to burn through them as fast as humanly possible. I rejected around fifty manuscripts in a little over an hour that day. I don't know how I managed to do that. The only answer I have is that I had to, so I did. I suppose you could argue I wasn't really reading the stories if I went through everything that quickly. Except ... "The Cold Drake" was one of those stories. Even in that frenzied pace of reading, there was no way I could let this jewel of a tale go unnoticed. A good story will always stand out, regardless of the circumstances. That's my story behind the story on this one.

But getting back to the story itself, our half-drake protagonist attempts to learn her origins and ultimately face them down as she attempts to reconcile the two warring halves that make up who she is. Art to this one was provided by Brian Horton, which marks his third illustration in the magazine. This artwork was selected for inclusion in the Editorial section of *Spectrum 13: The Best in Contemporary Fantastic Art.*

Next up we have "The Hero Shore" by Darrell Schweitzer, which marks his fourth appearance in the magazine. This was another story that was accepted before I joined the magazine, so the first time I read it was when it was published. This one is a weird fantasy that deconstructs much of the mythos surrounding being a Hero, as a man driven mad with grief reveals the true cost of bearing such a burden. Art to this one was provided by Chuck Lukacs.

Then we have "True North" by K.D. Wentworth, which marks her third appearance in the magazine. This one is a YA tale. In it, we are introduced to a world much like our own. Only in this world, nearly every adolescent will at one point experience "the Call," to "Journey" to "the North Lands." Most adolescents heed the Call and make the Journey. There are even way stations along the way for adolescents on the road to the North Lands. Each person's Journey is different–some beautiful, some dangerous–and this tale chronicles the Journey of one girl who receives the Call. When you try talking to an adult about their Journey, they're unable to relate their experiences, as it's not something that can be described or understood in this world. The big metaphor here is obvious, i.e. the North Lands are a physical manifestation of the highs and lows of adolescence, with all its beauty and scariness and ugliness and passion. But the imagination and imagery in the writing are rich, and the metaphor is not heavyhanded, and so it works quite well. Art to this one was provided by Peter Ferguson, which marks his fourth illustration in Realms.

Finally we have "Indigo with Distance" by E. Catherine Tobler. This would be my fourth slush survivor in this particular issue. As with Ken, I had known E. through an online writing forum (actually the same writing forum as Ken), but had never met her in person. This is one of the stories I'm most proud of pulling from the slush, for the simple reason that at this time I wasn't reading much of this kind of fantasy. So it would have been easy to let this piece slip past my guard. Luckily that didn't happen. As to the story itself, it has a bit of magic realism bent mixed with a fairy tale. In it, a young woman translating books in Japan falls in love with and has a secret affair with the boss' daughter, only to lose her in horrifying fashion. It's a story that poignantly illustrates how sometimes tragedy is the only means to achieve happily ever after. Art to this one was provided by Zela Lobb.

So that wraps up this issue. And my favorite story? "Of Metal Men and Scarlet Thread and Dancing with the Sunrise" by Ken Scholes? And my favorite illustration? Allen's accompanying illustration to Ken's story.

*Although the magazine has been defunct for several years now, a skeletal version of the website still remains intact at www.rofmag.com as I edit these retrospectives.

**And would remain so until the magazine's closure.

***Four books are now out in the series.

Originally posted on douglascohen.livejournal.com on December 21st, 2009

Part seventy-three in my comprehensive retrospective as I read the fiction in *Realms of Fantasy* and offer my thoughts. This time around I'll be going toe to toe with the October 2006 issue.

The cover to this one is by Gordon Crabb, which marks his second illustration in the magazine. It was originally the cover to *The Lightstone* by David Zindell.

A rundown of this issue's nonfiction is as follows:

In the Movie/TV column, Resa Nelson covers *Masters of Horror* on Showtime. In the Folkroots column, Hal Duncan writes about death and rebirth from world mythology to contemporary magical fiction. In the Books column, Gahan Wilson reviews *Feeling Very Strange: The Slipstream Anthology*, edited by James Patrick Kelly & John Kessel, *H.P. Lovecraft's Book of the Supernatural*, edited by Stephen Jones, *The Line Between* by Peter S. Beagle, *The Tough Guide to Fantasyland* by Diana Wynne Jones, and Paul Witcover reviews *Firebird* by R. Garcia Y. Robertson, *The Silver Bough* by Lisa Tuttle, and *Shuteye for the Timebroker* by Paul Di Filippo. In YA Books, Michael Jones reviews *Fly by Night* by Frances Hardinge, *The Sea of Monsters* by Rick Riordan, *Jennifer Scales and the Messenger of Light* by Mary Janice Davidson and Anthony Alongi, *Timetripper Book One: Yestermorrow* by Stefan Petrucha, *The Chronicles of Fairie Book One: The Hunter's Moon* by O.R. Melling, *Blue Bloods* by Melissa de la Cruz, and *Boys That Bite* by Mari Mancusi. In the Artists Gallery, A. Jaye Williams covers the art of the Hildebrandt Brothers. And in the Games column, Eric T. Baker reviews *X-Men III: The Official Game* for the PC, PS2, Xbox, and the Xbox 360, *The Da Vinci Code* for the Xbox, PS2, and PC, for the *Dungeons & Dragons* world of *Eberron*, a standalone adventure module, *The Voyage of the Golden Dragon*, *Exalted Second Edition: Storytellers Companion* from White Wolf Publishing, *Metal Saga* for the PS2, and the latest card set in the *Magic: The Gathering* line, *Dissension*.

On to the fiction ...

The lead story is "Marriage Game" by Susan J. Kroupa, which marks her fourth appearance in the magazine. This one is a lighthearted ghost story about a couple of ghost women who play a "Game" wherein they try to influence the lives of "Flesh & Bloods," earning mostly meaningless points for causing certain events to happen due to their influencing. But in this instance, a marriage could hang in the balance due to their meddling. Art to this one was provided by John Singer.

Then we have "Dead Man's Tale" by Billie Aul, which marks her second appearance in the magazine. Like her first story in RoF, this is a post-Flood tale, where the sea levels have risen to such an extent that many magical folks have been forced to come out from hiding deep in the earth and take their place among humans. This in turn has caused many undead and fey who have lived among humans in secret all along to reveal themselves. Now everyone lives together in the ultimate melting pot. In this particular tale, a gumshoe detective must determine whether a man's severed lover is truly undead and unable to reanimate. If he is, then this was something the lovers did for kicks and that means a spell is blocking the undead body from reanimating. But if the body isn't undead as the lover claims, then the lover will be tried for murder. Art to this one was provided by Joel Spector, which marks his second illustration in the magazine.

Next up we have "Sunday" by Alethea Kontis. This is the ultimate successful mishmash of famous fairy tales. In the story, Sunday Woodcutter finds herself falling in love with both a frog and a prince, only her kisses are failing to transform the frog back into a man, and the prince is considered an enemy of the family. In reading this, I detected influences from the Frog Prince, Cinderella, Snow White, and Jack and the Beanstalk to name a few. Yet the author manages to make this tale entirely her own. Art to this one was provided by Scott Grimando, which marks his twelfth illustration in the magazine.

Following this we have "Blood of Virgins" by David Barr Kirtley, which marks his third appearance in the magazine. In this young adult tale, dragons are like cars among teenagers, meaning they are status symbols. So of course almost everyone wants one. One problem, though. While the dragons are basically under control, they enjoy the blood of virgins. And wouldn't you know it, our protagonist is a virgin going into his first year of college. So not only does he wish to hide the fact that he is a virgin, but it's compounded by the fact that he's absolutely terrified of dragons. So what is the solution? Well, facing down your fear always helps. Meeting the right girl could help as well. This story appeared as podcast 088 on the *Escape Pod* website. Art to the story in RoF was provided by Huan Tran.

Then we have "Snake Charmer" by Amanda Downum. This one is another one of my slush survivors. It also marks an interesting (but minor) step for me as an editor. Back when the story was still under consideration, Amanda happened to post a comment on my blog and mentioned that I had passed along her story. I asked her which one and when she replied "Snake Charmer." I said something about the story that was, well, completely wrong in terms of what kind of tale it was. I realized the mistake much later on and was rather embarrassed about it. Since that sort of error was rather unlike me, I took some time to think about why I made it. And I realized that I had finally gotten to the point that I had read so many stories for RoF (published and otherwise) that I was occasionally getting them mixed up in my head. This includes the ones I like, such as this one. It's nothing personal to the authors, but after this happened I learned that sooner or later you reach a saturation point/critical mass as an editor. You just can't remember every story as well as you'd like to.

As to the story itself, this was gives off an urban gothic flare with a hint of a high fantasy undercurrent. In it, the character of Simon Magus seeks revenge for his dead wife. Simon Magus seems like a high fantasy name, only very early on we find ourselves in a club that would seem right at home in Manhattan. Other tidbits also let us know this is a modern setting, such as the guns the DJ has in the club, and the mention of Halloween. Yet there are also tidbits that leak into this story that seem to come from an older, almost forgotten time, such as Simon's name, the mention of the otherkind, a history between the characters that seems to go back far longer than it should ...and let us not forget the last dragon. All of these tidbits are skillfully interwoven, and you find yourself nodding along as Simon seeks the aforementioned vengeance for his dead wife, even if it means killing the dragon in the bargain. Shawna's editorial caption also sums this one up rather nicely: "Vengeance, they say, is a dish best served cold. But it can be hard to remember that when your veins are running hot with anger and despair." Art to this one was provided by Chris Cocozza, which marks his seventh illustration in the magazine.

After this was have "Myths & Legends" by Kathe Koja, another story that was accepted by the magazine before my time. This one is a rather quick tale about a high school girl who must finish her homework assignment about myths & legends that is due tomorrow while battling the ever-dangerous procrastination. Art to this one was provided by Kris Chau.

Finally we have "A Fish Story" by Sarah Totton. This is another one of my slush survivors. It also marks the first author I ever worked with on a rewrite of a story. The rewrite itself wasn't too extensive. The story itself was basically there in my opinion. It just needed a few tweaks. I suggested them to Sarah and she came through with flying colors. Interestingly enough, Sarah had submitted something to us at an earlier time that I had rejected. In the rejection, I gave her some feedback on the story. She applied that feedback, sent the story back out, and later informed me that she had sold it to *Writers of the Future*. So given the end results of these two stories, I guess it's fair to say that Sarah liked my editorial feedback. But if you need further proof, it came in the form of her next submission, i.e. the story she sent us after selling "A Fish Story." When I informed her that because she had now sold something to us her future submissions would be automatic passes to Shawna, she wrote back, "What? You mean I won't have Cohen's guiding touch on my stories going forward?" That one brought a big old smile to my face. Of course, a few years later, Sarah is once again under the spell of "Cohen's guiding touch," since a while back I accepted her short story collection as an an acquiring editor for Fantastic Books. It includes "A Fish Story" as well as "The Bonefisher's Apprentice," the story she sold to *Writers of the Future*. The collection should be coming out in the not-too-distant future. Ah, symmetry.

As to the story itself, let me start off by saying that I have always been a tough sell with funny fantasies. They have their place in our genre and I fully acknowledge that. But I also know my own likes and dislikes enough to know that most speculative literature that is meant to be funny just doesn't ring my bells. But this ...this was absolutely hilarious. In the first sentence I was reading about a world with cloud fishing and pink yaks. Wild stuff. As I kept reading, I found myself laughing aloud as a young woman pursues her "one true love" with obsessively hilarious determination, to the point that she seeks to catch the legendary Barbary Fish to impress him. While we were working on the rewrite, I remember mentioning to Sarah that reading this reminded me of reading Mervyn Peake, to which she replied, "Peake is my hero." It shows, but she was not for one moment derivative. The style and imagination may have been somewhat reminiscent of Peake, but I haven't seen a story like this one before or since. It was eventually reprinted in *Fantasy: Best of the Year*

2007, edited by Rich Horton. Art to this one was provided by Caitlin Kuhwald.

I should also note that each time I've passed along a slush story to Shawna that I consider funny or silly in tone (which admittedly hasn't happened often), it has sold to the magazine. So while I can't promise you that passing along your funny fantasy means Shawna will buy it, I do have an excellent track record here. Basically, if you can make me laugh with a speculative tale, you're really doing something right, because generally speaking, the humor falls flat for me. I am a very tough sell here.

So that wraps up this issue. And my favorite story? "A Fish Story' by Sarah Totton. And my favorite artwork? Gordon Crabb's cover illustration.

Originally posted on douglascohen.livejournal.com on January 1st, 2010

Part seventy-four in my comprehensive retrospective as I read the fiction in *Realms of Fantasy* and offer my thoughts. This time around I'll be putting a cap on 2006 as I discuss the December 2006 issue.

The cover to this one is by Joseph Corsentino. While I was unable to determine the origin of this illustration, it's worth noting that with this issue things took off in a different direction over at Sovereign Media in terms of how they handled their covers. Chicks in chain mail covers went out the window, as did high fantasy covers (mostly). Instead, things started trending toward a lot more urban fantasy. A number of covers also incorporated fairies, and media covers also remained prominent going forward. There were signs of this transition happening back in 2004 and 2005, but with this issue the new look really became the norm under Sovereign Media.

It's also worth noting that this image also appears in the Artists Gallery, which marks the first time an image in the Artists Gallery was used on the cover. This said, I'll also point out that the cover to the April 2006 cover of RoF appeared in a different edition of the Artists Gallery, though this is something I recall from memory, so I couldn't tell which issue.

A rundown of this issue's nonfiction is as follows:

In the Movie/TV column, Resa Nelson covers *The Prestige* (loved it) and *The Fountain* (hated it). In the Folkroots column, Terri Windling discusses the personification of Death. In the Books column, Gahan Wilson reviews *The Ruins* by Scott Smith, *Renfield, Slave of Dracula* by Barbara Hambly, *Havoc Swims Jaded* by David Schow, and Paul Witcover reviews *Shriek: An Afterword* by Jeff VanderMeer, *Soldier of Sidon* by Gene Wolfe, and *The Stolen Child* by Keith Donahue, and in this issue Paul also conducts an interview with Laurell K. Hamilton. In YA Books, Michael Jones reviews *Wuthering High* by Cara Lockwood, *Braced 2 Bite* by Serena Robar, *Chance Fortune and the Outlaws* by Shane Berryhill, *Life As We Knew It* by Susan Beth Pfeffer, *Leven Thumps and the Gateway to Foo* by Obert Skye, *Now You See It* by Vivian Vande, *The Wizard, the Witch, & Two Girls From Jersey* by Lisa Papademetriou, and *The Dark in the Woods*, edited by Ellen Datlow and Terri Windling. In the Artists Gallery, Christine Colby covers the artwork of Joseph Corsentino. And in the Games section, Eric T. Baker reviews *Dungeon Siege II: Broken World* for the PC, *Prey* for the Xbox 360 and the PC, *Blade Dancer: Lineage of Light* for the PSP, the RPG, *Kobalds Ate My Baby!*, and the *Dungeons & Dragons Eberron* supplement, *Secret of Xen'drik*.

On to the fiction ...

The lead story is "Lost Wax" by Leah Bobet, which marks her second appearance in the magazine. In this high fantasy tale, we are introduced to a world where magic is a rather wild and untamed thing. However, there are ways to shape and mold this magic, such as a wax factory, where wizards, casters, and molders shape the magic through the wax. In this factory, we are introduced to our young protagonist, Simon Lake, who helps sweep, shine, clean up the loose bits of wax, etc. All agree this is a great honor. However, Simon yearns for something more. Like so many adolescents, he dreams grand dreams that seem so real and attainable at his young age. He believes magic is the way to achieving something more than the life he lives. Each day he secretly sneaks loose bits of wax from the factory and spends his nights shaping the wax, trying to capture the magic. Always his efforts meet with failure. But there are other ways of finding the magic ...and sometimes, the magic finds you. And when it finds Simon, he gets far more than he ever bargained for. This story was reprinted in *The Mammoth Book of Extreme Fantasy*, edited by Mike Ashley. Art in RoF was provided by Hyejeong Park.

Next up we have "In the Lair of the Moonmen" by Jon Hansen. Jon is another slush survivor of mine. The story could be classified as sword & planet, a near-extinct subgenre of sword & sorcery. It was rather popular in the days of the pulps. For those who haven't heard of this subgenre, sword & planet is basically sword & sorcery, with the protagonist being transported by some means from Earth to another world, where s/he then proceeds to undergo a sword & sorcery adventure. Some people could trace its roots back to Edgar Rice Burrough's John Carter of Mars. Robert E. Howard tried his hand at this with his novel *Almuric* (posthumously completed). Other authors who have dabbled in this area are Leigh Brackett, C.L. Moore, and Michael Moorcock. I haven't heard much about sword & planet in some years, as most of the champions of this brand of literature have passed on, and few have stepped up to carry on the torch.

So it's probably not a surprise this this is the first sword & planet story to be published in RoF.

As to the story itself, as you might expect from a tale in this subgenre, this one is firmly in the tradition of the pulps. Being as I love the pulps, I mean this in the most complimentary way. Basically, we have a land that has been subject to air raids by the moon men. When it's discovered that these raiders are in fact laired on the moon, by order of his king our princeling protagonist joins forces with a wizard to lead an enchanted hot air balloon expedition to the moon to strike back at these raiders. So while a moon is not quite a planet, for the purposes of this retrospective I'll say it's close enough that I'll term this tale as sword & planet. There is a lot of wit and dry humor in this tale that brings to mind Fritz Leiber's sword & sorcery duo of Fafhrd and the Gray Mouser. Leiber was another one of the acknowledged sword & sorcery masters and was churning out S&S back when sword & planet was still kicking. I'm honestly not sure if Leiber ever wrote a sword & planet tale, but I wouldn't be surprised if he did. Art to this one was provided by Tom Kidd, which marks third illustration in the magazine.

Then we have "Echoes of Me" by Michelle Thuma. This is another piece that was accepted back when Carina was with the magazine. The story itself deals with a woman mired in the past after losing the love of her life. In fact, she has become so mired in this past that phantoms of her have become physical manifestations, thus enabling her to "stay in the past" as opposed to dealing with her grief. Art to this one was provided by Chi-Yun Law.

After this we have "Of Swords & Horses" by Carrie Vaughn, which marks her fourth appearance in the magazine. This one deals with a daydream that so many of us might have had when we younger: what if there was a fantasy world we could go to? Would you go? Would you leave everything behind to enter a world that until now you only entered through words? It's not a new idea, but what is new (at least to me) is how Carrie handles it. Instead of focusing on the youth faced with this choice, she focuses on the mother, after her child has left. Only as far as mom knows, her baby is missing and possibly dead. The possibility that she has left for some greater destiny in a magical realm hasn't occurred to her. Everything is handled in a rather believable manner, including how someone from our world could suddenly adapt to this fantasy world. Art to this one was provided by Zela Lobb, which marks her second illustration in the magazine.

Following this we have "The Valhalla Job" by Sandra McDonald, which marks her third appearance in the magazine. This one is a humorous take on home makeover programs, as one of them sets out to to give Valhalla a makeover. However, along the way the crew gets embroiled in the lives and politics of Valhalla's inhabitants. Makes perfect sense to me. After all, what's a reality TV show without a little drama? Art to this one was provided by David Leonard.

Then we have "Shelf Life" by Thomas Seay, which marks his second story in the magazine. This was another story that was accepted back during Carina's time. It's also the last story that was in inventory from her time. So being as I mentioned with the covers that this issue marks something of a transition, I suppose it's fitting that with the same issue the fiction department should finish publishing the stories that were accepted during the time of my predecessor. As to the story itself, it's another vignette. This one is a story for writers and folks who absolutely love to read, as it tells the charming little tale of one little book who dares to be different, calling himself 1985 (among other names). Art to this one was provided by John MacDonald.

Finally we have "Infants in the Lake of Fire" by M.K. Hobson. This is a tale of innocence and unfortunate knowledge. In this tale, we are taken to Limbo, a place for souls of various folks who don't belong in Heaven or Hell. In this story, the souls in question are a pair of very young children. As you might expect, such souls are rather innocent and have limited self-awareness. And while this may not be Hell, there are still dark and terrible things to be found in Limbo ...or at least they are dark and terrible when you come to understand them. And the more you understand the more awareness this unlocks, which in turn leads to a loss of innocence. And as with Adam and Eve and the Tree of Knowledge, such knowledge and loss of innocence comes with a cost, one that not even a very young child can avoid paying. Art to this one was provided by Erin and Kelly Carty.

So that wraps up this issue, as well as 2006. And my favorite story? "Shelf Life" by Thomas Seay. And my favorite illustration? Zela Lobb's illustration to "Of Swords & Horses."

Originally posted on douglascohen.livejournal.com on February 15th, 2010

Part seventy-five in my comprehensive retrospective, as I read the fiction in *Realms of Fantasy* and offer my thoughts. This time around I'll be butting heads with the February 2007 issue.

The cover to this one features the artwork of Wendy Froud. Wendy Froud is also one of the artists profiled in this issue's artist gallery, and, as with last issue, the cover illustration also appears in the artist gallery. As to the artwork itself, it was originally the cover *to The Art of Wendy Froud*.

A rundown of this issue's nonfiction is as follows:

In the Movie/TV column, Resa Nelson covers the movie, *Eragon*. In the Folkroots column, Midori Snyder writes about the magic of food. In the Books column, managing editor Laura Cleveland reviews *Peter Pan in Scarlet* by Geraldine McCaughrean, the first authorized sequel to J.M. Barrie's original story, Gahan Wilson reviews *Here Comes a Candle* by Fredric Brown, and Paul Witcover reviews *Tourmaline* by Paul Park, *The Ladies of Grace Adieu and Other Stories* by Susanna Clarke, *The Privilege of the Sword* by Ellen Kushner, and *Ex Cathedra* by Rebecca Maines. In YA Books, Michael Jones reviews *Fairest* by Gail Carson Levine, *Changeling* by Delia Sherman, *Troll Bridge* by Jane Yolen and Adam Stemple, *No Place For Magic* by E.D. Baker, *River Secrets* by Shannon Hale, *Peter and the Shadow Thieves* by Dave Barry and Ridley Pearson, *The Last Days* by Scott Westerfeld, and *Catalyst* by Nina Kiriki Hoffman. In the Artists Gallery, Ari Berk interviews the aforementioned Wendy Froud, and also Brian Froud. And in the Games column, Eric T. Baker reviews the board game, *War of the Ring*, based on Tolkien's *Lord of the Rings*, *Lego Star Wars II: The Original Trilogy*, "for the PC and every game system except the Wii and the PS3," *Spectral Souls* for the PSP, *Disgaea 2* for the PSP, *Yakuza* for the PS2, and *Test Drive Unlimited* for XBox 360 and the PC.

On to the fiction ...

It's worth noting that this is the first issue where all the fiction contributors have had stories that appeared in earlier issues of the magazine. Considering this is the seventy-fifth issue of RoF, that's quite an achievement. It clearly demonstrates the magazine was very consistent in publishing new talent and/or established authors who hadn't appeared in the magazine before. And since by this point there were a ton of regular contributors as well, RoF really did and still does strike a great balance between the regulars and the new. What makes this all the more interesting is that most issues contain five or six stories. But this issue contains *eight* stories. Not bad!

The lead story of these eight is "Three Wishes" by Bruce Holland Rogers, which marks his tenth appearance in the magazine. In this rather short piece, a man finds a genie in a bottle and is granted the standard three wishes. Only Rogers takes things in a somewhat different direction when the man doesn't use any of them. Art to this one was provided by William L. Brown.

Next up we have "Looking After Family" by Carrie Vaughn, which marks her fifth appearance in the magazine. This one is set in the same universe as her very popular Kitty Werewolf novels. In this piece, a young man father's hunted werewolves but was killed by one of them. The young man is taken in by his father's family. The son wishes to take up the father's work and perhaps wreak a little vengeance in the bargain, but when the opportunity presents itself, he must decide whether he is willing to follow through at the cost of the lives of his family. Art to this one was provided by Scott Anderson.

Then we have "Spare Change" by Chuck Rothman, which marks his second appearance in the magazine. It's worth noting that Chuck's first appearance in the magazine was in the very first issue. Interesting RoF factoid: to date, he remains the only author from the first issue to have a second story appear in the magazine. As to the story itself, a man has had his life ruined by a mysterious organization known as THEM. But when he has an opportunity to end his suffering by passing it along to another, unexpected results occur. This one had a science fictional vibe to me, at times reminding me of the movie, *The Matrix*. Of course, I like *The Matrix*, so this is hardly a complaint. Art to this one was provided by Janet Hamlin, which marks her second illustration in the magazine.

After this we have "Syren" by Graham Edwards, which marks his third appearance in the magazine. This is another one of his gumshoe detective tales, the third such to appear in the magazine. With this story, Graham really begins to open his universe up. Until this point (at least in RoF), his stories in this world mostly were mostly a blend of contemporary fantasy and mythology. And while these elements are still present, with this story, a decided cyberpunk bent also starts to emerge in this universe. It's with this story that I pretty much stopped thinking of the protagonist as the gumshoe detective, and started thinking of him as the cyber-detective. As to the story itself, our cyber-detective gets pulled into a case he'd rather not be a part of, but favors are owed and powerful people are doing some big-time arm-twisting. And so the detective must hunt down the son of a titan of industry, while navigating through golems, cybernetic syrens, temporal thieves, crooked cops, and of course, the perils of misguided love. Art to this one was provided by Scott Grimando, which marks his thirteenth illustration in the magazine.

Following this we have "The Devil and Mrs. Comstock's Snickerdoodles" by Eugie Foster, which marks her third appearance in the magazine. In this lighthearted tale, a reporter investigates reports of the Devil ...only when he arrives on the scene, he finds that the purported Devil is in the form of a cat. Very naturally, he is inclined to dismiss this report as a hoax. But as we all well know, the Devil can come in many shapes and sizes. Is this cat one of them? Perhaps. Art to this one was provided by Lori Koefoed, which marks her eleventh illustration in the magazine.

Then we have "Number of the Bus" by Jay Lake, which marks his sixth appearance in the magazine. In this world, wizards find their magic through stories. And in this tale, our young protagonist's magic is based around the stories of those people circulating through the transit bus. And not just the living people; there is a regular ghost on this bus as well. And when a living version of that ghost one day steps onto the bus, it throws everything into question. Numbers and particularly prime numbers factor heavily into this tale, for every bus has a number and follows its own schedule. Math was my worst subject in high school, so I took a lot of what the author told me at face value in this one, but I would imagine the math geeks out there will get an extra thrill from reading this one. Art to this piece was provided by Andrea Wicklund, which marks her fifth illustration in the magazine. The artwork was also selected for inclusion in the Editorial section of *Spectrum 14: The Best in Contemporary Fantastic Art.*

The next story is "Circus, Circus" by Eric M. Witchey, which marks his third appearance in the magazine. This also marks the 450th story to be published in RoF. As to the story itself, it's a rather touching tale. A young boy makes a request of the spirit of the circus, for all circuses have a spirit. He wants nothing more in the world than to be a circus. Not to run away with the circus, but to *be* a circus. It seems like an impossible request, but when tragedy strikes, we learn exactly what a circus is capable of. Art to this one was provided by Val Bochkov.

And finally, we have "In the Thicket, With Wolves" by Josh Rountree, which marks his fourth appearance in the magazine. In this one, a young woman is pregnant and the father has taken off. She's struggling to make enough money, and to add to her worries, it seems as though her child will be born with complications. Desperate, she turns to the mystical thicket wolves to strike a bargain that will ensure her child is born healthy. But like the oldest of fairy tales, we all know bargains such as these come with a steep price. Art to this one was provided by Patrick Arrasmith, which marks his fifteenth illustration in the magazine.

So that wraps up this issue. And my favorite story? "Circus Circus" by Eric M. Witchey. And my favorite artwork? Scott Grimando's illustration to "Syren."

Originally posted on douglascohen.livejournal.com on April 4th, 2010

Part seventy-six in my comprehensive retrospective as I read the fiction in *Realms of Fantasy* and offer my thoughts, right up to the present. This time around I'll be discussing the April 2007 issue.

The cover to this one features the artwork of Victoria Francés, which marks her second illustration in the magazine. I was unable to determine the origins of this illustration.

A rundown of this issue's nonfiction is as follows:

In the Movie/TV column, Resa Nelson covers the movie, *300*, based on the graphic novel by Frank Miller. In the Folkroots column, Midori Snyder discusses the ancient roots of the masked comic theaters. In the Books column, Gahan Wilson reviews *Adventures in Unhistory: Conjectures on the Factual Foundations of Several Ancient Legends* by Avram Davidson, *The Darkening Garden: A Short Lexicon of Horror* by John Clute, *The Salon of the Fantastique: Fifteen Original Tales of Fantasy*, edited by Ellen Datlow & Terri Windling, and Paul Witcover reviews *The Orphan's Tales, Volume I: In the Night Garden* by Catherynne M. Valente, *Dragon Avenger* by E.E. Knight, *Pictures from an Expedition* by Alexander C. Irvine, and *Three Days to Never* by Tim Powers. In YA Books, Michael Jones reviews *Beka Cooper: Terrier* by Tamora Pierce, *Spirits That Walk in Shadow* by Nina Kiriki Hoffman, *Flora Segunda* by Ysabeau S. Wilce, *Cupid* by Julius Lester, *Fangs 4 Freaks* by Serena Robar, *Larklight* by Phillip Reeve, *Water Song* by Suzanne Weyn, *The Salem Witch Tryouts* by Kelly McClymer, and Laura Cleveland reviews *Here, There Be Dragons* by James A. Owen. In the Artists Gallery, Karen Haber covers the art of P. Craig Russell, And in the Games column, Eric T. Baker reviews *World of Warcraft: Burning Crusade*, *Gears of War* for the Xbox 360, the RPG, *Neverwinter Nights 2*, the *Dungeons & Dragons* module, *Expedition to Castle Ravenloft*, and *Mage Knight Apocalypse* for the PC.

On to the fiction ...

The lead story is "A Touch of Hell" by Richard Parks, which marks his twentieth appearance in the magazine, making him the first author to have twenty stories appear in RoF.* This is another story about his far eastern samurai detective, Lord Yamada, the third such story to appear in the magazine. In this one, Lord Yamada is pressed for cash and accepts an assignment to deal with an ogre that has killed a young woman and is causing trouble along an important path. As is often the case with such stories, this assignment proves to be far less than straightforward. Art to this one was provided by Tiffany Prothero, and the artwork was nominated for a 2007 Chesley Award for Interior Illustration. It was also selected for inclusion in the Editorial section of *Spectrum 14: The Best in Contemporary Fantastic Art.*

Next up we have "The Rope: A New Tale of the Antique Lands" by Noreen Doyle, which marks her fourth appearance in the magazine. In this one, there is a rope-charmer of considerable skill with something of a mystery about him. For whenever the young boys climb up the rope that he causes to rise into the sky, they seem to vanish. Finally, a young woman endeavors to work with the rope-charmer and solve the mystery of where this rope leads. Well, wherever it goes, Rich Horton must have appreciated the location, because this piece was included in his anthology, *Fantasy, The Best of the Year, 2008.* Art to this one was provided by Paul Lee, which marks his fourteenth illustration in the magazine.

Then we have "Stephanie Shrugs" by Josh Rountree, which marks his fifth appearance in the magazine. In this urban fantasy, we are introduced to a young rock n' roller with dreams of stardom. Before his career takes off, he receives a visit from a beautiful and mysterious woman who seems to know more than she should and who ends up setting him along the path he has been dreaming of. Over the years, she shows up again and again at crucial points in his life. She might be his muse, but she might be something else entirely. Music lovers should get a particular kick out of this one. Art to this one was provided by Eric Fortune, which marks his fourth illustration in the magazine.

After this we have "Black Jack Davy" by Trent Hergenrader. In this Wild West fantasy, a newly made widow struggles to find happiness on the frontier while the ghost of Black Jack Davy haunts the land, stealing young women away with a method that seems more in keeping with the fey than with any sort of frontier shootout as you might first imagine based on the milieu. Art to this one was provided by Brian Horton, which marks his fourth illustration in the magazine. I will also humbly point out that Trent's story marks my tenth slush survivor to appear in the magazine.

Following this we have "Red" by Jackie Kessler. This is a retelling of the Little Red Riding Hood fairy tale. The big twist? Well, if Little Red befriends the Wolf, would that qualify as a big enough twist for you? Yes? I thought so. Art to this one was provided by Jada Fitch.

Next up is "Bottles" by Samantha Henderson. In this dark fantasy, a single mother is struggling with her recent divorce, her repressed anger, and the psychic abilities she's been repressing since adolescence. Things become even more convoluted when she discovers that her daughter, early into adolescence herself, has developed the ability to remove the souls of living beings and store them in glass bottles. This story can be best summed up by two words the author uses quite effectively: never assume. It's also interesting that I reread this story when I did, because some months back this story was adapted into a twenty minute independent film. It's since been making the indie film circuit and has been doing quite well for itself. Sam was kind enough to send me a copy of the film. I suspect this was a thank you for the part I played in helping this one get into print. While Sam's story isn't a slush survivor, suffice it to say this one took a rather unusual and circuitous journey before finally making its way into the magazine's pages, and I ended up playing some small role in making this happen. As to what exactly happened, I believe this is a story best left off the web**, but if you ask Sam really nicely, maybe she'll tell you some time. As to the film, I ended up watching it right after I reread the story. As I told Sam, I think she should be very pleased. There were obviously some changes made to translate this into another medium, but overall I thought the film stayed very true to the original story. Art to this story was provided by Tony Shasteen and it was selected for inclusion in the Editorial section of *Spectrum 14: The Best in Contemporary Fantastic Art*.

Finally we have "The Tao of Crocodiles" by Euan Harvey, another of my slush survivors. At the time Euan wrote this he was living in Thailand, and he does an excellent job of painting the picture of what this land is like for the readers, making it seem truly exotic if you're from the western world. As to the story itself, a woman's dead lover is haunting her dreams in the form of a sexual crocodile. Yeah, pretty dark, and things just get darker when they try to get rid of the ghost. Art to this one was provided by Rob Johnson.

So that wraps up this issue. And my favorite story? "The Tao of Crocodiles" by Euan Harvey. And my favorite artwork? Tiffany Prothero's illustration to "A Touch of Hell."

*And at the time of the magazine's final closure, the only one to ever achieve this milestone.

**Or in print

Originally posted on douglascohen.livejournal.com on June 20th, 2019

Part seventy-seven in my comprehensive retrospective as I read the fiction in *Realms of Fantasy* and offer my thoughts. This time around I'll be saying hello to the June 2007 issue.

The cover to this one features Karl Urban in his role in the fantasy movie, *Pathfinder*. This marks the magazine's eighth movie cover and tenth media cover.

A rundown of this issue's nonfiction is as follows:

In the Movie/TV column, Resa Nelson covers the aforementioned *Pathfinder*. In the Folkroots column, Heinz Insu Fenkl discusses Trickster tales. In the Books column, Gahan Wilson reviews *The End of the Story: Volume One of the Collected Fantasy of Clark Ashton Smith*, edited by Scott Connors and Roger Hilger, *The Further Adventures of Beowulf, Champion of Middle Earth*, edited by Brian M. Thomsen, and he provides coverage of the online magazine, *The Cimmerian*, which was dedicated to Conan and his creator, Robert E. Howard, while Paul Witcover reviews *Polyphony 6*, edited by Deborah Layne and Jay Lake, *Scar Night, The Deepgate Codex: Volume 1* by Alan Campbell, *Flora Segunda* by Ysabeau S. Wilce, and *Weatherwitch: Book Three of the Crowthistle Chronicles* by Cecila Dart-Thornton. In YA Books, Michael Jones reviews *Into the Wild* by Sarah Beth Durst, *Wildwood Dancing* by Juliet Marillier, *Tattoo* by Jennifer Lynn Barnes, *Dragon Slippers* by Jessica Day George, *Evil Genius* by Catherine Jinks, *Dragonfrigate Wizard Halcyon Blithe* by James M. Ward, *The Scarlet Letterman* by Cara Lockwood, and *The Faerie Path* by Frewin Jones. In the Artists Gallery, Karen Haber covers the art of Stephaniu Pui-Mun Law. And in the Games column, Eric T. Baker reviews *Star Trek Legacy* for the PC and Xbox 360, *Marvel Ultimate Alliance* for the Xbox, Xbox 360, PS2, and PC, Bionicle Heroes for the PS2, Xbox 360, and GameCube, and the *Dungeons & Dragons* supplement adventure, *Scourge of the Howling Horde*.

It should also be noted that this issue marks the last one for book reviewer, Gahan Wilson. Gahan had been part of the magazine since the very first issue, a very respectable run of seventy-seven issues, or almost thirteen years.

On to the fiction ...

The lead story is "Afghan Buddha Payback" by David Pinault. This story was plucked from the slush and marks it marks David's first fiction publication. It is also marks the first story I ever fished from the slush that went on to publication wherein the author had no fiction credits whatsoever (though he did have a number of nonfiction credits outside the genre). As to the story itself, this one is a quirky contemporary fantasy tale, in which a pair of art thieves become involved with the Taliban and a Buddhist djinn while hunting for art in Pakistan that they might sell on the black market. Art to this one was provided by Lori Koefoed, which marks her twelfth illustration in the magazine.

Next up we have "Companions to the Moon" by Charles de Lint, which marks his fourth appearance in the magazine. This story was the first in the "Charles Vess Project," in which Charles Vess allowed the magazine to pair his paintings with various well known fantasy authors who would each create stories around one of his paintings. In this one, de Lint tells the tale of a woman who suspects her lover is cheating on her, only to discover that he is a member of the fairy court. Art to this one was obviously provided by Charles Vess.

Then we have "The Hotel Astarte" by M.K. Hobson, which marks her second appearance in the magazine. You might want to term this one historical fantasy. It takes right before the Great Depression, and introduces us to an alternate America where magic is alive and kicking, and the land is dominated by figures such as the King of the Midwest and the Emperor of the East. As you might expect right before the Great Depression, things are becoming somewhat ominous. The King of the Midwest is seeking the death of the Emperor of the East, believing that this will help the farmers and crops of his own land. To accomplish this, he employs a dead warlock who is his wife's former lover from years ago, and who almost killed her before falling in love with her instead. He also sends along the Prince of the Midwest, treating both of them as little more than chess pieces. But the past has a way of catching up to the present, and when it does, it sends powerful repercussions that will be felt in the future. This story appeared online on the *PodCastle* website as podcast 006. Art in RoF was provided by Michael Gibbs, which marks his thirteenth illustration in the magazine.

After this we have "Pennsylvania Dragon" by Stephen Chambers. This takes place in a small dwindling town in Pennsylvania, and is a dark tale about the dark things that come from the old country and rule from the shadows. In it, a young man who is looking forward to the rest of his life must deal with a dangerous and enigmatic figure known as the chicken man while those closest to him are dying or are in danger of dying. But the chicken man is just the tip of the iceberg. There are things far more dangerous, and the chicken man amounts to little more than the messenger. Art to this one was provided by Chris Cocozza, which marks his eighth illustration in the magazine.

Finally we have "Princess Lucinda and the Hound of the Moon" by Theodora Goss, which marks her fourth appearance in the magazine. This one is a charming fairy tale that takes place in the fictional European country of Sylvania. In it, we learn that the queen is heartbroken when she learns that she is unable to bear children. Then out of nowhere she discovers a baby in a basket and raises the child as her own daughter. But when it turns out the child is in fact the daughter of the moon, well, it's safe to say this complicates matters. This story was reprinted in *Year's Best Fantasy 8*, edited by David Hartwell & Kathryn Cramer. Art was provided by Erin and Kelly Carty, which marks their second illustration in the magazine.

So that wraps up this issue. And my favorite story? "The Hotel Astarte" by M. K. Hobson. And my favorite artwork? Charles Vess's illustration, which provided the inspiration to "Companions of the Moon."

Originally posted on douglascohen.livejournal.com on September 4th, 2010

Part seventy-eight in my comprehensive retrospective as I read the fiction in *Realms of Fantasy* and offer my thoughts. This time around I'll be making nice with the August 2007 issue.

The cover to this one is a Harry Potter illustration by Tony Shasteen, which marks his second illustration in the magazine. It also marks the third Harry Potter cover for the magazine. I was unable to determine the origins of this illustration.

A rundown of this issue's nonfiction is as follows:

In the Movie/TV column, Resa Nelson covers *Harry Potter and the Order of the Phoenix*. In the Folkroots column, Terri Windling discusses the themes in the story of Rapunzel. In the Books column, Paul Witcover reviews *Day Watch* by Sergei Lukyanenko, *Endless Things: A Part of Aegypt* by John Crowley, *Worshipping Small Gods* by Richard Parks, *No Dominion* by Charlie Huston, and *When They Came* by Don Webb. In YA Books, Michael Jones reviews *Prom Dates From Hell* by Rosemary Clement-Moore, *The Dead Girls' Dance* by Rachel Caine, *Worldweavers: Gift of the Unmage* by Alma Alexander, *City of Bones* by Cassandra Clare, *The Game* by Diana Wynn Jones, *Why I Let My Hair Grow Out* by Maryrose Wood, *Alfred Kropp: The Seal of Solomon* by Rick Yancey, *Iris, Messenger* by Sarah Deming, and Laura Cleveland reviews *Vintage: A Ghost Story* by Steve Berman. In the Artists Gallery, Ari Berk covers the art of Charles Vess in Neil Gaiman's world of *Stardust*. And in the Games column, Eric T. Baker reviews *Supreme Commander* for the PC, *Galactic Civilizations II: Dark Avatar* for the PC, *Earth Defense Force 2017* for the Xbox 360, *Armored Core 4* for Xbox 360, *Ghost Rider* for the PS2 and PSP, *Atelier Iris 3: Grand Phantasm* for the PS2, and the *Dungeons & Dragons* supplement, *Dungeonscape: An Essential Guide to Dungeon Adventuring*.

On to the fiction ...

The lead story is "Waiting at the Door" by Cherith Baldry, which marks her second appearance in the magazine. In this one, a woman comes to the fairy court, begging the fairy queen to return her stolen child. During the course of this encounter, we meet the fairy lord who originally stole the child. He has reached a crossroads in his life, and is no longer satisfied with his callous decadent existence. When he starts experiencing guilt over his actions, it leads to a number of changes in his life. Art to this one was provided by Stephanie Pui-Mun Law.

Next up we have "Little Miss Apocalypse" by Christopher Barzak, which marks his fourth appearance in the magazine. In this piece, a shy college student falls in love with a brilliant classmate. Over time, she reveals to him that she has the ability to see and sense clouds of death around people. But when it's later revealed that she's bipolar, it puts into question what is true vs. what is not. But come the end of this story, the author makes a pretty convincing case as to which side of the fence we should stand on concerning her supernatural abilities. Art to this one was provided by Chris Cocozza, which marks his ninth illustration in the magazine.

After this we have "A Trade in Serpents" by Alan Smale, which marks his third appearance in the magazine. In this piece, Smale takes an actual quote from Benjamin Franklin and reinvents its meaning, so that Benjamin Franklin has called down a curse on Britain, causing them to become infested with a plague of snakes. He adds further credence to this reinvention by noting Franklin's associations with Salem, not to mention the respective time period is close to the time when the witch trials and burnings were taking place. When the story begins, Franklin has been captured by the British, and they're attempting to extract the truth from him. But there is more to this Benjamin Franklin than meets the eye, as he proves to be something of a schizophrenic, with a personality that goes along with the scientist in him, one for the politician in him, and so on. And perhaps, just perhaps, there is a personality associated with Franklin's dark sorcerer. Art to this one was provided by Tony Shasteen, which marks his second illustration in this issue and his third in the magazine overall.

Then we have "MetaPhysics" by Elizabeth M. Glover. This is another story I pulled from the slush, and it marks Elizabeth's first fiction sale. And in the interests of full disclosure, I'll note that she happened to be a personal friend of mine before she submitted this piece to the magazine. I rejected her first piece, encouraged her to submit again, and she sent along "MetaPhysics." I read it, asked her to tweak the ending, and to make a long story short, she ended up snagging her first sale when Shawna decided to take this one for the magazine. As to the story itself, this one is a lighthearted tale about a demon from Hell, seeking souls to collect and bring back to meet his quota. He happens along a potential couple. When the man proves to be devout, he turns his attention to the woman, a scientist who also happens to be an atheist. Atheists are prime targets, and so the demon believes he has found a likely victim. However, our atheistic target demonstrates that it's not about believing in God that can provide protection from Satan's minions. It is *believing* that is important. And if there is one thing a scientist believes in, it's in the immutable laws of science. She goes on to demonstrate these beliefs, with amusing results.

This story actually has three separate illustrations, by Mark Harmon, Cameron Munk, and Annika De Castro. As to why this specific story has three illustrations, I'll simply provide the following note that was included on the first page of the story: *Note: You may wonder why there are three illustrations for this story. Well, we ran a very successful experiment with the illustration class at Southern Utah University in Cedar City. The class, taught by well-known artist Ben Sowards, was given the challenge of illustrating this story on time and on budget, and eleven students submitted their work to* Realms of Fantasy. *We chose our three favorites and decided to print all of them. We'd like to thank all of the students for sharing their illustrations with us and we wish we could have shown all of them. We expect you'll see their work in future issues of* Realms of Fantasy. This story was also reprinted in the recent anthology, *Sympathy for the Devil*, edited by Tim Pratt.

After this we have "Restless in My Hand" by none other than Tim Pratt (ah, symmetry), which marks his eighth appearance in the magazine. In this one, a man with a family in modern times inherits a strange ax from an even stranger delivery man, who informs him that this ax is his birthright and is to be delivered to him now that the ancient curse on his line has expired. The ax proves to be sentient, and it wants its owner to resume wielding him in an alternate reality to resume a war against the enemies for which this ax was forged to kill. One problem: our protagonist experiences deep urges because of this ax, but he loves and is dedicated to his family. But that love gets put to the test at times, and while I'm not going to give away the ending to this one, our protagonist's struggle to resist the lure to indulge the ultimate adolescent fantasy of becoming a hero in another world makes him a hero in an entirely different way. This story appeared on the *PodCastle* website as podcast 84. Art to the story in RoF was provided by Rob Johnson, which mark his second illustration in the magazine.

Finally we have "Time Tells All" by Way Jeng, which marks his second appearance in the magazine. In this amusing tale, we are introduced to a seemingly simple man who has a karmic surplus, so the sisters Happiness and Fate attempt to improve his life. As you might guess, these names indicate they're more than just ordinary sisters. However, the man they're out to help is more complex than meets the eye, and when Happiness falls for him, and then Fate too, hilarity ensues. Art to this one was provided by David Leonard, which marks his second illustration in the magazine.

So that wraps up this issue. And my favorite story? "Restless in My Hand" by Tim Pratt. And my favorite artwork? Tony Shasteen's cover.

Originally posted on douglascohen.livejournal.com on September 16th, 2010

Part seventy-nine in my comprehensive retrospective as I read the fiction in *Realms of Fantasy* and offer my thoughts. This time around I'll be sharing some thoughts on the October 2007 issue. This issue is something of a milestone in my retrospective series. Back in August 2007, when I wrote my very first RoF Retrospective for the very first issue of *Realms of Fantasy*, the October 2007 was the magazine's current issue. Being as the current issue of the magazine is now the October 2010 issue, it's taken me roughly three years to get to this point, and a run of thirty-five issues. It would be thirty-six, but when Tir Na Nog Press took over the magazine, RoF missed one issue before resuming publication. So over the course of thirty-five issues, I've done retrospectives on seventy-nine issues (including this one). That averages out to a little over two retrospectives per issue. Not bad.

The cover to this one features Michelle Pfeiffer in her role in the movie adaptation of Neil Gaiman's novel, *Stardust*. This marks the magazine's ninth movie cover and eleventh media cover.

A rundown of this issue's nonfiction is as follows:

In the Movie/TV column, Resa Nelson covers the big-screen adaptation of Neil Gaiman's aforementioned novel, *Stardust*. In the Books column, Paul Witcover reviews *Acacia: Book One of the War with the Mein* by David Anthony Durham, *The Kingkiller Chronicle, Day One: The Name of the Wind* by Patrick Rothfuss, *The End of the Story: The Collected Fantasies of Clark Ashton Smith*, Volume One, edited by Scott Connors and Ron Hilger, *Softspoken* by Lucius Shepard, *Soon I Will Be Invincible* by Austin Grossman, and Jeff VanderMeer joins the magazine with this issue and reviews *Deadstock* by Jeffrey Thomas, *Dangerous Offspring* by Steph Swainston, *Ilario: The Lion's Eye* by Mary Gentle, *Vacation* by Jeremy C. Shipp, and *The Music of Razors* by Cameron Rogers. In YA Books, Michael Jones reviews *Ironside* by Holly Black, *The Titan's Curse* by Rick Riordan, *The Wizard Heir* by Cinda Williams Chima, *Nobody's Princess* by Esther Friesner, *In the Serpent's Coils* by Tiffany Trent, *Tantalize* by Cynthia Leitich-Smith, *The Good Ghoul's Guide to Getting Even* by Julie Kenner, and *Hex Education* by Emily Gould. In the Folkroots column, Terri

Windling discusses the orphaned hero in myth, folklore, and fantasy. In the Artists Gallery, Karen Haber covers the artwork of Scott M. Fischer. In the Games column, Eric T. Baker reviews *Pirates of the Caribbean at World's End* for the XBox, *Spiderman 3* for all consoles and the PC, *Penumbra: Overture Episode One* for the PC, *S.T.A.L.K.E.R. Shadow of Chernobyl* for the PC, and *Touch the Dead* for the Nintendo Dual Screen. This issue also marks the introduction of the Graphic Novel column, and its inaugural reviewer is the aforementioned Jeff VanderMeer. This first time around he reviews *Mouse Guard Fall 1152* by David Peterson, *Death by Chocolate* by David Yurkovich, *Wormwood, Gentleman Corpse: Birds, Bees, Blood, and Beer* by Ben Templesmith, *The Secret History, Book One: Genesis* and *Book Two: Castle of the Djinns* by Jeane-Pierre Pecau, Igor Kordeey, and Carole Beau, and *Dungeon: Twilight, Vol. 1: Dragon Cemetery* and *Vol. 2: Armageddon* by Joann Sfar and Lewis Trondheim.

On to the fiction ...

The lead story is "Everyone Bleeds Through" by Jack Skillingstead. In this story, we are presented with a universe filled with parallel worlds; a couple that have met in alternate realities meet each other again, and we see an attraction based on recognition through molecules. This story was reprinted in *Science Fiction, Best of the Year 2008*, edited by Rich Horton. To the best of my knowledge, this marks the first time a story from RoF was included in a Best of science fiction anthology. Art to this one was provided by Janet Hamlin, which marks her third illustration in the magazine.

Next up we have "Paper Cuts Scissors" by Holly Black. This was the second story in RoF's Charles Vess project, wherein authors write stories based around illustrations provided by Charles Vess. In this piece, after having a fight with her boyfriend, a young woman who is able to change what takes place inside a story flees into a book, taking refuge inside the story within its pages. Our young protagonist attempts to win her back by tracking her down at the ultimate literary party, with scores of characters come to life in a very special library. This story was reprinted in *Year's Best Fantasy 8*, edited by David Hartwell and Kathryn Cramer. It is also available on the *PodCastle* website, as podcst 116. Art to this one in RoF one was obviously provided by Charles Vess, which marks his second illustration in the magazine.

After this we have "Save Me Plz" by David Barr Kirtley, which marks his fourth appearance in the magazine. In this piece, a college student is trying to track down her ex, who had been so addicted to multiplayer online fantasy game it led to them breaking up. But it turns out that our protagonist is actually part of the online game in question and is stuck in a repeating quest that was started long ago by her ex. With each successive quest, she is helping shape a new reality, one that is more in line with the fantasy world in question. Hints to this revelation are provided throughout, and this far-fetched idea is set up set up rather nicely. This story was reprinted in *Fantasy, Best of the Year 2008*, edited by Rich Horton. It also appeared as podcast 124 on the *Escape Pod* website. Art to this one in RoF was provided by Hyejeong Park, which marks his second illustration in the magazine.

Then we have "Roger Lambelin" by Jay Lake and Ruth Nestvold. This marks Jay's seventh appearance in the magazine and Ruth's third appearance. It also marks their second collaboration to appear in the magazine. Their first collaboration in RoF was "Schwarze Madonna and the Sandalwood Knight," and "Roger Lambelin" is set in the same high fantasy universe, though the characters this time around are different. In this piece, a knight and his companion journey into the strange dangerous world of the fairies to save the lady knight he loves. As to what results from this quest, I will go ahead and steal Shawna's editorial tag to this piece: "In fairyland each day is like a year in our world, and love can conquer all. In the real world love sometimes has to take a different path, and it's often unclear just what love has conquered." Art to this one was provided by Dave Leri, which marks his sixth illustration in the magazine. This illustration was nominated for a 2008 Chesley Award for Interior Illustration. It also appeared in the Editorial section of *Spectrum 15: The Best in Contemporary Fantastic Art*.

Following this we have "When the Train Calls Lonely" by Devon Monk, which marks her eighth appearance in the magazine. In this piece, a young woman able to see the dead sees her sweetheart go off to war. When the nearby train passes the farm she works on, the dead come to her with its whistle, telling her their last words so she can write them down and mail them off to the loved ones of the deceased. During their time apart, the couple-to-be grow into adults as they each learn to deal with death in their own ways. Art to this one was provided by Paul Lee, which marks his fifteenth illustration in the magazine.

Finally we have "Honest Man" by Naomi Kritzer, which marks her fifth appearance in the magazine. In this piece a young woman during WWII runs into an "honest" con man, i.e. he only cons liars and cheats. This con man has the ability to read thoughts, which he often uses to his advantage while running his schemes. Since the woman in question is honest, their relationship never becomes adversarial. As the years go by, he pops into her life a couple of more times, the last one being when she's an old woman who has just been conned. With his help, they team up to con the con artist ...but just how far this con runs is a fun answer that you don't get in full until the end of the tale. This story appeared as podcast 039 on the *PodCastle* website. Art to this one in RoF was provided by Joe Kovach. It marks his third illustration in the magazine and it also appeared in the Editorial section of *Spectrum 15: Best in Contemporary Fantastic Art.*

So that wraps up this issue. And my favorite story? "Honest Man" by Naomi Kritzer. And my favorite illustration? Dave Leri's illustration to "Roger Lambelin."

Originally posted on douglascohen.livejournal.com on October 8ᵗʰ, 2010

Part eighty in my comprehensive retrospective as I read the fiction in *Realms of Fantasy* and offer my thoughts. This time I'll be polishing off 2007 as I discuss the December 2007 issue.

This marks the first retrospective I've written since Kim and William Gilchrist of Damnation Books took over as the new publishers of *Realms of Fantasy*, saving the magazine from cancellation a second time after it ceased operations under Warren Lapine of Tir Na Nog Press. It's been almost four months since I wrote the last retrospective. Part of that was due to me wanting a break from all things RoF after the magazine was cancelled once again. The rest of the layoff was due to the fact that since the magazine has come back I've been pretty busy getting RoF caught up. I'm not sure how regularly I'll be able to write these going forward, but I do intend to see this series through to completion. It would be a shame to stop after writing seventy-nine previous installments, and I'll certainly try to write more than one every four months!

So without further ado:

The cover to this one features a fairy silhouette by Julie Fain. I was unable to determine the origins of the illustration, but I *can* tell you it's the only silhouette cover the magazine has ever run.

A rundown of this issue's nonfiction is as follows:

In the Movie/TV section, Resa Nelson covers the 3D movie, *Beowulf*. In the Folkroots section, Virginia Borges discusses Hans Christian Andersen's "The Little Mermaid." In the Books column, Paul Witcover reviews *Devices and Desires* by K.J. Parker, *Winterbirth* by Brian Ruckley, *Gospel of the Knife* by Will Shetterly, *Territory* by Emma Bull, *The Imago Sequence* by Laird Barron, the anthology *Fantasy*, edited by Sean Wallance and Paul Tremblay, Laura Cleveland reviews *God's Demon* by Wayne Barlowe, and Jeff VanderMeer reviews *Mister Pip* by Lloyd Jones, *Red Seas Under Red Skies* by Scott Lynch, *The Kingdom of Bones* by Stephen Gallagher, *Not Flesh Nor Feathers* by Cherie Priest, and *The Coyote Road: Trickster Tales*, edited by Ellen Datlow and Terri Windling. In YA Books, Michael Jones reviews *Wicked Lovely* by Melissa Marr, *Vintage* by Steve Berman, *The Silver Moon Elm* by MaryJanice Davidson and Anthony Alongi, *Interworld* by

Neil Gaiman and Michael Reeves, *The Princess and the Hound* by Mette Ivie Harrison, *Alex Unlimited: The Vosarak Code* by Dan Jolley, and *The Secret Life of Sparrow Delaney* by Suzanne Harper. In the Graphic Novels column, Jeff VanderMeer reviews *Scarlet Traces: The Great Game* by Ian Edginton and D'Israeli, *Artesia Afield/Afire* by Mark Smylie, *B.P.R.D.: The Universal Machine* by Mike Mignola, John Arcudi, and Guy Davis, *Robotika* by Alex Sheikman, and *Hell Beasts: How to Draw Grotesque Fantasy Creatures* by Jim Pavelec. In the Artists Gallery, novelist and artist Wayne Barlowe conducts a discussion with himself. And in the Games column, Eric T. Baker reviews *The Darkness* for the Xbox 360 and the PS3, *Vampire Rain* for the Xbox 360, *Transformers the Game* for the PC, *Confessions of a Part-Time Sorceress: A Girl's Guide to the Dungeons & Dragons Game*, and *Project Sylpheed* for the Xbox 360.

On to the fiction ...

The lead story is "Still Point" by Graham Edwards, which marks his fourth appearance in the magazine. This is another tale about his cyber-detective, which is also the fourth such tale to appear in this magazine. In this one, our cyber-detective's business is in dire straits and he has just hours left before it shuts down. Then a case comes his way involving the Still Point of the Turning of the World, which is the most important bank in this universe. There is some debate concerning just what this bank holds, but when he learns some corrupt cops are threatening to break into the bank, which could in turn lead to the end of the world, he accepts the case. Of course, saving the bank poses problems of its own when you have to contend with undead cops and the last remaining Leviathan. Art to this one was provided by Tony Shasteen, which marks his third illustration in the magazine.

Next up we have "Hot Water" by Richard Parks, which marks his twenty-first appearance in the magazine, and his fourth Lord Yamada tale. This is another detective tale (of the Far Eastern variety) as Lord Yamada must unravel the mystery of a strange entity haunting a waterfall while figuring out whether it's a demon or goddess and what to do about it. But as usual in these Lord Yamada tales, all is not quite as it seems. Art to this one was provded by Tiffany Prothero, which marks her second illustration in the magazine.

Then we have "The Fireman's Fairy" by Sandra McDonald, which marks her fourth appearance in the magazine. In this story, we're introduced to a world where firemen's mascots are creatures out of myth, such as dwarves, minotaurs, satyrs, etc. We move from premise to twist when a newly minted firefighter discovers that his station's mascot is a little fairy in pink tights called TinkerBob, who is rather flamboyant and somewhat irritating. Given that most firefighters are men and it is often considered a macho job, dealing with TinkerBob proves an exercise not just of patience but also self-discovery, acceptance, and learning for our protagonist as he also struggles to overcome post traumatic stress syndrome from his recent stint in Iraq. This piece was appeared as podcast 074 on the *PodCastle* website. Art to this one in RoF was provided by Bruce MacPherson.

After this we have "Transformations" by David Barr Kirtley, which marks his fifth appearance in the magazine. In this one, we meet a robot named Carrus who is somewhat reminiscent of the Transformers (as is the title, for that matter). The most obvious similarity is the robot's ability to transform into a car. The similarities end there though, as we learn Carrus has been stationed on this planet for some time in secret, waiting to hear from his people. He breaks protocol when he reveals himself to a teenage boy, and from there this story becomes an exploration of love and friendship between the two of them. To me, this story has a science fiction feel, but as Shawna sometimes does with these pieces I consider to be science fictional, she justifies the fantastical element through the exploration of love. Given this, her editorial blurb for this story reads thusly: "Whether you're made of metal and oil or flesh and bone, love can be an incredible transformative force." Art to this was provided by Rob Johnson, which marks his third illustration in the magazine.

Then we have "On Tuesday it Rained Horned Toads" by Joe Murphy, which marks his third appearance in the magazine. This is another Sprokly tale, a wooden girl brought to life, his third such tale to appear in RoF (it would seem this is an issue for recurring characters). In this one, Sprokly has become something between wood and real and has run away from home, as she's becoming more determined to assert her own independence, which means getting out from under the thumb of Grampser, her creator and the paternal figure in her life. She ends up taking refuge with an older couple whose child is mentally challenged. While there, Sprokly attempts to help the boy overcome her disabilities. No doubt she feels a certain connection to him given that she would like to be something a little closer to normal as well. But when Grampser and his mechanical horned toads come looking for Sprokly, there might not be enough time to help her newfound friend. Art to this one was provided by Lori Koefoed, which marks her thirteenth illustration in the magazine.

Finally we have "The White Isle" by Von Carr. This is another tale I pulled from the slush and I worked with the author on some very modest edits before passing this up the editorial ladder to Shawna McCarthy. In this one, a young and naive merchant prince is shipwrecked on a nearly deserted island. He falls in love with the oddly quiet witch woman who lives there, and when he's rescued he brings her back with him, intent on making her his wife. They say love is blind, but it isn't love that blinds the prince to what the woman is, just his own sheltered upbringing. The author makes it plain that just about everyone else recognizes the danger this woman poses, and we witness what you might call a slowly unfolding train wreck as the story progresses in this richly detailed world. Art to this one was provided by Stephanie Pui-Mun Law, which marks her second illustration in the magazine. This illustration was nominated for a 2008 Chesley Award for Interior Illustration.

So that wraps up this issue, as well as 2007. And my favorite story? "The White Isle" by Von Carr. And my favorite illustration? Tony Shasteen's illustration to "Still Point."

Originally posted on douglascohen.livejournal.com on January 30th, 2011

Part eighty-one in my comprehensive retrospective as I read the fiction in *Realms of Fantasy* and offer my thoughts. This time around I'll be discussing the February 2008 issue.

The cover to this one features a scene from *The Golden Compass* movie, based on the novel of the same name, and it marks the magazine's twelfth media cover.

A rundown of this issue's nonfiction is as follows:

In the Movie/TV column, Resa Nelson covers the aforementioned *The Golden Compass*. In the Books column, Paul Witcover reviews *The Dog Said Bow-Wow* by Michael Swanwick, *Mainspring* by Jay Lake, *The Traitor* by Michael Cisco, *Pirate Freedom* by Gene Wolfe, *The Blade Itself* by Joe Abercrombie, and Jeff VanderMeer reviews *The Secret History of Moscow* by Ekaternia Sedia, *The Well of Ascension* by Brandon Sanderson, *Shadowbridge* by Gregory Frost, *In the Cities of Coin and Spice* by Catherynne Valente, and *Chronicles of the Black Company* by Glen Cook. In the Graphic Novel column, Jeff VanderMeer reviews *Sardine in Outer Space Vols. 1-4* by Emmanuel Gilbert and Joann Sfar, *Flight 4* by Kazu Kibuishi, and *Korgi: Book 1* by Christian Slade. In YA Books, Michael M. Jones reviews *Midnight Alley* by Rachel Caine, *Uninvited* by Justine Musk, *Book of a Thousand Days* by Shannon Hale, *Hero* by Perry Moore, *The Nixie's Song* by Tony DiTerlizzi and Holly Black, *Little (Grrl) Lost* by Charles de Lint, and *Fight Game* by Kate Wild. In the Folkroots section, Janni Lee Simner writes about the folklore of Iceland. In the Artists Gallery, Karen Haber covers the artwork of Adam Rex. And in the Games column, Eric T. Baker reviews *BioShock* for the PC and Xbox 360, *Blue Dragon* for the Xbox 360, *Two Worlds* for the PC and Xbox 360, *Halo 3* for the Xbox 360, the RPG, *Prime-time Adventures*, *Fury* for the PC, and for the *Dungeons & Dragons Miniatures Game*, *D&D Icons: Legend of Drizzt Scenario Pack*.

On to the fiction ...

The opening story is "The People's Republic of the Edelweiss Village Putt-Putt Golf Course" by M. K. Hobson, which marks her third appearance in the magazine. First of all, yes, the story is as silly as the title suggests. Jeremy is your local nice guy doormat who at the local miniature golf course. The golf course belongs to Marxist and feminist girlfriend, Becky, a big, domineering woman who excels at turning Jeremy into said doormat. While on the job one day, Jeremy discovers a colony of tiny people living inside the castle on one the holes of the course. Jeremy takes an interest in them, and it turns out this civilization is an autocracy, and Jeremy and the tiny princess even have the beginnings of romantic affection toward each other ...until Becky, the Marxist feminist girlfriend returns from her vacation. At this point, romance and politics are both thrown into a state of upheaval. Art to this one was provided by David Leonard, which marks his third illustration in the magazine.

Next up we have "Blood and Oil" by Josh Rountree, which marks his sixth appearance in the magazine. This one is a science fantasy piece, and it plays with the tropes of magic and machines. Simon Hallowmander is the Flesh King and the last hope of humankind. Their foes are Hallowmander's bastard son, Richard the Remade, who leads the clockwork armies of the Tinker King in the final battle meant to decide the fates of both man and machine. The machines and the destiny guiding Richard seem unstoppable, so Simon the Flesh King must draw on the darkest arts there are to give humankind its last chance at survival against this evil enemy. But are you truly good when you commit the worst kinds of evil to protect the good? And even more, are you still human anymore? These are the questions Josh tackles in this apocalyptic story, which is essentially one extended climax. Art to this one was provided by Allen Douglas, which marks his ninth illustration in the magazine.

Following this we have "The King of the Djinn" by Benjamin Rosenbaum and David Ackert. In this one, an Arab man in the desert blessed (or cursed?) with the ability to have visions is occasionally visited by a creature he has come to think of as the King of the Djinn. In the story, his latest encounter with the djinn leads our protagonist to a poignant and uncomfortable crossroads involving the life of his son. It must have pretty poignant indeed, because this piece was reprinted in *Year's Best Fantasy 8*, edited by David Hartwell & Kathryn Cramer, and also *Best American Fantasy 3: Real Unreal*, edited by Kevin Brockmeier. Art to this one was provided by Ben Sowards.

Then we have "Hobnoblin Blues" by Elizabeth Bear. In this one, Loki from Norse mythology has become mortal ...and a rock star. And no one can party quite like a god gone mortal as we learn through various article, interview, and story snippets. Art to this one was provided by Dave Leri, which marks his seventh illustration in the magazine. This illustration was selected for inclusion in the Editorial section of *Spectrum 15: The Best in Contemporary Fantastic Art*. The illustration really captures the essence of what Loki is supposed to look like in this story. But don't take my word for it. You can ask Elizabeth. It so happened that I ran into her at a literary reading while this was the current issue of the magazine. I commented to her how much I liked the illustration, to which she replied (paraphrasing here): "I know! That's Loki. That's exactly how I pictured him." Pat yourself on the back there, Dave. You successfully dipped into the author's head.

After this we have "And Spare Not the Flock" by Margaret Ronald, which marks her second appearance in the magazine. In this one, a priest of Christ leaves the Nordic realms and journeys to Rome in the hopes of lifting his exile. His companion during his travels is a varg, a human who turns into a wolf, or vise versa depending on whom you talk to. Their companionship makes for a strange one, and along the way many assumptions about the natural order of things are questioned, some on the surface, and others beneath. So it only makes that come the end the natural order is shaken up more than ever. Art to this one was provided by Kiriko Moth.

Finally we have "The Singers in the Tower" by Peni R. Griffin, which marks her seventh appearance in the magazine. In this high fantasy piece, King Ventor long ago conquered a neighboring land and locked his royal enemies in a tower in the hopes of extracting their secrets. But all his enemies did day and night was sing, and years later their ghosts continue to sing, as they're bound to the tower by Ventor's curse. But along come a brother and sister from the conquered land, who journey to the heart of the enemy kingdom, so that the brother might study at the university to become a mathematician. The sister earns a living as a dressmaker, and helps support her brother at the university ...and when the two of them become involved in royal affairs, these two commoners just might be the key to ending the ancient curse ...and maybe to freeing their homeland too. Art to this one was provided by Matthew Baek.

So that wraps up this issue. And my favorite story? "Blood and Oil" by Josh Rountree. And my favorite illustration? Dave Leri's illustration to "Hobnoblin Blues."

Originally posted on douglascohen.livejournal.com on April 4th, 2011

Part eighty-two in my comprehensive retrospective as I read the fiction in Realms of Fantasy and offer my thoughts. This time around I'm diving into the April 2008 issue.

The cover to this one features the fairy photography of Joseph Corsentino (i.e. he photographed someone in fairy garb), which marks his second piece of artwork to appear in the magazine. I was unable to determine the origins of this piece.

A rundown of this issue's nonfiction is as follows:

In the Folkroots column, Midori Snyder discusses the Swan Maiden. In the Movie/TV column, Resa Nelson covers The Spiderwick Chronicles. In the Books column, Paul Witcover reviews Thunderer by Felix Gilman, Amberlight by Sylvia Kelso, A Betrayal in Winter by Daniel Abraham, In a Time of Treason by David Keck, One for Sorrow by Christopher Barzak, Eclipse One, edited by Jonathan Strahan, and Jeff VanderMeer reviews Last Dragon by J.M. McDermott, The Man on the Ceiling by Melanie Tem and Steve Rasnic Tem, Wastelands: Stories of Life After the Apocalypse, edited by John Joseph Adams, Paper Cities: An Anthology of Urban Fantasy, edited by Ekaterina Sedia, Of Love and Other Monsters by Vanda Singh, and The Outlaw Demons Wails by Kim Harrison. In YA Books, Michael M. Jones reviews Uninvited by Amanda Marrone, Starcross by Philip Reeve, Unwind by Neil Shusterman, Peter and the Secret of Rundoon by Dave Barry and Ridley Pearson, Alcatraz Verus the Evil Librarians by Brandon Sanderson, The Tapestry: The Hound of Rowan by Henry H. Neff, Extras by Scott Westerfeld, and The Red Queen's Daughter by Jacqueline Kosolov. In Graphic Novels, Jeff VanderMeer reviews Three Shadows by Cyril Pedrosa, Therefore Repent! by Munroe and Salgood Sam, Fruits Basket: Ultimate Edition # 1 by Natsuki Takaya, The Demon Ororon by Hakase Mizuki, Warcraft: Sunwell Trilogy by Richard A. Knaak and Jae-Hwan Kim, and Jellaby by Kean Soo. In the Artists Gallery, Karen Haber covers the work of James Gurney. And in the Games column, Eric T. Baker reviews Mass Effect for the Xbox 360, the multi-player online RPG, Pirates of the Burning Sea, Portal for the Xbox 360, PC, and PS3, the Dungeons & Dragons module, *The Fortress of the Yuan-ti, and Kingdom Under Fire: Circle of Doom* for the Xbox 360.

On to the fiction ...

The lead story is "Gift from a Spring" by Delia Sherman. The illustration to this one was provided by Charles Vess, which marks his third illustration in the magazine. This story and illustration also marks the third and final edition of the Charles Vess Project, wherein authors were paired up with illustrations by Charles Vess, and created stories inspired by the illustrations. In this one, a young artist in France who is lacking inspiration and money takes a job as a bookkeeper at a secluded camp that is run by a former dancer and her younger husband, who is a stage director. Questions about art and love are raised as our young protagonist becomes entangled in the lives of the camp's owners, and gradually a mystery becomes unearthed and revealed. And the catalyst for these revelations? A dishwasher! This story was reprinted in *Year's Best Fantasy 9*, edited by David Hartwell and Kathryn Cramer, as well as *The Year's Best Science Fiction & Fantasy 2009*, edited by Rich Horton.

Next up we have "The Doom of Love in Small Places" by Ken Scholes, which marks his second appearance in the magazine. This story is pretty bizarre, as we're introduced to a world where everything is requisitioned out, even emotions. And it seems love and hope are in very short supply. And when you try to obtain emotions while cutting through the red tape of bureaucracy, well, it makes for quite the twisted pretzel, but not so twisted to prevent Jonathan Strahan from including it in *Best Science Fiction and Fantasy of the Year, Volume 3*. Art to this one was provided by Cat Scott.

After this we have "On the Banks of the River of Heaven" by Richard Parks, which marks his twenty-second appearance in the magazine. This one is a far eastern fable that dips into Chinese mythology. The Celestial Herder wants nothing more than to cross the Bridge of Birds to be with his lady-love. Mind you, he is the *Celestial* Herder because the River of Heaven is actually the Milky Way. But another jealous god is causing the rains to come down, preventing the Bridge of Birds from forming. Meanwhile, the Celestial Otter is destined to forever chase the fish of the River of Heaven. In a moment of kindness, the Celestial Herder presents Otter with a fish, allowing him to finally know what is like to capture what he has forever been chasing. Otter wishes to repay this kindness, but the Herder desires nothing but to reach the woman he loves. But a mere otter could never help with that ...could he? This story also appeared on the *Podcastle* website as podcast 059. Art to this one in RoF was provided by Tiffany Prothero, which marks her third illustration in the magazine.

Then we have "Girl in Pieces" by Graham Edwards, which marks his fifth appearance in the magazine. It also marks the fifth story about his cyber-detective. In this one, as so often happens to him, trouble comes stumbling into his office when a golem is on the run from the zombie cops and stands accused of being a serial killer. Our detective has never trusted golems and also kicks the golem out of his office, but this particular golem's extreme insistence of his innocence as well some decidedly un-golem-like traits convince the gumshoe to take on this case of horrors, vendettas, and revelations. Art to this one was provided by Tony Shasteen, which marks his fourth illustration in the magazine.

Finally we have "The Dinosaur Diaries" by Scott William Carter, which marks his second appearance in the magazine. In this one the farm is in trouble, Pa has been dead for over a year, Ma appears to be losing her mind, the older brother is off at college and refuses to pitch in with the harvest coming, Uncle Ed is after the farm, and our poor protagonist is getting by on four hours of sleep a night as he struggles to oversee the farm by himself, take care of his mother and his little sister, go to school, and maintain a relationship with his girlfriend who will soon be leaving for college. And if that isn't enough, suddenly there are footprints appearing in the cornstalks ...large footprints that seem to belong to a Tyrannosaurs rex. But surely this is some sort of prank. Surely this isn't connected to his dead father somehow. Surely there is a logical explanation for this. Surely? Or surely not? Regardless, I should mention that Scott also used this as the title piece for his story collection, *The Dinosaur Diaries and Other Tales Across Space and Time*. I feel this is worth mentioning because a few years earlier, I had plucked one of Scott's stories from the RoF slush pile. When I started doing some editorial freelance work for Fantastic Books, since I already had a working relationship with Scott, he approached me about this collection, which I ended up taking. His original slush tale that I found for RoF, "The Grand Mal Reaper," is also part of this collection. Art to this piece was provided by Eric Fortune, which marks his fifth illustration in the magazine.

So that wraps up this issue. And my favorite story? "The Dinosaur Diaries" by Scott William Carter. And my favorite illustration? Tiffany Prothero's illustration to "On the Banks of the River of Heaven."

Originally posted on douglascohen.livejournal.com on April 26th, 2011

June 2008 (Issue 83)

Part eighty-three in my comprehensive retrospective as I read the fiction in *Realms of Fantasy* and offer my thoughts. This time around I'll be doing just that with the June 2008 issue.

The cover to this one features the art of John Howe. It was originally the cover to *Chimeras* by Christopher Evans.

A rundown of this issue's nonfiction is as follows:

In the Movie/TV section, Resa Nelson covers *Nim's Island*. In the Books column, Paul Witcover reviews *The Hidden World* by Paul Park, *Evil for Evil* and *The Escapement*, the second and third volumes in K.J. Parker's *Engineer Trilogy*, *The Dragons of Babel* by Michael Swanwick, *Lace and Blade*, edited by Deborah J. Ross, and Jeff VanderMeer reviews *A World Too Near* by Kay Kenyon, *The Magician and the Fool* by Barth Anderson, *The Bone Key* by Sarah Monette, and *Before They Are Hanged* by Joe Abercrombie. In YA Nooks, Michael M. Jones reviews *Gods of Manhattan* by Scott Mebus, *Hallowmere # 2: By Venom's Sweet Sting* by Tiffany Trent, *The Sweet Far Thing* by Libba Bray, *Sun and Moon, Ice and Snow* by Jessica Day George, *Runemarks* by Joanne Harris, *Neptune's Children* by Bonnie Dobkin, *Verdigris Deep* by Frances Hardinge, and *Pandora Gets Jealous* by Carolyn Hennesy. In the Graphic Novel column, Jeff VanderMeer reviews *The Museum Vaults* by Marc-Antoine Mathieu and Nantier Beall Minoustchine, *Age of Bronze: Betrayal, Part One* by Eric Shanower, *The Dreamland Chronicles: Books 1 and 2* by Scott Christian Sava, *The Wind in the Willows* by Kenneth Grahame and Michel Pessix, and *The Nightmare Factory: Based on the Stories of Thomas Ligotti* by various authors. In Folkroots, Rafaella Benvenuto and Theodora Goss write about the fairy lore of Italy and Hungary. In the Artists Gallery, Karen Haber covers the artwork of the aforementioned John Howe. And in the Games column, Eric T. Baker reviews *Mana Khemia: Alchemists of Al-Revis* for the PS2, *The Witcher* for the PC, *Nights: Journey of Dreams* for the Wii, *Universe at War: Earth Assault* for the PC, *Dark Messiah: Elements* for the Xbox 360, and *Avencast* for the PC.

It should also be noted that this is the first time Theodora Goss's work has appeared in the Folkroots column, which I find noteworthy since she is currently the editor of the Folkroots column.

On to the fiction ...

The lead story is "The Snake: A Story of the Flat Earth" by Tanith Lee, which marks her fourteenth appearance in the magazine. In this piece, a man betrothed to the most beautiful woman in the world is bitten by a snake while on the way to marry his beloved princess. When he dies of the poison, the princess is so distraught that she is left hovereing between life and death due to a broken heart. Her father sends his men far and wide, seeking someone who can bring the princess out of her state. Failure is met time and again, until one messenger meets a sorcerer who is far more than what he seems. Art to this one was provided by Stephanie Pui-Mun Law, which marks her third illustration in the magazine.

Next up we have "Lest Our Passage Be Forgotten" by Bradley P. Beaulieu. In this pseuo-medieval Japanese tale, we are introduced to Yasuo, a humble man who holds the position of smokeman. In this world, smokemen capture memories of people in smoke jars, and when the remembered person dies, he brings those memories to life in a fireworks ritual that helps usher their souls into the Lands of the Dead. His simple life is about to become more complicated though, not only because of his infatuation with a local widow, but also because he has been hired by the local Daimyo to harvest memories of the Daimyo's aging mother. Unfortunately, the Daimyo's mother wants no part of this, but the more Yasuo comes to know her, the more he comes to understand that her reasons for this are far more complicated than they seem at first glance. Art to this one was provided by Kiriko Moth, which marks her second illustration in the magazine.

After this we have "The Self-Fulfilling Prophet" by Way Jeng, which marks his third appearance in the magazine. In this lighthearted tale, a man with a negative attitude who always believes the worst will happen becomes a self-fulfilling prophet. It's one of the lighter takes on prophecy you'll ever read. Art to this one was provided by Mark Harmon, which marks his second illustration in themagazine.

Then we have "The Good Neighbor" by Betsy James. In a village where adults wear masks known as good neighbors and wearing a good neighbor ushers one into godhood, a boy on the verge of undergoing his adulthood rites doubts the power of the good neighbors and the stories told to him by the adults. As you might expect, the lessons of adulthood can be difficult. Art to this one was provided by Darren Winter.

Following this we have "The Summer of Lucy" by Kate Riedel, which marks her seventh appearance in the magazine. In this story, a midwestern town is in the throes of a draught. Everyone is struggling to get by, but when a starving dog shows up on the doorstep of Margaret's family, they're quick to take the dog in. As time goes on, Lucy the dog proves rather extraordinary ...and in more ways than they think, for it turns out that Lucy holds one of the keys to ending the draught. Art to this one was provided by Laurie Harden, which marks her seventeenth illustration in the magazine.

Finally we have "Here's What I Know" by Dennis Danvers. In this piece, a science ficiton writer is being visited by the ghost of his father. It turns out dad had a child by another woman, and now he wishes to help take care of her (financially speaking) by passing along a collection of collectible premiums to her. In order to make this happen, Dad wants his son to hunt down his half-sister, which means meeting her for the first time. And in order to find her, he must go, of all places, to a science fiction convention. Art to this one was provided by Andy B. Clarkson, which marks his third illustration in the magazine.

So that wraps up this issue. And my favorite story? "Here's What I Know" by Dennis Danvers. And my favorite artwork? John Howe's cover illustration.

Originally posted on douglascohen.livejournal.com on September 15th, 2011

August 2008 (Issue 84)

Part eighty-four in my comprehensive retrospective as I read the fiction in *Realms of Fantasy* and offer my thoughts. This time I'll be discussing the August 2008 issue.

So obviously it's been a long time since my last retrospective, over a year and a half. When RoF was canceled for the third and final time in early November of 2011, it had already been a month and a half since my last retrospective. The magazine's ending didn't exactly provide me an impetus to start writing them again. If the previous two cancellations were any indication, I was more inclined to take long breaks. On top of that, there has been a lot going on since then. Since I learned about the magazine's cancellation, I've started selling short stories with semi-regularity. I put out my first anthology (and I'm working on making the second one happen). I finished my first novel and put it through several drafts (with another draft or two to come). Long story short, I had a lot of other stuff on my plate professionally speaking. I still do, but I always meant to return to this retrospective series and finish what I started. As a reminder to myself of my intentions, all this time I've kept the August 2008 issue on my dresser. The poor cover has actually become a little bit faded from so much exposure to sunlight, but it served its purpose. Every time I saw that issue, I knew I had unfinished business. I still don't have much time to work on these retrospectives, but I've found a way to budget a few minutes of reading time into my schedule each day. It's not even enough time to finish the shortest story in an issue in a single sitting, but right now it's all the time I can afford. But even if I'm reading piecemeal going forward, I think the important thing is that the project will finally reach its conclusion. Including this issue, there are nineteen retrospectives left, and since we shouldn't be counting on another RoF revival anytime soon, I can actually see the light at the end of the tunnel. So with this said, let's dive in.

The cover to this one features the artwork of Rebecca Guay. While the illustration is a reprint, I was unable to determine its origins.

A rundown of this issue's nonfiction is as follows:

In the Movie/TV column, Resa Nelson covers M. Night Shyamalan's *The Happening* ...I believe the infamous Comic Book Guy just might call this one "Worst. Movie. Ever." In the Folkroots column, Terri Windling writes about how the idea of heart and home permeates fairy tales, folklore, and mythology. In the Books column, Paul Witcover reviews *Black Ships* by Jo Graham, *Walking Brigid* by Francis Clark, Pamela Freeman's *Blood Ties, Book One of The Castings Trilogy, Wicked Game* by Jeri Smith-Ready, and Jeff VanderMeer reviews *Sharp Teeth* by Toby Barlow, *The Veil of Gold* by Kim Wilkins, *Renegade's Magic* by Robin Hobb, *God and Pawns* by Kage Baker, and *Elric: The Stealer of Souls, Volume 1* by Michael Moorcock. YA Books appears to be on hiatus this issue, but in Graphic Novels, Jeff VandeMeer reviews *Amulet, Book One: The Stonekeeper* by Kazu Kibuishi. In the Artists Gallery, Karen Haber covers the artwork of the aforementioned Rebecca Guay. And in the Games column, Eric T. Baker reviews *The Experiment* for the PC, *Turok* for the PC, 360, and PS3, *Ninja Gaiden Dragon Sword* for the DS, *Devil May Cry 4* for Xbox360 and PS3, and *Sins of the Solar Empire* for the PC. This issue also includes an article on faerie festivals by Robert Gould.

On to the fiction ...

The lead story this issue is "A Letter to Nancy" by Carrie Vaughn, which marks her sixth appearance in the magazine. In this quirky little tale, a nurse writes letters to on a wounded soldier's non-existent sweetheart on his behalf, and afterward she throws a bottle into the ocean with the letter inside ...and it leads to far more than anyone ever expected. Art to this one was provided by Laurie Harden, which marks her eighteenth illustration in the magazine.

Next up we have "Spiderhorse" by Liz Williams. It marks her tenth appearance in the magazine, and it is the 500th story to be published in the magazine. In this piece, a dead woman rides Sleipnir, the eight-legged horse—or Spiderhorse—in the Wild Hunt. She captures the attentions of Wotan, who impregnates our narrator, and come the story's end she has been carrying the child seventeen years with the birth drawing near. This story was selected for inclusion in *Year's Best Science Fiction and Fantasy 2009 Edition*, edited by Jonathan Strahan. Art was provided by Huan Tran, which marks his second illustration in the magazine.

After this we have "The Restroom Murders" by Peni R. Griffin, which marks her eighth illustration in the magazine. In this piece, rumor takes on a life of its own when temps at a bank make up stories about a ghost, and people's repressed emotions make the ghost a reality as it starts haunting the bank as a poltergeist. Art to this one was provided by Tony Shasteen, which marks his fifth illustration in the magazine.

Then we have "Daughter of Botu" by Eugie Foster, which marks her fourth appearance in the magazine. In this piece of Chinese mythology, a rabbit becomes a human woman who ends of marrying and experiencing love. All the while, she must contend with her husband's stepmother, who like the protagonist herself is far more than she seems. This story also appeared as podcast 63 on the *PodCastle* website. Art to this one was provided by Jada Fitch, which marks her second illustration in the magazine.

Following this we have "Light of a Thousand Suns" by James Van Pelt, which marks his seventh appearance in the magazine. In this chilling tale, a security guard beset by nuclear nightmares stumbles upon a secret group that sacrifices willing victims in order to prevent a nuclear holocaust. Art to this one was provided by Dale Rutter.

Our penultimate tale is "Someone Desperately Needed to be Neil Gaiman" by Way Jeng, which marks his fourth appearance in the magazine. In this heartwarming tale, a father makes his best attempt to write a novel that seems like it was written by Neil Gaiman, all to satisfy his young daughter, who loves Neil Gaiman's stories. Art to this one was provided by Natalie Pierandrei.

Last but not least we have "Our to Fight For" by Jim C. Hines, which marks his third appearance in the magazine. In this piece, elves are at war with men in the modern world and the Ku Klux Klan wields magic. Racism is explored as a confused adolescent wants to join the Klan, but things become further complicated when the Klan commits violence against his elven friend. Art to this one was provided by David Palumbo.

So that wraps up this issue. And my favorite story? "Daughter of Botu" by Eugie Foster. And my favorite artwork? Tony Shasteen's illustration to "The Restroom Murders."

Originally posted on douglascohen.livejournal.com on April 13ᵗʰ, 2013

Part eighty-five in my comprehensive retrospective as I read the fiction in *Realms of Fantasy* and offer my thoughts. This time I'll be delving into the October 2008 issue.

The cover to this one features the artwork of James A. Owen and as best as I can tell is original to the magazine. This cover came out four issues before I started overseeing the magazine's artwork, but I nonetheless had a hand in some of this issue's artwork. Some months before this issue's release, James A. Owen had posted in-process sketches on his LiveJournal account. I enjoyed his post and mentioned as much in a comment on his blog. James replied that he'd be happy to have this whole sequence appear in *Realms of Fantasy*. I thought it was a great idea, so I emailed the publisher. I never heard back from him, so I assumed they weren't interested. Then later on I learned from James that this email set the wheels in motion for him being the featured artist in the Artists Gallery. Then later on the stakes got upped once more when James's artwork appeared on the cover. Over the years, *Realms of Fantasy* has put out a lot of covers featuring or including dragons in one form or another (nineteen to be exact), but without a doubt this one is the most distinctive of the bunch. How often do you see a beautiful illustration of a bad-ass dragon drinking tea? Am I little biased toward this cover since I played a small hand in bringing it about and also consider James a friend? You betcha. Do I still stand by what I say? Absolutely.

A rundown of this issue's nonfiction is as follows:

In the Movie/TV section, Resa Nelson writes about the rise of 3-D movies. In the Books column, Paul Witcover reviews *An Autumn War*, volume three in the Daniel Abraham's *Long Price Quartet*, *The Court of the Air* by Stephen Hunt, *The Hounds of Ash and Other Tales of Fool Wolf* by Greg Keyes, *Havemercy* by Jaida Jones and Danielle Bennett, and Jeff VanderMeer reviews *Artists Inspired by H.P. Lovecraft*, edited Jerad Walters, *Bring Down the Sun* by Judith Tarr, *Midnight Never Comes* by Marie Brennan, *Filter House* by Nisi Shawl, and *Too Many Curses* by A. Lee Martinez. In YA Books, Michael M. Jones reviews *Generation Dead* by Daniel Waters, *Little Brother* by Cory Doctorow, *Nobody's Prize* by Esther

Friesner, *Percy Jackson # 4: The Battle of the Labyrinth* by Rick Riordan, *Princess Ben* by Catherine Gilbert Murdock, *Vampire Academy # 2: Frostbite* by Richelle Mead, *the dead & the gone* by Susan Beth Pfeffer, and *Alfred Kropp: The Thirteenth Skull* by Rick Yancey. In Graphic Novels, Jeff VanderMeer reviews *The Amazing Remarkable Monsieur Leotard* by Eddie Campbell and Dan Best, *Out of Picture 2: Art from the Outside Looking In* by Jim Munroe and Salgood Sam, *Rapunzel's Revenge* by Shannon and Dean Hale with Nathan Hale, *Dungeon: Monstres, Vol. 1, The Crying Giant* by Joann Sfar, Lewis Trondheim, Mazan, Jean-Christophe Menu, and Nantier Beall, and *Doctor Grordbort's Contrapulatronic Dingus Directory* by Greg Broadmore. In Folkroots, Terri Windling writes about why myth and mythic fiction matter, and why they matter to her. In the Artists Gallery, Mia Nutick covers the aforementioned James A. Owen. And in the Games column, Eric T. Baker reviews *Ninja Gaiden II* for the Xbox 360, *Okami* for the Wii, *Summon Night: Twin Age* for the DS, *Penny Arcade Adventures. On the Rain-Slick Precipice of Darkness* for the PC, Mac, Unix, and Xbox 360, and *Kung Fu Panda* for the Pc, DS, Wii, PS2 & 3, and Xbox 360.

It should also be noted that this issue marks the last issue with Folkroots being under the editorial direction of Terri Windling. Terri was the founding editor of this column after being recruited by Shawna McCarthy. She wrote or edited every single issue, an impressive run of eighty-five issues.

On the fiction ...

The lead story is "The Purple Basil" by M.K. Hobson, which marks her fourth appearance in the magazine. In this piece, we are given a detailed look at the life of a modern witch and the accompanying Satanic ceremonies. Along the way, we learn that for all their darkness, at heart they too are human beings with feelings. Art to this one was provided by Tiffany Prothero, which marks her fourth illustration in the magazine.

Next up we have "The Luckiest Street in Georgia" by Vylar Kaftan. This is another tale I pulled from the slush, and I worked with Vylar on some light revisions before passing it up the editorial ladder. In this piece, an old woman on a certain street in Georgia (duh!) is able to see future events occurring on this street and impact the lives of those living on said street—a peculiar but effective gift. She can't change the past though, where she has a sad history of being left at the altar. However, one man across the street remains a mystery to her, someone who she sometimes sees watching her through his window, and he seems strangely outside the established magical rules for her street. And it just might be that he can help fix the past the way she fixes futures. Art to this one was provided by Eric Dinyer, which marks his ninth illustration in the magazine.

After this we have "Under the Skin" by Greg O. Weatherford, another slush survivor of mine. It also marks Greg's first sale. This one is a rather unusual tale about a smart adolescent girl who lives with a controlling father who also happens to be a werewolf. While the werewolf side of him only comes out once a month during the full moon, the reality is that the werewolf side of him has come to dominate every aspect of their lives as he strives to maintain his secret. It's this secrecy that leads to him being so controlling, and ultimately our protagonist must face the difficult question of whether to betray someone she loves so she can have a life of her own. Art to this one was provided by Eric Westbrook, which marks his second illustration it the magazine.

Then we have "The Horned Toad in Hubcap" by Joe Murphy, which marks his fourth appearance in the magazine. It also marks his fourth tale about Sprokly, the wooden girl given life by the magical tinkerer, Grampser. This tale deviates some from the previous stories since it is told through the point of view of Walter, the autistic boy Sprokly befriended in her previous adventure, whom she helped gain the power of speech with some of the magic she'd learned from Grampser. In this piece, Walter's favorite toy is his hubcap, where he claims he can see a whole different galaxy of stars ...until the spirit of a horned toad gets inside his hubcap. When Spokly and and Walter set out to solve the mystery of the hubcap, they learn that Grampser has been creating wooden equivalents of the horned toads in his never-ending quest to create true life. These wooden horned toads are killing the real ones, and the only way for the real ones to contact Walter and Sprokly and get help is through the hubcap. Art to this one was provided by Lori Koefoed, which marks her fourteenth illustration in the magazine.

Following this we have "All Beautiful Things" by Sharon Mock, my third slush survivor tale to appear in this issue. In this decidedly dark tale, we are introduced to a fairy world that has been overrun by humans and their iron technologies, except for the Inner Court of the fairies. A spoiled fairy princess is interested in seeing the world beyond, and she seduces a human ambassador to spirit her away, with disastrous results. I have to admit that by the time I came across this one in the slush I was pretty burned out on fairy stories—we got so many of them. But I have a soft spot for dark fiction. Combined with the fact that the author subverted so many of the tired tropes that are prevalent in fairy fiction, it made passing this one along a no-brainer. Art to this one was provided by Dave Leri, which marks his eighth illustration in the magazine. This artwork was selected for inclusion in the Editorial section of *Spectrum 16: The Best in Contemporary Fantastic Art*.

Finally we have "The Claw Unseen" by Euan Harvey, which marks his second appearance in the magazine. In this sword & sorcery piece, a thief in debt come across a trinket of treasure he believes will get him cut of financial difficulties. However, it turns out to be a cursed item; one that fills him with steadily building rage. When his rage reaches certain levels ....he grows, and with his growth and his growing rage he becomes a bigger and bigger problem for those around him. It sounds like a simple enough premise, but the execution in this piece made it fascinating throughout. Art to this one was provided by Rob Johnson, which marks his fourth illustration in the magazine.

I should also mention that this is the first time I'm writing about Euan's work in my retrospectives since he passed away from cancer. I never met him (he lives overseas, first in Thailand and then in the U.K. after his sickness worsened), but we got to be online friends, as our tastes in the genre were very similar. Come his unfortunate end, he was one of the magazine's most prolific contributors. He actually had two stories in inventory with us in inventory that would have been published posthumously had the magazine not closed down. His death is a shame—chiefly because he was a good and funny person who left behind a loving family—but also because it also deprived the community of a talented writer who was improving with every story he wrote. I still think about him and what might have been.

So that wraps up this issue. And my favorite story? We have one of those rare ties, this time between "All Beautiful Things" by Sharon Mock and "The Claw Unseen" by Euan Harvery. Two very different stories, but they're equally effective in their own distinct ways. And my favorite artwork? Also a tie! This time the dual honors go to James A. Owen's cover with his tea-drinking dragon, and Dave Leri's illustration to "All Beautiful Things" by Sharon Mock.

Originally posted on douglasochen.livejournal.com on May 11th, 2013

Part eighty-six in my comprehensive retrospective as I read the fiction in *Realms of Fantasy* and offer my thoughts. This time around I'll be delving into the December 2008 issue.

The cover to this one is by Donato Giancola, which marks his third illustration in the magazine. It was originally the cover to issue 307 of *Dragon Magazine* and it depicts Melisandre, a character from one of my favorite topics: *A Song of Ice and Fire*.

A rundown of this issue's nonfiction is as follows:

In the Folkroots column, Phil Satyr Brucato discusses feet in myths, fairy tales, and pop culture. In the Movie/TV column, Resa Nelson discusses upcoming television programming for the fall lineup. In the Boooks column, Paul Witcover reviews *The Magicians and Mrs. Quent* by Galen Beckett, *The Word of God* by Thomas M. Disch, *Iodine* by Haven Kimmel, *The Long Look* by *Realms of Fantasy* regular, Richard Parks, and Jeff VanderMeer reviews *The Ant King and Other Stories* by Benajamin Rosenbaum, *Vicious Circle* by Mike Carey, *The Living Dead*, edited by John Joseph Adams, *The Mammoth Book of Extreme Fantasy*, edited by Mike Ashley, and *The Dragons of Manhattan* by John Grant. In YA Books, Michael Jones reviews *Out of the Wild* by Sarah Beth Durst, *The Dragon Heir* by Cinda Williams Chima, *Ink Exchange* by Melissa Marr, *Flora's Dare* by Ysabeau S. Wilce, *Gone* by Michael Grant, *Dead is the New Black* by Marlene Perez, *Vamps* by Nancy Collins, and *Heck: Where the Bad Kids Go* by Dale E. Bayse. In Graphic Novels, Jeff VanderMeer reviews *Flight Volume 5*, edited by Kaz Kibushi. In the Artists Gallery, Mia Nutick covers Folkroots regular Ari Berk's *The Secret History of Giants*. And in the Games column, Eric T. Baker reviews *Too Human* for Xbox 360, *Space Seige* for the PC, *Soul Calibur IV* for Xbox 360 and PS3, *Tales of Vesperia* for Xbox 360, and *Dracula 3: Path of the Dragon* for the PC.

On to the fiction ...

The lead story is "Harry and the Monkey" by Euan Harvey, which marks his third appearance in the magazine. In this dark fantasy tale, Euan explores an urban legend in Thailand, dealing with a mysterious black van that snatches children. He relies on various facts and news clippings to lend this urban legend a frightening reality. The urban legens proves itself true, and the narrator's son is almost lost to him, until a monkey comes to the rescue in mysterious fashion, which almost feels like a new urban legend come the end. This story was selected for inclusion in *Best Horror of the Year, Volume 1*, edited by Ellen Datlow. Art to this one was provided by Jada Fitch, which marks her third illustration in the magazine.

Next up we have "Achilles, Sulking in his Buick" by Jay Lake, which marks his eighth appearance in the magazine. This is a quick tale that takes Homer's *Iliad* and retells it as a high school drag race with a decidedly 1950s flavor. Art to this one was provided by Mark Harmon, which marks his second illustration in the magazine. Interestingly, Mark's first illustration for the magazine was back in the August 2007 issue, for Elizabeth M. Glover's "MetaPhysics." In that piece, Mark was one of three student artists who provided an illustration for the story in question as part of a student experiment that *Realms of Fantasy* ran in conjunction with an art class at Southern Utah University. This time around, Mark went from student to paid freelancer.

After this we have "The Milagroso Trail" by Clinton Lawrence, a contemporary fantasy tale about a group of travelers seeking the legendary city of Milagroso in the forest, only to find Milagroso and leave without ever realizing it. Art to this one was provided by Kenneth Callicutt.

Then we have "Late in the Day" by Gregory Frost, a story about the lover of the fairy Titania, who disguises himself as a human to learn the ways of humanity, only to forget who he is as he sinks into dimensia during his old age. Art to this one was provided by Kiriko Moth, which marks her third illustration in the magazine.

Following this we have "Fragments of a Fantasy Mind" by Josh Rountree and Mikal Trimm. For Josh, it marks his seventh appearance in the magazine. In this piece, after a tragic accident costs a woman her husband and son, she retreats into her mind in a story that blurs the lines between fantasy escape and full-blown insanity, as the protagonist fights against a demonic little creature known as Bandy Tam. Art to this one was provided by Kurt Huggins and Zelda Devon, and the illustration was selected for inclusion in the Editorial section of *Spectrum 16: The Best in Contemporary Fantastic Art*.

Our penultimate tale this issue is "Pumpkinjumper" by William H. Wandless, a slush survivor of mine. In this dark fairy tale, when the locals neglect to inform the new family in town about how one must always pay a simple offering to the crow known as Pumpkinjumper, Pumpkinjumper takes matters into his own hands, and takes his own price in the form of their daughter. Art to this one was provided by Eric Deschamps, which marks his fourth illustration in the magazine.

Finally we have "The Olverung" by Stephen Woodworth. This piece is historical fantasy set in medieval London, and while he brings the details alive, it should be noted that with a few tweaks, if the the author were so inclined, he easily could have set this story in a secondary fantasy world. As to the story itself, it deals with the olverung, a hideously ugly bird that makes beautiful music that brings people to tears whenever it's hurt. Enter our protagonist, a heartless rogue with gifts for illusion and deception, who at the behest of a nobleman pulls quite the caper as he steals the olverung from the royal court. But when he hears the olverung sing, he gets more than he bargained for. This story was reprinted in *Year's Best Fantasy 9*, edited by David Hartwell. It was also appeared as podcast 069 on the *Podcastle* website. Art to this one in RoF was provided by Tony Shasteen, which marks his sixth illustration in the magazine.

So that wraps up this issue. And my favorite story? "The Olverung" by Stephen Woodworth. And my favorite illustration? Kurt Huggins and Zelda Devon's illustration to "Fragments of a Fantasy Mind."

Originally posted on douglascohen.livejournal.com on June 19th, 2013

Part eighty-seven in my comprehensive retrospective as I read the fiction in *Realms of Fantasy* and offer my thoughts. This time around I'll be dealing with February 2009 issue.

This issue marks a significant turning point in the magazine's history. It was while the February 2009 issue was out that news broke that Soverign Media would be canceling the magazine. To put it lightly, the way this went down was a royal mess. When this happened, Shawna McCarthy—the magazine's founding editor and lone fiction editor in its entire history—was on vacation in Italy. I was holding down the proverbial fort in her absence. The problem here is that neither Shawna nor yours truly were informed of the magazine's closure before the news broke on the Internet. My involvement with the magazine wasn't as heavy as it would be in the coming issues, so of the two of us it was without question far more important that Shawna be informed beforehand. Still, it would have been nice if someone in the fiction department had been apprised of the situation. To make matters worse, the way Shawna learned about the news was that a reporter tracked down her number and called her while she was in Italy to ask her thoughts about the magazine closing down.

In a word? Ugh.

Now to be fair, I can understand why at least some of this mess happened. The publishers looked at the numbers and made a business decision that the April 2009 issue would be the last one. But meanwhile, magazines have ongoing production schedules, meaning there were deadlines in place for nonfiction and art for issues beyond April 2009. So they needed to get in touch with people to tell them to stop working on their assignments before they were handed in. That's all part of business. I get that. And I know the publishers did make several unsuccessful attempts to get in touch with Shawna before the news broke. The problem is that it was never made clear that this news should be kept quiet until the appropriate time. The appropriate time would obviously have been when Shawna and I were informed, and a thoughtful official announcement could be made. Since there were plans for another issue beyond February

2009, there would have been enough time to make this happen without a problem.

Instead, the news was leaked. I know who leaked the news too, because shortly after I (abruptly) learned about the magazine's closure (also from a phone call from someone not affiliated with the magazine), I did some online sleuthing, trying to see if this rumor had teeth. I found the source of the news pretty easily, but I will refrain from mentioning names. Even in retrospectives like these where I provide some behind-the-scenes information about the magazine, there is no need to needlessly hang someone out to dry. Since the magazine has suffered two more closures since then, good luck wading through the various online posts and articles if you want to track down the original bearer of bad news.

Suffice it to say that after seeing this I confirmed the news with the publishing office. Since the Internet was already raging with rumors mixed with facts at this point, I went online and confirmed the news, but declined to say anything more until Shawna was back and I had a chance to talk with her.

Needless to say I was pretty shocked, both at the magazine's closure and at how everything went down. From there the save *Realms of Fantasy* movements began while Shawna was still on vacation, which was a heartening thing to see, though I was uncertain if they would make a difference. The magazine would eventually be saved, but we'll get into that next issue.

As to the issue itself ...

The cover to this one features the artwork of Daniel Merriam and it was originally a galley piece. To be clear, I don't mean the magazine's Artists Gallery, but an actual physical art gallery.

A rundown of this issue's nonfiction is as follows:

In the Movie/TV column, Resa Nelson covers the movies *Inkheart* and *The Spirit*. In the Books column, Paul Witcover reviews *The Ten Thousand* by Paul Kearney, *The House of the Stag* by Kage Baker, *The Company* by K.J. Parker, *A Field Guide to Surreal Botany*, edited by Janet Chui and Jason Erik Lundberg, with illustrations by Janet Chui, *Psychological Methods To Sell Should Be Destroyed* by Robert Freeman Wexler, and Jeff VanderMeer reviews *Mr. Gaunt and Other Uneasy Encounters* by John Langan, *The Engine's Child* by Holly Phillips, *The Domino Men* by Jonathan Barnes, and *Things We Think About Games* by Will Hindmarcha and Jeff Tidball. In

Graphic Novels, Jeff VanderMeer reviews *The Good Neighbors, Book One: Kin* by Holly Black and Ted Naifeh, *The Invisible Man* by H.G. Wells, adapted by Rick Geary, *Swallow Me Whole* by Nate Powell, and *From the Shadow of the Northern Lights: An Anthology of Swedish Alternative Comics*, edited by Johannes Klennel. In YA Books, Michael M. Jones reviews *Hell Week* by Rosemary Clement-Moore, *How to Ditch Your Fairy* by Justine Larbalestier, *Skinned* by Robin Wasserman, *Rapunzel's Revenge* by Shannon Dean, and Nathan Hale, *Impossible* by Nancy Werlin, *Cybele's Secret* by Juliet Marillier, *Vibes* by Amy Kathleen Ryan, and *Cycler* by Lauren McLaughlin. In Folkroots, Stephen D. Winick writes about riddles. In the Artists Gallery, Karen Haber covers the work of the aforementioned Daniel Merriam. In the Games column, Eric T. Baker reviews *Star Wars the Force Unleashed* for Xbox 360 and PS3, the MMO *Warhammer Age of Reckoning*, the MMO *Wizard101*, *Mountain & Blade* for the PC, and *Dark Horizon* for the PC. Also in this issue is a profile of fantasy author, Joseph Nigg, provided by Jeff VanderMeer.

On to the fiction ...

The lead story this issue is "The Radio Magician" by James Van Pelt, which marks his eighth appearance in the magazine. In this piece, our protagonist is a boy stricken with polio back when this was still a prevalent illness. His favorite pastime is listening to on the radio to the program, *Professor Gilded's Glorious Magical Extravaganza*, our titular radio magician. In an act of sheer will, determination, bravery, and belief, our polio-ridden protagonist takes himself to the radio station, hoping that Professor Gilded can cure him. While no such cure is found, he learns that magic among other things is all a matter of perception. I promise you that it's not as depressing as it sounds. Art to this one was provided by Rob Johnson, which marks his fifth illustration in the magazine.

Next up we have "The Happiest Place" by Carrie Vaughn, which marks her seventh appearance in the magazine. In this piece, a young woman works as a fairy tale princess in an amusement park reminiscent of Disney World. However, while the venue is supposed to lend the vibe of the happiest place on Earth, our protagonist is in fact becoming emotionally worn down from constantly spending time with terminally sick children whose final wishes are to spend time with a "princess." She's granting wishes in a sense, but it's taking an obvious toll. Everything changes though when she comes upon across a tiara that can grant wishes in the magical sense of the word. But doing this comes with an emotional cost as well. Art to this one was provided by Jada Fitch, which marks her fourth illustration in the magazine.

Then we have "Joy is the Serious Business of Heaven" by David D. Levine, which marks his third appearance in the magazine. This one is a lighthearted tale about the beauracracy of Heaven, and how sometimes even angels can lose their way and need to be reminded about what truly matters. Art to this one was provided by David Leonard, which marks his fourth illustration in the magazine.

After this we have "The River of Three Crossings" by Richard Parks, which marks his twenty-third appearance in the magazine. This one is another Lord Yamada tale, the fifth such to appear in the magazine. In this piece, Lord Yamada and his drunken priestly sidekick help a young child put the ghost of her bandit father to rest, and their good deed yields some unexpected results. Art to this one was provided by Tiffany Prothero, which marks her fifth illustration in the magazine.

Last but not least we have "Fossil Fuels" by Alan Smale, which marks his fourth appearance in the magazine. This one takes place in underground mines of Yorkshire, England in 1937. In these dark depths, a tragic, ancient, and eternal battle is played out once again, as a pair of archetypes do battle, one representing the future and order, the other the past and chaos. Care to guess who wins? Art to this one was provided by Chris Cocoazza, which marks his tenth illustration in the magazine.

So that wraps up this issue. And my favorite story? "The Radio Magician" by James Van Pelt. And my favorite artwork? Tiffany Prothero's illustration to "The River of Three Crossings" by Richard Parks.

Originally posted on douglascohen.livejournal.com on July 25th, 2013

Part eighty-eight in my comprehensive retrospective as I read in the fiction in Realms of Fantasy and offer my thoughts. This time around I'll be discussing the April 2009 issue.

This was the last issue under original publisher Sovereign Media, a run of eighty-eight issues. For a while it looked like this would be the last issue in the magazine's entire run, but at some point while this issue was still on newsstands, the news broke that Warren Lapine—the publisher of the defunct DNA Publications, which had published such magazines as Weird Tales, Absolute Magnitude, Dreams of Decadence, etc.—had reached a deal with the current publishers to take over Realms of Fantasy with the next issue. In his return to magazine publishing, Warren formed a new company called Tir Na Nog Press, which would act as Realms of Fantasy's publisher. Before Warren announced the news online, he contacted both me and Shawna, and we both agreed to return to our old editorial positions. With this accomplished, when Warren announced that the magazine had been purchased/saved, he was able to simultaneously break the news that the old editorial team was returning.

That's the short version, and in the coming editions of these retrospectives, I'll be able to provide more of an insider's view concerning each issue, as I would be assuming new responsibilities with the magazine as time went on. But first we have to cover the final issue from Sovereign Media, so let's get to it.

The cover to this one features a scene from the cinematic version of Alan Moore's Watchmen, which marks the magazine's twelfth media cover. A quick perusal of previous media covers reveals that this is the first superhero movie to grace a cover of the magazine.

A rundown of this issue's nonfiction is as follows:

In the Movie/TV column, Resa Nelson covers the aforementioned Watchmen. In Folkroots, James Ryan Gregory explores otherworldly marriages through the lens of Welsh folklore and myth. In the Books column, Paul Witcover reviews Gears of the City by Felix Gilman, The Love We Share Without Knowing by Christopher Barzak, Tender Morsels by Margo Lanagan, Space Magic by David D. Levine, and Fast Ships, Black Sails edited by Ann and Jeff VanderMeer. Speaking of Jeff VanderMeer, prior to this issue he was Paul Witcover's partner-in-crime when it came to the book reviews, but the February 2009 issue was his last one in this department, a run of nine issues. Taking his place is Matt Staggs.

I have to admit that I was a bit tickled at the time to see that the first book Matt reviewed was *Lamentation* by Ken Scholes. *Lamentation* is set in the same universe as Ken's "Of Metal Men and Scarlet Thread and Dancing with the Sunrise," a story that I fished out of the slush in the early days of my time at *Realms of Fantasy*, and it appeared in our August 2006 issue. Parts of this story were even incorporated in *Lamentation*, and Shawna and I—as well as artist Allen Douglas—all received nice mentions in the book's acknowledgements page. *Lamentation* was actually the first in a five-book deal with Tor Books. As I write this, the first three books are out, though if memory serves correctly, I believe Ken has finished work on book four.* Without a doubt, this is one of the better success stories I've helped along during my time with the magazine, so when I thought this was the last issue of RoF, it felt rather fitting that I should see Ken's book being reviewed.

But I digress (not for the first time and probably not the last). The other books Matt reviewed this issue are *The Stormcaller* by Tom Llod and and *Duainfey* by Sharon Lee and Steve Miller. In YA Books, Michael Jones reviews *Eon: Dragoneye Reborn* by Alison Goodman, *Lament: The Faerie Queen's Deception* by Maggie Stiefvater, *Selkie Girl* by Laurie Brooks, *Palace of Mirrors* by Margaret Peterson, *Worldweavers: Cybermage* by Alma Alexander, *Chance Fortune in the Shadow Zone* by Shane Berryhill, *Revealers* by Amanda Marrone, and *The Crown of Zeus* by Christine Norris. In Graphic Novels, Jeff VanderMeer sticks around and reviews *The Dresden Files: Welcome to the Jungle* by Jim Butcher and Ardian Syaf, and *Dungeon Monstres Volume 2: The Dark Lord* by Joann Sfarr, Lewis Trondheim, Andreas, and Stephane Blanquet. In the Artists Gallery, Karen Haber covers the artwork of Bruno Mallart. And in the Games column, Eric T. Baker reviews *Fable 2* for the Xbox 360, *Fallout 3* for the PC, Xbox 360, and PS3, *Golden Axe: Beast Rider* for the PS3, the MMO, *The Wrath of the Lich King*, an expansion for *World of Warcraft*, and *Mines of Moria*, an expansion for *Lord of the Rings Online* for the PC.

On to the fiction ...

There are only four stories in this issue, which marks the first time an issue of the magazine would publish this small a number. On the bright side, since for a little while this was the magazine's final issue, I'm pleased to say that the fiction department finished strong, as it put out four strong pieces.

The lead story is "Impractical Cats" by K.D. Wentworth, which marks her fourth appearance in the magazine. In this contemporary fantasy piece, an elderly husband grows worried about his wife when she starts seeing cats that aren't there ...only you've already figured out that the cats are there, because this is a fantasy magazine. He just can't see them, so he thinks his elderly wife's mind is breaking down. Instead we're shown that magic is not something that is just for the young. Art to this one was provided by Stephanie Pui-Mun Law, which marks her fourth illustration in the magazine. One other tidbit worth mentioning is that some months later Warren Lapine invested in a new website for the magazine. As part of the launch for the website, I suggested to Warren and Shawna that we at long last introduce some reader choice awards for art and fiction to the magazine. Both of them liked this idea, so we went ahead and did this. The first reader choice awards honored original art and fiction published in *Realms of Fantasy* during 2009. Stephanie's illustration was the inaugural winner for Best Artwork.

Next up we have "Sails Above Greensea" by Adam Corbin Fusco. I admit to having a crush on this story. At almost 13,000 words (if memory serves correctly), it's one of the longest pieces ever published in the magazine. It's also exactly the kind of story that turned me into a full-fledged fan of fantasy literature all those years ago. Captain Absinthe Monteroy is a pyrate captain of the *Crimson Moon*, one of the last two greatships in the world. Greatships fly through the air and house massive populations in the lower holds, enough to fill entire towns. Most of the earth has been submerged beneath the ocean, or eaten by the great beast known as Leviathan. The pyrate captain of the other remaining greatship is Absinthe's greatest enemy and the former pyrate captain of the *Crimson Moon* before he betrayed everyone aboard the ship when he started worshiping Leviathan, none other than Abilairde Monteroy ...Absinthe's father. At the start of the story, the greatships are in a lull in an aerial battle, one that is extra heated because the two pyrate captains are in a race to claim the crown of the First and Last Pyrate King, which is on island that only comes up from beneath the waves once every hundred years. What follows is a rich tale of adventure, psychological depth, vivid imagery and world building, and unexpected plot twists.

One thing that disappointed me was the fact that while Adam used italics in this piece to brilliant effect—employing them in a manner that heightened the sensory input as one read his battle scenes—for whatever reason, these italics did not find their way into the published version of the story. Whether this was an honest mistake or Sovereign Media got a bit lax/sloppy because this was the last issue remains a mystery. Regardless, it's a very entertaining tale. I think one of the reasons I'm going on about this particular piece is that each time I've read it, I don't feel like I'm reading a shorter work—I get the same sensations I do when I'm reading a good novel, meaning I feel like I'm falling into something bigger and deeper. This doesn't make the piece any better or worse than other short fiction I've read that I've enjoyed, but it's an unusual experience for me. Reading short fiction feels different from reading a novel. I can't think of another story I've read in RoF that did this to me on this level, and given that the magazine published about 600 works of fiction and that high fantasy and sword and sorcery *are* my favorite areas of fantasy, I think that's reason enough to go on about this piece at some length. I've told Adam more than once that he should write a novel in this world. I hope he listens, because I'll be first in line to buy the book. Art to this one was provided by Kurt Huggins and Zelda Devon, which marks their second illustration in the magazine.

Following this we have "Name Day" by Garth Upshaw, another one of my slush survivors, and I'd be lying if I said I wasn't proud of the fact that two of the stories appearing in the then-last issue were stories that I discovered. This piece marks the first time we published a piece that might be classified as New Weird. In this piece, we have an island surrounded by an ocean of lifeforms. When a child becomes old enough—seemingly around the time of puberty or soon thereafter—each child undergoes his Name Day. At one's Name Day, you're essentially dipped into the lifeform-ocean, which creates various mutations in one's body. Usually these mutations lead to positive enhancements of one's body, though occasionally things can go horribly wrong and leave you as little better than a pile of goop. But assuming you're not left as goop, after you undergo the change, you receive your new Name, which tends to tie back into your mutation in some manner. But things go horribly wrong when our protagonist who has yet to undergo his Name Day is hanging out with an older crowd (read: teenagers) who are imbibing. Imbibing is drinking from the lifeform-ocean without permission, which seems to enhance one's enhancements. This is bad enough, and when our unassuming protagonist gets exposed to the lifeform-ocean before his official Name Day ceremony, suffice it to say that things quickly go from bad to worse. Art to this one was provided by Erin and Kelly Carty, which marks their third illustration in the magazine.

Finally we have "Sand Castles" by Desirina Boskovich, which marks the twentieth story I pulled from the slush. For a short while, this story held the dubious distinction of being the last story published in *Realms of Fantasy*, which would have made 527 stories total. It also marked her first sale, though she was actually published elsewhere first. I also want to mention that over the years I made a number of friends through the magazine, particularly with my slush survivors. But Des (as she's known to me) was the first friend I made through the slush that I hung out with on the regular. Elizabeth Glover was another friend of mine that I fished from the slush some years back, but I was actually friends with Elizabeth before she sold the story. Des came afterward, so the fact that we're friends—and that she became part of my old geek posse—is thanks to her strong writing, my eye for talent, and the fact that Shawna took the story for the magazine. Good work all around!

As to the story itself, "Sand Castles" is one of the more subtle fantasy pieces we've published in the magazine. It's not a religious tale, but as with religion, the fantastical element in this one comes down to belief. If you believe, this is a fantasy story. If you don't believe, then it's more of a mainstream literary story. And if you're not sure ...well, I suppose this would be the non-religious equivalent of agnosticism. In this piece, our protagonist has recently graduated and is feeling a bit lost as she must find her way in the real world. Enter her pothead artist friend Radley, along with his mysterious female companion, both of whom need our protagonist to use her car to take them on an even more mysterious roadtrip into Mexico. It turns out they're in search of a lost city on a beach, and while this city may or may not exist, in the larger view it can also be viewed as a metaphor for the protagonist's need for some magic in her life. This story subsequently appeared as Podcast 294 on the *PodCastle* website. Art to this one in RoF was provided by Natalie Pierandrei, which marks her second illustration in the magazine.

So that wraps up this issue, as well as the Sovereign Media era of *Realms of Fantasy*. And my favorite story? Yeah, you probably guessed this one already. "Sails Above Greensea" by Adam Corbin Fusco. And my favorite artwork? Natalie Pierandrei's illustration to "Sand Castles."

*He's currently working on book five as I write this.

Originally posted on douglascohen.livjournal.com on July 31ˢᵗ, 2013

Part eighty-nine in my comprehensive retrospective as I read the fiction in *Realms of Fantasy* and offer my thoughts. This time around we're going to kick off a new era in the magazine's history as I discuss the August 2009 issue. As it marked the first time the magazine changed publishers, there is a lot to discuss. It should also be noted the reason there is no retrospective for the June 2009 issue is because due to the transition process we had to skip putting out a June issue. In the magazine's entire publishing history, this marks the only time an issue was skipped during its publication schedule.

As mentioned in the previous retrospective, Warren Lapine—former publisher of DNA publications—became the magazine's new publisher, this time under the publishing company, Tir Na Nog Press. The former publishers of Sovereign Media—Carl A. Gnam and Marc Hintz—had a run of eighty-eight issues. With their departure and Shawna McCarthy remaining aboard as the fiction editor, Shawna became the only person to have been associated with the magazine since the first issue. I stuck around as well, and Warren handed me some additional responsibilities to go along with my role as assistant editor of fiction, giving me responsibilities as nonfiction editor and art director.

Since I know some people like to quibble about the definition of art director, I'll clarify that this meant I commissioned the artists for illustrations, engaged them in back-and-forth discussion regarding said illustrations and their sketches, I oversaw the covers, and the Artists Gallery. I did not handle layout and design. I've had people tell me this didn't make me an art director. I understand their point, but I can't entirely agree with it. First, I didn't pick out the title, Warren did. Second—and this one I've never bothered mentioning before—if one takes the time to flip through the back issues of RoF, they'll discover there is a precedent for other people being given the title of art director while a different person handles layout and design. Since Warren and his publishing predecessors have literally put out thousands of issues of magazines—both in the genre and outside of it—I'd say they have some experience in these matters. When illustrations I commissioned appeared in the award-winning *Spectrum* art series, its editors also had no qualms with crediting me as art director. I've also seen a lot of other people in *Spectrum* credited as art directors without handling design and layout. So while there may be more popular definitions concerning what an art director is, I feel perfectly comfortable in saying there is no blanket definition as some people in this industry like to believe.

Let's move on to the cover. The artwork here is by Dominic Harman, and as people familiar with RoF may realize, this particular cover sparked a controversy. Warren had a new way he wanted covers to be handled, but because the magazine was in major transition at this point, we wouldn't be able to implement his idea for a couple of more issues (we'll get to that idea in a later issue). So instead, Warren asked me to choose an illustration for reprint rights from Dominic's website, an artist he had worked with before (and also discovered some time back if memory serves correctly). Since it was the first issue under the new regime, I roped Warren and Shawna into helping me choose an illustration. The mermaid was the one we settled on, though Warren had Dominic crop the nipples before using it on the cover.

Since I was listed as the art director, I understandably took the brunt of the heat on this controversy I mentioned ...of course, had I kept a cooler head it would have been a much smaller issue. In a nutshell, someone I don't get along with and whom I had had run-ins with before, posted on his/her blog about the cover (yes, I'm being as intentionally vague as possible on this tidbit), and also wrote some things about me, doing their best to cast me in a negative light. It was pointed out to me, and I decided to respond in kind on my blog ...angrily, given what I read. Looking back, it was a huge mistake to respond at all to this person's pettiness. And if I didn't know this person off-line, I doubt I ever would've taken the time to address the post. But since I *did* know this person, it felt like a personal attack, and I reacted to that. Yeah, that was a big mistake. I had been involved in the occasional unfortunate flame war, but I had never been at the center of an online controversy before, and to suddenly find myself smackdab in the middle of one about female nudity on covers due to my comments online ...well, suffice it to say a lot of people were anxious to lend their two cents to the conversation, and it was a lot to digest/deal with.

While it wasn't fun for me, it was nonetheless an interesting experience. Basically, there was a contingent of people who believed that the nudity had no place on the cover. There were other contingents, including those who believed it was fine because it wasn't sexualizing the mermaid, and there were also those who believed it was fine, period. I also distinctly remember the artists that weighed in didn't really seem to have a problem with this cover. Basically a wide range of opinions all got thrown into the stew, though without question the loudest voices were those objecting to the cover. I did my best to listen and respond to everyone, and I learned a lot from the experience, both about online interactions and about how I would approach the magazine going forward. Now to be clear, yes, this is an abridged version of events. I have zero interest in dredging up every last detail and getting people riled up over ancient history, which is a big reason why I'm leaving names out of this. But if this series is a retrospective about the magazine, it would be dodgy on my part to not even mention this happened. If you don't like how I'm presenting the information, that's your right. And that's really all I have to say about this matter.

Moving on ...

There is one other tidbit worth noting on the cover as the magazine experienced its first price increase since the August 1998 issue. The previous price was $3.99. The new price is $6.99. (Don't shoot the messenger!)

Let's finally turn the page and get past the cover ...

Not surprisingly, we have some activity in the masthead. Carl A. Gnam Jr. and Mark Hintz were the previous published as already mentioned, and were listed in the last issue as the Editorial Director and Chief Executive Officer respectively. Warren Lapine replaces them this issue as Publisher. Shawna's title changed from Editor to Fiction Editor, though her duties remained almost exactly the same. Laura Cleveland was the Managing Editor and an employee of Sovereign Media, so the previous issue marked her last one. Laura actually had two stints with the magazine. Between the October 1998 and August 2004 issues, she filled the roles of Copy Editor, Associate Editor, and finally Managing Editor. Then she was no longer with the magazine for a stint (I don't know why) before returning to the magazine as Managing Editor once again with the October 2006 issue, a role she would continue until the April 2009 issue. All told, she contributed in some form to fifty-two issues, slightly more than half the magazine's run. I should also add that she was tremendously generous with her time to me, answering various questions I had between Sovereign's last issue and Tir Na Nog's first for RoF. Warren and I ended up splitting her various duties. Samantha DeTulleo is also no longer listed as the Art Director, a role she filled from the October 2000-April 2009 issues. Like Laura, this marked a run of fifty-two issues. Interestingly, while Sovereign Media had in past mastheads listed one person as Art Director and another handling design and such, Samantha only handled layout and design. Laura handled the artwork, much the way I would as her replacement. How Sovereign Media determined what title to assign to whom is a question you'll have to ask Soverign Media. While he's not listed in this issue as doing such, Warren ended up taking on the role of layout and design.

As to me, my titles in the masthead this issue are listed as Art Director and Nonfiction Editor. Warren and I had discussed what to do about listing my fiction duties, since I was still the Assistant Editor in the fiction department. Ultimately, I asked him to just leave that out of the masthead, as listing me three times over struck me as too excessive.

Let's turn our attention to the nonfiction. Warren was interested in preserving continuity with the magazine, so besides bringing me and Shawna back, he also brought all the old columns. Additionally, he wanted all the old columnists back, so he had me invite them to return to their old positions. Everyone but Eric Baker accepted. Eric handled the Games column, and when I contacted him he informed me that he was planning on stepping down from his post in the near future anyway, so this was as good a time as any to walk away from his position. All told his contributions extended from August 1998-April 2009, a run of sixty-five issues (plus he contributed one work of fiction that I covered many issues back).

One of my new duties after Warren took over was the hiring (and firing) of the nonfiction columnists. So it fell to me to hire Eric's replacement. While I looked at a few different candidates, like Warren, I wanted to preserve a certain level of continuity with the magazine. For this and other reasons, I ultimately chose Matt Staggs as the new Games columnist. Matt had joined RoF as one of the book columnists with the April 2009 issue, and when I contacted him about his old position, in addition to accepting, he offhandedly mentioned some of his other interests in the genre should the need ever arise with the magazine. One of those interests was games, so that's the genesis of Matt's role for the Games column. Since there was already a precedent with columnists contributing to more than one column—Jeff VanderMeer contributed to both Books and Graphic Novels for a time—I had no qualms about handing off these additional duties to Matt.

As to the nonfiction itself ...

In the Games column, the aforementioned Matt Staggs reviews *Player's Handbook 2, A Sourcebook for the 4th edition of Dungeons & Dragons*, *The Chronicles of Riddick: Assault on Dark Athena* for Atari, Xbox 360, Playstation 3, and the PC, the RPG, *Scion Companion, A Sourcebook for Scion*, and the RPG, *Summoners, A Sourcebook Mage: The Awakening*. In the Movie/TV column, Resa Nelson covers the movie, *Harry Potter and the Half-Blood Prince*. In the Folkroots column, SatyrPhil Brucato writes about the musical in the fantastical. In the Artists Gallery, Karen Haber covers the artwork of Michael Hague. In Books, Paul Witcover reviews *The Dark Volume* by Gordon Dahlquist, *The Red Wolf Conspiracy* by Robert. V.S. Redick, and *Sum: Forty Tales from the Afterlives* by David Eagleman, while Matt Staggs reviews *Green* by Jay Lake, *Blood of Ambrose* by James Enge, *Midwinter* by Matthew Sturges, and *The Mystery of Grace* by Charles de Lint; in YA Books, Michael Jones reviews *Percy Jackson and the Olympians # 5: The Last Olympian* by Rick Riordan, *Beka Cooper: Bloodhound* by Tamora Pierce, *Highway to Hell* by Rosemary Clement-Moore, *Soul Enchilada* by David Macinnis, *Fortune's Folly* by Deva Fagan, *The Amaranth Enchantment* by Julie Berry, *Zombie Queen of Ashbury High* by Amanda Ashby, and *Hottie* by Jonathan Bernstein. And in Graphic Novels, Jeff VanderMeer reviews *Dungeon Zenith Volume 3: Back in Style* by Joann Sfarr, Lewis Trondheim, and Boulet. At the back of the issue, Shawna also returns with an Editorial to commemorate our return and thank our new publisher, while Warren provides an accompanying Publisher's Note.

I'll also add a brief mention that the vast majority of nonfiction this issue was originally written for and/or purchased by Sovereign Media, and later transferred over to Warren as part the purchase of the magazine. My records are a bit spotty about which pieces were written for the magazine after Warren took over, though working from memory I know that Matt Staggs' Games column and Jeff VanderMeer's were both written after Warren took over, and I know that Resa's movie column and Karen's Artists Gallery column were both paid for by Sovereign Media. Beyond that, I couldn't tell you anymore. I keep pretty detailed records, but only to a point.

On to the fiction ...

As with the previous issue, there are only four stories this issue (though three of them are rather long). This marks the second and last time the magazine published as few as four stories in a single issue.

The lead story and first story in the Tir Na Nog era is "Our Lady in Scarlet" by Tanith Lee, which marks her fifteenth story in the magazine. This one is an historical fantasy about a scholar and alchemist who seeks a cure for the bubonic plague in medieval Europe who experiences a crisis of non-faith (i.e. he doesn't believe) when he starts receiving visits by a red goddess of death, known as the Red Virgin. He summons alchemic angels and such to defend him, but to no avail, and ends up learning more about his future than he wishes to from an entity he never expected to believe in. Art to this one was procured from Canstock Photo. Understandably, Warren wanted to kick off his first issue with the biggest authorial name we had in inventory. This was Tanith Lee. However, due to the transition, there simply wasn't enough time to commission original artwork, so he asked me to find something suitable on Canstock Photo. In the last retrospective, I mentioned how some months later we introduced Reader Choice Awards to the magazine for best ficton and artwork. Tanith Lee's piece was the inaugural winner for Best Fiction.

Next up we have "Healing Benjamin" by Dennis Danvers, which marks his second appearance in the magazine. In this one, a teenager inexplicably wills his dying cat back to life. The cat proves immortal and learns new skills such as human speech while its aging master takes care of it and tries to hide the truth about his extraordinary cat. This one is a lot better than I'm making it sound. Plus Shawna bought it, and as I've mentioned in the past, she always was rather picky about buying her cat stories (even if there was also a cat story in the previous issue). Art to this one was provided by Eric Westbrook, which marks his third illustration in the magazine. I'll be sure to let you know when the art that started appearing was solicited by yours truly, but this particular piece was commissioned by Sovereign Media.

After this we have "Digging for Paradise" by Ian Creasey. In this science fantasy, magic is employed through power-stones, and these stones build up their power by storing the earth's energies inside them. In order to harvest a massive amount of energy in one of the power-stones, a sorcerer buries one of them in the earth and brings a select crew untold millennia into the future to the End of Days, where they will unearth the power-stone, which has been accumulating energy all this time. Everyone but the protagonist is a servant to the sorcerer. The protagonist himself is a miner of sorts, and was tricked into journeying in this far-flung future, as the sorcerer will need his expertise to unearth the power-stone. In this future, the human race is seemingly dead, something that hurts extra for the protagonist because his wife is gone. But the sorcerer claims the power-stone will have so much energy they can all remake this future in whatever fashion they see fit. But as you might expect in this situation, trust issues arise, as seeds of doubt arise whether the sorcerer can be trusted with so much power. Art to this one was another piece commissioned by Sovereign Media and was provided by Rob Johnson, which marks his sixth illustration in the magazine.

Finally we have "Well and Truly Broken" by Bruce Holland Rogers, which marks his eleventh appearance in the magazine. This a brief story about some three girls who are sisters who stumble upon some fairies and wish to join them. But in order to do so, it is required to break a heart.

Unfotunately, the end of this story is cut off in the magazine. It was a series of unfortunate events that led to this happening. This story was not originally slated to appear in this issue. But since this was the first issue in the relaunch, there were a lot of moving parts. In this case, Warren made the call to shift a different story out and this one in right before going to press. For whatever reason, the file Warren received from Sovereign Media for this story had the ending cut off. Where it did end was abrupt and a little puzzling, but not blatant enough for the ending to be obviously missing. As to me, the version we received from Sovereign Media was the first one I had ever seen. Bruce was one of Shawna's clients for her literary agency, and these folks often submitted to Shawna directly. So I was in the dark as much as Shawna about this. As to Shawna, like I said, Warren made the call to switch this story in right before we went to press. I don't think she saw this "version" of the story until it appeared in the magazine. So like I said, a series of unfortunate events led to this happening, alas. I have to give Warren credit for being a standup guy about the whole situation though. Not only did Bruce get paid for appearing in the magazine, but Warren made Bruce's story—the full version of it—the first one to appear on the magazine's new website, and he got paid for that as well. While it wasn't the scenario we envisioned, Warren made the best of it and Bruce was quite pleased with Warren's handling of this matter as publisher. Art to this one was a classic illustration by Edward Reginald Frampton. We didn't have artwork in inventory at the time Warren made the call to run the story, so there was no choice but to run a reprint. Warren dug up the artwork for this one.

So that wraps up one of the longer (if not the longest) retrospectives I've written for this series. And my favorite story? "Healing Benjamin" by Dennis Danvers. And my favorite artwork? Eric Westbrook's illustration to the same story.

Originally posted on douglascohen.livejournal.com on August 31st, 2013

Part ninety in my comprehensive retrospective as I read the fiction in *Realms of Fantasy* and offer my thoughts. This time around I'll be diving into the October 2009 issue.

The cover to this one reprints the artwork of Antonis Papantoniou. Warren Lapine actually found this piece. He pointed it out to me, asking if I thought it would work for the cover. Now that it's four years later, I will let you in on my basic thought process here. We had just dealt with a cover controversy in the previous issue. I knew all eyes would be on this cover. I had yet to begin my search for a cover for this issue when Warren pointed out this art. I liked the artwork and nothing about it struck me as controversial. And if Warren was comfortable with the cover, that was good enough for me. So I gave the green light on this usage. Now in retrospect (pun not intended), I might have used a different cover if given another chance. Again, I like this artwork, but after another issue or two of character-oriented covers, I came to the conclusion that I preferred covers in this vein for the magazine. Again, I like this art, so I'm not casting judgment on the quality of the illustration. But it was only my second issue overseeing the artwork, a position I never expected. I freely admit I was still sorting through what direction I wanted to take the magazine. And one unrelated tidbit worth mentioning is that as the cover notes, with this issue the magazine has reached its fifteenth birthday.

There are a couple of noteworthy design changes to report this issue. Firstly, Warren did away with the longtime Contributors Page. Instead, brief author and columnist bios appear at the end of their respective stories and columns. In place of the Contributors Page, Warren provided an Advertiser Index.

There are also some changes to the masthead with this issue. The copy editors are now listed again for the first time in ages, these being Marty Halpern and Ian Randal Strock. Also, for the first time ever, the Folkroots editors are now listed in the masthead, these being Arik Berk and Kristen McDermott. (Since I don't believe I mentioned it earlier, I'll add that they actually assumed these duties with Terri Windling's departure.)

A rundown of this issue's nonfiction is as follows:

In the Games section (yup, Games is now listed first instead of its usual last), Matt Staggs reviews the RPG core rulebook to *HackMaster Basic*, the sourcebook *Trail of Cthulhu* to the *Shadows Over Finland* RPG, the RPG core rulebook to *Witch Girls Adventures*, the core rulebook to the RPG *Supernatural*, and *The Age of Conan* strategy boardgame. In the Movie/TV column, Resa Nelson covers *Final Destination 4*. In Folkroots, H. Talmat Halman writes about the Green Man al-Khidr. In the Artists Gallery, Mia Nutick covers the artwork of Lee Moyer. In the Books section, Paul Witcover reviews *Best Served Cold* by Joe Abercrombie, *Norse Code* by Greg van Eekhout, *The Age of Misrule* by Mark Chadbourn, *Naamah's Kiss* by Jacqueline Carey, and Matt Staggs reviews *The Magicians* by Lev Grossman, *Songs of the Dying Earth*, edited by George R. R. Martin and Gardner Dozois, *Child of Fire* by Harry Connolly, and Cat Rambo's collection, *Eyes Like Sky and Coal and Moonlight*. In YA Books, Michael M. Jones reviews *Eyes Like Stars* by Lisa Mantchev, *Dull Boy* by Sarah Cross, *The Demon's Lexicon* by Sarah Rees Brennan, *Kiss of Life* by Daniel Waters, *Once Dead, Twice Shy* by Kim Harrison, *Sea Change* by Aimee Friedman, and *Me, My Elf & I* by Heather Swain. There was no Graphic Novel column due to to an unexpected staff change.

On to the fiction ...

The lead story this issue is "Flower Fairies" by Kristine Kathryn Rusch, which marks her third appearance in the magazine. This one is a brief tale about a funeral director's place of business and the flower fairies that have haunted it since the days when his father ran the business. I don't know why, but when I write it this way it makes me think: HBO's *Six Feet Under*, with flower fairies. The story is too short to actually touch on all the themes of *Six Feet Under*, but for whatever reason I find this comparison amusing. I solicited the artwork to this one and it was provided by Michael Hague.

Next up we have "Tio Gilberto and the Twenty-Seven Ghosts" by Ben Francisco, another one of my slush survivors. In this piece, a young gay man goes to San Francisco for the summer to live with his Uncle Tio, who lives in a large house with twenty-seven ghosts who have all died from AIDS. While pursuing his comedy career, our protagonist gets involved in a romantic relation and is forced to confront the danger of AIDS after having unprotected sex. This story was reprinted in *Wilde Stories: 2010: The Best of the Year's Gay Speculative Fiction*, edited by Steve Berman. It also appeared on PodCastle as podcast 086 and was a selection of the IO9 Short Story Reading Club. This was another piece where I solicited the artwork, and it was provided by John Kaiine.

After this we have "Nell and the Devil" by S.E. Ward, another slush survivor of mine. This one is a fun retelling of the Cinderella fairy tale, with Cinderella's fairy godmother being an agent of the Devil. Art to this one was in inventory when the magazine was purchased from Sovereign Media and was provided by Lori Koefoed, which marks her fifteenth illustration in the magazine.

Then we have "Red Dirt Kingdoms" by Jay Lake, which marks his ninth appearance in the magazine. This is a short piece about a man called Proverbial Stranger who comes seeking the King of an Elfland that resides beneath the earth. Only the human man he comes looking for turns out to be the ugliest woman he's ever seen, while being every bit as big and burly as an imposing male. And to spice things up, Ms. Artemisia Cleminshaw has taken a fancy to Proverbial Stranger. Art to this one was provided by James A. Owen, which marks his second illustration in the magazine.

I have to admit that I was pleased to have come across a story to match up with James. As I discussed in my entry for the October 2008 issue, an unlikely series of events that started with a conversation on LiveJournal led to James getting the cover and a feature in the Artists Gallery, though this was some months before I was overseeing the art department. So to have a chance to solicit artwork from James felt like things were coming full-circle. And the results went over rather well with author. I remember Jay expressing some interest to me in purchasing the original artwork. The last I heard about this when I mentioned it to James was that he wanted to make a gift of it to Jay. I imagine this is what happened.

Finally we have "Bob and the Mermaid" by William R. Eakin, which marks his seventh appearance in the magazine, and also his seventh story in RoF set in the town of Redgunk, Mississippi. In this piece, the story is told through the eyes of Bob Delashmit's best friend, though as the title implies, Bob has a pretty critical role to play. We come to learn that when he was younger, Bob had a wild streak and was something of a ladies' man. This all changed when he met the love of his life, but Bob's wife has been sick for many years, basically entirely dependent on him for survival. Bob has been a good devoted husband to her the whole time, but when a beautiful mermaid washes up by his home in the swamps of Redgunk, old desires he hasn't dealt with in many a year come bubbling to the surface and test the devotion he has to his wife. Art to this piece was provided by Zak Pullen and was another illustration that was in inventory with Sovereign Media.

So that wraps up this issue. And my favorite story? It's pretty close, but I'll give the nod to "Tio Gilberto and Twenty-Seven Ghosts" by Ben Francisco. And my favorite artwork? John Kaiine's accompanying artwork to this story.

Originally posted on douglascohen.livejournal.com on October 9th, 2013

Part ninety-one in my comprehensive retrospective as I read the fiction in *Realms of Fantasy* and offer my thoughts. This time around I'll be digging into the December 2009 issue.

The cover to this one features a new direction for the magazine. When Warren Lapine took over the magazine, when possible, he wanted us to run one of the interior illustrations on the cover. His reasoning was that it would tie the cover more directly into the magazine's content. For various reasons, not every illustration can be considered for a cover, so the third issue of Warren's run as publisher ended up being the first issue we went in this direction. The cover itself is Carol Heyer's interior illustration to "Stories of the Sand" by Dirk Strasser. It marks Carol's ninth illustration in the magazine.

In the masthead, there is one change to report, as Trent Zelazny is now listed among the issue's copy editors. Trent is the son of famed sf/f writer Roger Zelazny, and also a writer. Considering that one of Roger Zelazny's stories appeared all the way back in the first issue of the magazine, it's interesting that his son ended up working on the magazine all these years later.

A rundown of this issue's nonfiction is as follows:

In the Games section, Matt Staggs reviews *Ghost Busters* for the Xbox 360, the RPG, *Geist: The Sin-Eaters* from White Wolf Publishing, and the RPG, *Adventurer's Vault 2: A 4th Edition D&D Supplement* from Wizards of the Coast. In the Movie/TV section, we ran an evergreen article by Resa Nelson from back when the magazine was still owned by Sovereign Media. It numbered among the inventory Warren acquired when he purchased the magazine. The topic for this piece was to pick our guilty pleasure movies. Resa sent the question out to people in RoF's staff, along with some of the regular contributors. The answers received were as follows: Shawna McCarthy picked Walt Disney's *Beauty and the Beast*, Richard Parks picked *The Last Unicorn*, Gene Wolfe picked *Who Framed Roger Rabbit?*, former managing editor Laura Cleveland picked *Somewhere in Time*, I picked David Lynch's *Dune*, Folkroots editor Ari Berk picked John Boorman's *Excalibur*, Jane Yolen picked *Truly Madly Deeply*, Andy Duncan picked *Chitty Chitty Bang Bang*, Resa Nelson picked *On a Clear Day You Can See*

Forever, James A. Owen picked *A Knight's Tale*, William Shunn picked *Baron Munchausen*, Jay Lake picked *Mary Poppins*, and like Shawna McCarthy, Eugie Foster picked *Beauty and the Beast*.

In the Folkroots section, SatyrPhil Brucato writes about demon lovers. In the Artists Gallery, Karen Haber covers the work of Jill Bauman. In the Book column, Paul Witcover reviews *Finch* by Jeff VanderMeer, *The Other Lands: Book Two of the Acacia Trilogy* by David Anthony Durham, *Hope in the Mist* by Michael Swanwick, *The Lees of Laughter's End* by Steven Erickson, and Matt Staggs reviews *The Sad Tale of the Brothers Grossbart* by Jesse Bullington, *The Red Tree* by Caitlín R. Kiernan, and *Boneshaker* by Cherie Priest. In YA Books, Michael M. Jones reviews *Ash* by Malinda Lo, *Libyrinth* by Pearl North, *Shiver* by Maggie Stiefvater, *Never Slow Dance with a Zombie* by E. Van Lowe, *Bite Me!* by Melissa Francis, *The Eternal Kiss*, edited by Trisha Telep, and *Gifted: Out of Sight, Out of Mind* by Marilyn Kaye. The Graphic Novel column makes its return this issue with new columnist, Andrew Wheeler (recommended by previous columnist, Jeff VanderMeer), and he reviews *Flight Volume Six*, edited by Kazu Kibuishi, and *Mercy Thompson: Homecoming*, written by Patricia Briggs and David Lawrence, painted artwork by Francis Tsai and Amelia Woo, and lettering by Bill Tortolini.

On to the fiction ...

The lead story is "Stories of the Sand" by Dirk Strasser. In this high fantasy piece, a man takes his daughter into the rymlands beyond the Red Desert to help his daughter reclaim her lost eyes after actions taken in her defense led to them being lost. Along the way he encounters strange creatures and his reality comes into question. Art to this one was provided by the aforementioned Carol Heyer.

Next up we have "A Road Once Traveled" by Richard Parks, which marks his twenty-fouth appearance in the magazine. In this grounded fairy tale, a man sets out in his fifty-sixth year in search of his fortune. Along the way he must use his smarts to overcome trolls, magic, giants, and the biggest threat of all: adolescents. Art to this one was provided by Tiffany Prothero, which marks her fifth illustration in the magazine.

After this we have "Felicity's Engine" by Sharon Mock, which marks her second appearance in the magazine. This piece is set in the same dark fairy universe as her previous story in the magazine, "All Beautiful Things." In this short piece, in a universe where the fairy world has been overrun by humans except for the Inner Court, a dog's loyalty and a cat's sense of self-preservation come into odds as the two of them entreat the cruel fairy queen to help their dead mistress. Art to this one was provided by Dave Leri, which marks his ninth illustration in the magazine.

Then we have "In Time of Despair and Great Darkness" by Ken Scholes, which marks his third appearance in the magazine. This piece takes place in the American Dust Bowl during the Great Depression. In it, our protagonist Arthur Lee has unknowingly brought back a sword from World War I that is in fact Excalibur. It's been stuck in the earth for years as a ploughshare, and no one is giving it much thought, until some agents of the rising Third Reich come looking for it. Art to this one was provided by David Michael Beck, which marks his thirteenth illustration in the magazine.

Finally we have "Narrative of a Beast's Life" by Cat Rambo. In this world beasts of all kinds are taken as slaves by humans. A young centaur is captured and sold into slavery and chronicles his story, a tale which examines the life of slavery through the lens of a fantasy. This story appeared in audio form on *Podcastle* as podcast 087. Art to this one in RoF was provided by Alan M. Clark. Another thing worth noting is that while we still had art in inventory acquired from Sovereign Media in the purchase, this is the first issue wherein all the stories featured original art that I commissioned.

So that wraps up this issue and also the 2009 stories. And my favorite story? "Narrative of a Beast's Life" by Cat Rambo. And my favorite artwork? Carol Heyer's illustration to "Stories of the Sand."

Originally posted on douglascohen.livejournal.com on November 16th, 2013

Part ninety-two in my comprehensive retrospective as I read the fiction in *Realms of Fantasy* and offer my thoughts. This time around we say hello to the February 2010 issue.

The cover to this one features Gallegos's interior artwork to "The Unknown God" by Ann Leckie. While this issue was out, we also launched a new website for the magazine. The website address on the cover is for the old website, so when we launched the new website we created redirect link that led to www.rofmag.com. (Being as this issue was already to print by the time the new site was ready to launch, including the new website address on the cover was impossible.) The magazine has been defunct for a little over two years now, but as of the time I write this the magazine's final owners still keep a pared down version of this website running.* It was a great site, and full credit for its design goes to E. Jay O'Connell. When we launched the website, I feel like that was when these retrospectives became part of the *Realms of Fantasy* cannon, as all the retrospectives I'd written to that point (and some afterward) were included on the website.

In addition to my retrospectives, there was some other interesting content we launched on the website that is worth a mention. First, at my suggestion, we relaunched the long defunct Editorial column. This column had been dead for many years, with the exception of when Shawna wrote a new one for the August 2009 issue, to commemorate our relaunch under a new publisher. Shawna wrote the first editorial for the website, this time commemorating the launch of the nicest website the magazine ever had. Following that, with each new issue of the magazine, we published a new editorial on the website. I wrote most of them, though Shawna wrote a couple more as well. I was happy to have her write as many editorials as she wanted, but after writing so many in the past, I think she was in turn happy to let me handle most of them, which I very much enjoyed doing. With a little bit of digging, you should be able to find these editorials on the website. The other feature worth a mention is that we launched a cover gallery, which at the time displayed every cover in the magazine's history. We actually kept this cover gallery up to date until the very end of the magazine's history, and as I write this the gallery remains intact. So if you want to see all 102 covers of *Realms of Fantasy*, it is but a few clicks away on your computer.

All right, let's get back to the magazine itself ...

In the table of contents page, one interesting tidbit worth noting is that editorial blurb written to Harlan Ellison's story was written by Harlan Ellison. To the best of my knowledge, it is the only time someone has written an editorial blurb to a story in *Realms of Fantasy* besides Shawna. At the very least, it was the only time this happened while I was with the magazine.

In the masthead, there is one change to report. With this issue I was promoted to the position of Editor. Shawna McCarthy remained in charge of the fiction department, and I remained her faithful assistant here, and I was already overseeing the nonfiction and the artwork. However, I had recently received additional responsibilities of overseeing the copyediting department, and was also made the equivalent of the content editor for the website. So Warren ended up rolling all of this under the title of Editor. When it came to my placement in the masthead, while Warren would obviously remain at the top as the owner and publisher, I made a point of requesting that Shawna's name remain above mine. I don't know what Warren was planning on doing, but this felt right to me. Shawna was the magazine's founding editor, the only person to have been with the magazine since issue one, she was the one who first hired me, and the fiction was always the heart of the magazine. Put all this together and requesting that Shawna remain ahead of me in the masthead was a no-brainer.

A rundown of this issue's nonfiction is as follows:

In the Games section, Matt Staggs reviews *Batman: Arkham Asylum* for the PC, Playstation 3, and Xbox 360, *Halo 3* for Xbox 360, the card game *Scary Tales, Deck One: Little Red vs. Pinocchio*, and he throws our readers a curveball by reviewing the book (gasp!) *Fantasy Freaks and Gaming Geeks: An Epic Quest for Reality Among Role Players, Online Gamers, and Other Dwellers of Imaginary Realms* by Ethan Gilsdorf. In the Movie/TV section, Resa Nelson covers *The Lovely Bones* and also delivers an article about the Harry Potter Exhibition Tour, which is basically a traveling museum featuring items from the Harry Potter movies. In the Folkroots column, Stephen D. Winick writes about the mythology of Jack and the Beanstalk. In the Artists Gallery, Karen Haber covers the artwork of Charles Vess. In the Books column, Paul Witcover reviews *The God Engines* by John Scalzi, *Big Machine* by Victor LaValle, *The Silver Skull: Swords of Albion* by Mark Chadbourn, *The Choir Boats: Volume One of Longing for Yount* by Daniel A. Rabuzzi, and Matt Staggs reviews *This Crooked Way* by James Enge, and *The Infernal City: An Elder Scrolls Novel* by Greg Keyes. In YA Books, Michael M. Jones reviews *Leviathan* by Scott Westerfeld, *Ballad: A Gathering of Faerie* by Maggie Stiefvater, *The Splendor Falls* by Rosemary Clement-Moore, *Hush, Hush* by Becca Fitzpatrick, *Devil's Kiss* by Sarwat Chadda, *Devoured* by Amanda Marrone, *Never Cry Werewolf* by Heather Davis, and *Once a Witch* by Carolyn MacCullough.

Andy Wheeler's Graphic Novel column for this issue appeared on the website instead. Being as these columns came down when a new issue was published, it's unavailable to be read. Nor do my personal records indicate which graphic novels he reviewed this time around, so I'm afraid it's mysteries upon mysteries.

On to the fiction ...

The lead story is "How Interesting: A Tiny Man" by Harlan Ellison. In this contemporary fantasy, a man creates a living breathing tiny man that he carries around with him, and his act of creation frightens and angers strangers who wish to destroy it/him. Things culminate with two possible endings, which were printed on their own page of the magazine: "The First Ending" and "The Second Ending." Along with Kij Johnson's "Ponies," this story was the co-winner for the 2010 Nebula Award for Best Short Fiction. Art to this was provided by Leo and Diane Dillon, and Harlan Ellison handled the art direction for his piece, which ended up being included in the Editorial section of *Spectrum 17: The Best in Contemporary Fantastic Art*. It should also be noted that Warren Lapine deserves some of the credit for this story's appearance in RoF. When Warren took over the magazine, Harlan Ellison owed Warren an original story from Warren's days of running DNA Publications. So when Harlan passed this story along to Warren, Warren in turn passed it along to Shawna, who made the final call about whether to include it in the magazine. But if not for Warren, there is the distinct possibility that Harlan's story never would have found its way to us in the first place.

After this we have "Mister Oak" by Leah Bobet, which marks her third appearance in the magazine. This short contemporary fantasy can be summed up rather easily: an oak tree falls in love with a woman, and then *literally falls for her* after having his heart broken. Art to this one was provided by Gary Lippincott, which marks his seventh illustration in the magazine. This piece was also selected for the Editorial section of *Spectrum 17: The Best in Contemporary Fantastic Art*. For me, this was very gratifying, as it marked the first piece of artwork I oversaw that received some sort of recognition. Considering I had only been overseeing the artwork since the August 2009 issue and that much of the artwork we published to this point was inherited from Soverign Media, this was more than a bit unexpected.

Next up we have "The Demon of Hochgarten" by Euan Harvey, which marks his third appearance in the magazine. This is a sword & sorcery piece that takes place in medieval Europe. In it, a knight who is also a werewolf investigates the murder of a baron and must fight demons and sorcery for his trouble. To me, it feels like Euan was setting this up to be a recurring character that would experience further adventures, but as I've mentioned in a previous retrospective, Euan passed away from cancer. To the best of my knowledge, this was the only tale he published featuring Stefan Von Stawy, Knight of the Bloody Spear. Art to this one was provided by Dave Leri, which marks his tenth illustration in the magazine. It numbered among the inventory that was transferred over to Warren Lapine from Sovereign Media when he purchased the magazine. It also occurs to me that in this issue we have artwork that was overseen by three different people: Harlan Ellison for "How Interesting: A Tiny Man," Laura Cleveland from Sovereign Media for "The Demon of Hochgarten," and myself for the other three illustrations.

After this we have "Melanie" by Aliette de Bodard. Aliette was actually one of my slush survivors back when she was first breaking onto the scene ...but while this is her first publication in *Realms of Fantasy*, it is actually the second story she sold to us, i.e. not the one I fished out of the slush. Sometimes publishing is funny that way. As to the story itself, this is a contemporary fantasy about a young man named Erwan who has a gift that allows him to see people's mathematical knowledge in glowing formulas that suffuse their body. He is shy and awkward, and he is infatuated with a beautiful fellow student who turns out to have a secret of her own, one that hides her own true nature of being a snake. Loving this serpent comes at a great cost though, too much for anyone else, though Erwan brings us back to that timeless theme of love conquers all. Art to this one was provided Frank Wu.

Finally we have "The Unknown God" by Ann Leckie, another one of my slush survivors. This piece is a high fantasy that deals with a god living in human form who must confront being human in two of the most difficult ways possible: a crisis in faith and a broken heart. Art to this one was provided by Gallegos, which as mentioned earlier was selected to appear on the cover of this issue. One interesting tidbit about this artwork is that in this piece the protagonist is chanting a spell, and it has taken physical form as a glowing string of symbols leaving his mouth. The spell the artist is illustrating was not a direct scene in the book, so I suggested to him that to tie this more closely into the narrative he should consider hiding the name "Saest" among the glowing symbols. Saest is the name of the human woman that our protagonist god fell in love with. We agreed this should be subtle, but if you pay attention you'll be able to find it. This artwork was the winner of the magazine's second annual Reader Choice Award for Best Artwork.

So that wraps up this issue. And my favorite story? "The Demon of Hochgarten" by Euan Harvey. And my favorite artwork? We have a tie between Gary Lippincott's illustration to "Mister Oak" and Gallegos's illustration to "The Unknown God."

*And as I prep these entries for book publication, the same holds true as of the middle of June 2015.

Originally posted on douglascohen.livejournal.com on December 28th, 2013

Part ninety-three in my comprehensive retrospective as I read the fiction in *Realms of Fantasy* and offer my thoughts. This time around I'll share some thoughts regarding the April 2010 issue.

The cover to this one is a reprint of Dominic Harman's cover art to *Blood of Ambrose* by James Enge. It marks his second illustration in the magazine. As mentioned in the previous retrospective, while the last issue was our we changed the website address to www.rofmag.com and provided a redirect link. With this issue, the new website address began appearing on the cover. Building on this thought, there is also one change to the masthead this issue, as E. Jay O'Connell is now listed as Web Master.

A rundown of this issue's nonfiction is as follows:

In the Games column, new columnist Tony Sims reviews *Heroes of Gaia* for the Firefox browser and *Duels of the Planeswalkers: Expansion for Magic: The Gathering* for the Xbox 360, and Matt Staggs reviews *Borderlands* for the Xbox 360, *The Dungeon Alphabet* by Michael Curtis, and *Pathfinder Roleplaying Game: Bestiary*. With this issue, we also introduced Entertainment Software Ratings Board (ESRB) ratings in the product information for all electronic games. When Tony handed in an old review column of his while applying to be Matt's co-columnist, I noticed that he included the ESRB with his review. This struck me as a good idea and when I asked myself why RoF hadn't been doing this all along, I couldn't come up with a good answer. Its inclusion also struck me as a sensible precaution, because if a child wanted his or her parent to buy a game based on our magazine's review and the ESRB for that game was "Mature," no irate parent would be able to accuse us of failing to provide the ESRB. Put all this together and including the ESRB going forward struck me as a no-brainer.

In the Movie/TV column, Resa Nelson examines how the unexpected success of the movie *Paranormal Activity* rodes the coattails of various ghostly TV series. In the Folkroots column, Maggie Secara writes about the rings of ancient times. In a special feature, Publisher Warren Lapine conducts an interview with the musical fantasy band, Blackmore's Night.

In the Artists Gallery, Karen Haber conducts a Q&A with artist, Silvano Braido. As memory serves, this was something that had been planned with Sovereign Media and I gave Karen the green light to follow through on this. In the Books column, Paul Witcover reviews *Sasha: A Trial of Blood & Steel* by Joel Shepherd, *The Hundred Thousand Kingdoms* by N.K. Jemisin, *The Spirit Lens* by Carol Berg, and Matt Staggs reviews *The Devil's Alphabet* by Daryl Gregory, *Total Oblivion, More of Less* by Alan DeNiro, and *Spellwright* by Blake Charlton.

There is actually a bit of a story how we came to review *Spellwright*. Back in 2009, I was attending the World Fantasy Convention. As often happens at conventions, I ended up sharing a room with a few other people to split costs. One of those people was Blake Charlton. I had never met him at that point, but he was friends with another of my con roommates, editor and anthologist, John Joseph Adams (who got terribly sick at that convention, though on the bright side he also met his future wife there). In talking to Blake, I learned that his first novel was coming out with Tor Books. In addition to this, I learned that Blake had dyslexia, and that his protagonist experiences something of a magical equivalent in Blake's novel. I found all of this fascinating, so upon returning home from the convention I contacted my reviewers, explained the situation, and asked if either of them would be interested in reviewing the book. Matt volunteered and the rest is history.

In YA books, Michael Jones reviews *Ice* by Sarah Beth Durst, *Lips Touch: Three Times* by Laini Taylor and illustrated by Jim Di Bartolo, *Beautiful Creatures* by Kami Garcia, *The Doom Machine* by Mark Teague, *The Shifter, Book One of the Healing Wars* by Janice Hardy, *Lockdown: Escape from Furnace* by Alexander Gordon Smith, and *The Seven Rays* by Jessica Bendinger. And in the Graphic Novel column, Andrew Wheeler reviews *This Ugly Yet Beautiful World, Volume 1*, original story by Gainax/Konomini Project, art by Ashita Morimi, *Moyasimon 1: Tales of Agriculture* by Masayuki Ishikawa, *Time and Again, Volume 1* by JiUn Yun, and *Raiders, Volume 1*, by JinJun Park.

On to the fiction ...

The lead story is "Just Another Word" by Carrie Vaughn, which marks her eighth appearance in the magazine. In this short piece, the rockstar Janis Joplin is presented with a chance to run away with the fairy queen and spend a life serving her with songs, but in the end she rejects it. Art to this one was provided by Peter Ferguson, which marks his fifth illustration in the magazine.

Next up we have "Hanuman's Bridge" by Euan Harvey, which marks his fourth appearance in the magazine. This is another short piece, in which ancient Hindu mythology comes to life in the real world and ushers in nuclear war when Sri Lanka is connected to India via bridge. Art to this one was provided by Frank Wu, which marks his second illustration in the magazine.

After this we have "The Hag Queen's Curse" by M.K. Hobson, which marks her fifth appearance in the magazine. This one is a funny fantasy that starts off in Maryland in 1798, operating under the assumption that magic is real. A witch known as the Hag Queen is enjoying her meal in her tavern, when her dinner is interrupted and ruined by a pair of men in the midst of a fight. One is John Rodgers, Warlock First Class, United States Navy. Rodgers is attempting to apprehend Hide-Pirate Captain Flâneur, a man who plunders bodies, essentially spirit-hopping from one to the next, staying in it until he must find a new host before the old body crumbles into dust. So for interrupting her meal, the Hag Queen sends these adversaries hurtling into through space and time, all the way to Newport, Oregon in 1986. Enter Kat and her best friend, Jeff. Kat and Jeff have been best friends since childhood and share a secret telepathic link, so when the hide-pirate inhabits Jeff's body, Kat immediately can tell that something is terribly wrong. Kat ends up joining forces with Admiral Rodgers to stop Flâneur and save Jeff. Along the way, they smoke some weed (or as Rodgers puts it, "General Washington's herb"), eat some culry fries, and endure the annoying antics of Kat's stoner boyfriend, Brody. Kat also happens to be a gay man in a woman's body, and while it's a less-than-friendly term, this makes Kat a "hag," making her the key to breaking the hag queen's curse.

I don't by any means want to sound like I'm accusing the author of anything discriminatory. Quite the opposite; the story is a lot of fun and Hobson is quite respectful in her handling of the terms and all the characters (including Jeff, who is gay, and Rodgers, who develops a mutual attraction toward Kat). This story appeared as podcast 99 on the PodCastle website. Art to this in RoF was provided by Peter Ferguson, which marks his sixth illustration in the magazine. Of additional interest is the fact that this artwork includes the magazine's first illustration with drug paraphenelia, as you can see Admiral Rodgers sitting on a couch with his eyes closed and holding a bong, clearly stoned out of his mind. When Peter first handed in the sketch for this one, I thought it was hysterical and a perfect representation of the story. However, I wanted to make sure it wouldn't cause any problems because of the paraphenlia depiction. So I ran this past Warren. His basic response? "I don't care." At that point, I went back to Peter and suggested we up the ante. Since he made Rodgers look so high, I suggested that he add some smoke floating around the ceiling to indicate the copious amounts of marijuana that had been smoked. Peter loved the idea, and we ended up adding in. A big thanks to Warren for allowing this illustration, as it is simply perfect for the story in question.

Then we have "A Close Personal Relationship" by Thomas Marcinko, which marks the 550th story to appear in the magazine. This story comes with an interesting back-story. Back in the early days of the magazine, Shawna had accepted it for the magazine. However, the publishers overruled her, refusing to publish it in the magazine as they believed it too controversial. A few months after Warren took over as the new publisher, Thomas got in touch with Shawna to see if she still might be interested in using this for the magazine, as almost fifteen years later it remained unpublished. Normally I would see just about every story before it found its way to Shawna, but in this case Shawna asked the author to email the story to her directly. So Shawna gave the story another read and still wanted it. But given what happened last time, she understandably wanted a second opinion. So she emailed the story to me and told me about the story's interesting past (and to the best of my knowledge, this was the only time in the magazine's history where a publisher overruled Shawna's desire to purchase a story). So I read the story, liked it, and agreed that we should buy it. I also doubted that publishing it would stir up any controversies (which it didn't) and said as much. But as with the art in the previous story, I erred on the side of caution and suggested to Shawna that she show the story to Warren and clear this with our publisher. So Shawna sent it along to him, explained the back-story, and Warren gave it a read. His basic response? "I don't care." This makes twice in this issue that Warren said "I don't care" when asked if something was all right. But don't take that to mean that he didn't care about the magazine in general. He simply trusted his staff and believed in allowing us much creative freedom as possible. It's something we all very much appreciated.

As to the story itself, basically Jesus has returned to Earth, and it turns out His values and ideas match up with those of right wing Christian conservatives. Since Jesus now walks the Earth, everyone is expected to worship Him, and at some point everyone has a private meeting with Him so that He has a "Close Personal Personal Relationship" with them. This includes folks who were Jews, Muslims, Hindus, Buddhists, and yes, atheists and agnostics. In this piece, our protagonist Ted is a good person who has a deep affection for dinosaurs. His faith also deserted him long ago. Needless to say, Jesus (or as he's referred to in this story, "Junior") has a problem with this. It is not enough for Ted to live his life as a morally good person when he doesn't give his worship to Jesus. Feel free to take a guess which of the two loses when they confront the "problem." To be clear, I put the word "problem" in quotes not to disparage religion, but more because whether it's a problem or not really depends on who each particular reader is siding with.

At first glance, this piece is a contemporary fantasy. However, this is also a matter of interpretation. I'm an atheist, and I found that reading this piece was rather like reading a horror story. Again, I don't say this to disparage religion, but I've been a non-believer for many years. If were confronted with the idea in real life that Jesus exists, and more than that I *have to* worship him (even though I was raised Jewish), well I won't be shy in saying this is a pretty scary notion. I rather imagine it would be the equivalent of someone devoutly religious being presented irrefutable proof that God in any shape or form *does not* exist. If I can wax philosophical for one more moment, I would add that just as beauty can be found in the eye of the beholder, so too can horror or fear. Art to this one was provided by John Kaiine, which marks his second illustration in the magazine.

Finally we have "The Fortuitous Meeting of Gerard van Oost and Oludara" by Christopher Kastensmidt. This sword and sorcery piece was another one of my slush survivors, and its discovery marks one of the high points of my career with *Realms of Fantasy*. Sometimes I come across something in the slush that I just know Shawna is going to take for the magazine. This was such a piece (despite the fact that Shawna was always a tough sell with sword and sorcery). This was reason enough to make me smile. Then the story got nominated for the 2010 Nebula Award for Best Novelette. Slush stories very rarely never get nominated for Nebula Awards. Sword and sorcery stories almost *never* receive such nominations.

So when you put these things together, this nomination very much defied the odds. And on top of this, it also marked Christopher's first pro sale. Yup—he pulled the trifecta on this one. Nice job, Chris. Added bonus? It was also the co-winner for the Realms of Fantasy 2010 Reader Choice Award for Best Fiction. My understanding from Chris is that this story and its success have also opened a number of doors for him in Brazil.* Put all this together and it's with good reason that this is one of the prettiest feathers in my editorial cap.

As to the story itself, it takes place in a colonial Brazil where magic is real. Gerard van Oost is an adventurer from Europe who wishes to carve a name for himself as an adventurer in the new world. However, the only European company in Brazil worth joining belongs to Antonio Dias Caldas, and he refuses to let Gerard join his company because of Gerard's Protestant beliefs. It is around this time that Gerard meets Oludara, a recent slave fresh off the boat from Africa. Gerard is struck by the man's bearing and intelligence and believes he would make an excellent traveling companion in the wilds of Brazil. He then endeavors to to acquire enough money to purchase Oludara, not to be his slave but rather to free the man in the *hopes* that he will join Gerard as a companion, friend, and equal. In order to acquire the necessary coin, Gerard must outwit a forest creature out of Brazilian mythology, and after he buys Oluadara's freedom, Oludara agrees of his own volition to travel with Gerard for five years if at the end of this time Gerard helps him return to Africa. With an agreement struck, the two of them form their own two-man company, under the Elephant and Macaw Banner.

As you might expect based on this summary, this is the first in a series of adventures for the dynamic duo. I've since read a few of the others, and there is even a chance that down the road a sword and sorcery story of my own—one read and critiqued by Chris long after he published in *Realms*—might be appearing alongside another one of Chris's van Oost and Oludara, in the same venue.** Chris would probably lay a curse on me from distant Brazil if I say more than this, but if it does happen it would be something that I would get a kick out of as an editor, a writer, and subsequently as Chris's friend. Art to this one was provided by Federico Piatti, and it marks another piece that was part of the inventory inherited from Sovereign Media.

So that wraps up this issue. And my favorite story? "The Fortuitous Meeting of Gerard van Oost and Oludara" by Christopher Kastensmidt (and honorable mention to "The Hag Queen's Curse" by M.K. Hobson for leaving me breathless with laughter). And my favorite artwork? Peter Ferguson's illustration to "The Hag Queen's Curse."

*Indeed, there is now a board game, a graphic novel, the novel is being readied for publication in Brazil, and Chris recently released some of the stories in the coming novel as Kindle singles.

**Alas, Chris withdrew his story from this venue because they were taking forever to publish him. (I know the feeling!)

Originally posted on douglascohen.livejournal.com on January 16th, 2014

Part ninety-four in my comprehensive retrospective as I read the fiction in *Realms of Fantasy* and offer my thoughts. This time around I'm tackling the June 2010 issue.

The cover art features Marc Roland and Alan M. Clark's interior illustration to "Fallen." There is an interesting story behind this one, but I'll get into that when I discuss "Fallen."

A rundown of this issue's nonfiction is as follows:

In the Movie/TV section, Resa Nelson examines how video games, comics, and classics inspire the spring fantasy movies. In Folkroots, H. Talat Halman writes about Hermes as a magician, messenger, and guitar god. In the Artists Gallery, Mia Nutick covers the art of Virginia Lee. In the Books column, Paul Witcover reviews *Horns* by Joe Hill, *Empire in Black and Gold* by Adrian Tchaikovsky, *Bloodroot* by Amy Greene, *Petrodor* by Joel Shepherd (this particular review was moved to the website), and Matt Staggs reviews *Mr. Shivers* by Robert Jackson Bennett, *Soulless* by Gail Carriger, and *Tails of Wonder and Imagination*, edited by Ellen Datlow. In YA Books, Michael Jones reviews *I Kissed a Zombie, and I Liked It* by Adam Selzer, *The Iron King* by Julie Kagawa, *Firespell* by Chloe Neill, *Fallen* by Lauren Kate, *Undead Much?* by Stacey Jay, *Wish* by Alexandra Bullen, *Hearts at Stake* by Alyxandra Harvey, *The Dark Divine* by Bree Despain, and *Magic Under Glass* by Jaclyn Dolamore.

This issue also introduces a new column, this being Paranormal Romance and Urban Fantasy Books. We decided to introduce this column because at the time both of these subgenres (which crossover with each quite a bit) were exploding on the market in a big way. So while our other book column reviewers were not precluded from reviewing books in these subgenres, we deemed it a good idea to introduce a column devoted specifically to these areas, thus ensuring they received enough coverage each issue. Credit the idea for this column to Publisher Warren Lapine, though he left the hiring process to me. I put an open call for the position on my blog and the magazine's website and received an absolutely phenemonal response. There were a number of excellent candidates, but ultimately I settled on Elizabeth Bear as our inaugural columnist. As to her inaugural reviews, she reviews *Kitty's House of Horrors* by Carrie Vaughn,

The Better Part of Darkness by Charlie Madigan, *Spiral Hunt* by Margaret Ronald, and *The Sorcerer's House* by Gene Wolfe.

The Games column this issue was shifted online. In it, Matt Staggs reviews *Runequest II*, *Dungeons & Dragons 4ᵗʰ Edition*, *Plane Below Sourcebook*, and the RPG, *The Cursed Chateau*, and Tony Sims reviews *Babel*, an expansion to *Heroes of Gaia*, *Bayonetta* for Xbox360, and *Torchlight* for the PC. I assume the Graphic Novel column was also shifted to the website this issue, though my records here are oddly blank.

On to the fiction ...

The lead story this issue is "Desaparacidos" by Aliette de Bodard, which marks her second appearance in the magazine. As mentioned previously, this was the first story we bought from her and was one of my slush survivors (my twenty-fifth), but her second story, "Melanie," ended up getting published first in February 2010 issue. Sometimes publishing is funny like that. Mostly it comes down to matters of space in terms of word counts, though when an illustration is ready for publication also factors in. As to the story itself, we are presented with a contemporary fantasy wherein a young woman returns to where her lover presumably died in prison, but it turns out his soul (and many others) are still imprisoned and in desperate need of release ...and so too is a grounded angel. Art to this one was provided by Rob Alexander. As I recall, Aliette was very happy with it, as she expressed an interest in acquiring the original art. I believe I provided her the artist's email address, though I'm uncertain what came of this.

Next up we have "Sultana Lena's Gift" by Shweta Narayan, another of my slush survivors. This is a rare steampunk story in the magazine, only our second and final by my count. As I'm not the biggest steampunk fan (said the guy who is putting the final polish on his steampunk novel), I find it ironic that of the almost 600 stories we published, I should discover one of the two stories we published in this vein. In this piece, a young shah struggles with whether to go to war and he relies on the advice of his clockwork bird. Most of the bird's advice comes through the form of a story, wherein we meet Sultana Lena, who can grant wishes to any boy or man before her as long as he did not touch her in any way. Needless to say, this sort of power leads to some unexpected results. Art to this one was provided by Stephanie Pui-Mun Law, which marks her fifth illustration in the magazine.

Interesting side note about the artwork in this one: when Warren Lapine bought the magazine, this story was stuck in transition. I had plucked it from the slush during the days of Sovereign Media as publisher and passed it along to Shawna for further consideration. It languished there for some time along with many other stories while Warren was in negotiations with Sovereign Media, and further months passed before we had need of enough new fiction that Shawna could do a buying run. At some point during this time, Warren put me in charge of overseeing the magazine's artwork. Once he did, the very first thought I had was that if Shawna purchased "Sultana Lena's Gift," I wanted Stephanie Pui-Mun Law to illustrate it. I didn't know Stephanie at the time, but I had seen a number of her earlier illustrations in the magazine, and I was seized by this instant association between her artwork and the way I envisioned the story. So when Shawna purchased this piece, when it came time to find an illustrator, I wasted no time contacting Stephanie. I didn't even have a backup plan—I was convinced in my gut that this pairing was meant to happen. Thankfully, Stephanie's schedule agreed with my gut. And I'm happy to add that her illustration pretty much matched up with how I envisioned she would tackle the imagery. This initial association between Shweta's work and Stephanie's skills created the template for how I would go about my story/artist pairings going forward. I'm a fairly visual reader, so when looking for an artist for a particular piece, I tried to find someone whose illustrations were reminiscent of the imagery in my head. Of course, not all stories provide a lot of imagery, so in these cases I relied more heavily on matching up the feel of the story with the feel of the artwork.

Next up we have "The Well of Forgetting" by Meredith Simmons. This was another story that got caught in transition hell after the magazine's closure, and I remember that when Shawna decided she wanted to purchase it, for whatever reason we had a devil of a time getting in touch with the author. We were just about ready to give this story up for lost when we finally tracked her down. As to the story itself, this one is a high fantasy. In it, we are introduced to the Well of Forgetting, a place where people go to forget their darkest dreams, memories, thoughts, etc. Enter Hepta, a young girl who is plagued by far darker thoughts than anyone her age has a right to be. When her mind is purged, she is forced to return again several years later. This pattern repeats itself several times until it's discovered that she's a living well, a person able to perform the same function as the Well of Forgetting. She has been unknowingly absorbing the darkness of her fellow villagers. She is sold into a life of prostitution, but despite her beauty her true value is her function as a living well. Over time, so much absorption of others' darknesses begins to take its toll on her. But she is able to use this very thing to gain her freedom, for in absorbing such darkness, she is also learning people's darkest secrets. Art to this one was provided by Carol Heyer, which marks her tenth illustration in the magazine.

After this we have "The Hearts of Men" by T.L. Morganfield, another one of my slush survivors. This one is swords & sixguns piece that delves into Aztec mythology. The heyday of the Aztec empire is long over, and America is in full expansionist mode during its Wild West period, as the clues dropped by the author seem to indicate this piece takes place not long after the end of the Mexican-American War in 1848. In this piece, the Aztec god Huitizilopatchli—also referred to as the Blue Hummingbird of the South—is reborn to continue his endless battle with his sister, Coyolxauhqui, who has once again stolen the moon. With the aid of a young Aztec boy, he must seek out his sister and stop her, all the while fighting his mounting desire to feast on the boy's heart, for human hearts are the only thing that can sate his otherwise bottomless hunger.

I worked with T.L. on a revision before passing this one along, and while we worked rather well together, it's safe to say that it was an unusual experience for both of us. While reading this, I found myself reminded of my own piece published in *Interzone* a few years earlier, "Feelings of the Flesh." By no means did I think that T.L. was in any way imitating my story—the world-building and themes were entirely different from my own, as were the characters. But every so often in the plot (which was also pretty different from my piece overall), the characters did something that made me think of my own piece. It was all surface stuff, but I couldn't shake this feeling. So anyway, while I enjoyed the piece, I thought it could benefit from a few revisions. So I reached out to T.L. and asked her if she would be amenable to this. Naturally, she was. (I say naturally because we had actually worked on a revision to a previous submission of hers to the magazine, called "Morning Star Falling," and the editorial process here also went very smoothly. Shawna *almost* bought that one ...and I'll also add that T.L. has subsequently published a novel called *The Bone Flower Throne* that incorporates aspects of this story).* Since we knew each other a little bit already from the last time we worked together, I couldn't help but remark to her that her story reminded me a little bit of my own. T.L. confessed to me that when she'd read my story in *Interzone*, she had also noticed some of these surface similarities, and that it actually made her hold off on submitting this particular piece to *Realms of Fantasy*. I can understand her thinking here, as she realized her story would have to go through me first, which would be ...for lack of a better word, I'll say weird. Regardless, at some point she decided to submit to us anyway, and I'm obviously glad she did, as it led to a story for the magazine, it led to T.L.'s first pro sale, and it led to a friendly acquaintaince becoming a friend.

As to the revisions I requested, I was very conscious of trying to remain as objective as possible given the perceived similarities. This was T.L.'s story, not mine, so I wanted her to realize *her* vision of this story without my own piece coming into play. Thankfully, none of the revisions I requested concerned any parts of the story that shared any similarities with my own piece, but I remember reading over my notes quite a number of times before passing them along to her, because I wanted to remain absolutely certain I maintained my objectivity. I even explained all this to Shawna, because I wanted her to let me know if anything seemed off thanks to my editorial tinkering. But I'm glad to say all was well in the end. Artwork to this one was provided by Kurt Huggins and Zelda Devon, which marks their third illustration in the magazine. This illustration was another piece that was inherited from Sovereign Media. It was also selected for inclusion in the Editorial section of *Spectrum 17: The Best in Contemporary Fantastic Art*.

Finally we have "Fallen" by Bruce Holland Rogers, which marks his twelfth story in the magazine. This one is a rather short piece about giant angels falling from the sky, and the lengths to which people are going to eat their flesh when it's discovered that doing so is a form of luck. Art to this one was provided by the aforementioned Marc Roland and Alan M. Smale. For Alan, it marks his second illustration in the magazine. The interesting story I promised about this illustration is the following: this artwork was actually submitted to the magazine *with* the story. Since Bruce was a client of Shawna's literary agency, he submitted the story directly to Shawna, along with the artwork, so Shawna saw both pieces before I did. So she decided to purchase the story, at which point she passed along the story and accompanying artwork to me, explaining that she already planned on taking the story and thought we should take the artwork as well. The artwork struck me as pretty gorgeous, but to be sure that I wanted it I read the story in question. Afterward, accepting the artwork was a no-brainer. During my six and a half years with the magazine, this marks the only time a story and illustration were submitted in conjunction to the magazine with both leading to an acceptance. It's certainly possible this had happened previously during the magazine's run, though you'd have to ask Shawna.

So that wraps up this issue. And my favorite story? We have a tie between "The Well of Forgetting" by Meredith Simmons and "The Hearts of Men" by T.L. Morganfield. And my favorite artwork? Stephanie Pui-Mun Law's illustration to "Sultana Lena's Gift."

*And as it happens, a few years later I joined T.L.'s critique group (which actually also includes Aliette) and critiqued the sequel to *The Bone Flower Throne*, *The Bone Flower Queen* (both are available for purchase).

Originally posted on douglascohen.livejournal.com on February 16[h], 2014

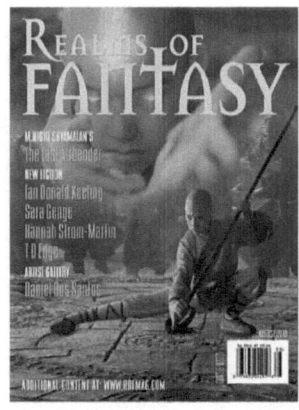

Part ninety-five in my comprehensive retrospective as I read the fiction in *Realms of Fantasy* and offer my thoughts, right up to the final issue. This time around I'll be dissecting the August 2010 issue.

There's a lot to discuss regarding the cover to this one. It features a montage image from M. Night Shyamalan's *The Last Airbender*. This marks the first movie cover published under Tir Na Nog Press. It's also the first montage cover published during the magazine's run. Credit for putting together the montage goes to E. Jay O'Connell. Jay was our webmaster after putting together a new website for the magazine that went up during December 2009 issue, but with this issue he took on additional duties of design and layout for the magazine, which were handed off to him by publisher, Warren Lapine.

Now one nice thing about doing this retrospective series is that you can go back and revisit certain events that took place during the magazine's run and shed additional light on them. For example, I can discuss why we ran a cover to a movie that received some understandable flack for whitewashing the lead character. But before I get into that, a quick bit of background on *The Last Airbender*: the movie is based on the wildly popular cartoon, *Avatar: The Last Airbender*. It's written for kids, but the storyline is sophisticated enough that adults who are open to cartoons can and will appreciate this one. The main character, Ang, is of a decidedly Far Eastern persuasion. In the movie version, he was recast as being white, and thus the accusations of whitewashing.

And now that you have the necessary background, I'd like to address why we ran such a cover, because I was neither deaf nor blind to some of the comments we received regarding this choice when it happened. There are actually a number of reasons this happened, and I'll relay them as best I can (don't forget that it's been almost four years between now and the publication of this issue). First, I know that for some months Warren Lapine had been saying he'd like for us to try out a movie cover to see how that impacted sales, so right there my radar was up for a possible media cover. Now anytime we run a media cover, we're also covering the featured item in the Movie/TV column of the magazine. Resa Nelson was our

longtime columnist here, and our normal routine was for her to pitch me
a set of choices for upcoming movies or TV programming and have me
pick something. So some months before this issue, she mentioned *The Last
Airbender* as a possible candidate for this issue. At this time, I hadn't seen
the cartoon, but I was aware of the tremendous positive buzz surrounding
it, along with the excitement of there being an upcoming movie. So this
led me to selecting *The Last Airbender* to be cover in the Movie/TV
column.

With me so far? Good. So at some point during the process, Resa
conveyed to me a request from the publicist for *The Last Airbender* to be
given the cover. Remembering Warren's interest in running a movie cover,
I passed along this request to him. (Warren gave me a lot of freedom
regarding the cover selection, but he was also the publisher—if he had a
desire for us to try out a media cover, of course I was going to mention this
to him). So Warren expressed a desire for us to try out this cover, which
is how it came about.

Now before I go any further, I'd like to make it clear that I am not in
any shape or form trying to pass the buck. I am simply relaying the chain-
of-events. So several different images were passed along to us to choose
from for the cover, and Jay took two of them and created the montage, and
I think he did quite a good job with it. Now here's something you may not
know: besides the fact that I'd never seen the cartoon, neither had
Warren. Neither had Resa. I'm fairly certain Jay hadn't either. So when
this movie was chosen for the cover, none of us were aware that this white
lead in the movie was in fact Far Eastern in the original cartoon. The first
I heard about the whitewashing was when Warren sent me an article he
came across online, and by this time the magazine had already gone to
press.

Other than the four of us, the only other people that would have been
seen the magazine before it went to press were the copy editors when they
reviewed the pdf, and our advertising director. I can't tell you if any of
them were familiar with the cartoon or had read articles about the
whitewashing before we went to press. I've never asked them. However,
given their professionalism and the character of these people, I feel
confident that if they were aware of any of this they would've brought it
to my or Warren's attention.

Now if you'd like to say I'm at fault for not researching the movie before greenlighting that cover, I'll accept that criticism. I could have looked into it further. But the idea that the movie would be whitewashed never even occurred to me. Call me naïve, but why would it? M. Night Shymalan was attached to direct, and while I don't care for most of his work, there is no denying that he was and is one of the more influential non-white directors in Hollywood. So I would never have expected him to attach himself to a movie that would become embroiled in this sort of controversy. And if you want to say I should have looked into the movie on a general basis beforehand, again, I'll accept that criticism. But once again, it never occurred to me that such a thing would be necessary. The original cartoon aired on Nickolodean, a TV channel for kids. The movie in turn would be targeting kids above all others (thus its PG rating). With this in mind, I couldn't envision too much controversy resulting from the adaptation.

Oh, how wrong I was. It wasn't a full-blown controversy regarding our cover, but we received a number of comments. We could have addressed those comments at the time, but the truth of the matter was that I understood from past experiences that the more you try to explain yourself online the more you risk someone misinterpreting something you're saying, and fanning the flames into a full-blown controversy. So even though a number of unflattering things were said about me, I bit my tongue and made no reply. Nor did anyone else (as best as I can remember), and as a result this whole matter went away far more quickly as opposed to escalating, which it almost certainly would have with people posting in the heat of the moment.

So why am I saying something now? Quite simply, this is a retrospective series about the magazine, and I prefer not to rewrite that history but rather examine it, and, where warranted, explain it. Obviously these explanations are through my perspective, but alas, I can only be me. So with the magazine canceled and this being several years in the past, I have no qualms about revisiting this matter in more detail. And if after reading this explanation you have a problem with me or anyone at the magazine for running this cover, then you have no tolerance for honest mistakes, however unlikely they might be. I'll personally vouch for every last person on the staff who was aware of the cover before it went to press that they didn't allow this to happen because of racial hatreds or insensitivies or anything remotely along these lines.

Hindsight is 20/20. If Warren or I learned about these accusations of whitewashing before the cover went to press, I am quite certain there would have been a serious conversation about whether to pull the cover. And before you ask, "What is there to talk about?" the answer is quite a bit. If we pulled the cover, we ran the risk of offending the publicist or studio, which could have prevented us from covering future movies of theirs, which could in turn hurt potential revenue avenues. And let's say Resa had yet to conduct her interviews and we changed our mind about the cover. If the publicist or studio was upset enough, they might cancel the interview, leaving us without an article. It takes weeks and weeks to set up these interviews, sometimes more. Now please don't misinterpret this to mean that any of this would have prevented us from pulling the cover. It simply illustrates the fact there would be enough factors at play to warrant a conversation. If you have a problem with a conversation taking place, kindly take two steps back and refrain from commenting. Conversation is pretty damn essential to proper communication. For my money, if I had all the facts in front of me, at the end of the conversation I would have voted for pulling the cover and dealing with any possible fallout as best we could. As to Warren, since this was his business I'd imagine he would have weighed everything even more carefully than I would have. And knowing Warren as well as I do, I can say that he is a very principled person, and I would have been shocked if he also didn't vote for pulling the cover.

As to the movie, I've seen it. It was terrible. It was after this that I swore off all future movies by Shymalan. I've also subsequently seen the original cartoon series. It is awesome. I haven't seen *The Legend of Korra*, another cartoon series set in the same universe, but I hear it too is awesome. I'll check it out at some point.

There is one other detail about this cover worth noting. We always listed our website, but you'll notice that with this issue, we started listing it as follows: "Additional Content at: www.rofmag.com." The reason we did this is simple. For some issues now, Warren had occasionally been moving various columns to the website because there wasn't enough room in the magazine (yes, this comes down to financial considerations). But with this issue, Warren and I made the decision to move the Games column to the website fulltime. This was a tough decision to make, one we'd been weighing and discussing for a long time. But as Warren put it, the true value of the Games column was the ad revenue it helped generate. Unfortunately, the ad revenue from the Games column dried up soon after Warren took over the magazine. We had the same advertising director from Sovereign Media, and the columns were as a strong as always, so my honest assessment here is that the revenue dried up due to changing marketplace. The gaming companies were simply allocating their advertising dollars elsewhere. We could go into the wheres and whys, but that really isn't germaine to this retrospective beyond saying that this ties into how the print markets were already undergoing radical changes at this time, something that has yet to stop as I write this. Quite understandably, these changes also impacted print advertising. So with this in mind, the Games column was no longer pulling its weight in the magazine. But rather than cancel it entirely, we shifted it to our website. And as long as the column was going to be there fulltime for the foreseeable future, I asked that we include the "Additional Conent" note on the cover.

All right, let's finally open up the magazine, shall we? There is one change to note in the masthead. As already noted, E. Jay O'Connell took over layout and design. So to cover this and his contributions as our website designer, his new listing in the masthead is Design & Production.

A rundown of this issue's nonfiction is as follows:

In the Movie/TV column, Resa Nelson covers the already thoroughly discussed *The Last Airbender*. In the Artists Gallery, Karen Haber covers the work of Dan Dos Santos. In Folkroots, SatyrPhil Brucato writes about the temptress in mythology. This issue also marks the last one for Ari Berk and Kristen McDermott as the Folkroots editors. Their stewardship lasted from December 2008-August 2010, a run of eleven issues. In the Books column, Paul Witcover reviews *Dragonfly Falling* by Adrian Tchaikovsky, *The Left Hand of God* by Paul Hoffman, and Matt Staggs reviews *The Gaslight Dogs* by Karin Lowachee, *Choices Meant for Kings* by Sandy Lender, and *Divine Misfortune* by Lee A. Martinez, though this last review was moved to the website. And in Paranormal Romance and Urban Fantasy Books, Elizabeth Bear reviews *A Local Habitation* by Seanan McGuire, *Mind Games* by Carolyn Crane, *How to Make Friends with Demons* by Graham Joyce, and *Changes* by Jim Butcher.

The YA Books column by Michael M. Jones was moved to the website this issue, though my records do not indicate which books he reviewed. Andy Wheeler's graphic novel column was also moved to the website this issue, and my records once again fail to indicate which books he reviewed. As already mentioned earlier, the Games column made an official move to the website with this issue. Matt Staggs reviews *Dungeons & Dragons: Martial Power II*, the RPG *Amethyst: Foundation*, and the RPG *Death Dealer: Shadows of Mirahan*, and Tony Sims reviews *Dante's Inferno* for the Xbox360, the expansion pack for *Borderlands* for Xbox360, and *Mount & Blade: Warband* for PC.

On to the fiction ...

The lead story this issue is "Super. Family." By Ian Donald Keeling, which marks his second appearance in the magazine. This one is a superhero piece in which Magnet Man tries to balance being a superhero with a dysfunctional family life. And things only become more complicated when his past comes back to haunt him at the same time as his rebellious teenage daughter struggles with the recent discovery that she has superpowers of her own. Art to this one was provided by Eric Fortune, which marks his sixth illustration in the magazine. This also marks the final piece of art we had in inventory from the purchase of the magazine from Sovereign Media. Interestingly, this piece also appeared in *Spectrum 16: The Best in Contemporary Fantastic Art*. Normally when a piece from *Realms of Fantasy* appears in *Spectrum*, it appears in the Editorial section. In this case, the piece appeared in the Unpublished section. Having never spoken to anyone in the know about this piece, I can only surmise that Eric submitted this piece to *Spectrum* following the magazine's cancellation by Sovereign Media but before Warren Lapine purchased it, and that he marked it down as being submitted for the Unpublished section.

I should pause here and also note that this issue marks an excellent example of how after seven issues under our new publisher, the magazine was still very much in transition. In this one issue, we published the last of our art solicited by the previous art director, we moved the Games column to the website, we had a new person working on design and layout, and this marked the last issue for our Folkroots editors. This all comes on the heels of launching a new column in the previous issue, and a new website not too long before that. My point here is that at this juncture I think the magazine was still rediscovering itself. It was still absolutely recognizable as *Realms of Fantasy*, but at the same time we hadn't fallen into a true rhythm yet. This isn't a complaint, but an observation. It wasn't until the publication of this issue that I felt as though we had fully transitioned away from Sovereign Media, but as you can see we were still tinkering with the magazine, trying out new things to make it work. And it's good that we tried all these things. Magazines need to evolve. If they remain exactly the same for too long, they run the risk of growing stagnant. But at the same time, I know that it was very much in my mind that I was looking forward to the magazine falling into a rhythm. Not too lighten my workload or make my life easier, but simply because I wanted a complete picture of what the magazine had evolved into, and also because while change is good, you never want *too much* change too soon. Right until the very end, I don't think we ever changed things up so much that it hurt the magazine—most of our changes were quite good in my biased opinion. But I know that with this issue, I let myself take half a breath, because barring any curveballs we had reached a point where I knew exactly when the magazine could start falling into its rhythm. It would have been with the February 2011 issue, but there were in fact some curveballs thrown our way before then, some big ones. But we'll get into that later. For now let's keep the focus on this issue by continuing with the fiction.

Next up we have "Father Peña's Last Dance" by Hannah Strom-Martin, another one of my slush survivors (and an Odyssey almumni—I always enjoyed discovering stories by writers from my old workshop). The story marks Hannah's first pro sale, and it deals with a rare vampire piece for the magazine, one dealing with a young woman and an aging priest in modern Buenos Aires, Argentina, attempting to recover their lost loves, both of whom were kidnapped by vampires. In order to find them, they rely on mastering the tango. Yes, you read that correctly. The vampires in this world are very much attracted to passion, and when the tango is mastered and you truly give yourself to it, our main characters have discovered that it generates enough passion to attract the vampires, leaving them hopeful this can lead them back to their lost loves. But the young woman Cole has secret motives of her own for wishing this reunion to happen, and in helping her, Father Peña encounters another obstacle he must contend with, something he never expected to find again: love for a living woman. Art to this was provided by Tony Shasteen, which marks his eighth illustration in the magazine. I remember when I told Hannah that Tony would be illustrating the story she was rather elated, as she had been a fan of his works in the magazine for some time. It was rather gratifying helping her indulge her inner fan girl, even if I did so inadvertently.

Then we have "Seagull Girl's Butterfly Tongue" by Sara Genge. In this piece, zombies have overrun the planet, only the zombies are an intelligent organism comprising and somewhat homogenizing Earth's various lifeforms—like semi-zombie-borg, I guess. When they come across a holdout in America who is inexplicably alive all this time later, they attempt to absorb him into their collective, not through eating or biting, but by swaying him through intelligent conversation. Art to this one was provided by Jill Bauman.

This is one of those rare issues with only four stories, so finally we come to "[Dragon]" by T.D. Edge. This one is a young adult piece about a girl on in a fantasy kingdom on the verge of adolescence who, to become a princess—the first in a hundred years—must meet the dragon. She doesn't want to be a princess and doesn't believe in the dragon, but everything changes soon enough. Along the way, she learns that the dragon is far from what one would imagine, and that while she wishes to be a princess after all, the price is far steeper than she could have guessed. Art to this one was provided by Scott Altmann.

So that wraps up this issue. And my favorite story? "Super. Family" by Ian Donald Keeling. And my favorite artwork? Scott Altmann's illustration to "[Dragon]."

Originally posted on douglascohen.livejournal.com on March 15th, 2014

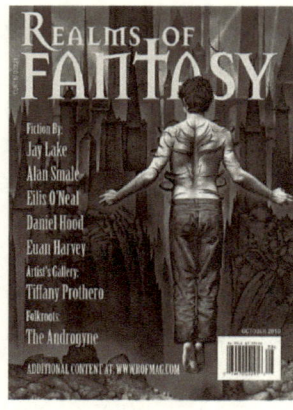

Part ninety-six in my comprehensive retrospective as I read the fiction in *Realms of Fantasy* and offer my thoughts. This time around I'll take a whack at the October 2010 issue.

It was while this issue was out that I learned from Warren Lapine that the December 2010 issue would be the final issue under Tir Na Nog Press. Warren had plans to put the magazine up for sale, but being as it had suffered one death already back in 2009, neither Shawna nor myself were expecting much to result from this. I'll get into this more with the December 2010 issue, but for now we'll keep the focus on October.

The cover to this one is a reprint of an illustration by John Jude Palencar. Two things I'll always remember when I think of this cover: first is that when I emailed John about acquiring reprint rights of this illustration, he emailed me his phone number so we could talk, and he proved quite generous with his time, far more than you would expect from someone so successful (not to say there aren't other folks in the industry like this, just that you never expect it). And second, while I'll refrain from mentioning names, I'll always remember how a certain literary critic referred to this as a "BDSM cover" when reviewing this issue. I wonder what s/he would say if s/he were to learn this illustration originally appeared on the cover of a YA novel? But never mind that: apparently magical tattoos equal kinky sex. Who knew?

In the masthead, the only change to report is that the Folkroots editor is no longer listed. Ari Berk and Kristen McDermott finished their run with the last issue. I had already hired Theodora Goss to take over the column, but if memory serves correctly, while she was interested, during that time was working on a thesis paper for her PhD. So our solution was that I would oversee the column on an interim basis, and Theodora would take over with the February 2011 issue.

A number of candidates were considered to take over Folkroots—all of them quite good—but the truth is that when I learned that Ari and Kristen were stepping down, Theodora's name immediately came to mind as their replacement. The reasons for this are myriad, and Theodora had enough ties to the magazine on different levels that it's worth sharing my thinking here. First, I had known Theodora since we both attended the Odyssey Fantasy and Science Fiction Writing Workshop, all the way back in 2000. Both of us were newbies to the professional scene at this point, without a writing or editorial credit to our respective names. This workshop runs six weeks, so during this time I got a pretty good feel for a number of her interests, which led me to believe in 2010 she would be an excellent fit for Folkroots.

Of course, this is just the beginning of Dora's connections to the magazine. A year later in 2001, she attended the Clarion Writing Workshop. Shawna McCarthy, the magazine's longtime and founding editor, was one of the teachers that year, and she actually decided to purchase one of Dora's workshop stories for the magazine, which resulted in Dora's first sale. (That story was "The Rose in Twelve Petals" in the April 2002 issue.) She ended up selling three more stories to us, so in addition to being to her being a known quantity to both Shawna and myself, this also made her a known quantity to the magazine's readers. She also wrote a Folkroots article as a guest columnist in an earlier issue, providing further proof she would be a good fit for the position.

And if all this wasn't enough, she also had a connection to our publisher at the time, Warren Lapine. When Dora applied for the Odyssey Workshop back in 2000, Warren wrote a recommendation for her, as she had submitted to the magazines at his old DNA Publications several times. While Warren hadn't bought anything from her, he was familiar enough with her writing that he was comfortable writing said recommendation. Put all this together and despite the other excellent candidates Dora and the Folkroots column was clearly a match made in heaven.

Moving on, a rundown of this issue's nonfiction is as follows:

In the Movie/TV section, Resa Nelson provides a rundown of the fall movies. In the Artists Gallery, Karen Haber covers the work of Tiffany Prothero. In Folkroots, SatyrPhil Brucato writes about the androgyne lover in fantastical fiction. In the Books column, Paul Witcover reviews *The Bird of the River* by Kage Baker, *The Loving Dead* by Amelia Beamer, *Blood of the Mantis* by Adrian Tchaikovsky, *The Office of Shadow* by Matthew Sturges, and Matt Staggs reviews *Pariah* by Bob Fingerman, *Metrophilias* by Brendan Connell, and *Our Lady of the Absolute* by Resa Nelson. In Paranormal Romance/Urban Fantasy Books, Elizabeth Bear reviews *Thief Eyes* by Janni Lee Simner, *Black Blade Blues* by J.A. Pitts, *White Cat* by Holly Black, and

Discord's Apple by Carrie Vaughn. In YA Books, Michael Jones reviews *The Boneshaker* by Kate Milford, *Passing Strange* by Daniel Waters, *Perchance to Dream* by Lisa Mantchev, *The Mermaid's Mirror* by L.K. Madigan, and *For the Win* by Cory Doctorow.

Andrew Wheeler's Graphic Novel column was moved to the website for this issue, and he reviews *Graphic Classics, Volume 1: Edgar Allen Poe*, and *Melvin Monster*. And in the Games column, Matt Staggs reviews *Steve Jackson's Sorcery! The Shumanti Hills* for the iPhone, *Contagion Infected Human Zombie Cards*, the *Dungeons & Dragons Player's Strategy Guide*, and Tony Sims reviews *Prince of Persia of Persia: The Forgotten Sands* for the Xbox 360, *Legio* for the PC, and *Darkness Within 2: The Dark Lineage* for the PC.

This issue also marked the last one for columnists Matt Staggs and Tony Sims. Matt was with the magazine since the April 2009 issue, a run of eight issues as a book columnist, and a run of seven issues as a gaming columnist. Tony was with the magazine since the April 2010 issue, a run of four issues.

On to the fiction ...

The lead story this issue is "Cutter in the Underverse" by Daniel Hood, which marks his second appearance in the magazine. This one is an urban fantasy about the Underverse of NYC, a place of memories, ghosts, and monsters. Detective Cutter is one of the few from the real world that is able to visit the Underverse without complications, but in this story he ends up going there somewhat against his will when someone from the Underverse buys up all his gambling markers in the real world. The buyer turns out to be the ghost of Arnold Rothstein, a criminal figure out of history best known as the man who fixed the 1919 World Series. He wants Cutter to do him a favor, but as you might imagine when dealing with such a shady character, all is not as straightforward as it seems. Art to this one was provided by John Kaiine, which marks his third illustration in the magazine.

Next up we have "Middle" by Eilis O'Neal. This one feels like magic realism to me, and it deals with the classically neglected middle family, only her family is a bit extraordinary, as her older perfect sister has fallen asleep and won't wake up while her dreams remain visible in a kind of cloud above her while she sleeps. Meanwhile, her younger brilliant brother has a pretend llama for a pet that might not be so pretend. Nothing fantastical seems to be going on with the middle child, which of course would only add to the classic neglect ...and also lead to a cry for attention in rather spectacular fashion. Art to this one was provided by Kurt Huggins and Zelda Devon, which marks their third illustration in the magazine.

Then we have "The Fall of the Moon" by Jay Lake, which marks his tenth appearance in the magazine. This one is quirky high fantasy tale about a man who builds a boat with the bones of his dead grandfather so he might sail the Sea of Murmurs and live forever. Along the way, he must overcome obstacles such as monsters, neighbors, and family. Art to this one was provided by Allen Douglas, which marks his tenth illustration in the magazine.

Next up is "Saint's-Paw" by Alan Smale, which marks his fifth appearance in the magazine. This one takes place in medieval Europe and portrays an adolescent girl on the run after curiosity led to her dissecting her dead father, which in turn led to accusations of witchcraft. When she takes shelter in a church housing the hand of St. Stephan while fleeing some vengeful soldiers, we learn that the hand is not what—or who—it seems to be. Art to this one was provided by Alan M. Clark, which marks his third illustration in the magazine.

Finally we have "Halloween: Comprising a Cautionary Acrostic of Nine Bedtime Stories for Reading to the Tiresome or Disobedient Child" by Euan Harvey, which marks his sixth appearance in the magazine. Euan is also hereby given the unofficial award for longest fiction title to ever appear in the magazine. Right before the story begins, Euan included the following note: "To Jack Slay, Jr., with respect. (And apologies.) A quick search online revealed that Jack Slay, Jr. had a story appear in the magazine *Cemetery Dance* called "Halloween: An Acrostic of Little Horrors." So presumably Euan took his inspiration from this story, and perhaps followed a somewhat similar narrative structure. As to that structure, it features nine loosely connected flash fiction pieces about kids in the same neighborhood on or around the day of Halloween, with each kid's name beginning with a different letter from the word Halloween. (For example, the first flash piece begins with "H is for Hugh ...") Art to this one was provided by Jill Bauman, which marks her second illustration in the magazine.

So that wraps up this issue. And my favorite story? Euan's Halloween Acrostic tale. And my favorite artwork? Jill Bauman's illustration to the same story.

Originally posted on douglascohen.livejournal.com on April 22nd, 2014

Part ninety-seven in my comprehensive retrospective as I read the fiction in *Realms of Fantasy* and offer my thoughts. This time around I'm diving into the December 2010 issue.

This issue represents another turning point in the magazine's history, as for a short time it was the last issue in the magazine's run (which would mark the second time this happened). During the previous issue, I heard from Warren Lapine that the December issue would be the last one. Originally it was only released for free on the website in PDF form. Shawna and I both wrote some farewell editorials on the website, which was nice since no one had a chance to issue any kind of official goodbye when Sovereign Media pulled the plug. Both of us were disappointed of course about RoF coming to an end once again, but neither of us was terribly surprised by this development. While everyone from Warren on down gave it their best on the magazine, print had been struggling for years, and genre magazines were no exception. *Realms of Fantasy* in particular was hard to keep profitable, as it was more expensive to produce than the digests, demanding better quality paper, interior color illustrations, etc. Warren had also kept me fairly well informed concerning the magazine's financial situation, so when he shut things down we were ready for it. More than that, while I would certainly miss the magazine, I was at peace with it coming to an end. As best as I can tell, so was Shawna.

So when the magazine was once again sold, it came as a big surprise. Granted, Warren had put the magazine up for sale and done so publically, but no one was expecting anything to come of it. The magazine had been canceled twice in a market that was becoming ever more electronic.

It seemed as if RoF had run its course ...except Kim Richards Gilchrist and William Gilchrist of Damnation Books and Eternal Press had other ideas. They struck a deal with Warren to purchase the magazine and all that went with it, including the website, inventories, subscription list, etc. However, in order for the deal to go through, they wanted the December issue to go to press so that it could reach the subscriber base. I imagine there was some back and forth that I wasn't privy to, but ultimately Warren agreed to this condition, so the December 2010 issue ended up going to press with Warren Lapine as the publisher under the Tir Na Nog Press banner. In total, Warren put out nine issues of the magazine as publisher, and Kim and William were slated to take over with the February 2011 issue. As best as I can recall, Warren ended up selling the magazine about two or three weeks after the magazine's cancellation.

And the science fiction and fantasy community being what it is, a high level of scrutiny naturally followed this announcement. For starters, while Warren Lapine was something of a known quantity from his days of publishing genre magazines with DNA Publications, it was not the case with the new owners. While Kim and William had their own small press dealing with horror and dark fantasy, not too many of the people reading and writing for *Realms of Fantasy* were terribly familiar with them, and at the time we were one of the better known magazines.

People were also uncertain what to make of this development because there was no mention about what would happen concerning the magazine's staff, including myself, Shawna, our columnists, and so on. This was very important to the community, particularly when it came to me and Shawna. Now I'm not going to be so naïve as to believe that everyone loved me as the editor—I made a few mistakes along the way. But with an unknown publishing team taking over the magazine, one thing Shawna and I represented was stability. Considering that the magazine would now be on its third publisher in less than two years, this was rather important. Shawna was the only person remaining who had been with the magazine since the beginning. And I had been with the magazine for five and a half years, working closely with Shawna in the fiction department while also overseeing a number of other departments as time went on. Say what you want about me (and people have said quite a few things over the years), but in six and a half years with *Realms of Fantasy* (total) no one ever called me lazy. I did quite a bit with the magazine, and if the combined editorial team was no longer with the magazine, it would have left a big void to fill since the new publishers planned on keeping the publishing schedule intact. You may recall that when Warren took over the magazine, even after he brought back the editorial team, we didn't publish a June issue as there was just too much to square away as we changed publishers. So understandably people were left wondering if the magazine would still feel like *Realms of Fantasy* under this tight schedule if the same editorial team wasn't there to smooth over the transition.

The third concern among the community was that there were some stories circulating online that cast the new publishers in a less than positive light. As we're only human, naturally people seized upon this and it became a big talking point, raising concerns about these new publishers.

So what do you ask was the editorial team doing while all this controversy raged? Quite simply, we were being very smart about this whole situation. Shawna and I had both closed the door on the magazine. But now it was back, and it turned out the new publishers wanted us to return to our old positions. This was by no means a given—I've seen people get bent all out of shape in our community when new publishers take over magazines and replace the editorial team, but the truth is that publishers are perfectly within their rights to replace the editor if they believe a change is warranted. But being as Kim and William wanted us back, Shawna and I needed to decide if we *wanted* to return. Having been through one relaunch for the magazine already, we knew exactly how much work it would take to get the magazine up and running once again. We also didn't want to return to the magazine only to see it fold after another issue or two. And lastly, while we weren't rushing to judgement, word had gotten back to us about some of the concerns raised about the new publishers. So before we came back to the magazine, we also wanted to make sure these were people we would be comfortable doing business with.

But at the time all of this was behind the scenes. Shawna happened to be out of town when the sale took place, attending a convention I believe. So I was keeping her in the loop as things developed, via email and phone. As to me, I wasn't about to comment on anything involving *Realms of Fantasy* until my status with the magazine was sorted out. I didn't think it would be appropriate to do otherwise. So when I received emails from various people asking me what the deal was, I basically told them all the same thing: "I can't really comment at this time."

But eventually I had a chance to speak to the new publishers and ask them some questions, at which point I spoke to Shawna and spoke to the publishers again ...and so on. And in the end, Shawna and I decided we were comfortable working with these folks and would come back to the magazine. At that point I set about bringing back as many of my columnists as possible, and made an online announcement. I guess I learned a thing or two from earlier online mishaps, because in this instance my announcement did not fan the flames but helped settle them down. Now let s turn our attention to the December 2010 issue.

The cover to this is another movie montage by graphic designer E. Jay O'Connell, as he took an image from *Harry Potter and the Deathly Hallows Part I* and added several images in the background from the movie that created a movie reel effect. This marks the fourth time Harry Potter has graced the cover. Appropriately/ironically enough, the following words appear on the cover: "The Beginning of the End." Of course, this is in reference to the end of the Harry Potter movie franchise, and how the final book was being split into two movies. But looking back on it, this issue was sort of the beginning of the end for *Realms of Fantasy*—it's just that no one knew that for certain at that time. On the bright side, if this marked the beginning of the end for the magazine then I'm proud to say we went out in style during that last year.

As long I mentioned E. Jay O'Connell, I should mention that this was his last issue with the magazine. Jay designed the website (which is still up and running at the time I write this), and also handled design and layout for the magazine for three issues, but the new publishers ended up splitting his duties between them, Kim handling the design and layout and William taking over the webmaster duties. If we include the time from when the new website launched, Jay was with the magazine for a total of six issues. If we include all the time spent working behind the scenes to construct the website, it was probably closer to eight issues.

There are a couple of changes to report in the masthead here. Jeff Kight, the longtime
advertising director for the magazine, was offered a chance to return to the magazine but ended
up declining for personal reasons. So while he was responsible for generating the advertising
this issue, Kim Richards Gilchrist was listed as the advertising director. This was done with the
idea that if anyone reading the magazine wanted to purchase advertising, they would be able to
get in touch with Kim, as she would be handling the advertising going forward. The customer
service address was also changed this issue so that anyone with a problem could get in touch

with the new publishers. Jeff Kight was with the magazine since the October 2005 issue. If we

include this issue (and we should), he was with the magazine for thirty-one issues.

Moving on to the nonfiction, more of it than usual was moved to the website this issue. Obviously there were financial considerations in doing this, but I wasn't privy to these conversations, so I can't enlighten you much beyond passing along the surface details.

I'll start off my providing a rundown of the nonfiction in the actual issue:

In the Movie/TV column, Resa Nelson covers the aforementioned *Harry Potter and the Deathly Hallows Part I*. In the Artists Gallery, Karen Haber covers the work of Terese Nielsen. In the Books column, Paul Witcover reviews *The Third Bear* by Jeff VanderMeer, *Twelve* by Jasper Kent, *Salute the Dark* by Adrian Tchaikovsky, and with Matt Staggs having moved on with the previous issue, paranormal romance/urban fantasy reviewer takes on dual duties as she joins this column and reviews *Burton and Swineburne in: The Strange Affair of Spring Heeled Jack* by Mark Hodder, and *Who Fears Death* by Nnedi Okorafor. And in Paranormal Romance/Urban Fantasy Books, Elizabeth Bear reviews *Sparks* by Laura Bickle, *Dark Oracle* by Alayna Williams, and *A Wild Light* by Marjorie M. Liu.

And a rundown of the nonfiction on the website for this issue is as follows:

Part of the Books column got shifted to the website so over here Paul Witcover reviews *The Man with Knives* by Ellen Kushner. Part of Paranormal Romance/Urban Fantasy Books also got shifted to the website, so over here Elizabeth Bear reviews *Waking the Witch* by Kelley Armstrong. In the Games column, new columnist Matt London reviews the *Harry Potter Legos* game for multiple formats. In YA Books, Michael Jones reviews nine titles, but I'm afraid my files don't indicate which ones and the information is no longer available to me on the website. In the Graphic Novel column, Andrew Wheeler reviews *Flight, Volume Seven* by Kazu Kibuishi and *The Extraordinary Adventures of Adele Blanc-Sec, Volume One: Pterror Over Paris/The Eiffel Tower Demon* by Jacques Tardi. And in Folkroots, Stephen D. Winick writes about the mythology of unicorns.

I'll admit that when I learned Folkroots was being shifted to the website for this issue, it left me somewhat concerned. At its heart, the features that always made *Realms of Fantasy* the magazine it was were the fiction and accompanying artwork, the Artists Gallery, and Folkroots. This isn't meant to disrespect the other columns or columnists in any shape or form. I simply believe the features I mentioned had the most to do with *Realms of Fantasy* assuming its own unique personality. Anyway, because of my concern, I specifically requested that on the table of contents page we insert a note informing our readers that Folkroots would return to the print publication with the next issue. This issue also marked my last issue as the interim editor of Folkroots, a whopping two issues total.

One other feature we introduced with this issue was listing the materials on the table of contents page that could be found on our website. Before we learned that this was to be the last issue under Warren, I suggested this change to Jay since he was our not only handling layout and design, but was also the webmaster. My thinking was that by listing the online materials in our print publication, it could drive more traffic to the website. Jay liked this idea and incorporated it. While Jay and Warren moved on from the magazine after this issue, it still proved a worthwhile suggestion as we ened up incorporating it under the new regime (although in retrospect I wish this idea had occurred to me sooner).

On to the fiction ...

This issue we only have four stories, the third and last time in the magazine's history we ever published fewer than five stories in a single issue. The lead story is "Queen of the Kanguellas" by Scott Dalrymple. This piece takes place in Angola, right on the cusp of the twentieth century. In it, a young man sets out to find his father. All the while, he behaves like his dead sister, as grief has driven him to blame himself for her death when they were children. The revelation that our protagonist is in fact a he doesn't come until the end of the story. Along the way, our protagonist and his companions must contend with witch magic and the dangers of the native terrain. Art to this one was provided by Petar Meseldžija.

Next up we have "Maiden, Mother, Crone" by Ann Leckie and Rachel Swirsky. For Ann, it marks her second appearance in the magazine. In this secondary fantasy piece, we're introduced to a world where women born with birthmarks wield magic and are branded as witches. When such a woman who has hidden this secret all her life becomes worried her secret will be discovered, she flees into a brewing winter storm. Oh, did I mention that she's pregnant? And that she goes into labor? That should complicate matters. Art to this one was provided by Kristina Carroll. Before Kristina ever submitted her portfolio to me, I remember I once attended an art show featuring a lot of speculative illustrations by art students who had recently graduated. My thinking was that I might come across a few names that I could work with in the future. So I scribbled down the names of some of the artists whose works caught my eye ...and sure enough, when Kristina sent me a sample of her work and I checked out her website, I came across an illustration of hers from the art show. The very fact that I remembered her illustration so clearly, and remembered where I had seen it without consulting my records, decided me on the spot to assign her to this piece since I thought she would prove a good match.

Then we have "The Banjo Singer" by Dennis Danvers, which marks his third appearance in the magazine. In this piece, a young woman in twentieth century America before the rise of television wants nothing so much as to sing. However, her overbearing and physically imposing father is deadset against the idea, believing singing an unseemly practice fit only for nightclub singers. Instead, he has his daughter take up the banjo, believing this far more proper. But Marie is determined to sing and when the hummingbirds inlaid into her banjo magically come to life they lend her the confidence to start singing. Her voice proves nothing short of magical, making men practically fall in love as her voice pours through the radio. This in turn leads to a greater confidence in herself, and those men who meet her in person are instantly smitten. But all is not sugar and gumdrops as more than one man seeks to keep her from singing, most notably of all her father. Art to this one was provided by Andy B. Clarkson, which marks his fourth illustration in the magazine.

Finally we have "Tools of the Devil" by Jerry Oltion. In this piece, a teenage girl has overbearing religious parents who refuse to let her be photographed, believing that each picture steal a piece of her soul. Our protagonist Mary basically considers her parents nothing short of religious freaks and wants to be free of them, and she wants a life of fame and fortune. This leads her to looking for the devil in the hopes of making a deal. When the devil finally takes notice and visits her, it turns out Mary has done her homework and then some, as she words her wish incredibly carefully to prevent Lucifer from screwing her over. In fact, she words it so carefully that she believes she has in fact outwitted him ...but while the devil honors their deal, Mary ends up learns that when you try to outsmart the devil, you might end up outsmarting yourself in the bargain. Art to this one was provided by David Palumbo, which marks his second illustration in the magazine. This illustration was also selected for inclusion in the Editorial section of *Spectrum 18: The Best in Contemporary Fantastic Art.*

So that wraps up this issue, along with 2010 and *Realms of Fantasy*'s run under Warren Lapine and Tir Na Nog Press. And my favorite story? "Tools of the Devil" by Jerry Oltion. And my favorite artwork? David Palumbo's accompanying illustration to this piece.

Originally posted on douglascohen.livejournal.com on May 9th, 2014

Part ninety-eight in my comprehensive retrospective as I read the fiction in *Realms of Fantasy* and offer my thoughts. This issue marks the first one under new publisher Damnation Books, and while it represented a new chapter in *Realms of Fantasy*'s history, it proved to be a brief run, as *Realms of Fantasy* would last just another five issues total under its new publishers. However, during these five final issues we accomplished quite a bit with the magazine, and looking back I couldn't be happier that we extended our run just a tad longer.

You can read the previous entry concerning the particulars about how the sale of the magazine came about following its second cancellation. As I noted already, the new publishers bought the magazine on the condition that the previous publisher, Warren Lapine, went to press with the previous issue so that it would reach the existing subscriber base. This meant that unlike the transition from Sovereign Media to Tir Na Nog Press, there would be no skipped issues. In turn, this meant that the entire staff would be under a tighter schedule to put out the February 2011 issue while transitioning publishers. However, having been through such a transition once already less than two years back, going through it again proved far easier for everyone involved, which allowed the new publishers to hit the ground running and put out their first issue in a timely fashion.

The cover to this issue is by Lori Koefoed, which doubles as an interior illustration to "Magpie" by Mark Rigney, one of the stories inside. Interestingly enough, I remember exactly how I got the idea for Lori to do this illustration. Once I finished reading "Magpie," I asked myself, "Who did the artwork to 'Fable from a Cage?' That's who I want to illustrate this." "Fable from a Cage" was a story that appeared in the magazine some years back by Tim Pratt. I remembered the story, and I vividly remembered the artwork. However, I couldn't remember the artist or the issue it appeared in. However, I keep extremely detailed logs concerning the magazine's art and fiction, so hunting down the right issue took me a matter of minutes. Once I discovered the artist was Lori and I took another look at the illustration, I wasted no time contacting her. I had a strong feeling she would take her approach in "Fable from a Cage" and apply that same technique to "Magpie." She fulfilled my expectations 100% and it led to her piece gracing the cover of the first issue under our new publishers.

In the masthead, there are a few changes to report this issue. William Gilchrist and Kim Richards Gilchrist replace Warren Lapine as the Publisher, and while Kim took over as Graphic Designer, this listing was dropped from the masthead since she was also listed as the Advertising Director. Under Copy Editors, Trent Zelazny is no longer with us. He was offered the chance to return but opted to move on. His run with the magazine lasted seven issues. Theodora Goss also takes over this issue as the Folkroots Editor, replacing me as the interim editor of this section after two issues. Otherwise, besides Webmaster and Graphic Designer E. Jay O'Connell and Advertising Director Jeff Kight who I discussed in the previous issue, I'm pleased to say that everyone else on the staff returned to their old positions. The relatively small turnover also made putting the February 2011 issue out on time much easier, as many on the staff had been through one transition already, and they were all already working on columns for this issue at the time of the magazine's cancellation.

One design change worth noting is that our new publishers did away with the Advertising Index.

All right, let's move on to the actual content. A rundown of this issue's nonfiction is as follows:

In the Movie/TV section, Resa Nelson discusses the best foreign horror movies in recent years. In the Artists Gallery, Karen Haber covers the artwork of Dominic Harman. In Folkroots, Theodora Goss's inaugural column deals with the Femme Fatale at the Fin-de-Siècle. As I mentioned already, one of the reasons I was disappointed when the magazine was canceled was that I had recruited Theodora months earlier to take over the Folkroots column with this issue. Had our new publishers not stepped in, Theodora never would have had the chance to oversee Folkroots. Instead, she was afforded that opportunity, and she not only met my lofty expectations, but she exceeded them.

Continuing with the rundown, in the Books column, Paul Witcover reviews *The Habitation of the Blessed* by Catherynne M. Valente, and *Entangled* by Graham Hancock, while Elizabeth Bear reviews *The Heir of Night* by Helen Lowe and *Vampires Not Invited* by Cheyenne McCray. In Paranormal Romance and Urban Fantasy Books, Elizabeth Bear reviews *Rogue Oracle* by Alayna Williams, *Hunger* by Jackie Morse Kessler,

Midsummer Night by Freda Warrington, and *Sleeping Helena* by Erzebet Yellowboy. In YA Books, Michael Jones reviews *Enchanted Ivy* Sarah Beth Durst, *Hold Me Closer, Necromancer* by Lish McBride, *Solitary: Escape from Furnace 2* by Alexander Gordon Smith, *Black Hole Sun* by David Macinnis Gill, *Low Red Moon* by Ivy Devlin, *Behemoth: Leviathan, Book Two* by Scott Westefeld, *Torment: A Fallen Novel (2)* by Lauren Kate, *The Candidates: Delcroix Academy, Book 1* by Inara Scott, and *Personal Demons* by Lisa Desrochers. In the Graphic Novel column, Andrew Wheeler reviews *Toys in the Basement* by Stéphane Blanquet, *The Littlest Pirate King* by David B. and Pierre Mac Orlan, and *RIP, M.D.* by Mitch Schauer, Mike Vosburg, Michael Lessa, and Justin Yamaguchi.

Meanwhile the Games column remained on the website, where Matt London reviewed *Lord of the Rings: Aragorn's Quest* and *Dead Rising 2*, both for the Playstation 3.

Let's move on the fiction ...

Fittingly, the first story published by our new publishers is "The Swan Troika" by Richard Parks, the magazine's most profilic author. This story marks his twenty-fifth appearance in the magazine, making him the first author to reacht this milestone. It would also mark his final story to appear in RoF. He would go on to sell another one to us, but the magazine would fold before it could be published. As to the story itself, this one is a historical fantasy that takes place in Russia some years prior to the Bolshevik Revolution. While on the way to pay his respects at his aunt's birthday, a young man encounters a rusalka who is trapped outside a river because the ice has frozen over. In folklore, rusalka are young women or girls who died in or near a body of water. Afterward, they tend to haunt that body of water as type of succubus/water demon/etc. In this story, the rusalka has matured into a beautiful young woman, and the protagonist Pyotr is so smitten that despite the danger to him, he turns on the charm and actually manages to convince the rusalka to come with him to his aunt's party. But once there, it turns out the rusalka has a dark connection to his elderly aunt, and her presence threatens to unearth old family secrets. Art to this one was provided by Ruth Sanderson, and it was subsequently selected for inclusion in the Editorial section of *Spectrum 18: The Best in Contemporary Fantastic Art.*

Next up we have "Thirteen Incantations" by my old slush survivor, Desirina Boskovich, which marks her second appearance in the magazine.

This one is a young adult piece about a girl named Elizabeth in her senior year of high school that is coming to grips with her sexual preferences. This process is accelerated when she becomes infatuated with her new classmate, Ana Celina. They begin spending time together, but fearful that her feelings will not be reciprocated, Elizabeth keeps these matters of the heart secret from Ana Celina. The two girls spend the summer together, trying different blends of perfumes created by Ana Celina's mother. Ana Celina's mother is a bit of a witch though, so trying each perfume is literally a magical experience. Come the end of the summer, Ana Celina leaves for college without saying goodbye, leaving Elizabeth heartbroken ...but she leaves behind one final perfume for Elizabeth, one that *she* made instead of her mother ...and this perfume contains the greatest magic of all. This story was reprinted in *Heiresses of Russ 2012: The Year's Best Lesbian Speculative Fiction*, edited by Connie Wilkins and Steve Berman. It also appeared as podcast 337 on the *Podcastle* website. Art to this one in RoF was provided by Kurt Huggins, which marks his fifth illustration in the magazine.

Then we have "Magpie" by Mark Rigney, which is another one of my slush survivors. This one is a dark fairy tale about a young girl who loses her family and home to a flood. Soon afterward she is befriended by Jackdaw, a man with wings, and something of a rogue. Soon she is given wings of her own by Jackdaw, and becomes Jackdaw's partner as he pulls off capers and lives the high life of a thieving prince. But over time Jackdaw grows old while she grows up, and upon his death she soon finds a boy and continues the cycle. The arc of this story was something I've encountered a number of times before, but the language made this one entirely fresh, enough that I was instantly compelled to pass it along. Art to this one was provided by the aforementioned Lori Koefoed, which marks her sixteenth illustration in the magazine.

After this we have "No Tale for Troubadours" by Pauline J. Alama. This one is an historical fantasy that takes place in medieval times. In this piece, we are introduced to a woman who was a legend as a maiden knight when she was younger. Now she is settled down with a husband and several young children. But with all the men including her husband off to war, when a village is in need of protection from some trolls, Lady Ursula of Veronne must don her old armor and pick up the sword once more to protect some innocents. Along the way, she recruits her old sorceress companion who has retired to a nunnery, and the two of them set off for one final adventure. But things are not as they were, as they're both haunted by their actions from the Crusades, and they've become very different people in the interim. Nor is their mission to fight trolls what it seems on the surface, further illustrating to both of them that in matters of war things are rarely black and white. Art to this one was provided by Walter Velez, which marks his third illustration in the magazine.

Finally we have "The Time of His Life" by another old slush survivor, Scott William Carter, which marks his third story in the magazine. In this piece, a man discovers a hidden room in his new house. When he's inside it, time in the outside world slows to a crawl. At first it seems like the perfect room, as it allows him all the time in the world to get everything done, from personal projects, being a good husband, a good father, and so on. But this becomes one of those classic examples of too much of a good thing. The room becomes addictive, and while at first it seems to allow him to do anything, come the end of the story it threatens to rob him of everything he has. Art to this one was provided by Tomislav Tikulin.

So that wraps up this issue. And my favorite story? It's a tie between "Thirteen Incantations" and "Magpie." And my favorite illustration? Ruth Sanderson's illustration to "The Swan Troika."

Originally posted on douglascohen.livejournal.com on June 24th, 2014

Part ninety-nine in my comprehensive retrospective as I read the fiction in *Realms of Fantasy* and offer my thoughts. This time around I'll be discussing the April 2011 issue.

The cover to this one is by Brom, which marks his fourth illustration in the magazine. This was a previously unpublished piece that we included as part of the Artists Gallery (as a two-page spread that you could remove as a mini-poster if you were so inclined—credit the poster idea to our publisher/graphic designer, Kim Richards Gilchrist) that I also ended up selecting for our cover. It ended up winning the Silver Award in the Editorial Section in *Spectrum 18: The Best in Contemporary Fantastic Art*. As you might imagine, this was a huge thrill for me.

The cover also notes this is a "Special Dark Fantasy Issue." This marks the magazine's first themed issue. We had plans for a Halloween issue back with Sovereign Media, but the magazine was canceled before this could take place and it was agreed by everyone that trying to make this issue happen while also transitioning a new publisher would be too much of a hassle, so we tabled this idea indefinitely (although the dark fantasy issue would probably have quite a bit in common with the Halloween issue). Then under Tir Na Nog Press we once again had plans for a themed issue, this time a Women in Fantasy issue. But once again the magazine was canceled before this issue could take place, and we tabled this idea under the new publishers for the exact same reason ...along with the fact that the dark fantasy issue had already been announced.

When news broke that Warren Lapine had sold the magazine to RoF's final publishers, the April dark fantasy issue was part of that announcement. Since our publishers also ran Damnation Books—a small press focusing on dark fantasy and horror—doing an issue such as this made perfect sense for them to help promote their product. At this time, neither Shawna nor I were back with the magazine, and while we didn't have a problem with doing a themed issue (obviously—we had tried to do themed issues twice before), it did mean that when we returned we were on a limited timeline to put this issue together. With the previous two attempts for themed issues, we had started the preliminary planning probably about a year in advance, although if we'd done that for this issue, there never would have been a dark fantasy issue, due to the magazine's final cancellation coming with the October 2011 issue. So it's actually a very good thing the publishers went ahead and did this, because we never would've had a themed issue otherwise, and I'm very proud of the work we did on this one, short timeline and all.

So our vision for this themed issue was pretty straightforward. The fiction would be dark, meaning by extension the accompanying artwork would be dark. For the Artists Gallery, we would feature an artist who excelled in illustrating the dark fantastical, and the other nonfiction columns would also focus on dark subject matter. With the review columns, I decided it was unreasonable to expect the reviewers to only review dark materials—they can only review what happened to be current at the time after all. So I told them to do their reviews as usual, but when possible give preference to reviewing dark fantasy and horror should the opportunity present itself and it was something they believed was worth reviewing.

So with all this in mind, a rundown of this issue's nonfiction is as follows:

In the Movie/TV section, Resa Nelson writes about *The Walking Dead* and "the most disturbing zombie movie you've probably never seen" (*Deadgirl*). In Folkroots, Theodora Goss writes about vampires. In the Artists Gallery, Karen Haber covers the work of the aforementioned Brom. In the Books column, Paul Witcover reviews *Half-Made World* by Felix Gilman, *The Desert of Souls* by Howard Jones, *The Last Dragon* by J.M. McDermott, while Elizabeth Bear reviews *The Golden Age* by Carrie Vaughn and *The Bone Palace* by Amanda Downum. In Paranormal Romance and Urban Fantasy Books, Elizabeth Bear reviews *Among Others* by Jo Walton, *Red Glove* by Holly Black, and *Soul Hunt* by Margaret Ronald; in YA Books, Michael Jones reviews *The Emerald Atlas* by John Stephens, *The Iron Queen* by Julie Kagawa, *The Painted Boy* by Charles de Lint, *Out For Blood* by Alyxandra Harvey, *The Goddess Test* by Aimee Carter, *Fallen Angel* by Heather Terrell, *Night School* by Mari Mancusi, and *Hexbound* by Chloe Neill. In the Graphic Novel column, Andrew Wheeler reviews *Castle Waiting Volume II* by Linda Medley and *Grandville Mon Amour* by Bryan Talbot. In the Games column online, Matt London reviews *Minecraft* and *Lego Universe*, though my notes fail to indicate for which systems and the column itself is no longer online.

We also had a one-shot column this issue, about the Addams Family on Broadway, written by yours truly. I don't remember how I got the idea, but at some point during the process it occurred to me that we'd never really covered the fantastical on Broadway, and a column about the Addams Family on Broadway would be a perfect fit. Since we were on a short timeline to put this issue together and I had dreamed up the idea, I decided I wanted to write this article myself. However, since I was also overseeing the nonfiction, I didn't like the idea of arbitrarily assigning myself to write the piece, especially since I had never done this before for the magazine. My solution was to pitch this to my publisher as if I were just another writer pitching the nonfiction editor. So Kim went for it, at which point I sent an email to the publicist for the Addams Family on Broadway to see if I could score some free tickets. My efforts won me two free tickets and my first nonfiction article in the magazine. I remember working really hard on the research for that article, as I was determined that the piece should measure up with the other nonfiction features (read: I had and have great respect for the work done by our columnists). I even asked Shawna McCarthy to take a look at it and felt a lot better after she gave me the green light concerning the content (and even added some helpful ideas to incoporate).

This brings us to the fiction. I should note that when the dark fantasy issue was announced, as soon as we reopened to fiction submissions we started receiving submissions for this issue. That's no surprise, but given the short timeframe we had to put this issue out coupled with the delay in reopening to fiction submissions, we were never able to consider these stories for the issue in question, which is why we never at any point said we were accepting submissions for this issue. Instead, we had to use whatever was already in purchased inventory to cobble together this issue I will note though that while we couldn't consider the submissions we received for the dark fantasy issue, we did consider them for other issues instead.

Anyway, the lead story in the dark fantasy issue is "A Witch's Heart" by Randy Henderson, another one of my slush survivors. This marked Randy's first professional sale, and it also marked my thirtieth slush survivor to appear in the magazine. This one is a dark retelling of the Hansel and Gretel fairy tale, in which the witch trains Gretel as her protégé while Hansel is locked away. Art to this one was provided by Thomas Canty.

Next up we have "The Sacrifice" by Michelle M. Welch. If ever a story deserved to be published in the magazine, it's this one. It was originally submitted to us during the Sovereign Media era, and while it was accepted, it ended up slipping through the cracks and finding itself in "transition hell" as the magazine shifted publishers to Tir Na Nog Press. It wasn't properly uncovered until more than six months after the fact ...and before it could be published, the magazine was canceled a second time. But third time is the charm, as it finally found its way into our pages with this issue. As to the story itself, this one is a high fantasy piece about how the king's daughter gets raped by invading soldiers while he's out to war. The rape happened because she made the ultimate sacrifice, putting herself in front of the soldiers, knowing what would happen, but making this sacrifice bought enough time for his precious runestone to be saved. Afterward, the king acts as if his daughter is dead, refusing to acknowledge her living but damaged body next to him on the floor. Ultimately a myth forms around this woman, as she leads soldiers against the enemy while calling herself the Dead One. But even this is not enough to win back her father's love. It takes a careful reading to unravel exactly what is going on in this story, because the author spells out very little of this. But all the clues are buried in the text, and when you put them all together you're able to lay out the thrust of the tale as described above. Art to this one was provided by Carol Heyer, which marks her eleventh illustration in the magazine. If you look at this illustration you'll notice that is drop of blood, hanging off the woman's jawline. I had suggested to Carol that she incorporate this into her illustration, as a metaphorical teardrop, since the king's daughter seemed best able to express herself through violence (and understandably so after what was done to her). Carol liked the suggestion and we ended up incorporating this small addition.

After this we have "Little Vampires" by Lisa Goldstein, which marks her third appearance in the magazine. This one is a contemporary fantasy that deals with the metaphorical aspects of being a real-life vampire. In this piece, we are introduced to two Jewish sisters, about a decade apart in age. Both of them were in Hungary during WWII, and the older sister sacrificed herself, entering a concentration camp to spare the younger sister having to do this. Ultimately the older sister survived, but expected her younger sister to take care of her going forward. All these years later (the 70s), the younger sister still feels obligated to take care of the older sister, sacrificing her social life and so on. Put simply, the older sister has become a little vampire, as she sucks the metaphorical life out of the younger sister in order to keep living. Art to this one was provided by Billy Norrby.

Then we have "By Shackle and Lash" by Euan Harvey, which marks his seventh appearance in the magazine. In this high fantasy piece, a pair of elite soliders demoted to prison duty encounter a strange prisoner who can choose who is able to enter her cell. To those allowed in, she fills their minds with dreams of beauty and freedom, and the need to take her to a dead city that she came from centuries ago. Art to this one was provided by Cyril Van Der Haegen.

Finally we have "The Strange Case of Madeleine Marsh (Aged 14 ¼)" by Von Carr, which marks her second appearance in the magazine. This one is a funny fantasy, which spoofs the writings of H.P. Lovecraft in hilarious fashion. When Madeleine Marsh's parents go away for the weekend, trouble soon follows when the Dark Gods of H.P. Lovecraft manifest in her basement. Fans of Lovecraft reading this retrospective will instantly interpret this as a mistake, as his stories involve the Elder Gods, but the author makes it clear this was an intentional deviation, and it factors into the story. As usual when I laugh at a story, I knew Shawna would take it, because every story I ever laughed at that was submitted to us, Shawna ended up buying. Art to this one was provided by Peter Ferguson, which marks his seventh illustration in the magazine.

I also want to note that while there would be more tweaks and such with future issues it was with this issue that I started feeling the magazine was no longer in transition following its closure under Sovereign Media. Old inventories had been burned through, the staff was mostly settled in, there were no more changes in publishers or editorial responsibilities, and so on. To put it another way, I felt like the magazine had found its groove. Had we had had a little more time, I feel like we could have done some amazing things, as we had some great plans in place for the future, but I'll get into that down the road.

So that wraps up this issue. And my favorite story? "A Witch's Heart" by Randy Henderson. And my favorite artwork? I'm giving the nod to Brom's cover illustration.

Originally posted on douglascohen.livejournal.com on July 20th, 2014

Part one hundred in my comprehensive retrospective as I read the fiction in *Realms of Fantasy* and offer my thoughts. This time around I'm tackling the milestone June 2011 issue.

A hundred issues is an achievement not too many magazines in our genre achieve, especially when the magazine is on a bimonthly schedule. Given that RoF was canceled twice before we reached this point under our final publisher, Damnation Books, more than once it looked like we would fall short of this important milestone. Happily it worked out otherwise, and while we didn't get to do every last thing we would have liked for this issue, we still included quite a number of special features to celebrate the occasion.

So as usual, I'll start off with the cover. While selecting covers was my domain, for the hundredth issue it felt right to me that the choice be a group effort, so I included founding editor Shawna McCarthy along with publisher Kim Gilchrist in the conversation. After some discussion, we selected an illustration by Thomas Canty, which also doubles as an interior illustration for Sharon Mock's "The Economy of Powerful Emotion." When we were discussing the possibilities, when Canty's piece came up, I did raise an initial concern about using it, though it had nothing to do with the quality of the illustration. Instead, I mentioned how the interior illustration was a two-page spread. The back cover had always been reserved for advertising and we'd never a run a two-page cover before, so we might have to consider cutting off the illustration and limiting it to the front cover if we decided to use Canty's piece. Kim's basic response was to e-shrug and tell me, "I'm the publisher. We can run a two-page cover if I want to." So that settled that, and after seeing the mock-up for this piece, it was obvious that if we'd just run what is depicted on the front cover and cut off the rest of it, the artwork still would have worked just fine. But I'm glad we ran the whole illustration, as breaking this new ground made for a nice touch for the hundredth issue. The choice also went over well with *Spectrum 19: The Year's Best in Contemporary Fantastic Art*, as they singled out this cover and the previous one as two strong covers in the magazine's final year.

At the top of this issue, you'll also note the banner informing readers that we're "celebrating 100 issues with 100 pages!" It was a nice touch, though you might be surprised to learn this is not the longest issue in the magazine's history. That would be the October 2003 issue, which runs 116 pages. The June 2011 issue was longer than most in the magazine's run though, and the longest since the December 2007 issue, which weighed in at 106 pages. (As to the shortest issue, several issues during the magazine's run numbered sixty-six pages.)

Also worth noting is that the back cover has a QR code. At the time, QR codes were only just starting to become regularly scanned with smart phones, so after some discussion it was agreed that if were going to introduce QR codes on the cover, for the first issue we would do so on the back cover.

Turning our attention to the *inside* of the magazine, we added a number of special features for this issue. Shawna McCarthy wrote an editorial to mark the occasion, her first to appear in the magazine since the August 2009 issue, and also the last to appear in the pages of RoF (although online editorials by both of us would continue until the final issue).

This issue also saw the return of the Letters Page, which had last appeared in the August 2003 issue. But for this edition, we did something a little different. All the letters were written by previous fiction contributors to the magazine. In most cases, the author landed his or her first pro sale with the magazine (or their first sale ever) and went to carve some bigger mark for themselves in the field, often the sale of a novel with a major publisher. In each case, the author expressed appreciation to Shawna (and sometimes yours truly) for helping along their career. We did our best to track down all the authors we believed might fall under this umbrella of accomplishment, though we can make no claims that our job was comprehensive. Still, the authors who contributed to the Letters Page were as follows: Richard Parks, Christopher Rowe, Naomi Kritzer, Paul Melko, Theodora Goss, Margaret Ronald, Ken Scholes, Alethea Kontis, and Christopher Kastensmidt. In the case of Richard Parks, we felt it was appropriate he contribute since he was the magazine's most published fiction author by a wide margin, and had been contributing his imagination to our pages since the third issue.

Another feature this issue was "Little Known Facts About Realms of Fantasy." Late into the process of laying out the issue, our publisher/graphic designer informed us that she needed to fill some space in the issue, and so she asked us to come up with some little known facts about the magazine.

I won't list all ten facts here; instead, I will admit for the first time anywhere that mistakes were made on two of these facts. One mistake took place in fact one, when we said we would be publishing our 600th story in the October 2011 issue. This one is my fault. I did the math several times, and each time it worked out that our 600th issue would appear in the October issue. I'm not sure how I got it wrong. The only reason I discovered the error is because I keep an Excel story log file, listing each story, along with other pertinent information. I've been filling out this story log as I write up new retrospectives. If you're familiar with Excel, you know that on the far right there are numbers next to each cell. This is how I've always been able to tell readers exactly when we published our one hundredth story and so on. So a couple of issue back, I happened to notice that the count seemed as if it would fall short of 600 total stories come the October issue. Getting all squinty eyed, I proceeded to investigate, and discovered that the final count come the end of the October issue would in fact be 597 stories. As this was the magazine's final issue, we ended up falling short of 600 published stories by three (alas).

The other mistake was that in fact eight, in which we listed our awards and nominations, we claimed to have won one World Fantasy Award, when in fact we were only nominated for one.

I debated whether or not to share these mistakes with those reading these retrospectives; after all, had I chosen to omit any mention of them, I doubt anyone would notice. It's three years after the magazine's cancelation and I've yet to hear from anyone pointing out these mistakes. But the fact that it's three years later also makes me shrug these mistakes off. Everyone makes them, whether they admit it or not. I choose to acknowledge them, which I hope adds a bit more authenticity to these retrospectives.

We also added a new feature to this issue, this being poetry. Our new publisher wanted to add a poetry section, and being as Shawna had previous experience selecting poetry during her editorial stint with *Asimov's*—with several pieces winning Rhysling Awards—and so she was a natural fit to add these duties to those of selecting fiction. We intentionally chose to premiere this feature with this issue as part of the overall festivities, and we did so in style, as our premiere poetess was none other than the grand dame of science fiction and fantasy, Ursula K. Le Guin.

Now while Shawna was responsible for selecting the poetry—an area I admittedly had and have very limited experience with—I will nonetheless pat myself on the back for helping us land Ursula's poetry. Every year I attend a publishing event in NYC called the SFWA Reception (aka the Mill n' Swill) in which various parties in publishing all get together for a few hours and talk shop in a relaxed environment. It's similar to the atmosphere you might find in the suites or bars at a convention. So while I was there in late 2010, I happened to be chatting with Le Guin's agent, someone I had known for several years, as she often submitted her clients' work to Realms. During the course of our chat, she mentioned that Le Guin hadn't been writing much fiction lately, because she had been on a poetry kick. So of course the editorial lightbulb went off over my head, and I mentioned how Realms would be launching a new poetry section, and it would be wonderful if we could possibly premiere with some poetry from Le Guin. You might think I was overstepping my bounds here, except I knew Shawna appreciated Le Guin's work, and after working with her for so long, I also knew she would like the idea of premiering the section with some poetry from Le Guin (and besides, Shawna would still have the final call as whether or not we used poetry, so there was no real harm being done). So several emails ensued, and ultimately two of Le Guin's poems were submitted for publication, and Shawna ended up accepting both.

We ended up running both poems this issue. The first was "Distance," a short fantastical piece examining the notions of "away" and "far," and our refusal to acknowledge the distances we create within ourselves. The second piece was "Mendenhall Glacier," which tells of the first time someone spotted a cold dragon.

Let's move onto the nonfiction ...

In the Movie/TV column, Resa Nelson covers Marvel Studio's *Thor*. In the Artists Gallery, Karen Haber covers the work of Peter Meseldžija. In the Folkroots section, Theodora Goss writes about fairies and fairylands. In the Books column, Paul Witcover reviews *Blood and Honey* by Stina Leicht, and *Hidden Cities* by Daniel Fox, while Elizabeth Bear reviews *God's War* by Kameron Hurley, and *The Cloud Roads* by Martha Wells. In the Paranormal Romance & Urban Fantasy Books column, Elizabeth Bear reviews *Welcome to Bordertown*, edited by Holly Black and Ellen Kushner, and *Desdaemona* by Ben Macallan. In YA Books, Michael M. Jones reviews *The Iron Thorn* by Caitlin Kittredge, *Teeth*, edited by Ellen Datlow and Terri Windling, *Rage* by Jackie Morse Kessler, *Tiger's Curse* by Collen Houck, *Angel Burn* by L.A. Weatherly, *Falling Under* by Gwen Hayes, *After*

Midnight by Lynn Viehl, and *A Long, Long Sleep* by Anna Sheehan. The Games column makes a return from the website to the magazine this issue, with Matt London reviewing *Marvel vs. Capcom 3: Fate of Two Worlds* for Playstation 3 and Xbox 360, and *Dragon Age II* for Microsoft Windows, Playstation 3, Xbox 360, and Mac OS X, and after several issues away, Matt Staggs returns to the Games column, reviewing the Wizards of the Coast board game, *Wrath of Ashardalon*, the RPG *Kingmaker*, *Bookhounds of London*, an RPG supplement for *Trail of Cthulhu*, and an RPG supplement adaptable for various formats called *Soldiers of Fortune*. Going forward, this would be the breakdown when it came to the Games column, with Matt London covering video games, and Matt Staggs covering RPGs and other non-video games. And last but not least, in the Graphic Novel column, Andrew Wheeler reviews *Patricia Briggs' Mercy Thompson: Moon Called, Volume One*, written by Patricia Briggs and David Lawrence, artwork by Amelia Woo, and *Dungeon Quest, Book Two*, by Joe Daly.

We also added an additional feature to the Artists Gallery with this issue. One day I happened to be flipping through one of my copies of *Spectrum: The Year's Best in Contemporary Fantastic Art*. One of the many features this fine series of art books includes is, with each illustration, in addition to the piece's title, they list the size of the original illustration, along with its medium (watercolor, oil on masonite, etc.). This was something I had noticed before, but on this particular occasion I found myself thinking what a good idea this was. Then I asked myself why we weren't doing this very thing with the Artists Gallery. Unable to come up with a good answer, I made the change starting with this issue. I'd imagine it was an interesting feature for fans, and artists in particular would surely appreciate the inclusion of such information. Either way, if this column focused on the artist and their work, it only made sense to include this information.

I should also note that with the return of Matt Staggs to the Games column, this would mark the last change to our nonfiction staff prior to the magazine's closure. Some of these columnists were inherited, others I hired, but, and I say this with all due respect to each and every columnist I've worked with over the years, I could not have asked for a better staff to end the magazine's run with.

Let's move onto the fiction ...

The lead story is "The Ground Whereon She Stands" by Leah Bobet, which marks her fourth appearance in the magazine. In this contemporary fantasy, a witch-woman in Idaho near the Canadian border is unable to express her feelings toward another woman who is her neighbor. Our neighbor and protagonist's work is going to take her away for a while, and so the witch-woman casts a spell on her from afar, one that causes flowers to start growing from her. I rather like Shawna's editorial byline to sum this one up: "Florists tell us to say it with flowers. But sometimes you just can't say it all." Art to this one was provided by Gary Lippincott, which marks his eighth illustration in the magazine.

Next up we have "Escaping Salvation" by Josh Rountree and Samantha Henderson. This marks Josh's eighth appearance in the magazine and Samantha's second. This one takes place in a post-apocalyptic Texas overrun by dirt angels, creatures whose body parts can magically replace the corresponding lost human parts. But there is more to these creatures than meets the eye, and much of that is revealed when an angel bounty hunter stumbles upon a woman who holds the key to bringing back the lost water angels. Art to this one was provided by David Palumbo, which marks his third illustration in the magazine.

After this we have "The Economy of Powerful Emotion" by Sharon Mock, which marks her third appearance in the magazine. This one is a short piece about a princess who is cursed as a baby, so that every time she cries, her tears are diamonds, cutting her skin. But instead of sympathy for his daughter, the king only experiences greed, to the point that the economy becomes saturated with diamonds. It makes for a sad situation, except when a princess is in distress in a fairy tale, there is often a prince waiting in the wings. Art to this one was provided by the aforementioned Thomas Canty, which marks his second illustration in the magazine.

Then we have "The Good Husband" by Thea Hutcheson. This one is another of my slush survivors, and I confess it makes me proud to see a story I plucked from the piles appearing in issue one hundred. This piece takes place in the days after the American Civil War, and focuses on Keeler, an aging woman magically tied to her land. When there is a man around to be a husband and mind the land, Keeler regains her youth and beauty, and the land prospers. Enter Jody, a young soldier who recently left the fighting behind. At first all seems to be bliss, but Jody is haunted by nightmares of war, and also fears that he is unfairly sacrificing his youth to Keeler and the land. Love becomes tested when Jody must confront his own fears and past ghosts. Art to this one was provided by Laurie Harden, which marks her nineteenth illustration in the magazine.

Following this we have "The Equation" by Patrick Samphire, which marks his seventh appearance in the magazine. This is a short contemporary piece about magic being erased from the world by things such as logic, science, and mathematics. One of the few remaining wielders of magic runs into an old high school flame, only to discover she is among those responsible for erasing magic from the world. Magic has no chance of winning this battle, but the magic of love just might. Art to this one was provided by Tony Shasteen, which marks his ninth illustration in the magazine.

Our penultimate tale this issue is "Wreathed in Wisteria, Draped in Ivy" by Euan Harvey, which marks his eighth appearance in the magazine. This one is a Far Eastern fantasy about a man deprived of both his manhood and his son, both at the whim of the same cruel lord. In this tale, he relates through to a letter to the perpetrator of these crimes the impossible tale of how he cheated death and will be able to claim his unexpected vengeance. Art to this one was provided by Dave Leri, which marks his eleventh illustration in the magazine. When I saw the mockup to this piece, it was very detailed (as is all of Dave's work, which is one of the things I love about it). I thought it was great, but I did have one suggestion: while reading the story, I had a very vivid image in my mind of the way Euan described some red maple leaves, and I suggested to Dave that he incorporate a few such falling leaves into the illustration. Dave liked this idea, believing it would break up some of the empty space. It proved a good working relationship between us, as this piece ended up being selected for inclusion in the Editorial section of *Spectrum 19: The Year's Best in Contemporary Fantastic Art*. To the best of my knowledge, this was the last work of any kind published in RoF that earned itself special recognition, i.e. awards, nominations, inclusion in year's best compilations, etc. Given what a strong piece this is, it was a fine way for the magazine to leave its final mark.

Our final tale this issue is "The Tides of the Heart" by David D. Levine, which marks his fourth appearance in the magazine. In this modern piece, we are introduced to a lesbian plumber who is gifted in working with the element of water, but whose romatic relationship skills are in need of work. When she meets an imprisoned undine who holds the keys to the city's existence, she seeks a way to help the undine escape. While trying to set her free of her prison, our protagonist falls in love with the undine and learns to escape the prison of her tempermental heart. Art to this one was provided by Lori Koefoed, which marks her seventeenth illustration in the magazine.

So that wraps up this issue. And my favorite story? Euan Harvery's "Wreathed in Wisteria, Draped in Ivy." And my favorite illustration? Dave Leri's accompanying artwork to this story.

Originally posted on douglascohen.livejournal.com on October 19th, 2014

Part 101 in my comprehensive retrospective as I read the fiction in *Realms of Fantasy* and offer my thoughts. This time around I'll be discussing the August 2011 edition, the penultimate issue of the magazine.

It was while this issue was out that the magazine's final set of publishers informed me the next issue would be the magazine's last. The magazine had been losing money, and with no end in sight they had decided to throw in the towel. I make no denials that my opinion here is biased, but even as I look back years later, I don't believe the creative end was to blame. We were still winning Nebula Awards as recently as the previous year. The magazine's artwork continued to win awards and recognition as well. The nonfiction staff was everything I could have asked for, both in terms of their professionalism and their creative efforts. We were still running new feature articles along with the usual ones to keep things fresh (right up to the final issue), and we'd put out our first themed issue in the magazine's history two issues earlier. We also had some exciting plans concerning the magazine's future (something I'll get into, but not with this particular retrospective). All the feedback we had received during the magazine's third life had been very positive.

But while I don't lay the blame on the creative team, nor do I lay the blame at the feet of the publishers. I was not privy to the day-to-day operations of how they ran the magazine, but I do know they were extremely supportive and enthusiastic about our product, they always paid everyone on time, they were receptive to suggestions/feedback, and they cared about the details. They were dedicated to putting out a quality product to the best of their ability.

So if I had to point to something regarding the magazine's demise it would be the realities of a changing print market. Everyone and their mother know that the rise of digitial publishing has changed the publishing landscape. Newspapers and magazines are among those that have been hit the hardest. In today's American speculative fiction market, the only remaining pro print magazines are in digest form. These are cheaper to produce than a full-sized color magazine like *Realms of Fantasy*. Perhaps just as importantly, it is easier to convert these magazines to digital formats.

The remaining American digests—*Asimov's*, *Analog*, and *The Magazine of Fantasy & Science Fiction*—can all be found in Kindle editions in addition to their usual print editions. It has helped extend their runs and stabilize them to some extent, as they might otherwise now be extinct.

Converting a magazine like *Realms of Fantasy* represented a number of headaches because of the color artwork accompanying the stories, the Artists Gallery, and the various design elements. Perhaps it would be easier to do now with 2015 almost upon us and constantly improving Kindle technology, but at the time? It was mindbogglingly difficult (not to mention the difficulties in getting Amazon to sell your magazine in their magazine department, but that's another story). Yes, we could (and did) offer pdfs of each issue for sale, but the truth is the sales generated from these proved negligible. Kindles are where worthwhile electronic sales were being generated at the time, and it just wasn't in the cards.

So the publishers were planning on making an announcement shortly after informing me and Shawna of the magazine's closure. However, at this time it was mid-October. The World Fantasy Convention was just a couple of weeks away, and Shawna was the editorial guest of honor. Given this, it would have put a serious damper on her being honored for her editorial work on *Realms of Fantasy* just weeks after the announcement of the magazine's cancelation, so at my suggestion the publishers delayed the cancellation announcement until after the convention was over, giving Shawna a chance to enjoy the weekend as opposed to having everyone offer her their condolences about the magazine's impending closure. I was in attendance at World Fantasy that year as well in support of Shawna, and our first night there we got together at one of the local bars and had several drinks in which we toasted the magazine's memory and reminisced about our time together. It was a great evening, one I'll always treasure when I look back at my time with the magazine.

So having shared all this, let's turn our attention to the issue in question. The cover to this one is by Kristina Carroll, and it doubles as her interior illustration to "Leap of Faith" by Alan Smale. It marks her second illustration to appear in the magazine. In this issue, the publishers also moved the QR Code from the back cover to the front cover.

Also of note is that the publishers dropped the price this issue. The previous price was $6.99, whereas the price with this issue became $5.99. All these years later, I can give you a little backstory on what happened here. I happened to be browsing online one day when I came across an article mentioning how DC Comics had dropped prices across the board for their comics. Intrigued, I passed the article along to the publishers. I mentioned to them how under the original publisher, the price of the magazine had for many years been $3.99, and how when the second publisher took over it immediately went up to $6.99, which marked a big increase. I didn't advocate lowering the price, but at this time I knew the magazine was struggling financially. Presumambly DC Comics had dropped their prices in an effort to stimulate sales. I emphasized to them that I had no idea if such a tactic would work for *Realms of Fantasy*, but I wanted to pass along the article and bring it to their attention so that at the very least they could consider the notion in case they should deem it a good idea. Apparently they decided it was in the magazine's best interests to make this change, as they dropped the price by $1.00, the first time in RoF's history the price was lowered. Whether this change actually helped the magazine or not, I don't rightly know. But if it did help, it was too little too late as the next issue proved our last. Still, I give the publishers credit for trying anything and everything to save the magazine.

A rundown of this issue's nonfiction is as follows:

In the Movie/TV section, Resa Nelson covers *Harry Potter and the Deathly Hallows Part 2*. In the Artists Gallery, Mia Nutick writes about Women in Fantasy [Art]. In Folkroots, Theodora Goss provides a brief history of monsters. In the Books column, Paul Witcover reviews *The River of Shadows* by Robert V.S. Redick, *The Enterprise of Death* by Jesse Bullington, *The Company Man* by Robert Jackson Bennett, *Vintage Vampire Stories*, edited by Robert Eighteen-Bisang and Richard Dalby, while Elizabeth Bear reviews *Wolfsangel* by M.D. Lachlan and *Mechanique: a Tales of the Circus Tresaulti* by Genevieve Valentine. In Paranormal Romance & Urban Fantasy Books, Elizabeth Bear reviews *Akata Witch* by Nnedi Okorafor and *Jim and the Flims* by Rudy Rucker. In YA Books, Michael M. Jones reviews *Huntress* by Malinda Lo, *Eona* by Alison Goodman, *The Girl Who Circumnavigated Fairyland in a Ship of Her Own Making* by Catherynne Valente, *Red Glove* by Holly Black, *The Girl in the Steel Corset* by Kady Cross, *Supernaturally* by Kiersten White, *Born at Midnight* by C.C. Hunter, *Queen of the Dead* by Stacey Kade, and *Always a Witch* by Carolyn MacCullough. In the Graphic Novel column, Andrew Wheeler reviews *Lost & Found* by Shaun Tan and *Anya's Ghost* by Vera Brosgol. And in the

Games column, Matt Staggs reviews the RPG *The Mutant Epoch*, the RPG *Red Tide: Adventure in a Crimson World*, the RPG *Black Bag Jobs*, Cubicle 7, and Matt London reviews *Portal 2* for Microsoft Windows, Mac Os X, Playstation 3, and Xbox 360.

I should also mention that Mia Nutick's article about Women in Fantasy [Art] was originally slated to be part of a Woman in Fantasy themed issue. Back with the previous publisher, Mia had pitched me the idea of this article, and I liked it enough that I decided we should do an entire themed issue about women in fantasy. Unfortunately, the magazine suffered its second closure before we could bring this idea to fruition. When the magazine was revived for the second time, the brain-trust collectively agreed to scrap this idea, as it was agreed that it would be too problematic to make this issue happen while we sorted through the transition to a new publisher. You may recall that the exact same thing happened once before, as the magazine ended up abandoning its plans for a Halloween issue when it was canceled and subsequently rescued by our second publisher.

Further complicating matters to make the Women in Fantasy themed issue happen was the fact that the new publishers had already announced a dark fantasy issue before they had brought back me and Shawna. As this issue was *definitely happening* and would (finally) mark the magazine's first themed issue, none of us were in a rush to plan another themed issue on top of this. Besides, the February issue would mark the first one under the new publishers, the April issue would produce the dark fantasy issue in question, and the June issue would see the publication of issue one hundred. As these would be the first three issues under the new publisher, this marked more than enough special issues to kick things off. (At least for a little while, but that's a retrospective for another day ...) Even so, I reasoned that we could still do Mia's original idea for her column in the Artists Gallery, so everything ended up coming full circle when we published her original idea in this issue and nothing else on this topic.

Let's move on to the fiction ...

The lead story this issue is "The Progress of Solstice and Chance" by Richard Bowes. In this brief mythological story where the gods and goddesses are such beings as Solstice, Chance, Life, Death, etc., two adolescent goddesses struggle to find their place in the world as they develop intimate feelings for one another. Art to this one was provided by Raoul Vitale.

Next up we have "Isabella's Garden" by Naomi Kritzer, which marks her sixth appearance in the magazine. In this one a little girl has the ultimate green thumb, as anything she plants takes root and blossoms, including jelly bean trees and money trees. However, things become a tad more complicated when little Isabella decides she wants to plant herself a baby sister. Art to this one was provided by Stephanie Pui-Mun Law, which marks her sixth illustration in the magazine.

After this we have "Collateral Damage" by Kate Riedel, which marks her eighth appearance in the magazine. In this piece, a teenagers's younger sister disappears in a temporal anomaly during a snowstorm and reappears many years later, when the older sister is now a grandmother. Further complicating matters is that this temporal anomaly has a history with this family, as the older sister is married to a man from the past who also came through the anamoly. Everyone is forced to make adjustments to each other, due to changes in time periods and revelations from the past coming to fruition in the present. Art to this one was provided by Joe Kovach, which marks his fourth illustration in the magazine.

Then we have "Snake in the Grass" by W.R. Thompson. This one is a lighthearted story in which our protagonist agrees to sell his soul to the Devil in return for happiness. Satan helps our protagonist meet the woman of his dreams, except Satan has plans of his own, for it turns out that their son will be the AntiChrist ...or so Satan thinks, until he learns that God stopped paying attention to Earth centuries ago and never bothered to tell his most fallen son. Art to this one was provided by James A. Owen, which marks his third illustration in the magazine.

Finally we have "Leap of Faith" by Alan Smale, which marks his sixth appearance in the magazine. This one is a piece of alternate Christian mythology, in which Levi is God's faithful servant, doing strange and fabulous works beyond the wicked city of Shadom. Lilith exists in this alternate world and is seen as the great evil, as she attacks the city incessantly. However, all is not as it seems, and this slowly comes to light when Levi and his family meet strange and beautiful servants of the Lord who may or may not be angels. While this is an alternate version of our mythology, ultimately the author ties into our own mythology when we learn that this is an earlier version of the biblical Earth, one doomed to destruction while God tinkers to perfect his creations. But for Levi and perhaps some of his family, God has other plans. Art to this one was provided by the aforementioned Kristina Carroll.

So that wraps up this issue. And my favorite story? "Leap of Faith" by Alan Smale. And my favorite artwork? Kristina Carroll's accompanying illustration to "Leap of Faith."

Originally posted on douglascohen.livejournal.com on December 15th, 2014

Part 102 in my comprehensive retrospective as I read the fiction in *Realms of Fantasy* and offer my thoughts. This time around I'll be discussing the October 2011 issue, the final issue in the magazine's run.

I covered most of the relevant details surrounding the magazine's closure in the previous retrospective. What I'll add is that Shawna and I both wrote farewell editorials that were posted on the magazine's website alongside the publisher's cancellation notice. There was also a ring of finality to this closure that the previous two hadn't had. Perhaps it was because we accomplished so much in our final year of publication—a Nebula Award, a Nebula nomination, publishing a cover that won Spectrum's Editorial Silver Award, publishing our first themed issue, followed by our hundredth issue, and our fiction editor being honored at the World Fantasy Convention as the Editorial Guest of Honor. I can't say that we went out on our terms, especially when we had so much more planned for future issues, but I can say that creatively we went out strong. I'd like to think this knowledge made the closure a little easier for both Shawna and myself.

And while we were disappointed to see the magazine reach its end, I have a feeling that had someone else stepped in to save RoF yet again, Shawna and/or I would have passed on returning a third time. Three sets of publishers and three closures in less than two years can be kind of exhausting. Enough was enough. For a brief time there was discussion among the publishers of possibly taking the remaining materials we had in inventory and publishing them as some sort of of .pdf, but this never came to pass. And so RoF passed into magazine history, though we did enough in our time that we'll be leaving our mark on the speculative field for years to come. And with this said, let's dive into the final issue.

The honor of the magazine's final cover goes to Ruth Sanderson's interior illustration to "Sweeping the Hearthstone" by Betsy James, which marks her second illustration in the magazine. As coincidence would have it, I actually met Ruth in person at the World Fantasy Convention in 2011, only days before we made the magazine's cancellation public.

A rundown of this issue's nonfiction is as follows:

In the Movie/TV column, Resa Nelson writes about the plethora of forthcoming fairy tales movies. In the Artists Gallery, Karen Haber covers the work of Ruth Sanderson. In Folkroots, Theodora Goss writes about the myth and magic of Narnia. In a Special Feature column, Elizabeth Bear provides a brief history of urban fantasy. In the Books column, Paul Witcover reviews *A Dance with Dragons* by George R. R. Martin, *Raising Stony Mayhall* by Daryl Gregory, *A Crack in Everything* by Daniel Marcus, *The Edinburgh Dead* by Brian Ruckley, and Elizabeth Bear reviews *The Snow Queen's Shadow* by Jim C. Hines. In Urban Fantasy and Paranormal Romance Books, Elizabeth Bear reviews *Kitty's Big Trouble* by Carrie Vaughn, *Hellbent* by Cherie Priest, and *No Hero* by Jonathan Wood. In YA Books, Michael M. Jones reviews *So Silver Bright* by Lisa Mantchev, *Death Sentence: Escape from Furnace 3* by Alexander Gordon Smith, *Spellbound* by Cara Lynn Shultz, *Fairy Bad Day* by Amanda Ashby, *Starcrossed* by Josephine Angelini, *Awaken* by Katie Kacvinsky, *Shift* by Jeri Smith-Ready, and *The Throne of Fire: The Kane Chronicles, Book Two* by Rick Riordan. In the Graphic Novels column Andrew Wheeler reviews *Blood Work* by Kim Harrison, illustrations by Pedro Maia and Gemma Magno and *The League of Extraordinary Gentlemen, Volume III: Century: 1969* by Alan Moore and Kevin O'Neill. And in the Games column, Matt Staggs reviews the RPG *Advanced Fighting Fantasy*, the RPG *Book of Drakes*, while Matt London reviews *Final Fantasy III* for the Nintendo Wii Virtual Console and *Hunted: The Demon's Forge* for Miscrosoft Windows, Playstation 3, and Xbox 360.

There are two things I'd like to note concerning our final nonfiction offerings. First is that I'm very proud of the fact that in our final issue we had a special feature column. It demonstrates that right until the end the magazine was trying new things on a creative level. Second is that while by the time this issue came out *A Dance with Dragons* had been out for several months, when Paul Witcover read and reviewed it, the book had not yet been published. More importantly to me, this meant that I as the editor would be reading and reviewing his work before the novel came out ...the novel by my favorite author ...the novel I had been waiting over six years to read ...the novel that I was scared to death was going to get spoiled to me by Paul's review. Well, I reasoned, there is only one thing to do. I need to do my job and read Paul's review, but I need to partition my mind so that once I'm done reading this I will forget *everything*. I'm not quite sure how I managed this, but I'd say I managed this with about a 90% succees rate, with the remaining 10% focusing on smaller details I was able to live with. But by the Seven of Westeros, I never hated working with the nonfiction except for that one moment when that review came across my e-desk.

Let's move onto fiction ...

The lead story this issue is "Return to Paraiso" by Rochita Loenen-Ruiz. It is another one of my slush survivors, which made thirty-two stories in total that I pulled out of the slush during my time with the magazine that were published in the magazine. In this contemporary fantasy, an island is ruled from afar by a despot, and his soldiers do constant sweeps of the island, removing anyone deemed as a threat to the regime. But when the government dares go after one young woman with magical ties to the Earth and take things too far, they awaken her wrath and pay the consequences for defying what can be interpreted as a version of Mother Nature. Art to this one was provided by Verónica Casas. As with the special feature nonfiction column, I admit to some pride at seeing one of slush survivors appearing in the magazine's final issue. The first story I ever plucked from the slush was purchased by Shawna, and it feels right to me that in the magazine's last issue, one of my slush survivors appeared within its pages. I can rightly say that when it came to finding up-and-coming authors, I was on my game from beginning to end.

Next up we have "The Man Who Made No Mistakes" by Scott William Carter, which marks his fourth appearance in the magazine. In this contemporary fantasy, a young man discovers he has a time traveling talent that he calls "switchbacking," which allows him to go back to an earlier point in time of his life and impact the way events play out. Once he does a switchback he can never visit an earlier point in his life, but it still lends him a tremendous amount of power, one he takes full advantage of until his mother dies and he falls into a drunken depression. He snaps out of it when he meets and falls hard for a young woman. When things fizzle out between them, he commits a terrible crime against her with the knowledge that he can always do a switchback to undo the crime. But to his horror, he learns that if this crime doesn't come to pass, it will have worldwide repercussions nothing short of disastrous. Art to this one was provided by Billy Norrby, which marks his second illustration in the magazine.

After this we have "Second Childhood" by Jerry Oltion, which marks his second appearance in the magazine. In this lighthearted piece, a woman's mother comes back from the grave ten years after she died, spontaneously appearing in the kitchen, happy, healthy, and all of thirty years old. The entire family unit must adjust to this unexpected visitor, as our protagonist must deal with her mother coming back and being younger and prettier than she is, her husband must deal with having his mother-in-law back in his life, while their daughter is meeting her grandmother for the first time. But more importantly, everyone is intent on figuring out why she has come back and what it means. Art to this one was provided Laurie Harden, which marks her twentieth illustration in the magazine.

Then we have "Sweeping the Hearthstone" by Betsy James, which marks her second appearance in the magazine. In this high fantasy piece, a young woman in search of new start takes a job as a barmaid. She is a virgin and has reached an age where she has grown sexually curious, to the point where there is a deep longing in her ...but only for the right man. And as it turns out, this man may not be walking through the door, but rather sleeping beneath the massive hearthstone in the inn, where he has slept for thousands of years. Art to this one was provided by the aforementioned Ruth Sanderson.

Finally (and I do mean finally) we have "Barbie Marries the Jolly Fat Baker" by Nick DiChario. This one is a funny fantasy set in a world where dolls and action figures are alive, only to suffer the "Little Death" when humans are around, meaning they go back to being inanimate. Paladin is a knight who is in love with Princess Barbie. The problem is Paladin is too knightly and courtly for her, and she needs someone who will fulfill her womanly needs. Enter the jolly fat (and repugnant) baker. Paladin is understandably shocked and dismayed at this tragic turn of events. Heartbroken, he resolves to venture out into the real world and learn the meaning to life's burning questions. Art to to this one was provided by Peter Ferguson, which marks his eighth illustration in the magazine.

When I look at the contributors for our final issue, I think it is an excellent representation of the kind of talent we published. We had slush survivors, former slush survivors, award-winning and prolific pros, and an award nominee being published in our pages for the first time. The same sort of variation could be found among the artists, and this blend of new and established talent was something we did as well as anyone, right until the end.

So that wraps up this issue, along with the magazine series as a whole. And my favorite story? "Barbie Marries the Jolly Fat Baker" by Nick DiChario. And my favorite artwork? Ruth Sanderson's illustraton to "Sweeping the Hearthstone."

Originally posted on douglascohen.livejournal.com on December 19th*, 2014*

PUTTING THE RETROSPECTIVE IN PERSPECTIVE

Welcome to part 103 in my comprehensive retrospective of *Realms of Fantasy*, the final installment in this series. In previous editions, I would share some thoughts on the fiction in each issue, along with the accompanying departments. However, there are no more individual issues to discuss. Installment 102 in this series covered the October 2011 issue, which was the final issue in RoF's publishing history. Even so, this series calls for one last installment to boil down this vast overview, to, as the subtitle states, put the retrospective in perspective, not to mention the magazine itself. As such, the format for this final installment will be somewhat different from previous editions. So let's jump in, shall we?

There is no better place to start with than the fiction. The first issue of *Realms of Fantasy* was the October 1994 issue. The final issue was the October 2011 issue. During this seventeen year period, the magazine only missed one issue, good enough for 102 issues total. 596 stories were published during this time by 280 different authors. That's good for a shade over two stories per author. Of these 596 stories, fourteen were reprints, leaving 582 original pieces of fiction to appear in the magazine's pages. These fourteen reprints were written by ten different authors, leaving 270 authors who submitted original fiction. When we consider only original fiction, the numbers still work out to slightly more than two stories per author on average. At 596 stories divided up over 102 issues, the magazine published approximately 5.8 stories per issue during the course of its history. Over the course of a year, that works out to about 34.8 stories.

The magazine's most published author is Richard Parks, with twenty-five stories, about 4.2% of all fiction. That's good enough to fill up 4+ issues. The next most published author is Tanith Lee with fifteen stories, about 2.5% of all fiction. That's good enough to fill up 2+ issues. In third place is Bruce Holland Rogers with twelve stories, about 2% of all fiction and enough to fill up two issues. The only other authors to have hit "the Double Digits Club" are Jay Lake and Liz Williams, each with ten stories, and each representing about 1.67% of all fiction. Any author who published six or more stories produced enough fiction for at least one entire issue and accounted for at least 1% of all fiction. There were nineteen such authors in total. The remaining authors from this group are Peni R. Griffin,

Devon Monk, Carrie Vaughn, Tim Pratt, Euan Harvey, Kate Riedel, Josh Rountree, and James Van Pelt with eight stories a piece, breaking down to about 1.34% of the fiction each and 1+ issues each; Patrick Samphire and William R. Eakin with seven stories each, breaking down to about 1.17% of the fiction each and 1+ issues each; and Alan Smale, Naomi Kritzer, Jane Yolen, and Bruce Glassco with six stories each, breaking down to about 1% of the fiction each and about one issue each. Combined, these authors accounted for 174 stories, about 29.19% of all fiction. That's good for thirty issues, about 29.41% of the 102 issues, and enough to fill up the magazine for five years.

During my six and a half years with the magazine, I pulled thirty-two stories from the slush that were published in the magazine, about 5.37% of all fiction. That's good enough to fill up about five and a half issues. These thirty-two slush survivors went on to publish fifty-two stories total, about 8.97% of all fiction. That's good enough to fill up just shy of nine issues total, about 8.79% of all issues, or just shy of filling up the magazine's fiction for a year and a half. For those keeping track, Euan Harvey not only published eight stories, he was also a slush survivor, so there is some crossover between these stats and those outlined in the previous paragraph.

Of the 280 authors to publish in RoF, 141 were male and 139 were female. That works out to approximately 50.375% male vs. 49.642% female. The fact that these numbers come so close to an exact 50/50 split is nothing short of amazing. Among my thirty-two slush survivors, nineteen were women vs. thirteen for men. That works out to 59.375% female vs. 40.625% male. Obviously this is a smaller sample size, and being as I passed stories along to Shawna for final consideration, it means I didn't have final say over what/who we would publish. But the fact that the slush results favor women by about 20% doesn't surprise me. As a general rule, the stories submitted by women to RoF's slush were stronger during my time with the magazine. I imagine that if I had been making the final calls on the slush stories, the results still would have favored female writers. Please note than I am speaking in *generalities only*, and am in no way comparing the merits of the work concerning male and female slush survivors who went on to publication.

Further research supports this supposition that I would (and to the extent of my responsibilities did) favor female writers when it came to the slush. Of the 186 slush stories I passed along to Shawna, 185 were considered before the magazine's cancelation. 105 were by women (the one that went unread was also by a woman). Of the remaining eighty-one submissions, seventy-nine were by men. One submission was by an author whose sex I am uncertain of despite online research, and one by an author whose sexuality doesn't define with traditional male/female pronouns. If we focus on the 184 submissions as defined by authors carrying male and female labels, 57.05% of what I passed along was by women vs. 42.93% by men. Of the 104 submissions by women that Shawna had a chance to read, 19.23% were accepted (including one story that never saw publication). Of the seventy-nine submissions by men, 17.72% were accepted (including one story that never saw publication). The author of unknown sex and the author who didn't define with traditional pronouns both ended up getting rejected. You'll excuse me if I pass on providing similar data concerning the automatic passes—sifting through that information represents a headache of epic proportions.

I would be interested in providing data concerning stories that deal with characters or issues important to the LBGT community. Unfortunately, I am not confident the data I could provide here would be accurate. I keep a master story log of all the stories published in RoF, which I filled out as I read issues and did retrospectives. This log includes one or two-line summations of each story, meaning they're rather brief. I don't trust the summations to always inform me about whether a story touches on LGBT matters in a meaningful way. Even with these summations (and my retrospectives series as a further source), there are a number of these 596 stories that I have absolutely no recollection of. If my data is off a percentage point or two here or there, I feel as if this is a forgiveable offense. But I refuse to grossly misrepresent any numbers on these matters. It would be unfair to everyone.

On minority writers, I run into a similar problem, i.e. when there are so many writers I don't know and never met, I don't believe I can state with any degree of accuracy which of them are minorities.

I will however consider a much smaller sample size, this being my thirty-two published slush survivors. Naturally the results here cannot be attributed to all the fiction and writers in RoF, but it does provide something, insufficient though it is. Three stories focus or touch on LBGT themes in a meaningful way, with a fourth being cleverly ambiguous regarding a homosexual relationship. Having read this story twice, my personal opinion is that the relationship *was* homosexual. With this in mind, 12.50% of the published slush survivors focused on or dealt with LBGT issues in some meaningful way. Five of my slush survivors come from minorities, or 15.63%. If you are interested in cross-referencing this data, the total number of stories dealing with LBGT issues combined with the total amount of minority authors would come out to eight, of 25% of the fiction.

I'll add that to the best of my recollection, Shawna was always rather open to LGBT fiction, so consider it an educated guess when I say I think her percentage is a bit higher than 12.50%. I couldn't guess one way or the other about her numbers regarding minority authors, but I see no reason to assume they would be significantly lower than my own percentage here, and would be pretty shocked if it proved otherwise. At the very least, I would imagine the numbers are comparable.

Now let's take a look at submissions. There were some submissions that were accepted but never published in the magazine due to its closure. Where applicable, I'm going to include those figures here to provide as much relevant data as possible. So instead of published stories, I'm going to create a wider net by discussing accepted stories. Those stories passed along to Shawna from the final two batches of submissions never received their final decisions and will only be included in some of the following tabulations.

Toward the end of the magazine's run, we had closed to submissions with the intention of reopening to electronic submissions several months later, but the magazine folded before we could make this happen. Instead, Shawna and I considered the fiction the old-fashioned way, i.e. via snail-mail. On top of this, there was no office for RoF where the two of us worked. She worked from home in NJ, I in NY. Every so often we would meet in Manhattan, where she would give me the latest batch of submissions to sort through, while I gave her everything that made the cut from the last round.

I started working with magazine back on May 10th, 2005. The last time we did a slush exchange was on September 11th, 2011 (with my last official day with the magazine being November 2nd, 2011). During this time, I sorted through 9,231 submissions, including a number of manuscripts submitted to RoF before I started working for the magazine. Of these submissions, there were 784 automatic passes (meaning they went directly to Shawna regardless of my opinion on them) and 186 slush stories that I passed along for further consideration. The combined number of stories that were passed along during this time for further consideration was 970, or approximately 10.51% of all stories submitted to the magazine. I also know of eight stories by automatic passes that were submitted directly to Shawna via email, all of which were accepted for publication.* So the adjusted numbers for *all* submissions received during this time that I know of works out to 9,239, with 792 of them being automatic passes, 186 being slush stories, and 978 stories total that reached Shawna, or 10.59% of all submitted stories. Of these stories, Shawna made a decision on 942 of them.** The remaining thirty-six stories were either withdrawn due to various reasons before they could be considered, or the magazine suffered its final cancelation before Shawna passed along her final decision. Of these 942 stories, 191 were accepted for publication. 157 were accepted automatic passes, which came from a total of 757 automatic passes, and thirty-four were accepted slush survivors*** from a total of 185 slush stories. That works out to a combined 20.28% acceptance rate.

80.36% of all stories that Shawna considered were automatic passes, 19.64% were slush stories. Of the 757 automatic passes Shawna considered, 20.74% were accepted. Of the 185 slush stories, 18.38% were accepted. The difference in acceptance rates between automatic passes and slush stories works out to a mere 2.36%. Shawna and I didn't always agree on which stories to take, but I always believed we worked well together. According to these numbers, that belief bears out, because during the course of six and a half years I was passing along enough fiction to essentially match the acceptance rates from more established writers.

If we subtract all of the automatic passes, that leaves us with 8,458 slush stories I considered during my time (though I read everything not submitted to Shawna via email and offered her my thoughts/opinions). At the time of the closure, I had already considered every last piece of slush, so these numbers are all-inclusive. Of these 8,458 stories, 2.20% were passed along for further consideration. Given Shawna's 18.38% acceptance rate of slush stories, once a story got past me the chances of landing a sale went up significantly. (This is of course to be expected, as my chief responsibility with the slush was to cull it down to the best possible candidates for the fiction editor to choose from.) Of these 8,458 slush stories, 8,457 received their final decision from Shawna. Only .4% of these stories were accepted for publication, or less than half a perecentile.

Anyone who passed muster with both me and Shawna should give themselves a hearty pat on the back. Both of us are very picky (if it were otherwise we'd have been awful at our jobs). I have no idea about the amounts of slush stories my predecessors were passing along to Shawna, but based on these numbers, it seems like a safe assumption than *anyone* who clawed/earned their way out of the magazine's slush and went on to publication *at any point* defied the odds in a serious way and should be very proud of themselves. I should add that even rejected authors who got out of the slush seriously beat the odds. Anyone who isn't brand new to the field obviously knows the odds are stacked against them when submitting to a magazine's general slush pile, but the sheer volume of data here may demonstrate it in a way that you might not have considered before.

If we consider the accepted slush within the framework of *all* the fiction that was submitted and considered by myself along with *everything* that reached Shawna that was *also* considered—and factoring in a reasonable estimate of about twenty stories that were withdrawn from the general slush over the years for various reasons—this number will bring us to 9,182. (My response times always remained rather acceptable during the days of postal subs despite handling all the slush on my own, and I therefore never had to deal with many withdrawals.) Of these, only .37% of stories were accepted. If we consider all of the accepted automatic passes out of everything submitted and considered, the number jumps to a 1.71% acceptance rate. If we consider *all* the fiction she accepted out of these 9,182 submissions—which is to say slush stories and automatic passes—the acceptance rate jumps again to 2.08%.

There are a lot of little things that pop up when you sift through as many stories as I have for as long as I did, so while I double-checked these numbers before posting them, for the sake of full disclosure I will mention it wouldn't surprise me if something here or there may be *slightly* off. However, the volume of fiction covered here is such that any such discrepencies can be considered negligble when considering the final data.

Let's now turn to special recognition the magazine's fiction has received. Credit belongs where credit is most due, meaning I will focus on the stories that were originally published in RoF. I'm also not going to include RoF stories that received reader awards or were published on the magazine's website, as RoF stories automatically end up getting selected by default. But over the years, the magazine's fiction received two Nebula Awards and six Nebula nominations for its fiction. It received one World Fantasy nomination for its fiction, while Shawna also received one World Fantasy nomination in the Special Award—Professional category for her editorial work on *Realms of Fantasy*, and was additionally honored at the 2011 World Fantasy Convention as the Editorial Guest of Honor. Our fiction also received one Bram Stoker Award, one Gaylactic Spectrum Award, and two Gaylactic Spectrum Award nominations. Thirty-nine stories were included in various Year's Best anthologies, and I know of an additional eight stories that were reprinted in other significant venues.**** Twenty-seven stories were podcast on what I would consider significant podcast venues. Four stories were longlisted for the Locus Award, and one story was shortlisted for the James Tiptree Jr. Memorial Award. Also worth mentioning is that I know of at least two stories first published in our pages that featured characters of stories that were later expanded into book deals with major publishers.

Naturally this list can never be comprehensive. There will always be more stories that get reprinted, more stories that get podcast. You never know when an author will turn a story into a major novel deal. Nor will I claim the reprints I've mentioned are absolutely comprehensive—I'm sure I missed some news about worthwhile reprints, particularly with stories reprinted before I started working at the magazine. But I did my best to note them. As you might also expect, when it comes to good stories there is also crossover in more than one instance, with stories earning nominations while also being reprinted, and so on. Still, based on the available numbers I know of eighty different stories received some sort of special recognition. This means of the 582 original stories the magazine published, 13.75% were judged by some editor, jury, or vote as deserving of special recognition, being brought to the attention of a new audience, or worth being turned into a novel to reach a new and bigger audience. Put another way, that's more than one out of every ten stories. Over time, this number should only rise.

As is always the case when discussing the slush, we're obviously considering a much smaller sample size, but of the thirty-two slush stories I discovered that saw publication, one story provided the springboard for a big novel deal with a major publisher, one was nominated for a Nebula

Award, two appeared in Year's Best anthologies, one was reprinted in another significant venue, and two appeared in significant podcast venues. There is some crossover with one of these stories, but 18.75% of these stories went on to receive special recognition, close to one of every five stories. And as with the rest of the published stories, it is certainly possible that over time this number will rise.

It's important to add that in some major award categories, fantasy has often been treated as the ugly stepchild as compared to science fiction. This would explain the lack of a single Hugo nomination in my opinion, and likewise the limited Nebula recognition. Eight combined Nebula awards and nominations are certainly nice, but it's not all that much considering how many stories we published. I can understand only receiving one Bram Stoker Award as Shawna's tastes never ran too dark overall (though she published more than one beauty in her time), but when it comes to the World Fantasy Awards, I consider it patently ridiculous that the magazine's fiction received only nomination and not a single award. Of course, every industry that provides special recognition is subject to this sort of scrutiny and I don't wish to take away anything from those who *did* earn awards or nominations, so I'll say no more on this subject except that matters such as these are all part of the business.

Let's move onto the artwork. All but four stories received some sort of illustration during the magazine's history, which adds up to 592 interior illustrations. Including covers (but not including the Artists Gallery, which I consider a separate beast), the magazine ran 679 illustrations. If you're thinking this number should be 694 due to there being 102 issues, I will remind you that RoF ran a number of media covers over the years featuring stills from movies and television (fifteen, obviously) and these should not be considered illustrations. In the magazine's final years, a number of interior illustrations and images from the Artist Galleries also doubled as magazine covers, so the adjusted number for *different* illustrations run by the magazine is 668. Including the cover to each issue and not including the art found in the Artist Galleries, there were about 6.6 illustrations per issue. Over the course of a publishing year, that works out to about 39.6 illustrations.

Not including the Artists Gallery, there were 177 different artists who had their art appear in the magazine. 135 were male, forty-one were female, and the sex for one is an unknown. If we focus on the remaining 176, we're left with a number of 76.70% male vs. 23.30% female.

Obviously this is a tremendous disparity. I am guilty of it as well, though my sample size as compared to the overall artwork is much smaller. I started overseeing the artwork with the August 2009 issue. A number of illustrations were inherited from preexisting inventory from the previous publisher, two illustrations were overseen by someone other than me during my tenure, and one illustration was a stock image with no attribution from the website of origin. Several illustrations also doubled as covers, and I'm only counting them once for the purposes of these percentages. Of the remaining illustrations during this time, I ended up working with sixty-four, both original and reprints. If we included the stock image, I worked with 9.43% of all illustrations, or less than one tenth. Over time, the numbers I'm about to share would unquestionably change, though to say with any certainty whether they would change one way or the other amounts to little more than conjecture. With this said, I will discuss my personal numbers in this department.

Sometimes there were artist teams working on these illustrations and I also hired artists to work on the same piece more than once, so the total number of *artists* attached to these illustrations is thirty-nine, with thirty-one men and eight women. That breaks down to 79.49% men vs. 20.51% women, which comes fairly close to the work of my predecessors (both men and women have overseen the artwork over the years if anyone is curious).

So while my work with the fiction favored the women by a wide margin, my work with the art favored the men by a much wider margin. I find this tremendously interesting, though I admit my knowledge of the speculative illustrative field isn't as wide as that of the speculative authorial one, so attempting to decipher what this all means based on the relatively small sample size wouldn't reveal all that much in the way of illuminating information. In case anyone considers it relevant data, of the sixty-three illustrations I worked with, nineteen of them had at least one woman involved (again, some pieces had artist teams), which would bring my personal percentage up to 30.16%. Interestingly enough, of the seven interior illustrations that I ended up using as a double for the magazine's cover, four of them were by women, or 57.14%. So of the eight female illustrators I worked with, half of them had their work featured on the magazine's cover. Also worth noting is that in the magazine's last issue, three of the five illustrations were by women, with one of them doubling as the cover. Given the unlikelihood of this many women appearing in a single issue based on the raw data, I'd like to believe this was indicative that my percentages concerning female illustrators would have climbed had the magazine's run continued.

I am going to pass on working up similar figures for *all* the artwork due to all the hair-pulling that would cause me, but it's a safe assumption that the percentage for female artists would again go up if you calculated everything according to female artists working on *any* piece.

When it comes to figuring out the LGBT art, I will point out that all the interior art was based on the accompanying stories. And as I'm uncertain about all the LGBT fiction, I'm not about to sift through all 596 stories to see which illustrations tap into these themes. Doing so would certainly be worthwhile, but even I have my limits to how comprehensive I'm going to be in this final retrospective.

As to minority artists, it is much the same case as with minority writers, i.e. I hesitate to provide numbers for fear of gross misrepresentation. Among the artists I worked with, I'm afraid I don't know them well enough to feel comfortable providing any kind of numbers (though I can certainly pick out a couple of minority artists at a glance).

In terms of covers, the artist with the most cover illustrations is Luis Royo, with twelve, or 12.24% of all covers. Over the years, the magazine ran nineteen covers (about 18.62%) that included a dragon.***** There were also nineteen covers that included warrior women of some kind (about 18.62%), most of them of chicks in chain mail (including a couple of media covers). As previously stated, the magazine ran fifteen media covers (about 14.71%). Seven covers doubled as interior illustrations (about 6.86%) and six covers either appeared in the Artists Gallery or were provided by the featured artist in the Artists Gallery (about 5.88%). There were five Lord of the Rings covers (about 4.9%)—all traditional media covers—and there were four Harry Potter covers (about 3.9%), though three were illustrations rather than traditional media covers. There were four Elric covers (about 3.9%) as well as three Conan covers (about 2.9%).

Based on my research, the vast majority of covers were reprints. Unfortunately, the original publishers were very uneven when it came to providing information concerning the covers. Where I could, I researched the answer on my own, either finding the answer on the artist's personal website, through a Google image search, or through miscellaneous means. These were not fullproof methods though, even when I visited an artist's personal website; artists do not always include all their artwork on their websites, and even when a piece is posted, they don't always include all the relevant information.

With this in mind, fifty-three covers were reprints (51.96%), it's unknown to me whether nineteen of them were reprints or being published in the magazine for the first time (18.63%), fifteen were previously unpublished (14.71%), and as previously mentioned, fifteen were media covers (17.65%). Of the 579 illustrations, 503 saw publication for the first time in RoF, or 86.87%. As a reminder, this number may be higher since I was unable to determine the origins of eighteen covers.

Our most published illustrator is Web Bryant, with twenty-two illustrations, (about 3.25% of all illustrations).****** That's good enough to fill up 3+ issues. In second place is Laurie Harden, with twenty illustrations (about 2.96%), good enough to fill up three issues. Third is Lori Koefoed with seventeen illustrations (about 2.52%), good enough to fill up 2+ issues. Fourth are Paul Lee, Patrick Arrasmith, and Janet Aulisio with fifteen illustrations a piece (about 2.2% each), good enough to fill up 2+ issues. Fifth are Michael Gibbs and Luis Royo with fourteen illustrations a piece (about 2.07% each), good enough to fill up 2+ issues. Sixth are Scott Grimando and David Beck with thirteen illustrations a piece (about 1.9% each), good enough to fill up 1+ issue. Seventh are Carol Heyer, Dave Leri, and Mary O'Keefe Young with eleven illustrations a piece (about 1.6% each), good enough to fill up 1+ issue. Eighth (and the final members of the "Double Digits Club") are John Berkey, Ken Graning, J.K. Potter, Chris Cocozza, Allen Douglas, and Charles Demorat with ten illustrations a piece (about 1.49% each), good enough to fill up 1+ issue. Anyone who contributed at least seven illustrations was responsible for at least 1% of the magazine's illustrations and filled up at least one issue with their illustrations. The remaining authors are Michael Whelan, Eric Dinyer, and Tony Shasteen with nine illustrations, Steve Adler, Gary Lippincott, and Peter Ferguson with eight illustrations, and Annie Lunsford, John Monteleone, and Joel F. Naprstek with with seven illustrations. Combined, these twenty-eight authors provided 313 illustrations, which represents approximately 46.37% of all illustrations, enough to fill up 47+ issues, or almost half of the magazine's run. It's interesting to note that such a relatively small amount of artists provided close to half the magazine's art, though I'll leave it to others to pontificate upon what this might mean.

Not much would be accomplished in discussing unsolicited art submissions—they were few and far between, even after the magazine began to officially accept them via electronic submission. I did learn of a few artists through this route (including the artist of our last illustration ever) but mostly it fell to me (and my predecessors) to solicit the artists. If you'd like to argue this makes me more culpable regarding the disparity in male vs. female artists, I suppose that is fair. But again, I will point out that I worked with a relatively small amount of art and artists, especially as compared to my work with the fiction.

In terms of recognition, thirty-seven pieces were published in various editions *of Spectrum: The Best in Contemporary Art*, including one piece that won the Gold Award in the Editorial Section, and another piece that won the Silver Award in the Editorial Section. For the Chesley Awards, the magazine twice won in the Interior Illustration category while also receiving five additional nominations, along with another five nominations in the Cover Illustration, Magazine category. The art directors were also nominated for a Chesley Award on three separate occasions, twice for Managing Editor Laura Cleverland, and once for Editorial Director Carl Gnam. In total, the art or its art directors received awards or recognition fifty-three times. The art itself received awards or recognition forty-nine times. Three pieces of art received both Chesley and *Spectrum* recognition, meaning forty-six separate pieces of art received recognition. Chesley rules are a bit funky, as they seem to permit reprinted work to win the award provided it's appearing in a particular medium for the first time (for example, a book cover appearing for the first time as a magazine cover). With this in mind, I will provide percentages out of all 679 illustrations to appear in RoF, meaning 6.77% of them received recognition of some sort.

As to my own tenure, I oversaw five pieces that appeared in three different editions of *Spectrum*, including one previously unpublished piece that won the Silver Award in the Editorial Section. While none of the work I oversaw earned Chesley recognition, it may surprise some to learn that based on my small sample, 7.81% of the artwork earned recognition, 1.04% higher than the established rate overall. And if we remove the artwork I oversaw while at the magazine from the overall totals, forty-one pieces received awards or recognition, dropping the percentage to 6.67%.

Also worth noting is that of my thirty-two published slush survivors, six of them had accompanying artwork that appeared in various editions of *Spectrum*, while a seventh piece was nominated for a Chesley Award for Interior Illustration. That is roughly 22% of all my published slush survivors, and a little over 15% of *all* illustrations that received recognition. As it happened, I never handled the art direction on any of these pieces. That may seem a bit coincidental, but far more interesting to me is the fact the stories I plucked from the slush should account for such a high total of the art that received recognition. The chances of that happenening seem astronomically high, and it's an odd enough statistic that I wanted to point it out.

Let's move onto the magazine staff and nonfiction. Five columns were part of the magazine from the first issue to the last, these being Book reviews, the Movie/TV column, the Folkroots column, the Artists Gallery, and Games.******* During the course of its run, four other columns were introduced to the magazine, three that lasted until the final issue, one that experienced a briefer run. The Past Lives column was introduced with the April 2003 issue and appeared in eight issues total. Young Adult Books was introduced with the April 2006 issue, and appeared in thirty-three issues. The Graphic Novel column was introduced with the October 2007 issue, and appeared in twenty-three issues. Paranoromal Romance and Urban Fantasy Books was introduced with the August 2010 issue and went on to appear in seven issues total. If you wish to view the Letters Page and the Editorials as feature columns, the Letters Page appeared in fifty-three issues, while the Editorials appeared in forty-seven issues. If we include the online editorials as well, the number increases to fifty-eight.

There were also six one-time special feature columns that appeared over the years. Two were interviews, one was about festivals, one profiled an author, one examined the history and definitions of urban fantasy, and I also contributed an article in writing about the Addams Family on Broadway for the special dark fantasy issue. If we include the special Publisher's Note from Warren Lapine in the first issue of *Realms of Fantasy* under his tenure, the special feature columns would increase to seven. There were also a couple of what might be termed as featurette columns over the years, though I never took the time to write about these, as they mostly dicussed books to look out for, or what books a certain known author happened to be reading at the time. Additionally, while it's not nonfiction, I'll note that we had poetry appear in issue one hundred; had the magazine continued, this would have become a more common feature.

In terms of staff who contributed to the magazine, my focus will be on people who helped put together the content that made people purchase the magazine for its creative content. In other words, I'm not including people who worked in subscription departments, business managing departments, ad departments, etc. These numbers *will* include publishers, editors, copy editors, art directors, and graphic designers, as well as columnists. Additionally, over the years there were a number of people listed as editorial assistants in the masthead who weren't in fact assistanting Shawna in the fiction department. These were folks assisting the Sovereign Media publishers in some capacity. Since I also noticed nonfiction contributions from these people appear in the magazine more than once, I am including them as well. In total, there were 118 people who contributed to putting together these 102 issues. Often there were people involved in more than one department, sometimes in the same issue and sometimes over the course of different issues.

In terms of publishers, six different people held this title. The last publishers were William Gilchrist and Kim Richards Gilchrist, who were publishers for the final five issues. The longest publisher was Carl A. Gnam for eighty-eight issues. He was most often listed as editorial director, but Shawna confirmed more than once that he was a publisher. Most of the time his co-publisher was Mark Hintz, but for a few issues Mark's name was mysteriously absent from the masthead and Joe Varda was listed as the publisher, someone who had previously been listed as the Advertising Director. Shawna doesn't remember the details behind this odd occurrence, so I'm afraid I can't shed any light on the matter as it all took place before my time. But based on the little I know, I consider Joe's tenure as publisher more of a technicality than anything else.

In terms of the fiction department, the magazine only ever had one fiction editor for its 102 issues, founding editor, Shawna McCarthy. She had three assistants over the years, the final one being myself. I joined the magazine during the June 2005 issue, but I don't count myself as being part of that issue since it was already out, so I was part of the last thirty-six issues (though it wasn't until the April 2006 issue that the publishers finally got around to listing me in the masthead, and like many others, my titles would change over the years). Rebecca McCabe was Shawna's assistant the longest though, as she was listed as being part of forty-two issues. I admit that one of the personal milestones I'd been looking forward to with the magazine was surpassing Rebecca in my tenure—close, but no cigar.

In terms of the Folkroots column, the column had five different editors at one time or another (though one of these people happened to be myself on a two-issue interim basis). At the time of the magazine's demise the editor was Theodora Goss, who held the position for the last five issues, and also handled writing the column during each issue under her stewardship (along with another issue before she became the editor). The longest tenured Folkroots editor was Terri Windling, who oversaw the column for eighty-five issues. And having written forty-three of the columns, she wrote the most columns of the twenty-two different columnists.

The Movie/TV column had thirteen columnists during its run. The final and longest tenured columnist was Resa Nelson, who handled sixty-three issues. The Games column had five columnists during its run. The longest tenured columnist was Eric T. Baker with sixty-five issues. At the time of the magazine's closure we had two columnists handling Games, Matt Staggs and Matt London. Matt Staggs contributed to ten issues, Matt London six.********

The Books column had nine columnists during its run. The longest tenured columnist was Gahan Wilson, who contributed to seventy-seven issues. The final columnists were Paul Witcover who contributed to fifty-two issues, and Elizabeth Bear who contributed to six issues. The Young Adult Books column lacked an attribution for its first issue, but it seems reasonable to assume the columnist was Michael M. Jones since he handled the other thirty-two issues. The Paranormal Romance & Urban Fantasy Books column had one columnist during the course of its eight issues, this being Elizabeth Bear. The final columnist for the Graphic Novel was Andrew Wheeler, and he also wrote the most columns with twelve. The final columnist for Past Lives also wrote the most columns, this being Emma Bull with seven issues.

Last but not least, there is the Artists Gallery. This column had twenty-five different columnists over the years, with no one contributing more columns than Karen Haber with fifty-three issues. At the time of the magazine's closure, she was handling most of the columns, though Mia Nutick contributed occasionally as well and totaled four columns. In terms of the artists, seventy-nine different artists were profiled (including two separate artist teams). The reason for this disparity between the amount of artists and the amount of issues is that some artists were profiled multiple times, and occasionally the Gallery would cover a topic in the art field as opposed to an artist. The artist whose artwork received the most gallery coverage was Brian Froud with four issues, sometimes profiling his general art and sometimes his work for a specific book.

Of these seventy-nine artists, sixty-four were men, and that works out to about 81%. This number feeds into the male/female disparities I touched upon earlier with the illustrations, but here the details are somewhat different. In my time overseeing this column, I rarely assigned my columnists to cover anything. I occasionally suggested things, but most of the time they would tell me what they wanted to cover and the *vast* majority of the time I would tell them, "That's fine." I've always been under the impression that my predecessors handled the columns in similar fashion. Most of the Artist Galleries were handled by female columnists during the course of the magazine, so assuming everything was handled in the same fashion throughout the magazine's history they would have been pitching these columns to whoever was overseeing the nonfiction and basically getting their choices approved. I doubt our female columnists would have carried this overwhelming bias toward male artists, either on a conscious or subconscious level. So this begs the question: why the disparity?

Alas, I don't have that answer. I'm willing to entertain the possibility that I or any of my male predecessors may have carried an unconscious bias toward male artists (though I never felt as though I did while working at the magazine), but if any of us did carry such a bias it doesn't explain the coverage breakdowns in the Artists Gallery (or why I carried this bias toward illustrations but not toward fiction). As with the interior illustrations, I am researching and learning about these numbers for the first time, years after the magazine's cancelation. I don't have enough information to make any authorative statements here—I am only presenting the data onhand. But if nothing else it is food for thought. Hopefully someone else is able to present more comprehensive data on the matter of male and female artists working in the speculative illustrative field, as the focus here will remain on *Realms of Fantasy*.

Moving on to art and design staff, fourteen people were at one point or another listed in the masthead as having Art Director, Assistant Art Director, Graphic Designer, Assistant Designer duties, or some variation of these titles. No one held down these duties longer than Samantha DeTulleo, who was listed as Art Director and handled the magazine's design for thirty-nine issues. When the magazine reached its end, I had been overseeing the artwork for fourteen issues, while Kim Richards Gilchrist had been handling layout and design for five issues. It should also be noted that while they were never credited for such in the magazine, both Carl A. Gnam and Laura Cleveland had stretches where they oversaw the magazine's artwork.

In terms of copy editors and other editorial staff outside the fiction department, twenty-two people received such listings over the years. No one contributed more than Laura Cleveland, who held titles of Copy Editor, Associate Editor, and ultimately Managing Editor over the course of forty-seven issues. At the time of the magazine's closure, Marty Halpern and Ian Randal Strock had both been listed as Copy Editors for fourteen issues. I had been listed as Editor for eleven issues, which covered my duties concerning fiction, art, nonfiction, miscellaneous managing editorial duties, and miscellaneous website duties.

With all this having been covered, I'd like to now spend a couple of paragraphs talking about the value of *Realms of Fantasy* in its final few years. To be sure, the original publishers deserve tons of credit for launching the magazine and keeping it going as long as they did. And including the original cancelation announcement, the magazine suffered three cancelations in the space of two and a half years. From afar, that's not a good look.

Even so, this final run was unquestionably worthwhile. During this time we published fourteen issues. Those fourteen issues consisted of seventy stories and seventy-seven original illustrations. One story was nominated for a Nebula Award, a second received a Nebula nomination. Two stories were reprinted in Year's Best anthologies and three others were podcast on significant venues. Four of the authors who published with us achieved their first pro sale. Our fiction editor was honored as the Editorial Guest of Honor at the World Fantasy Convention for her work on the magazine. One piece of artwork won *Spectrum*'s Silver Award in the Editorial section, and seven other pieces were published in various editions of *Spectrum*. We launched one new nonfiction column, and launched a poetry section featuring the work of none other than Ursula K. Le Guin. We published our first themed issue along with our hundredth issue, the latter being no small feat on a bimonthly schedule. We launched the nicest website the magazine ever had. And of course we published the usual variety of excellent nonfiction columns.

We did all this in two and a half years, despite changing publishers twice and missing an issue due to one of the transitions ...and this is why the final issues of the magazine were indeed worthwhile. Warren Lapine—the publisher who bought the magazine from Sovereign Media and rescued it from extinction the first time around—recently commented to me on Facebook that he wished he could have saved the magazine. I told him he did. If not for him, the magazine would have died much earlier and none of these fourteen issues would have happened. Everything ends, but the fact the magazine lasted another two and a half years allowed us to accomplish an incredible amount in a very short time.

So I've spent 102 retrospectives discussing the magazine's past, and all of this retrospective so far has done the same. Now it's time to discuss what the magazine held in store for the future had it continued. First I'll share with you the stories we had in inventory that would have been published. If I know of another venue where the story was subsequently published, I'll list that in parentheses, which will allow fans of RoF to have a chance to track down these stories if they're so inclined:

—"Wetwork: A Tale of the Unseen" by Matthew Rotundo (Issue 35 of *Intergalactic Medine Show*)

—"Seeking Captain Random" by Vylar Kaftan (Issue 240 of *Interzone*, and also podcast 240 on *PodCastle*)

—"The Transmuted Engine" by Lee Moan

—"In the Realm of Legend" by Richard Parks

—"In the Palace of the Jade Lion" by Richard Parks (Issue 100 of *Beneath Ceaseless Skies*)

—"The Pretty Knife" by Tanith Lee

—"Beasts" by Elizabeth Bourne (Issue 240 of *Interzone*)

—"Leviathan's Hooks" by Euan Harvey

—"Long is the Shadow in the Moonlit Hills" by Euan Harvey

—"This Gray Rock, Standing Tall" by James Van Pelt (Issue 9 of *Unlikely Story*)

—"Desperate Love" by Dennis Danvers (*See the Elephant*)

—"The War Between the Water and the Road" by William Alexander (Issue 3 of *Unstuck*)

—"Bozegeest, Wereldzee Stad, and My Revenge" by Garth Upshaw

—"Side Effects" by Susan J. Kroupa

With fourteen pieces slated for publication and thirty-two additional pieces still under consideration by Shawna, it is easy to see why we closed down to submissions while we made the switch to email subs (which never came to pass due to the magazine's cancelation).

Matthew Rotundo, Lee Moan, Elizabeth Bourne, and William Alexander all would have been published in the magazine for the first time. Lee Moan and Elizabeth Bourne were the two unpublished slush survivors who I referenced earlier. "Seeking Captain Random" actually had accompanying artwork by Zelda Devon and Kurt Huggins (though it was completed after the mag's death) that was also accepted by *Interzone*. It's the closest you'll ever come to expererincing a *Realms of Fantasy* story without reading an issue of *Realms of Fantasy*. "The Pretty Knife" also had finished artwork by John Kaiine, "In the Palace of the Jade Lion" had finished artwork by Tiffany Prothero, and "Side Effects" had finished artwork by Ben Sowards. Cyril Van Der Haegan had been assigned to "Leviathan's Hooks," Andy B. Clarkson had been assigned to "Desperate Love," and Scott Altmann had been assigned to "The War Between the Water and the Road." Had the December issue come to fruition, our fiction would have consisted of "Desperate Love," "In the Palace of the Jade Lion," "Leviathan's Hooks," "Seeking Captain Random," and "The War Between the Water and the Road."

While I don't know whether they would have been available, I had planned on approaching Rebecca Guay to illustrate "Beasts," and Raoule Vitale for "In the Realm of Legend." As best as I can remember, I didn't yet have anyone in mind for the other pieces at the time of the magazine's closure.

I can also reveal the future of the nonfiction columns. For the Books column, Elizabeth Bear had turned in reviews or planned to review *The Cold Commands* by Richard K. Morgan, *The Devil's Diadem* by Sarah Douglass, *Ganymede* by Cherie Priest, and *The Crescent Throne* by Saladin

Ahmed, while Paul Witcover had turned in reviews or planned to review *Low Town* by Daniel Polansky, *The Traitor's Daughter* by Paula Brandon, *Stories forNighttime and Some for the Day* by Ben Loory, *The Bible Repairman* by Tim Powers, *The Folded Word* by Catherynne Valente, and *Kafkaesque*, edited by James Patrick Kelly and John Kessel; in the YA Books, Michael M. Jones had turned in reviews for *Variant* by Robison Wells, *Drink, Slay, Love* by Sarah Beth Durst, *The Shattering* by Karen Healey, *The Death Catchers* by Jennifer Anne Kogler, *Wildfire* by Karsten Knight, *Texas Gothic*, by Rosemary Clement-Moore, *Forever* by Maggie Stiefvater, and *Blood Feud*, by Steven A. Roman; in Paranormal Romance and Urban Fantasy Books, Elizabeth Bear had turned in reviews for or planned to review *White Tiger: Dark Heavens Book One* by Kylie Chan, *Another Kind of Dead* by Kelly Meding, *The Drowning Girl* by Caitlin Kiernan, and *Conquer the Dark* by L.A. Banks; in the Graphic Novel column, Andrew Wheeler had turned in a column on *Velveteen & Mandala* by Jiro Matsumoto, and *Orcs: Forged for War*, written by Stan Nicholls, illustrated by Joe Flood; in the Artists Gallery, Karen Haber had turned in her column on David Palumbo and had planned to do a column on Lori Koefoed; in the Movie/TV column, Resa Nelson had turned in a column on *The Woman in Black*, along with a sidebar on holiday season movies, and she had planned on doing a column on *The Hunger Games*; in the Games column, Matt London had turned in reviews for *LIMBO* for the Xbox 360, Playstation 3, and Microsoft Windows, *Catherine* for Playstation 3 and Xbox 360, and Matt Staggs had turned in reviews for the RPGs *Savage Worlds Deluxe Edition* and *The One Ring: Adventures Over the Edge of the Wild*; and in Folkroots, Theodora Goss had turned in her column with a topic of "Planting a Magical Garden." Theodora's column can be read on cabinetdesfees.com or on her personal website.

The information I've spent the past few paragraphs relating only tells you about the plans for the magazine's immediate future. But now I'm going to share with you the magazine's longterm plans had we continued. I wasn't blind to the fact that print was struggling, nor was I living in some kind of bubble where I refused to acknowledge it. Quite the contrary, I was very much interested in a proactive approach to help bring the magazine in the black. Warren Lapine had started publishing the magazine in pdf form, but the money this brought in was negligible. The final publishers were looking into expanding the magazine into various e-reading devices, but the size of the magazine combined with the color illustrations, the ads, and the design elements made this a hefty challenge. So the answer had to come elsewhere. And to this day I believe I had that answer figured out ...unfortunately we ran out of time to implement it.

The answer was author-themed issues. Not just any authors though. What we were planning on was building occasional author-themed issues around writers with major followings. For example, at the time the magazine closed, our plan for the June 2012 issue was to put together a special Charlaine Harris issue. Harris had already agreed to deliver us an original story, and we planned on tailoring the nonfiction to her Sookie Stackhouse universe as much as possible; the Movie/TV column would cover HBO's *True Blood*, the Artists Gallery would provide revelant artwork to her series, be it interpretations of the world or art about vampires, Folkroots would tackle a topic that fed into the Stackhouse books as well, we wanted to conduct an interview with Harris ...you get the idea.

Fans of these big commercial authors often rush out to buy an anthology if it contains a story in the universe they love. So if an entire issue of a magazine was built around their favorite author, would they want to add this issue to their collections? Of course they would! And if they were unable to acquire the print issue for whatever reason, what would they would they do? Well naturally they would buy the .pdf version, which would always be available for purchase, and suddenly that would become a lucrative revenue stream.

The amount of money just one of these author-themed issues could have (*would have*) generated for the magazine would have provided an immense boost to RoF financially. Feel free to freak out when I tell you this, but back when Warren Lapine was the publisher, there were even some preliminary discussions with George R. R. Martin about doing such an issue revolving around him and a certain franchise you might have heard of. (Shawna being friends with George was a huge perk to opening up these discussions!) Alas, we never got past the initial conversation stage; not because George said no, and not because we lost interest (there's a laugh!), but rather because the magazine started to struggle and ended up folding for the second time. Had the magazine continued under Warren, while I can't guarantee this issue would've come about, it was certainly on the table, and things had certainly progressed beyond being a harebrained scheme. Anyway, by the time the final publishers took over, we knew it went without saying that between his books and the HBO series becoming a breakout hit, George had become much too busy for us to pursue such an issue anytime soon.

But George wasn't the only person we wanted to work with for issues like these, which brings us back to Charlaine Harris. Of course we couldn't pursue this immediately. The February 2011 issue was the first one under the new publishers and the transition required way too much work to also take on a themed issue of this sort; before the publishers brought back Shawna and me, they had already announced plans to do a special Dark Fantasy issue for the April issue; and the June issue was issue one hundred, which had its own set of special demands. After all this, we wanted to let a few issues pass before doing another special issue, because if every issue was a "special issue" we risked burning out our regular readers on what might start seeming like gimmicks.

So we targeted the June 2012 issue, which would have given us enough time to get an original story from Charlaine Harris along with the accompanying artwork. Everything seemed to be in place to keep the magazine going for a long while yet ...except that the October 2011 issue ended up being our last one due to financial losses. But had we managed to last *just four more issues* it's quite possible we'd still be going strong. Because again, this wasn't a one-shot idea; this was something we hoped to do every so often, basically whenever it made sense to all parties involved. With the right authors, we could have kept the magazine afloat a long time. Between an original story from the right author, the accompanying artwork, and our varied nonfiction columns by some excellent columnists, *Realms of Fantasy* was uniquely qualified to put such author-themed issues together.

But as we all know, it wasn't meant to be. Regardless, the work everyone did at *Realms of Fantasy* was stellar, and we did it for a long time. We can take pride in our past, and having revealed what the future held in store, we can also take pride in the fact that had we continued, our future would have been bright indeed.

So that wraps up this retrospective. Now at the end of each retrospective in the past, I would share with you my favorite story and favorite artwork in that particular issue. Except with this retrospective, there is no one issue that I've been discussing. Quite the opposite, I've been discussing *all* the issues. So what better way to end this series than provide you with my picks for a year's worth of fiction in RoF? As established earlier, an average year of RoF would see the publication of 34.8 stories. For the purposes of this list, I'll round up to thirty-five and keep it only to pieces that were originally published in RoF. Choosing my favorite thirty-five stories from 582 possible candidates is hard enough; trying to then rank *these* thirty-five stories would be borderline impossible. So I'm simply going to list them in order of publication.

I should add that I'm not going to do this with the artwork. I don't remember what each piece of artwork looks like. Even with the ratings I keep for the artwork in my personal files, I would need to lay out all the contenders in such a manner that I could walk around and consider them all at once. Being as this would involve laying out each magazine, I really don't have the space to make this happen ...not to mention that sometimes an issue would contain more than one piece of artwork I'd have to consider, and I'm not about to literally tear up my collection to spread out the artwork. So I'm afraid I won't be offering my picks for the illustrations.

As to the fiction, now I know what it's like when an editor chooses stories for a Year's Best anthology. You have to leave out *a lot* of great stories. Sometimes it rips your guts out to do so. So my hat goes off to every editor who has ever been faced with such choices ...and my hat goes off to every author who appeared in RoF. At the end of the day it doesn't matter whether you make this list or not. What *does* matter is that you were deemed worthy of publication in one of the most important speculative magazines to come along since 1994. So without further ado:

—"The Year of Storms" by Judith Berman, February '95
—"The Ruby" by Beverly Suarez-Beard, August '95
—"Tale of a Fish Who Loved a Bird" by Geoffrey A. Landis, October '95
—"Diana of the Hundred Breasts" by Robert Silverberg, February 96
—"Sarah's Window" by Janni Lee Simner, April '96
—"Lawnmower Moe" by William R. Eakin, April '97
—"Lost Girls" by Jane Yolen, February '98
—"The Grammarian's Five Daughters" by Eleanor Arnason, June '99
—"Aftershock" by F. Paul Wilson, December '99
—"Night Sweats" by James Van Pelt, February '01
—"Artie's Angels" by Catherine Wells, December '01
—"Stegosaurus Boy" by Steven Popkes, February '03
—"A Hunter's Ode to His Bait" by Carrie Vaughn, February 03

—"The Tao of Flynn" by Eric M. Witchey, April '04

—"Charlie the Purple Giraffe was Acting Strangely" by David Levine, June '04

—"In a Glass Casket" by Tim Pratt, October '04

—"The Good Doctor" by Melissa Lee Shaw, February '05

—"The Language of Moths" by Christopher Barzak, April '05

—"Moments of Grace" by Aaron Schutz, June '05

—"The Queen's Wood" by Josh Rountree, August '05

—"Countless Screaming Argonauts" by Chris Lawson, August '05

—"Uncle Vernon's Lie" by Patrick Samphire, February '06

—"Pavel Petrovich" by Daniel Hood, June '06

—"Of Metal Men and Scarlet Thread and Dancing with the Sunrise" by Ken Scholes, August '06

—"A Fish Story" by Sarah Totton, October '06

—"The Hotel Astarte" by M.K. Hobson, June 2007

—"The White Isle" by Von Carr, December 2007

—"The Olverung" by Stephen Woodworth, December 2008

—"Sails Above Greensea" by Adam Corbin Fusco, April 2009

—"Healing Benjamin" by Dennis Danvers, August 2009

—"The Hag Queen's Curse" by M.K. Hobson, April 2010

—"The Fortuitious Meeting of Gerard van Oost and Oludara" by Christopher Kastensmidt, April 2010

 —"Thirteen Incantations" by Desirina Boskovich, February 2011

 —"Magpie" by Mark Rigney, February 2011

 —"Leap of Faith" by Alan Smale, August 2011

This retrospective series runs 158,122 words long.********* This breaks down to an average of about 1,535 words per retrospective. Every last retrospective was first posted on my personal blog. The first one went up on August 14th, 2007, and the final one on January 13th, 2015, meaning it took about seven years and five months to complete this series in its entirety (the original version anyway—subsequent edits would lengthen the timeline). And with this final scrap of information, I believe I have accomplished exactly what I set out to do with this retrospective series as a whole: examining the magazine inside and out to the best of my ability, while with this final retrospective taken on its own, I'd like to think I've also accomplished my other goal, i.e. I have put the magazine and this retrospective series in perspective.

Thanks for reading.

*During the course of my tenure, Shawna *very occasionally* accepted email submissions from select authors. (Yes, the truth comes out all these years later!) Not all of these stories are accounted for in my calculations, but the body of work is large enough that the numbers reflect a meaningful study, especially as I am aware of all such stories she accepted, and I'm quite certain the amount of stories she would have rejected in this instance would be rather neglible.

**For the sake of my sanity, I am including stories that Shawna accepted only to see them published elsewhere for various reasons (usually because of cancelations to the magazine). It is a small number, but calculating things this way makes things easier, and also provides a greater sample size of relevant data concerning acceptances.

***While I stated earlier that I had thirty-two slush survivors, these were only the published ones. I had two additional slush survivors that were never published due to the magazine's cancelation.

****Alas, my research/records here encompass very few foreign market reprint sales.

*****A couple were judgment calls about whether they were dragons or some kind of demon.

******Due to there being artists who had interior illustrations as well as separate cover illustrations, the easiest percentage to go by here and in most cases for all the artists are the 675 different illustrations the magazine has run.

*******As noted in previous retrospectives, while the Games column was with the magazine until the end, toward the end of its run, there was shifting of the column back and forth between the magazine and the website.

********As noted above, several times toward the end of the magazine's run the Games column appeared on the website. This happened with other columns too on occasion, but it happened with the Games column the most often. Because the website and the magazine became rather interlinked toward the end of the magazine's run, I am counting all column appearances on the website as part of the overall count for the Games column, along with any other column this happened with.

**********The total word count is after I went through this entire series and did some edits.

Originally posted on douglascohen.livejournal.com on January 13th, 2015

Douglas Cohen is the editor of *Oz Reimagined*, as well as *What the #@&%
is That?*, a forthcoming anthology from Simon & Schuster to be released
in August 2016. He proudly worked at *Realms of Fantasy* for six and a half
years, starting off as Assistant Editor and working his way up to the title of
Editor (though if there is one *true* Editor of *Realms of Fantasy*, it will always
be Shawna McCarthy). During his time with the magazine, he discovered
numerous stories by new and unpublished authors in the general
submissions pile, including pieces that earned Nebula nominations and led
to major book deals. During the magazine's final years, he also oversaw the
artwork, including multiple illustrations that landed in the prestigious
Spectrum art series, and one piece that earned the Silver Award in the
Editorial section. Douglas is also a writer, and his fiction has appeared or
is forthcoming in such venues as *Space and Time Magazine*, *Fantastic Stories
of the Imagination*, *Interzone*, and *Weird Tales*.

Shawna McCarthy began her publishing career at *Firehouse Magazine* as
an editorial assistant and moved up to Editor before switching genres by
becoming Assistant to the Editor at *Isaac Asimov's Science Fiction Magazine*
where she eventually became Editor and won the Hugo Award for Best
Professional Editor. From there she moved to Bantam Spectra as Senior
Editor where she acquired books from writers such as Robert Charles
Wilson, Connie Willis, and William Gibson. After some time off for the
birth of her first child, she went back to work at Workman Publishing as
Senior Editor. While at Workman she acquired that company's only
novel—*Good Omens*, by Neil Gaiman and Terry Pratchett. Four years
later, after another child, she began a new career as a literary agent with
Scoville Chichak Galen while at the same time founding *Realms of Fantasy
Magazine* with Sovereign Media of Virginia. *Realms*, which folded in 2011
after seventeen years in print, was the world's most successful magazine
devoted solely to fantasy. As an independent agent for more than twenty
years, she represents Robert Charles Wilson, the estate of Tanith Lee, Eric
Flint, Liz Williams, Sarah Zettel, and many other well-known fantasy and
science fiction writers. She resides in coastal New Jersey.

www.ingramcontent.com/pod-product-compliance
Lightning Source LLC
Chambersburg PA
CBHW030930020726
47498CB00001B/183